Path to Freedom

The Path Volume 1

by

James Copley

Dedication:

To all my friends
both online and off
who encouraged me to
Create
both with words
and
otherwise

Prologue:

The End of the Beginning

"I'm telling you, Lieutenant Vulkeshson. You need to take this deal."

The interrogation room was cold. Not quite cold enough to cause my breath to fog up, but nearly so. Of course, as soon as the huge naval space station spun around its axis in another six hours, things would warm up enough to be decidedly uncomfortable. I glanced at the mirrored window, knowing we were being watched even though it was entirely against Confed Navy regulations. My genetically engineered fox-like ears could pick up the muffled voices through the double pane window, even if I couldn't quite understand them.

"Are you even listening to me?"

My eyes focused back on the human officer in front of me, seated on the other side of the table. Clad in his Class "A" dress uniform, the lieutenant commander was a stark contrast to my prisoner's dark blue utilities. Shoulder boards displayed the Judge Advocate General device in silver and gold thread, and only a bare minimum of campaign and deployment ribbons decorated his chest. *This guy's never even been within three light years of combat*, I thought to myself.

"I heard you." Arms crossed against my chest, I glared at the JAG officer.

"And?"

"What about Spurgle?" I swept my arm towards the mirrored glass. "What are they going to do about him?"

"*Lieutenant Commander* Spurgle-Saint-John is no longer your concern," the JAG officer said, pronouncing the name in its full 'correct' form. He grimaced even as he chided me for failing to include the man's rank. It was apparent even he couldn't stand the little asshat. Not that it was going to help me any. He was clearly in the odious little turd's pocket, regardless of his personal opinion.

"He got my RIO killed, goddammit!" I shouted. "We rotted in that damned Snake prison for weeks because that jackass couldn't keep his mouth shut! Buckley DIED in that prison!" My fur bristled and rage radiated from my body like a bonfire as I vented at the legal counsel. "I saw the intel report!"

"And who showed you that *classified* intel report, Lieutenant?" the officer's eyes sharpened again.

I clammed up. I wouldn't throw anyone else under the bus on this. It was my actions, *my temper,* that got me into this legal mess, but I just couldn't take it anymore. I stared balefully at the table in front of me in helpless anger.

"Regardless, the investigation is still ongoing," came the bland reply to my silence. I didn't believe a word of it. It was just going to be swept under the rug, just like any other issues the fully human officer had been confronted with. That's how things went in the Human Confederation. But I could no longer ignore the sleights, the insults, both subtle and not-so-subtle, which I had endured for the entire war against the Serpentia Empire.

Kin like myself were just cannon fodder to be expended, like equipment or ammunition, I thought bitterly. They hadn't even let me attend the funeral. I wasn't even sure there had even *been* a funeral. And when that jackass Spurgle showed up at the debriefing I just acted. Decked the man with a right cross, sending him flying into the wall. I'd then proceeded to send blow after blow into the man's gut, over and over, until the security personnel pulled me off. I'd witnessed the fear in the man's eyes. *Worth it.*

That wasn't the end of it, of course. I could still remember the asshole's wheezing voice as I was dragged away in handcuffs. "You'll pay for this! You'll never fly again, you hear me Vulkeshson? NEVER!"

And so here I was. As far as I knew, no one had even questioned him about the leak which got my flight shot up and my crews captured. They ignored our testimony about the prison camps, the torture, the lack of food or water, how my Radio Intercept Officer, a Weasel-Kin named Joseph Buckley, had died in captivity from untreated wounds. No, they only cared about a human officer getting a beating, no matter how richly deserved.

Maybe Mongoose was right, I thought. *Perhaps Terra isn't worth fighting for anymore.* My anger deflated as I realized there was no way to come out ahead, not here, and not now.

"Fine," I grated out. "What's the deal?"

*****

"...as the defendant has entered a plea of 'guilty' to striking a superior officer, therefore, it is the decision of this court martial that the prisoner, Lieutenant Vulkeshson, shall be stripped of his rank, remanded to the penal camp at Olympus Mons for a period of ten years, at the end of which he will be dishonorably discharged for conduct unbecoming of an officer." Rear Admiral Bates didn't even look up as he read off the sentence.

"What the hell, Lieutenant Commander?" My hackles rose as I snarled menacingly at my legal counsel. "This wasn't the deal!"

"You'll never prove it," he whispered back. The smug look on the asshole's face made me want to lash out again, this time at him, but before I could move, two burly Wolf-Kin with security brassards had already latched onto each arm and were pulling me towards the door.

You'll regret this, I seethed silently. *You'll ALL regret this!* The banging of the gavel echoed throughout the courtroom over and over. BANG! Bang. bang...

Ch 1: Eleven years later

Bang! Bang! Bang!

Rage and adrenaline suffused my system as I startled awake, my mind still whirling from the nightmare that haunted my sleep for the third time this week. But instead of the raw red-rock walls I'd endured for a decade in the Martian prison camp, my eyes saw a ship's painted metal bulkhead. A wave of relief washed through me as I recognized it. *Goddammit, another nightmare. And here I thought they might start becoming* less *frequent when I got out...* The thudding on the far side of the hatch sounded again, this time accompanied by a familiar voice.

"Rise and shine, buddy," Mongoose called. "We're about an hour from the first jump point, and I want you in the second seat when we translate."

"Right," I called back, stamping hard on the spike of anger that seemed to come from nowhere. "Be right out." *It's just Goose,* I told myself. *It's not a prison guard.*

Rubbing the sleep out of my eyes, I rolled off the bunk and pulled out a fresh set of socks from my small carry-bag. Looking at my feet, I examined my toe-talons for anything that might snag the fabric. When I'd been in the navy, they issued the pilots specially made socks which were tear resistant and strong enough to resist the slightly acidic musk that served as sweat for my Fox-Kin species. These were just thin synthetic cotton. But even stuff like this was going to be hard to get on an alien planet. Expensive at the very least. I pulled the stockings over my toes and up my fur-covered legs, making sure the reddish-brown hairs settled comfortably under the sheer fabric. *And thank all the gods that the geneticists solved the seasonal shedding issue,* I mused. I couldn't imagine how frustrating, not to mention *dangerous,* all that hair floating around was for the first few generations of Wolf and Fox-Kin, having to work and fight in microgravity while *also* having to battle contaminated seals and clogged enviro-filters constantly, even when *not* in actual combat. The human scientists were quick to solve the problem, if only to preserve their own precious hides from the dangers posed by contaminated hatch seals. As a result, fur-skinned Kin no longer had the ability to grow a thick winter coat, but realistically, that was what *clothes* were for.

I gave the second-hand flight suit a quick sniff. *Meh, it's not too bad.* I only had two of them. I'd have to run this one through an enzyme cycle before too long, though. We Fox-Kin tended to stink if we marinated in airtight clothing like a flight suit for too long. And even though we didn't sweat over our entire bodies like humans did, and *seasonal* shedding was no longer a chronic problem, we did still tend to shed under long-term physical or emotional stress. As I'd been 'stressed' for the last decade, it was now second nature to run the lint brush along the inside of the suit to get the loose red-brown hairs out, or it would end up a matted mess the next time I took it off. Wolf-Kin were even worse, which was why they were almost never tasked with full-time space operations. The whole ship would quickly be filled with *eau 'du chien mouillé*. And no one liked the smell of 'wet dog', not even the puppies themselves.

It was all part and parcel with being Kin. Larger brains meant more energy was used. That heat had to be shunted out of the body somehow, and most Kin were notoriously lacking in sweat glands around the cranium. I once saw a Wolf-Kin actually panting to dump heat, which while comical and ridiculous looking, was relatively effective. *Nature always finds a way*, I thought idly, trying hard not to dwell on the ghosts of my past.

My eyes sprang fully open as the savory aroma of freshly cooked bacon wafted in through the cracked-open hatch. *Wait, what?* I finished dressing in a rush and started to follow my nose, but the vestiges of my nightmare still bothered me. I shook my head in an attempt to dispel my personal ghosts. Stamping my stockinged feet into a pair of old EVA boots, I clomped out of the cabin and into the tiny galley of the old military surplus ship where Mongoose was scarfing down a huge bacon and cheese sandwich.

'Mongoose' was a former scout pilot, just like I was. We met when I had been pulled from piloting cargo shuttles, a job which I quite enjoyed, told I was now a Radio Intercept Officer, thrust into a two-man *Ferret* class reconnaissance scout ship and told to go scope out the Serpentia defenses along the constantly changing battlefront between our two military forces. Even now, nearly twenty years later, I still didn't know the old Weasel-Kin's real name. Everyone, even his commanders, just called him 'Mongoose', or 'Goose' if they were close friends.

"Hey, Goose, I don't suppose you..." I started, suddenly interrupted by a loud growl from my stomach.

"Yours is over there," the old pilot waved at a covered dish sitting next to the cooling microstove. "You didn't think I'd make one of these things and not offer you one, did you? I could hear your stomach from all the way up in the pilot's seat." He took a couple more bites as I levered my lanky frame down into the only other seat, my bushy tail sliding perfectly into the cutout on the back. *Thank god this thing was designed for Kin.* I thought gratefully. Nothing was worse than sitting down, only to discover the chair wasn't built with Kin in mind. More than once, I'd sat down only to nearly bend my tail in half on human-designed furniture.

Size was another issue. I was pretty average for Fox-Kin, standing at around 170 centimeters, or five and a half feet tall as the pure humans insisted on calling it, even though inches and feet hadn't been used as a standard of measurement for literally centuries. Thankfully, the *Ferret* class scout ship was designed with pure humans in mind, which averaged quite a bit taller than either Fox-Kin or Weasel-Kin, so there was no danger of me smacking my head on a hatch coaming. I truly felt sorry for the occasional Wolf-Kin who got assigned to one of these things, as they averaged quite a bit taller than even humans, at around seven feet.

The plate contained an unnatural monstrosity of a sandwich, piled with at least seven pieces of fresh-cooked, crispy bacon, interlaced with alternating strips of three different cheeses, all encompassed by a thick tortilla-like bread. Most full humans I'd known tried to describe it as a ham and cheese shawarma, but Goose always called it 'The Bacon-ator'.

We ate in companionable silence for a few minutes, neither of us wasting any time devouring the greasy, gooey, but delectable feast before us. I sighed as I wiped bits of bacon from my facial fur, ensuring none was lost. Goose just looked at me intently, waiting for the inevitable discussion.

"I never figured out how you do that so well," I stalled, gesturing at the minimalist kitchen. "Every time I try, and I follow every exact step I've seen you do, I just end up with burnt bacon bits."

"It's all in the wrist," the genetically engineered mustelid replied, waggling his expressive eyebrows. My face screwed up in confusion. *What the hell does your wrist have to do with... Never mind.* I sighed.

"Fine, keep your secrets," I shot back. "You sure I can't convince you to go halves with me on this?"

"You know why, Red. I still have... things to take care of. I know you and Joe had those really awesome dreams, and I was sick to hear how he bought the farm, but..." He showed an uncharacteristic reluctance to speak on the subject. He was usually quick to let someone know if their plan was complete bunk. I wasn't going to pry.

"Yeah, I figured." I stared down at my empty plate, dismally brooding over the tortuous path that led me to this point. "Yesterday was six months."

He sighed, knowing exactly what I meant. Six months since I'd finally been released from Olympus Mons Disciplinary Barracks, the military prison I had been sentenced to. He tried to change the subject.

"I know you want to work in space, but are you absolutely sure about this?" he asked, concern written all over his face. "I can still get you a job at Beeker's place."

"You know me better than that, Goose." I trailed off in silence. "Being a bouncer in a bar isn't working in space, even if the bar is *in* space."

He grimaced for a second, then moved on again, this time looking intently at me across the table. "So, now that we're outside *Internal Affairs* jurisdiction and you've finally got some rest, you mind telling me everything *else* that's going on?" Goose inquired, his rounded ears flicking in mild annoyance. "You say you were blacklisted. Fine, I accept that. By who, though? It wasn't the whole bureaucracy. There has to be a source for that sort of thing, it's not something they do, officially."

I sighed in exasperation, throwing my hands up. "That's the thing. I don't know, exactly. I spent nearly four months trying to get hired on for anything; pilot, navigator, all the crew positions. Hell, I even applied for *cargo handler*! But no one would hire me. It was all rejections with no reason given. And it's not like the positions were being filled by others. The *Astral Explorer* sat in port for nearly three weeks because they didn't have a qualified navigator."

"That does sound awfully suspicious, but I've been out-system for a while, so I haven't heard the latest scuttlebutt."

"Yeah, it was the first clue I had that something weird was going on, so I started digging. You remember that Volk-Kin, Polina?"

Goose's eyes lit up for a moment. "Yeah, she was fun! Intel section, if I remember. Never did understand why she called herself Volk-Kin, instead of Wolf. I mean, I get that she was from Siberia, but it's not like Old Russia still exists, and the genetics are damn near indistinguishable. But yeah, I have fond memories, for sure."

"She works for AstralCorp now," I said. "Data entry for their hiring department. She saw my name pop up in some internal emails, remembered that I was your old RIO, and decided to break some rules. She copied it and sent it to me when she got out of the datacenter."

"And?"

"I was blacklisted by the Confed Licensing Board. The CLB was flat out denying even a temporary crew license, without which none of the companies could legally employ me," I growled.

"But..." his expressive eyebrows drew down.

"Yeah, I know it's not supposed to be legal, but apparently they're doing it anyway. Only way around it is if I work on a privately owned vessel, rather than a Corporate one. But when I tried that, I discovered yet another issue. Every supplier and vendor which provides services to those same Corporate shipping companies are contractually obliged to require the same licensing standards for all their customers, not just the Corporate ones. And there *are* no suppliers which don't service the Corporations, there's just not enough privately held shipping to make it profitable. If the private ships bucked the CLB, they would lose access to their ability to operate."

"Wow," he said morosely. "I knew the Corpos were a virtual monopoly, but I had no idea they had *that* kind of stranglehold on everything."

"Trust me, there's no such thing as non-Corporate competition in space anymore. The Corporations may play like they're against each other, but once you get above the middle managers, you can tell they're all playing on the same team. And there's no room for bit players in *that* game."

Goose gave me a look that spoke volumes but held his tongue, knowing the internal turmoil I was probably going through.

The whole situation really pissed me off. Sure, I could go down to the surface and join the general labor pool. Work in the factories and 'ponics-farms which still dotted the landscape on Old Terra. But I knew in exquisite detail the kind of back-breaking, soul-destroying work such jobs entailed. I watched my parents get slowly worn down to mere shadows of themselves as they struggled to escape what was essentially debt slavery. They were one of the last generations to be "made" from a Fox-Kin production line, and fought their entire lives against the compound interest of the "cost" of their creation. Although my own birth was "debt free", I was intimately familiar with the ways the Agri-Corpos had to restart the debt cycle once again, with "required equipment purchases" and "mandatory maintenance protocols". All specifically designed to lock their employees into crippling and lifelong debt to the Corpo. I joined the Confed Navy as soon as I met the age requirements specifically to escape that trap, it being one of the only ways open for our kind to have any kind of normal life. Add in the crap that happened to end my military career, and at present my life was a complete shit-show.

After everything that happened, the only reason I was able to survive this long without work was through the generosity of people like Goose, who knew the whole story behind my conviction and incarceration. Of course, pretty much all of them were full-blood Kin, and had very little influence or resources in the 'Human' Confederation. No. Prosperity, control, and influence were decidedly a *human* thing. Even now, three decades after the Kin were supposedly "fully emancipated" and allowed some measure of control over their reproductive lives, we were still effectively third-class citizens. Not even second-class. At least a second-class could vote, not that the vote of a half-breed ever mattered in the *Human* Confederation.

My life was a mess. But it wasn't over. Not while I still had friends.

"By the way, I never said thank you for picking me up at Ceres," I said softly. "I know you have stuff going on. You could have just sent me credits for a ticket, you didn't have to actually come get me."

"Meh," he shrugged. "My shit's not all that time-sensitive. The Snakes'll still be there when I get done with this run."

"You still think they're the ones responsible for the missing colonists?" I asked skeptically. "I thought Force Intel had ruled them out ten years ago. That's why we signed the Armistice, anyways."

"Those weren't *human* settlers," he snarled softly. "You, better than anyone, should know how little the Confed cares about anyone but *pure humans* unless it impacts their bottom line."

I couldn't argue with that.

It *was* disgusting, especially considering it was Kin like myself, Buckley, and Goose who pulled the humans' asses out of the fire, not just in the latest war, but from the one six hundred years ago, and every single war in between. The only reason humans still had even their home planet was because of their biological slaves picking up the slack when the human numbers grew too few to maintain the world's infrastructure. Or crew the warships. Or carry the rifles. It was always the Kin who were sacrificed to the altar of war. Very rarely, these days, was a human killed by anything but stupidity or old age.

He abruptly stood and headed for the bridge. "Come on, let me get you checked out this bucket of bolts, 'cause sure as shit, I'm not piloting the whole way there when there's another full-qual pilot aboard, and I don't give a frak what the   CLB   says."

Ch 2: One Small Step for Fox

The electronics had been upgraded from a standard military scout. Instead of physical multi-function displays with actual buttons and dials, almost everything was converted to virtual holograph. Tiny light emitters dotted the entire cockpit, with only the regulation-mandated analogue backups still present on what used to be an incredibly busy instrument panel. I still remembered how confusing the array was to the brand new Fox-Kin RIO I was twenty years ago. I was kind of surprised to see a standard heads-up reflective panel in front of the pilot, though. With all the holo-screens, Goose could easily replace the front viewports with cerama-steel and just have a completely virtual outside view.

I still couldn't believe he'd obtained the *Ferret*-class scout ship as military surplus. For one thing, most of the original mil-spec systems were still installed. Goose had changed all the labeling on the virtual displays, marking them as *load-balancing*, and other innocuous functions, but even after a decade in prison, I immediately recognized the pattern of command trees on the holo-screens. *I wonder what other hidden surprises he has on this thing? It's not like he could hide a particle cannon or missiles on this thing, could he?*

I didn't see any physical weapons lock-out, so if he *had* heavy weapons besides the civilian-legal point defense clusters I saw mounted when I boarded, they were well concealed, and apparently heavily shielded.

As I sat down in what would be the RIO's position, I could no longer hold back my curiosity. "Okay, Goose. Level with me. How the hell did you manage to get one of these things as *military surplus*? And don't think I can't recognize that stealth/ECM package you have labeled as *ballast control!*"

He smirked at me from the left seat. "Spotted that, eh? You do remember how to work those, right?" I rolled my eyes.

"How about your nav skills?"

I chuckled. "I won't say it's like riding a grav-bike, because I never owned one as a kit, but I doubt I've lost too much. Back on Mars, I used to keep my mind busy with translation equations when it got too quiet."

He winced in sympathy, but quickly moved on, explaining changes from the military controls I was used to. Almost everything except offensive weapons were set up pretty much the same, just holographic instead of the normal 2-D screens. He even had me do the calculations for the translation, making me re-do it twice more before he was satisfied with my speed and accuracy. Finally, we shut down the anti-grav, charged the jump drives, and waited for the clock to wind down before jumping out of the Sol system.

Translation to Alpha Cetauri went smoothly. Nothing showed up on scan within three mega-klicks, so Goose checked in with Gateway Traffic Control and got a vector for our next leg of the journey. He smoothly oriented the ship and applied a steady, fuel efficient thrust before re-engaging the anti-grav. The jump point for the Hoth System was about ninety degrees from our entry vector, on nearly the same plane of the ecliptic, but we had to deflect six degrees to keep clear of the outbound traffic lane. It wasn't like we were in a hurry, as the next gravitational congruence wouldn't happen for another three days. Our hydrogen-3 fuel stores were down to nearly half from the high-energy jump we had to take out of Sol, but we planned to wait to take on more until Hoth, as it was much cheaper there.

I couldn't help but stare out of the side viewport at Alpha Centauri. Even after passing through dozens of times, I was still struck by how unique the system was. Officially referred to as the "Gateway to Terra", it *was* pretty special. It had a multitude of low-energy jump points leading to local stars along the ecliptic plane, available once every eleven days, each, and several high-energy ones to systems *much* further away, stretching nearly into the next cluster, but only in the direction antipodal to Proxima Centauri's orbit. *That* corridor was kind-of available all the time, but to get the best efficiency we would still need to wait for the eleven-day cyclical conjunction of the two primaries.

Why Alpha Centauri when we were headed nearly forty-five degrees away from that line of sight? The answer was fuel efficiency.

While it was certainly possible to jump directly from the Sol system to any of the local group stars, it was much less energy intensive to jump *back* from Gateway. The larger the total stellar mass, the more gravity our jump drives had to "push" against. It wasn't actually a *push*, per se, but it was a close enough analogue for most purposes. The Gateway system had *two* stellar masses close to the same size as sol, Rigil Kentaurus with one-point-one solar mass and Toliman at point-nine solar mass, plus another point-twelve from Proxima. Sure, we could jump to Barnard's Star from Sol. It was only six light years away, after all. But getting anywhere else would be nearly impossible without really *big* capacitors and a full refuel at turnaround. It only had sixteen percent of Sol's mass in the *whole system*, making the energy required to jump back over *ten* times as high. Most ships, even military ones, didn't carry capacitors large enough to store that much energy.

But as unique as Gateway was, there was one type of system which was even more sought after. Stable quadruple-star systems, called 'Quad-hubs'. Only a handful of them had ever been discovered, as multi-star systems like that tend to wobble about and toss out stars until they finally got down to just two, and the orbits stabilized. But finding a *Quad-hub*, especially one with fast orbits? That was considered the real prize. The Serpentia Empire had one on the far side of their territory, located 136 light-years away in the constellation Aries, although its inner orbital periods were measured in decades, not days, and the outer ones in millenia. It even had a planet or two, as I remembered.

I was personally thankful none of its low-energy jump points pointed this way, or the Confed Navy would have been wiped out a century ago, and I likely would never have been born. Considering their empire's focus on colonization and resource gathering, it was mostly Gateway that the Snakes were probably interested in. With two such massive hubs, they could literally steal half the easily extracted mineral and biological wealth within several hundred light years, and no one would be able to do a thing about it. Terra was just inconveniently in the way. Having Gateway so close to Sol was one the biggest, if not *the* biggest reason Terran shipping Corpos were so dominant in the local group.

Of course, all this was academic to me. I could grasp the logistics, sort of. And navigation was really just a matter of practice and precision. I could visualize it, and I could do the equations, but I really didn't understand the underlying principles of jump dynamics. I just plugged in the destination coordinates and made sure the ship's positioning was as exact as I could make it. Being as little as a hundred-thousand klicks out of position could cost you upwards of five percent in fuel, not to mention the added complications to navigation. *Hell,* I thought. *Screw it up badly enough, and you could even end up at the wrong star!*

It took several minutes, but I finally tore my eyes away from the view and started doing the post-jump checklists. We couldn't afford to pay for repairs, so keeping on top of maintenance was critical.

*****

After seeing the grandeur of Alpha Centauri, Hoth was a letdown.

Hoth was a binary star system featuring a pair of red dwarfs, six small rocky planets and one ice giant that used to be called Groombridge 34 before some schmuck human surveyor from half a thousand years ago decided that any ice ball he found *had to be called Hoth*, which is why there are fifteen or sixteen planets with that name now. But this was the *first* to be named such, so it was the only one called the

Hoth 'System'. The two stars had a mass of point-four and point-one-six SM respectively. Were it not a binary star with a stable, and predictable orbit, it would have been skipped by most traders. As it was, its two jump corridors were perfectly positioned to get us to the next major hub, a trinary on the edge of Confed space. The gas giant orbiting the larger star also had fuel scoops and refineries where we could top off on H^3 before arriving at the major hub. Fuel was always more expensive in busier systems, of course.

Goose and I played lots of cards while he caught me up on the Kin rumor mill. The biggest news was an update on the Dog Star Colony disaster. One of the other local jump points from Gateway went to Sirius, also known as the Dog Star. I found the name pretty appropriate, but also sad.

The Sirius system itself was downright beautiful. The two gorgeous blue-white stars shone like a pair of jewels. The first all-Kin orbital colony, composed mostly of Wolf-Kin, had been established almost three decades ago in a long, convoluted orbit around the binary pair. There were no planets in the system, as the stars' orbits were far too eccentric to allow them to develop. It also made it unsuitable as a regular trade route, as the jump points created by their resonance swung all over the place. It was predictable, of course, since the orbits themselves didn't change much, but the shapes of the orbits meant that the jump points rotated in odd directions, only coming back to the same spot once every eleven years or so. Getting there was easy. Getting right back was not. Also the mass difference between the two stars was considerable. Sirius A was nearly double the mass of Sirius B, meaning your jump drives had to be perfectly calibrated *but asynchronously tuned* or you would never be able to translate out.

But the colony went forward with the launch anyway. Eleven years later, when the next survey ship arrived to check on them, they were gone. The entire orbital platform was missing, as if it had never been constructed at all. No ships, no mining tugs, nothing. That was nearly eighteen years ago, now.

A few privately funded, and thus small-scale, missions were launched to investigate, but communication back was limited to either light-speed transmissions or a long, tortuous route through several single-star systems with no existing infrastructure. It meant having to scoop and refine your own fuel from the occasional gas giant, which were thankfully relatively common in single-star systems, but the added time and effort to make the return journey raised the already high cost of the trip to astronomical proportions. The latest communication from one of the private expeditions had arrived six months ago, but didn't contain much in the way of hard evidence, just trace elements detected in the colony's expected orbital path, and some odd spectrography readings from the smaller primary.

Goose was convinced that the Snakes were responsible. It was one of the reasons he'd joined up for a RECON posting to begin with, even before the latest spat of hostility. His theories ran from unknown Dark Matter jump points, which I seriously didn't believe existed, to massive rogue planets, all being used by the Serpentia Empire to sneak into human space, ambushing ships and destroying new, defenseless colonies.

I didn't put it past the Snakes to do such things, I just doubted they had much in the way of secret routes into human space. Their technology wasn't that different from ours, after all. And humans had very thoroughly explored their surroundings after having nearly been wiped out six hundred years ago. Any "secret passage" that didn't involve a brute force approach of hopping from single-star to single-star was ludicrous. Gravimetrics was a field in which humans had been forced to get very good at, and I seriously doubted anything was left undiscovered after so many years.

Besides, if they *did* have such a passage, why didn't they use it to bypass our fortified systems and wreck our infrastructure during the war? It would have been an immediate knockout blow.

Docking at the fuel station was a welcome change in routine.

*****

"Fueling is complete, Goose," I commed. "Five-point-seven-three metric tons liquid H3 and Five-point-seven-one metric tons of liquid H2 on board. Cryo is stable at thirty-two-point-six Kelvin, pressure stable at one-point zero-one kilopascals. Bucky bags show no breaks. Leak detectors show clear as well. Looks like we're done here."

Goose waved from inside the station where he was set to pay the fuel bill. I cringed at the cost, but there was no help for it. I'd given him all I could spare. I had to save enough for when we reached our destination. I had the inheritance money that *finally* got released a couple months ago, but I really needed that for later.

Goose popped back on the comm quicker than I expected. "Hey Red, you're clear to undock. Just pull her around to the hab module and meet me in the restaurant. I want to have at least one meal that I didn't have to cook."

"So you're saying you want me to cook?" I joked. Goose gave me a one-finger salute through the viewport, which was all the answer I needed. Neither of us wanted to eat my cooking. It was one thing I really sucked at, no matter how much I tried to practice.

The zero-G airlock let out into a clearly marked transition tube, with giant arrows pointing "down", and a yellow and black caution line demarking where the grav plates would take effect. I oriented myself and gracefully landed on my feet just as I passed the line. I was getting back to thinking and reacting like a spacer, finally…

The little diner was relatively empty. While the route we'd chosen through the jump points was efficient, it wasn't really the fastest route. Of course, the system was crowded with bulk carriers from all the major Corpos, but they used their own refueling facilities on the far side of the planet. This little station was for the local residents and asteroid miners that plied the system's belt. Not much in the way of amenities, but the dress code was relaxed, and the people were nice.

An old Beaver-Kin wearing a faded leather jacket adorned with a multitude of colorful patches, was holding court at the small bar at one end of the establishment. His raspy voice echoed through the room like an old buzz saw.

"I'm telling ya, eh? Them Corpo-cicles is after 'ar loot!"

"An 'am telling you right back, Grandpa, ViaCorp has nothing to do with it," a vaguely familiar voice argued back. To my surprise, the pup arguing with his elders was actually wearing a Corporate officers uniform. A ship-suit no less! I'd never heard of a Corpo letting Kin become officers, but apparently this one was solidly on the side of the same ones that hung me out to dry. I had little sympathy for the delusional pup as he continued to argue with his elder.

After a moment I realized I'd misjudged the young Beaver-Kin's age. He had to be at least in his mid to late twenties. Like their French-Canadian Otter-Kin cousins, West-Canadian Beaver-Kin tended to look young for most of their lives, until they didn't. Their sleek fur would quickly go gray and scraggly, their muscles would atrophy, and they suddenly looked positively ancient. As I listened to the argument, I began to recognize a pattern.

"Jorge, Philippe, Michael, Émile," the old Kin grated out. "And that's just in the last year! I told you they're waitin' fer us ta fill up 'ar holds, then BAM!" he smacked his hand on the bar with a dull thud. "They swoop in, pop a hole in t' canopy, and WHOOSH! They take every'ting, even the minin' pod."

"Grandpa," the young lieutenant almost pleaded. "The Corporation doesn't even have a smelter in the system. And shipping ore to another star for processing would cost more than the ore would be worth. We don't do mining here.

There's not enough material in the system to make a decent profit!"

"Bah! You think it's all aboot profit? It's costin' us 'ar lives! They're tryin' ta take us outa te picture, so's they can bring in more slaves. We's FREE here, an dey don't like that!"

"But where would the money be in that? Besides, none of the Corporation's ships have even BEEN on this side of the planet. I know, because I'm the one that does all the traffic control!" The young Beaver-Kin was clearly getting frustrated, but I finally realized where I'd heard his voice before.

"You know, the kid's right." Goose's voice chimed from behind me, startling me so much I nearly fell on my ass, I spun so hard.

"Shit, don't sneak up on me like that, Mongoose!" I nearly screeched.

Goose gave me an odd look at the use of his full nickname. "What are you, my mom?" He then turned back to the argument. "The Corpos don't do anything unless there's profit involved. It may not be monetary, but if they do something, they're gaining something from it." He turned to the old Kin. "What's your name?"

"Frances," the old guy answered. "Frances McGill."

"So, tell me something, Old Timer. Did you actually see a Corpo ship? Did your people ever get any scans?"

Frances shook his head reluctantly. "But who else could it be? No one else comes through here, not even the crabs."

"What about other ships that don't belong to you out there? Have you seen anything out of the ordinary besides the missing pods?" Goose looked around the room. "Anyone? Please don't be shy."

A voice called out from the back of the restaurant. "Nothing recent I think, but Frankie, remember that weird, dark-looking thing I told you about three years ago? The one that you told me was a sensor ghost?"

Goose zeroed in on the speaker. I could tell that something had triggered my friend, and he was in full hunt mode. "And your name, Miss?"

"Gwen Barlee," the small Otter-Kin replied. "I run the water purification plant, and do ice mining on the side."

"Could you give me a description of what you saw? Spectrograph readings?"

"I can do better than that. I saved the sensor logs. I *knew* something was weird with that thing," she glowered at Frances who was grimacing back at her.

Goose got a manic look on his face as he stepped towards his new best friend.

"Well, isn't that grand!"

I had no idea what had gotten his tail in a knot, but I knew someone, somewhere, would eventually have a really, *really* bad day.

Ch 3: A Race to the Start

Goose spent the next hour all but interrogating the residents of the small refueling station. I tried to listen in, but the smell of wonderful, greasy, protein-laden meat caught my attention. My nose told me it was *real, actual meat*, and beef, at that. It shocked the hell out of me. The nearest source was four jumps away, which really made me wonder who was shifting frozen steaks across a twelve day transit.

I mean, it wasn't like they were hard to keep frozen, and they didn't take up that much space, but there wasn't much demand for it, either. Most species in galactic society had transitioned to manufactured protein sources long before they even left their planet of origin, just due to population pressure. Even within the Human Confederation it was rare to see. Since the near-total destruction of Terra's biosphere, most of humanity had switched to vat-grown protein, and the farms had all transitioned to hydroponics due to the sheer volume of food needed to feed the billions of Kin who sustained the Confed economy. The amount of work involved in raising the animals, not to mention raising the feed for them, was pretty much a zero-sum game on heavily populated worlds. There was just not enough *room* to raise cattle on any kind of scale.

I just sat down at one of the tables with the biggest, juiciest, most *mouth-watering* rib-eye steak I had ever seen, when I heard a voice behind me.

"We're leaving," Goose said, his no-nonsense tone setting off alarm bells in my head.

"But..." I was stricken with grief. I opened my mouth to complain, but the look I saw on his face brooked no argument. "Now?" I whimpered.

To my horror, he grabbed the meal and dumped the whole thing into the recycler, plate and all.

"Now."

Less than three minutes later, we were undocking and boosting at maximum for the next jump point. I tried to get Goose to tell me what he found that was so urgent, but he kept silent on the matter, only speaking when necessary. I was beginning to get concerned. Whatever was bothering him was obviously serious, and I wanted to help, but I couldn't do anything when he just ignored my entreaties. Finally, he just told me to shut up.

I started to say something again, but realized I was just digging a hole for myself. He'd talk when he was ready, I figured. In the meantime, all I could do was just offer my silent support.

Handing over the controls, he instructed me to keep to the least-time flight profile he'd programmed into the nav. Without even looking in my direction, he unstrapped from the pilot's seat and disappeared into the hold of the ship, locking the hatch behind him.

The only thing I could think of that would set him off like this was the Snakes, but nothing I overheard in the fueling station above Hoth made me think they were directly responsible for the disappearing miners. Just like the old Kin back on the station, I would have immediately thought the Corporations were behind it. I had to admit I was heavily biased, but considering that kind of skulduggery usually *was* the human Corpos, there was little reason to think otherwise. But, like Goose said, there really wasn't any profit in it, and the Corpos were all about the bottom line.

"Ten minutes to threshold," I reported through the ship's intercom. A minute later, the hatch reopened and Goose emerged, smudges of grease and other space-rated lubricants now staining the sleeves of his ship-suit. He strapped in and took a look at the holo-screens before speaking his first sentence in nearly four hours.

"My ship," he said brusquely, taking over the flight controls from my station.

"Your ship, aye."

He looked over at me, but I studiously ignored him. If he wanted a conversation at this point, he'd have to start it. I was more than a bit resentful at this point, and I was sure he knew it.

"I can't tell you," he started hesitantly. I gave him a bland stare in return.

"It has to do with that thing I'm looking into, and right now I'm not sure you wouldn't consider me a nutcase. I don't know who to trust."

My eyes narrowed at this. I knew I had been out of the loop for ten years, but he'd known me for over a decade prior to that. We'd flown together for nearly four years, two of them in the same ship. We'd been in crazy situations together, and I trusted him with my *life*. If he seriously felt he couldn't trust me after all of that, then... *to hell with him*, I thought furiously.

"It's not that I don't trust you to have my back," he clarified. "I just don't trust you to not think I'm crazy." He finally looked at me. "And if you thought I was crazy, seriously 'round the bend' nutzoid, you might start talking to old friends and piecing together what made me that way. You don't need my headaches on top of yours."

"I don't know, Goose," I replied, my hackles finally starting to settle. "Crazy is kind of relative to the two of us. Some of those stunts we pulled in the war went right past that tube station and pulled up to 'bat-shit-insane', if you ask me. Who's to say I wouldn't believe you?"

"Doesn't matter," he sighed looking down at his hands on the controls. "Because even if you did, I don't have anything else to go on but a gut feeling. The NTK on this is a steel-plated bitch, and you're not going to be able to help me back in Confed space with that blacklist hanging over your head anyways. I'm going to have to go silent on this one, and having you aboard would just cause questions that I really don't need asked."

Shit. Yeah, that stopped me cold, right there. I lost one of my best friends and ten years of my life because of a lack of operational security. I understood the consequences of 'need-to-know' more than anyone, after that.

"Fine," I groused. "But did you have to toss my steak in the recycler? I haven't had steak in fourteen years!"

"Sorry." And to be fair, he actually *did* sound apologetic this time.

"So what now?"

"Now?" He looked at the nav screen showing the nearby jump point. "Now we set for silent running."

He hit a pair of buttons and waved at the holo-screen I'd recognized when he first briefed me on running the ship. "I reset the menu labels back to the default, just in case you can't remember what the little buttons do," he smirked.

"Ooookay..." I grew a little leary at the sudden cloak-and-dagger routine. "Why now?"

"Two reasons," he explained. "One, I'm thinking it would be better for you if everybody and their brother didn't know where you were headed. You already have people gunning for you, if you hadn't figured that out. This way, they'll have to look harder to find your destination, instead of just checking the sensor logs."

"I can understand that, I guess, but I haven't had people actually shooting at me that I've noticed." I booted up the stealth system and began to go through the checklist. ECM wouldn't be used unless we got targeted by fire control, and if that happened, we weren't being stealthy anymore, but I brought them up anyways, as Goose's statement got me thinking defensively again.

"The second reason has to do with that steel-plated NTK," he continued. "I'll tell you this much; that sensor ghost came from this sector of the sky."

"So why not go stealth from the git-go?"

"There's no chance the sensor watch on the Corpos station would miss having us fly into the Hoth system, then never leave, but there's two different trade routes we can reach from this jump corridor. The one headed to Ross 154 doesn't have an active control station, just the automated one for emergencies, which wouldn't necessarily pick us up, even if we weren't in stealth. But that one doesn't go the direction we want.

"So what we're gonna do is stealth up just before we jump, and translate to 61 Cygni. It's not a major hub, but they have an active sensor watch, since it's got mining and a refueling station. We'll come out and coast for a couple hours till we clear the jump point, then a short, low burn to get us headed to the jump point for Wolf 424. When Cygni control doesn't report us as having gone through the system, anyone watching for our trail will think we went to Ross 154, and maybe on down to the Pav system, since it would look like we were trying to drop off the radar. Based on the standard range of this ship type, they'd start looking for us to show up in Guniibuu or something for refueling. It's a reasonable assumption, really, if you assume we're headed to the frontier systems.

"Instead, we'll be staying in stealth through the whole Cygni-Ophiuchi chain till we get to the Ophiuchi jump point, and drop out of stealth before we translate there."

"Why there?" I asked. "I mean, I get the whole idea about dropping off sensors, but why end it there? We could just keep going. The Confed would never even know we left."

"That's as far as our fuel will take us, even with the boost we'll be getting from using the binary star routes and going slow through the transits."

"Oh, duh." I felt a little stupid. It really had been a while since I'd had to worry about fuel consumption.

"That, and it's the current border between the Confed and the Phoneck Alliance. We have to check in with Phoneck Customs. They won't care as long as we show we have no cargo. That's what I was getting rid of back there. It's got a radar reflector so I can pick it up later, and a stint in vacuum won't hurt it."

"Are the Confed going to care about me being on ship without a crew license? I don't think they'd accept us calling me a passenger." I wondered.

"Nah, Confed customs only look at inbound so they can tax it before it hits the market. They don't really monitor outbound traffic, other than to record transponders. However, if we didn't get clearance from Phoneck customs, we'd be screwed. Pop out of a jump point at Ophiuchi without a valid customs transponder, and the Phoneys will light you up and ask questions later. Terrans aren't really liked too much there since we have a stranglehold on their trade, and they already have a huge smuggling problem."

"That's fair. We kinda do contribute heavily to both issues, I guess."

"And before you ask, I'd only give even odds of our stealth being good enough to slip by undetected. The Phoneys have pretty good sensors, even if their weapons aren't all that great."

"All right," I agreed.

"Oh, one last thing." He finished, pulling out a small tray that looked like it was just a cup holder, giving a slight twist, then pulling it another three inches out. "Here's the heavy weapons lockout. I figured you should know in case things go sideways. Two concealed tubes, one loaded in each, and one reload each. Once the covers are blown off, we ain't hiding that we're armed, so last resort, eh?"

"Why does this not surprise me?" I sighed, shaking my head.

"Meh," he shrugged with a grin. "I'd have more reloads, but it would have cut too much into the cargo space. Can't say you're a cargo ship without actual cargo space, after all."

"This," I said, pointing at my deadpan expression. "This is my shocked face."

Ch 4: Arrival

"Docking in thirty minutes." Goose called back to me.

The Commercial Conglomerate of Cranotia was a single-system polity, and for now, my destination. It had taken twelve jumps to get here, and I was eager to be on my way. Goose was a great guy and all, but being cooped up with him for nearly two months was pushing things.

Even in RECON we'd never had to spend more than a couple weeks on a mission. That was done by the LRP teams. You really had to be a super-duper stable personality to handle long range patrols, with nothing but the two of you for conversation for months on end, literal weeks of boredom combined with the constant threat of discovery as you shadowed an enemy formation or fortification. Thankfully, the psychs said I was too twitchy to be a "Lurper" and I never had to test the absolute limits of my friendship with my RIO, Buckley. I doubt our friendship would have survived.

As this trip proved, I was just not cut out for long periods of solo activity. I needed to interact with a crew for more than just a few minutes a day. The first four jumps till we hit the Confed border had been insanely boring. We didn't have to worry about enemy action, but in some ways that made it worse. In order to thread the needle between all the sensor nets, Goose and I had swapped on watch every six hours, that being pretty much the maximum either of us could focus on the finicky task of stealth piloting. By the time we got to Ophiuchi Prime three weeks later, both of us were thoroughly exhausted, and we holed up in a station-side crew rest hotel on the Phoneck side of the border for three days to recuperate and just take a break from each other.

The rest of the trip was not as tiring, and entirely uneventful, but equally boring. At least without the need to dodge sensor nets we could just set the autopilot to collision avoidance and just relax together. When we tired of playing cards or rehashing old stories, Goose tried to educate me on alien customs and quirks. I smiled a bit at the memory.

"One thing you gotta remember, Red," Goose pontificated as he gestured with the half-empty glass of bourbon. "Aliens don't use the words 'shit' or 'frak', at least not the same way we do."

"Seriously?" I asked, nursing my own glass of rather watered-down whiskey, my tolerance for alcohol having suffered from ten years of enforced abstinence. "How else do you say something's all fraked up?"

"Well, they don't look at copulation in a negative context, for one," he started. "The human context of non-consensual sex is almost non-existent in most alien cultures. Many just don't have a sex drive like we do, so there's no reason to link the act of procreation with anything negative. Or positive, for that matter. It just 'is'."

"Okay, that's just weird," I concluded. "I guess aliens are just alien. But that doesn't explain the other one. Everybody shits, it's pretty much a universal constant!"

"Sure, sure," he agreed. "But for one, a lot of them consider it pretty vulgar to just call it out like that, and second, not all of them actually excrete solid waste like us."

"Ok, so kind of like in the high society movies, where everyone talks in euphemism?"

"Not really, it's just that most alien earbugs translate 'shit' into their equivalent of 'excrement' which never comes out right on their end. Aliens usually don't get human metaphors or hyperbole."

"So what do you do?" I slurred, more than a little drunk at that point. "I seriously doubt I can excise the ten.. tendency from my vern... Shit." I winced. "See? I can't stop using the phrase."

"So do some substitution." he answered. "There's one thing pretty much everyone but aquatics do when they expel waste. Even the avians do it."

I looked at him, puzzled.

"They squat."

I'd literally fallen to the deck laughing. But it made sense, if you looked at it from the right perspective. I'd countered again with the whole "aliens are alien" truism, but he replied with something a little more profound than I'd expected. *"You need to stop thinking of them as aliens. You're not in Confed space anymore. Technically, YOU are the alien here, not them."*

I finished cleaning up the galley, having just enjoyed one last "bacon-ater", courtesy of Goose's amazing cooking skills and headed back to my cabin to pack up. It wasn't like I had a lot of belongings, just a couple ship-suits, a small collection of civilian clothing, and a small pulser I'd picked up in a pawn shop in Ceres. That got put into the bottom of my carry bag, as I wasn't sure of the regulation for weapons on the Cranotian station.

Besides miniscule physical items, I had the savings I'd managed to accrue over six months working odd jobs before finally asking Goose for help. The rest of my nest egg, the capital I hoped to use to restart my life, had come in the form of an inheritance from my parents' death, seven years into my incarceration. My father had died of a stroke while laboring on one of the hydroponics farms, and my mother soon followed, stricken with grief, I supposed. I never got to talk to her. I wasn't told of their deaths until months later, their assets liquidated and their bodies already cremated and their ashes added to the Agri-Corp's compost pile. *Yet another thing to lay at the feet of that damned Spurgle and that back-stabbing JAG officer.*

After all the remaining "debt" had been deducted from their estates, there was barely enough to purchase a new skimmer. But given the right time, place and opportunity, it *might* be enough to start a new life, somewhere outside the confines of the stifling Human Confederation. I hoped.

I packed the last of my items into the carry-bag, slinging it over my shoulder. The small storage locker was almost completely empty, now. There was only one last thing.

I gently picked up the set of identification tags, known from time immemorial as 'dog tags' for some forgotten reason so far back it was lost to history. Humans hadn't had domestic dogs as pets for over five hundred years, and the native wolf population on earth, along with most other large predators on the planet's surface, existed only as cryogenically frozen genetic samples, but the nickname for the data-laden titanium and silicon sandwich still stuck.

The first two had *"Rodrick A. Vulkeshson"* engraved along the top edge. Below that was my service number. They were mine, the only things I was permitted to keep from my military service. The other two said, *"Joseph K. Buckley"*. They belonged to my RIO, the Reconnaissance Intercept Officer who'd died in the Snake prison camp we'd been thrown into. I was sure that if Spurgle had known I kept Buckley's dog tags, he would have found a way to take them too. It was just in his nature to be as vindictive as possible. *That damned sanctimonious, incompetent prig.*

Heading to the portside airlock, I waited patiently for the docking light to go green. I heard a soft *clank* as the docking collar engaged. Goose appeared a few seconds later, giving me a slight nod. I was never one for long goodbyes, and getting Goose to acknowledge even a short one bordered on futile. As soon as the airlock showed a good seal, he hit the actuator, gave me a slap on the shoulder and started heading back to the tiny utilitarian bridge.

"Hurry up, I don't have all day," his gravelly voice called back. "The fuzz doesn't like me here for some reason."

"I wonder why that could be?" I muttered sarcastically, stepping over the ship's pressure threshold out onto the orbital station's concourse. I couldn't help but gawk at my surroundings, and nearly got my satchel caught in the sliding hatch when it abruptly snapped closed behind me.

The airlock design was fairly standard outside Confed space, as I'd found when reading up on my destination. A seal formed between the two thresholds using what was essentially an inflatable tube which lined the station's hatch, filled with a sort of non-newtonian fluid. Instead of just being sensitive to impact, it was also made to solidify when it detected a pressure differential, so while there was vacuum inside the docking face, it remained the consistency of maple syrup allowing the tube to conform its shape to any number of hatch types. The tube itself was just a long continuous pressure switch with electronically-actuated variable adhesive skin. Once it detected mechanical pressure around the entire loop and the skin of the tube attached itself to the hull of the ship, verifying a seal, the dock's software would start to release nitrogen into the now sealed gap, which the fluid kept from seeping out by becoming rigid as it reacted to the pressure differential. It was an ingenious system, and a simple, inexpensive solution to a very old problem, as it didn't require a standardized lock design. But it looked kinda fragile to me, from a military standpoint. I wondered what happened when a ship came in too hard and broke the tube.

My question was answered only a couple docks down. The hatch was open, as if a ship were docked, but instead of a ship's interior, all I saw was a large cube surrounding the hatch. A retractable fabric ribbon was stretched across the hatch with bright purple and yellow letters in what I supposed was the equivalent of an "Out of Order" sign, and a short crab-like alien, a native Cranotian if I remembered the pictures in the brochure correctly, was inside ripping off a damaged tube which looked to have been pinched a little too hard. A replacement loop hung over one of the alien's four manipulators, and a vacuum-rated adhesive sprayer hung from its utility belt.

Apparently these were just personnel docks here, paid for by the minute, according to the large multi-language marquis prominently displayed at regular intervals along the wide corridor. Which also explained something about why Goose was in such a hurry to cut loose. Only the first three minutes were free, starting when the lock was opened. If you went beyond that before initiating undocking procedures, you either had to have an automated payment account, which I seriously doubted Goose would submit to, or were forced to come out to one of the little kiosks set up next to each placard. The kiosks also offered knickknacks and doodads commonly seen in spaceport terminals and travel centers. I spotted advertisements for at least three charging adapters and six locally made versions of the auto-translation earbugs I was already wearing, a final gift from Goose before we docked.

Considering I had no local currency yet, and was not about to pay the insane exchange rate I saw posted, I saw no reason to dawdle any longer. I pulled my slate from its clip and brought up the free map I'd downloaded on our approach. It wasn't very detailed, but it did allow me to figure out generally where I was.

There was a whole list of things I had planned. Find a bank, get my slate linked to the local payment applications, and get a ride down to the surface. But first, the bank. The map showed a bank terminal or branch was located next to the food court, so I accessed the routing function and pinged for directions. And ran into my first snag.

Invalid network credentials? I scowled at the small touch screen as it returned the same error message a second time. "Son-of-a-bitch," I growled softly. *I guess I have to do this the hard way and ask for directions. Spinward, maybe?*

The station was an old 'legacy' design. Nearly every species had at least one or two stations like this orbiting their home planet, and like every other example, it was based on large concentric rotating rings held together by spokes and connecting modules. Sometimes the rings were even stacked vertically as they expanded. This one consisted of three nested 'stacks' of three rings each, for a total of nine rings. Each stack had an outer, middle, and inner ring, and was anchored to the next stack by dozens of cross-connecting tubes and bays.

The entire ring structure was originally designed to spin on its axis to provide pseudo-gravity for the inhabitants, as most species required gravity to maintain their health. When those species finally developed anti-grav, the old stations were almost always converted to use grav plates and their spin halted. This allowed the massive real estate of the outer rings to be converted from living quarters to docking rings, as they were no longer moving targets. With how large those rings had to be to generate pseudo gravity, they provided the perfect platform for large trading hubs.

The docks were nearly deserted. I really had no idea what the local time was, so I couldn't tell if this was the normal state of things. As I continued to look around, I realized the only person I'd even seen was the maintenance guy back at the hatch. Retracing my steps, I headed back to look for him, her, or whatever they referred to themselves as.

I found them just as they were finishing up. As I walked up, their eyestalks swung my way jerkily, and their whole body froze up for an instant. I was no expert on alien body language, but that looked like a fear response to me, so I slowed my pace to a crawl and held up the map displayed on my slate.

"Excuse me, Sir," I ask politely. "Could you help me for a moment?"

Upon seeing the application on my slate, the maintenance guy seemed to deflate a little, their segmented carapace beginning to move again as whatever it used for lungs resumed their function. Its voice sounded like a series of clicks, scratches and gurgles, but my earbugs quickly translated it to Terran Common for me.

"No scare like that!" it protested, waving a small claw at me. "Close molt when rapid approach late-night! You luck not station-security call!" Clearly my earbug programming left much to be desired, but it was supposed to be chock full of learning algorithms, so I would wait and see if it got better over time. And it was night shift, apparently, which sort of explained the lack of traffic.

Asking the same question again didn't get a much better result, as the little guy apparently didn't have a translation device on them that understood Terran. However, it turned out they did understand Imperial Serpentian, which irked me to no end, considering the circumstances in which I learned what little I knew. Eventually I got my point across and he got me headed in the right direction.

"Follow guide. Look *cha-li-klik* sign that way, not miss." pointing at a small sign on the wall.

I had no clue what *cha-li-klik* meant, but they were right. You really couldn't miss it. Had I been paying attention I might have noticed the discrete signage with what in retrospect was an alien crab-claw pointing to the exit with a word written below in the hashtag-like script that just had to be the local written language. As it was, the large green sign above the archway was a dead giveaway, as it included universal pictograms of food, beds, and what were probably shuttles, along with several more for which I had no clue.

As I passed through the archway, noise blasted me in the face. Some kind of active noise canceling had been blocking it in the docking concourse, and the transition was decidedly jarring to my sensitive ears. Dozens of different aliens were strolling through the oversized compartment. Neon colored signs cheerfully blinked and flashed, peppy music streamed from storefronts and above all, shouted "prosperity" across the artificial environment. More than anything else, it reminded me of one of the huge shopping malls in the human-only retail districts back on Old Terra.

I'd only ever been to one once, while acting as personal security for a senior officer's daughter during my flight training. Kin were not permitted except in performance of their duties, be it janitor, bathroom attendant, or as in my case, security-guard-slash-pack-mule. It had truly been an eye opener on the realities of "social strata", and where I fit within them. It wasn't that the teenage girl was particularly demanding or insulting. As far as she was concerned, I didn't exist unless she needed something carried. I was a piece of furniture. A walking, self-directing shelf for her to place her purchases. I managed to avoid further additional duties like that for the rest of my training, but the experience left a residue of resentment, like a bad taste in my mouth.

Glancing at the map again, I tried to figure out where to go. The bank was listed as being open 36/8, which I guessed was the equivalent of 24/7 on Old Terra. Actual, physical banking terminals in the Sol system were actually kind of rare, as most everybody used their slate for everything. This wasn't to say there weren't lots of different banks located in the system, there were literally hundreds, but I knew of only three Terran banks that had actual, physical terminals you could sign into without a slate, and only one of those operated off-planet, let alone interstellar.

Finding the bank turned out to be more of a chore than I anticipated. I walked right past the entrance at least three times before I finally spotted the small, nondescript hatch with the human-style letters FCSICU engraved across the faux wooden facade. The logo above the letters was the familiar stylized orbital path I recognized from their ads. I sighed in relief.

First Ceres Spacers Interstellar Credit Union was a financial institution run by spacers, for spacers. They were one of the oldest banks in the Sol system, originally established to serve the growing belter communities before humans developed FTL communications. But what really made them unique in Confed was their clientele. They were the only ones that openly catered to Kin customers.

Sure, lots of human banks would allow Kin to establish accounts. It was pretty much required now that Kin were finally being born rather than manufactured in cloning facilities. But those accounts were always inextricably linked to whichever company "employed" those Kin. Deposits and withdrawals were restricted and purchases could only be done through "approved channels", forcing those trapped in the vicious cycle of debt slavery to essentially finance their own prisons. Perhaps things would change over time, but I wasn't holding my breath.

Speaking of holding my breath, the smells which were assaulting my nose had my stomach grumbling again in spite of the gigantic bacon-ator I consumed on the ship. But I needed money first.

"How can I help you, Sir?" the Cranotian at the service window asked. Either my earbug was getting better at parsing Cranotian, or the person at the desk was using a language it was already programmed for, but that was not the first thing that went through my mind. I was quite startled to find an actual person manning an actual teller window. I'd expected an automated terminal with biometric login, but after a few moments I finally realized the problem. Facial and fingerprint recognition wouldn't work the same with other species. It was while I was pondering all this that I was nudged back to reality by a repeat of the same question as before.

"Um, oh, sorry..." I stammered, a bit embarrassed at being caught woolgathering. "I just arrived and need to establish a local account, I guess. I tried using my slate, but I gather they don't have guest access here."

"Do you have an account with FCSICU?" they asked, pronouncing it "Fix-you", or at least, that's what came through the earbug. As the bank's name easily turned into the acronym "Fix-you", it was only a short leap to an incredibly effective advertising slogan, "We'll Fix You Up!", which hadn't changed in centuries.

"Yes," I replied quickly, focusing on my slate as I pulled up the account information on the screen. It was essentially a giant QR code, which instead of acting like a hyperlink to a network address, was actually a time-based encryption key. That along with my account number would allow a normal banking terminal to unlock access to my account. This was usually backed up with biometric data to prevent a stolen slate from being used to hack accounts, but I had yet to see a normal facial recognition scanner in the small room.

"Place your slate on the desk here so I can get a scan, please." They pulled a handheld data scanner from behind the desk and waited patiently for me to comply.

I had decided to assume this Cranotian was a female equivalent, but I couldn't really pin down why. It just felt right. But I still resolved to do a bit more research into the local culture, especially if I was going to be here for a while.

"Name, and timestamp of birth?"

"Rodrick Vulkeshson," I answered, followed by my birthdate and time in universal timestamp format.

"Vole... kesh... son," she sounded out as she searched for my name to match the data on the slate.

"No, it's 'Vul', from the word 'vulpine', 'Kesh', my father's name, and 'son' because I'm a male..." I corrected her. I didn't know how many Kin she'd ever run into, but I suspected it probably hadn't been more than one or two. But even then, the addition of a surname was probably strange sounding. "Made" Kin weren't given a unique surname, usually just having their inventory class designation as a placeholder. In my dad's case, it was "NA-Vulpine106", referring to North American KinLab, the company which "built" him, their breed, and the specific genetic profile on which his "model" was based. My mother's was "NA-Vulpine82". As the first generation of "born" Fox-Kin, I had been able to actually choose a surname, and followed the ancient Norse tradition of honoring my immediate filial ancestor. My younger sister had chosen something similar, but had dropped the breed reference, going with "Lilisdötter".

The receptionist tapped at her console for a bit then asked a couple more questions which I recognized as the security prompts I had been required to set up when I made the account. I quickly provided the correct answers, and soon my account balances were being shown on the crystal display in front of me. There was also a table of exchange rates, much better than the ones listed at the dock terminal, as well as a list of services provided, the first of which I figured was going to be one of the more important ones. After getting about five hundred credits worth of Confed transferred onto a cash card, I asked about the other options.

"Does the network service extend to dirtside, or just the station," I asked, as it wasn't explicitly stated. "And does that include point of sale for purchases?"

After getting a basic explanation of the various services on offer, I decided on the minimum I could reasonably get away with, as I needed to keep my expenses down. Network services, which did not include point of sale, banking support, which did, and emergency service support, a catch-all for dealing with local medical, rescue and law enforcement, were the only ones I picked. That last was actually required by bank policy, which I guessed was reasonable. I also got an update for my earbug that would help with the local dialects.

Syncing my slate took only a few minutes and I was ready to go get something to eat, as my stomach was still complaining that it hadn't been satisfied yet. As I started for the exit, the Cranotian bank teller gave me one last piece of advice.

"Fox-Sir, be careful if you go down to the planet." I turned back to look at her questioningly. "Humans aren't very popular down there. Well, not anywhere, I suppose, but especially dirtside."

"But I'm not human." I replied, confused.

"As you say, Sir," she said, one eyestalk cocked sideways in a manner that my new earbug update translated as 'doubtful agreement'. She didn't say anything after that and I stepped back onto the main floor of the mall concourse, wondering what she'd meant by that statement. Perhaps it was just that Cranotians didn't like foreigners, I supposed, but it still caused me a bit of worry. Not that I intended to stay in the system for that long. I had big plans.

Ch 5: Bad Food and Angry Drivers

The first of those plans was to get something to eat. Having network access meant that I could link to the vendors menus which were helpfully annotated with species compatibility ratings for the various items available. Like most off-planet kitchens, the majority of the protein was various forms of synthmeat. The non-synth ones didn't have any compatibility labels, which caused me to hesitate. I could experiment later, I figured, once I got a place to sleep off any indigestion.

I finally found something that resembled a kabob from a place that smelled delicious and placed an order through my slate. While it was being prepared, I browsed through the advertising links to see about catching a shuttle to the surface.

My slate pinged when my food was ready and I headed to the pickup window to get my food. It was then that I first became aware of the hostile stares. Several different patrons, a few of which whose species I didn't recognize, were all glaring at me as I made my way forward. I looked behind me to make sure it was actually me they were directing their hostile gaze, but the rest of the crowd seemed to have backed off, almost as if they knew a fight was brewing.

My instincts started screaming at me to run. I began to back away, my eyes darting about, looking for an escape path. As I turned away, I heard a loud chittering voice yell behind me.

"Hey, human," it called tauntingly. "You forgot your food." I turned toward the voice just in time to catch a loosely wrapped package of wretched-smelling glop with the side of my face. The soggy paper wrapper burst on impact, and its vile contents smeared across my fur. Every one of the other patrons had risen to their feet, their aura of menace clear. The voice continued its harangue. "Now get the squat out of here, and don't come back, or I'll have security in here."

I was unsurprised to find it was the establishment's cook, as I could not imagine anyone else having something *that* disgusting ready-to-hand in normal circumstances. As I quickly retreated out of the restaurant I could hear the grating sound of laughter. I was no longer hungry.

Why are they calling me a human, though? I couldn't help but wonder as I brushed off as much of the goop into a trash receptacle in a public washroom. It wasn't like the reddish fur and the huge ears weren't a huge clue that I was anything but *human*. The shuttle schedule I'd found said the next run was in thirty minutes. Getting as clean as I could without soap and water, I made my way through the corridors to the departure bay.

Where I was refused a ticket. Apparently I smelled bad.

What the actual frak? I fumed. I tried to explain what had happened, but the asshole at the ticket desk didn't give a shit. He wasn't going to let some "reeking human" into his "pristine passenger compartment". Stinking, frustrated, and at the end of my patience, I nearly punched him in the face. Luckily, however, I spotted the trap in time. A pair of armed and armored troops in what looked like security brassards were lurking on the far side of the bay, and seemed to be paying far too much attention to their data slates. I suspected that as soon as I showed any kind of aggression, they would suddenly find me much more interesting.

More and more, I was beginning to realize some things. Either the entire planet had a thing against Terrans in general, or it was a setup.

*****

Much as I wanted to, I couldn't just call Goose to come pick me back up. His ship was likely well past parking orbit and headed for the jump point by now, and I already knew he didn't really have the fuel to spare to turn back around for yet another round trip. Besides, I wasn't about to take this lying down. Finding a bench in a deserted corridor, I pulled out my slate. I then opened my carry bag and pulled out something I'd hoped not to need, my hacking kit.

When I first joined RECON and became a RIO, long before I earned a slot as a scout pilot, part of the training was network intrusion and data retrieval techniques. Scouts didn't just fly around gathering sensor data, after all. We also infiltrated enemy cities and government institutions. I'd even been part of a mission to data-suck operational plans from a Snake military base, which had been quite a bit more exciting than I really wanted at the time. While no Confed Corporation would ever dream of hiring me for a network security position, the RECON branch of Space Corp had no compunctions with letting us take such risky actions against the enemy. And to be honest, the training was pretty thorough. You had to have the right equipment, though.

The compact and highly illegal intrusion module was something I'd picked up from another old friend after learning I was blacklisted. While designed to penetrate alien networks, it worked on human ones as well. I'd used it to hack into the Licensing Board's email servers to figure out why I was being blacklisted. I hadn't found much, as a security protocol I'd never seen before kicked me off-net before I was able to download more than a few Gigs of data, but it was enough to confirm that I was indeed blacklisted, if not enough to figure out by whom.

Now I was going to use it for its original intended purpose to find the link between myself and whatever was laying these traps. I already had my suspicions, but first I needed to make sure the slate itself wasn't contaminated or compromised by malware or spyware. I donned the small headset with its tiny heads-up screen and plugged the module to the port on my slate while pressing the power and volume buttons simultaneously, forcing it to reboot. Using the rootkit on the module, I opened up the files for the operating system and scanned for known hacks. I generally did this every couple of weeks, but since I had connected to a new network and installed the bank applications earlier, I figured it was better to be safe than sorry.

Nothing showed up, so I put in the command to let the slate boot up the rest of the way. Now the module would act as filter, firewall and data packet sniffer, all in one. I had it monitor the network for packets that matched specific parameters, then switched to a special diagnostic tool I'd written for myself over a decade ago, designed to ferret out patterns in the data my module would capture. I was looking for anything that looked like a shuttle reservation, and I didn't have to wait long to capture one.

I opened the packet and stripped away the payload, digging into the metadata, where I suspected the problem lay. Not every bit was tripped, which didn't surprise me, but it, and the several other packets I looked at over the next ten minutes, gave me a good baseline of what a normal reservation packet should look like.

Hacking into the station's network was time consuming, but relatively straightforward. I penetrated the shuttle company's servers through a maintenance protocol which really should have been disabled. I scraped the cache then pulled up the logs from my own shuttle reservation.

And there it was, buried in the metadata. A single bit was tripped that had not shown up in any of the other packets I'd used as a baseline. Tracing back through the central routers, found the origin of the flag that set the bit in question. The bank.

Anger and disappointment warred for supremacy in my mind. The FCSICU was one of the cornerstones of my entire adult life. To think the same institution which had been the strongest proponents of Kin freedom for the last two centuries was actively sabotaging me was a real kick in the teeth.

Suddenly worried, I pulled out the cash card I had gotten from the bank and scanned its embedded chip. If they'd somehow flagged that too, I would have to resort to something seriously illegal to get off the station. Thankfully, the card seemed clean. I shut down the slate completely, even removing the power source, and placed it in my carry bag. I didn't want anyone tracking me at this point as I started to plan my next move.

Now that I knew the score, I had to figure out how to drop off the radar, or this crap would keep following me everywhere I went. And the best place to find what I needed was a *bar*.

Which wasn't really all that hard to find. I just followed my nose.

One of the strangest things the entire galaxy has puzzled over for millenia was the seemingly universal ability for intelligent life to consume alcohol. Even more puzzling was that it generally had the same effect on all of them. Of course, there were exceptions, and some of the flavorings different species used were downright toxic to Terran physiology, but the general rule held true. Anywhere you went, alcohol was served and consumed. And that meant bars.

And bars were where you went to get the local gossip. And make shady deals. The dingier the bar, the shadier the deals.

Heading towards the industrial section of the station, I soon found myself in a series of progressively dirtier and more utilitarian corridors as I traveled further from the well-lit and tastefully decorated retail concourses. As I'd suspected, the cargo and trash haulers weren't really welcome in the tourist ring, as an entirely different set of shops and businesses came into view as I entered the area around the cargo docks. Gone were the colorful vaulted ceilings and tasteful decor. Instead, the walls were lined with pipes and conduit, the bones of the station clearly visible and easily accessed for maintenance or repair. The myriad of warnings and painted signs on the floors were scuffed and faded from countless composite tires shredding the pigment with their passage. The heavy scent of lubricants and spilled chemicals lingered in the air, with a faint hint of sweat and carbonization adding just a bit of flavor to the mix.

The docking ring was huge, easily wide enough for a pair of medium cargo haulers to pass each other. Large hatches lined the outside of the ring, some of them opening into the cavernous holds of various bulk cargo carriers. On the inside of the ring, several wide corridors led deeper into the station where goods could be temporarily stored for cross-shipping. Smaller hatches led to numerous small businesses catering directly to the ships. Parts shops, machine shops, stores for food and supplies. All of them boasted brightly lit signs in hashtag squiggles advertising their wares. But the one I was interested in had none of that.

The dimly lit opening was unnamed, and the hatch looked like it hadn't been shut in years. The seal was cracked in at least two places. I was pretty sure what it was, just from the odor wafting my way, but the pair of crabs stumbling out confirmed it. It was a bar, or as my father would have once said, "a dive".

A set of public lock-boxes were arrayed along the wall just outside the hatch. Most were open, their keys hanging from the locks. Picking one that looked to be in good condition, I stashed my carry bag inside and closed it, swiping my cash card to release the key, which I slid into my pocket. Carrying a bag into a bar would make me stand out. And since it looked like the lockers weren't network connected at all, that meant I wouldn't be leaving electronic breadcrumbs for whoever at the bank had set the flag on my account, if there was some other method the station had for tracking cash cards.

Stepping through the hatch, I paused to let my eyes adjust to the low lighting. Just like the prevalence of alcohol across the galaxy, bars like this tended to look the same no matter which species was running it. Pay-to-play table games lined the back bulkhead, and a few tables with various barstools of different heights were scattered around the compartment. A few Cranotians and a couple of species I didn't recognize were spread out among them, no more than two or three in a group. A long counter lined one side, behind which worked the bartender.

To my surprise, they weren't Cranotian. Instead, a spider-like Shigothe was leaning up against the counter, two of its spindly appendages idly wiping down mugs and glasses, its dexterous three-pronged pincers handling the delicate task with ease, while two more were manipulating a slate propped up against a condiment dispenser. Based on the many holovids made about the war, I was vaguely familiar with the differences between the various castes, and this one looked like it might be a merchant-caste. I wasn't too sure about that, though. The old vids tended to get a lot wrong about the Kin, so it would be no surprise for them to mislabel the different Shigothe castes as well. Besides, it was really hard to tell between merchant and warrior castes without all the equipment the warriors were usually depicted carrying. The hump of the ovipositor under her cloak was a dead giveaway that she was female, however. Very few Shigothe left their core worlds anymore, at least not since 'The End of Innocence', the war between Terra and the old Protectorate which concluded nearly six centuries ago. I wondered to myself what convoluted path led them such a long way from home.

I couldn't ignore such an obvious opening and bartenders, as a rule, usually had dozens of cab drivers on speed dial. Considering that I was looking for a ride to the surface, it was a good chance that they'd know a way besides using the regular shuttle service.

"So," I started casually as I slipped onto a stool that was just about right for my stature. "Your story must be interesting. You're a long way from home."

The Shigothe looked over from her tasks with only one of the three sets of jet-black, unblinking eyes. I'd never met any Shigothi in person before, and the stare was making me a little nervous. She finished wiping the last mug and finally turned to fix me with the other two sets.

"As are you, Kin-Warrior," she said, her four legs propelling her across the floor smoothly as she stored away the slate.

"Not a warrior anymore, I'm afraid. Haven't served in ten years."

"A warrior without a battle is a warrior still. Your eyes give you away." She gestured at my body. "And your muscles are tense, ready to spring at the enemy. I wonder what foe has you so ready to do battle today?"

"Is it that obvious?" I asked, curious that she was so easily able to read my mood. I was a bit suspicious as well, considering the kind of welcome I'd gotten so far on the station, but I was willing to give her the benefit of the doubt, as she hadn't shown the same immediate hostility as the others. When she answered, I began to suspect my guess of her caste was a bit off the mark. Way off.

"My kind has always been sensitive to the moods of others," she answered calmly, snatching a shot glass from under the counter and looking at me expectantly. "What can I get you?"

"I'm going to guess you don't have a lager or pilsner that would work for me?" I sighed a little morosely. If I was telegraphing my emotions that badly, it didn't bode well for my plans. "Bourbon if you have it, vodka if you don't, I suppose."

"You'd guess wrong, young one. You are not the only human to frequent this place." She placed the shot glass back under the counter and grabbed a chilled mug from a cooler under the bar. Turning back to the unmarked taps on the bulkhead behind her, she quickly and efficiently filled the mug with a golden colored liquid that frothed just a bit as it poured down the side of the glass. She stopped the pour an inch short of filling it and waited for the head to settle before topping it off. She turned and set it in front of me with brisk efficiency, not a single motion wasted. "This is a local brew, but a favorite of those humans who patronize my establishment."

"Thanks," I said, my eyebrows raised in mild surprise. I'd figured there were at least *some* humans around here, but didn't realize they'd be so common as to have a local brewery catering to their needs. It still kind of bothered me to constantly be referred to as a human though.

"Hey, not to be pedantic or anything," I asked, keeping my tone as friendly as I could. "Why is it that everyone keeps calling me a human? It's not like we look anything remotely alike, other than general shape and stuff. I mean, I look more like an extra large rorr-ixian than a human."

She gave a close approximation of a human-style shrug by raising two appendages slightly, which really clued me in that she must have spent a lot of time with humans, or had studied them extensively. To be able to give that impression without a neck or shoulders was a true feat of body language brilliance. *Hell,* I thought. *I'm usually pretty good at picking up on alien body language, but that's some serious skill!* She answered in the same manner as everything else she'd done, quickly and efficiently, and her logic was razor sharp.

"Your kind are created by humans using their own genetic structure as a base, are you not?"

I shrugged back in semi-agreement. It wasn't a quibble I was going to make, as it was mostly true. Misleading, I thought, but true. "I was born of Kin parents, my family's first generation to be so, but I'll admit that our original genetic structure used a lot of the human genome."

She jumped a bit at hearing it. I got the impression she was surprised. "So the human masters finally recognized that natural breeding was more effective than manufacturing their slave armies? That could be worrisome."

"We're not slaves anymore." I countered, a mite offended at the 'slave' moniker.

"Are you?" she stared intently at me again. "And you are free to do as you wish in your own society, without impediment?"

I winced at that. She'd nailed the problem right on the head. We still weren't a "free" people, and probably wouldn't be until we finally gained a planetary home of our own, completely severed from human control. The Dog Star colony had been the first attempt at that, and it had disappeared without a trace, as far as anyone could tell.

"Fine," I admitted. "We're working on that, I guess. But sharing some genes still doesn't make me human. All mammals on Old Terra used to share the majority of their genetic structure before The End. It's why the bio attack killed off so much of the planet."

"Ah yes," she murmured. "That bottleneck in your genetic history was a major weakness in your physiology that we had not anticipated. For that I apologize."

"Meh," I brushed it off. It wasn't like she'd done it personally. That had all happened six centuries ago, or so. Ancient history, really. And given my current opinion of humans in general... "They probably had it coming."

"Hmm," she said noncommittally. "I think I have identified your problem. You equate the term human to refer to a specific, very narrowly defined genetic combination, with allowed variation limited to a tenth of a percent, true?" She waved a spindly arm at my ears and tail. "The fact that you share over ninety-five percent of it has no bearing?" She continued without letting me reply, as the answer was readily apparent. "Regardless, the answer is actually much simpler. You are suffering a failure in correct terminology. Though you do not claim 'human' to be one of your identifying characteristics, do you then reject the term 'Terran', as well?"

I wilted slightly at the thought. Regardless of how poorly I'd been treated by the Confed *government*, I was still proud of my origins. I was born on Old Terra of loving parents. No matter how corrupt the leadership of the Confed Navy, I was still proud to have served with my brothers and sisters in arms. There were even a few humans, a *very* few, I actually respected from that time period. Not like I was best buds with any of them, but I wouldn't go out of my way to spit in their beer. You could respect the man's abilities without liking the man himself. But in the end, I had to admit it to myself. *I am a Terran, and yes, I'm proud of it.*

And that's what I told her, at which she nodded with a slight bob of her body. "It is mainly a matter of semantics, as you are aware, but semantics are central to who and what we are. If you were to ask me what I was, having met me without knowing who or what I was, I would say I was 'Shigothi', the plural term for my people that equates to your word, 'humanity'. But my people and our birth world are semantically linked. Shigothi are originally from the planet Shigo," she explained further. "Most species self-identify with their species' birth world this way.

"But when your progenitors were discovered six-hundred and thirty two of your years ago and asked what they were, they did not say they were 'Terrans'. In fact, initially they didn't even say they were human. That came out later.

"No, they identified themselves as Americans. The next time, it was Russians. Then British, then Chinese, Indian, Japanese, African, and so on. It was not until after The End had begun that we finally realized that, despite the apparent visual differences between the various human sub-types and the constant state of low-grade warfare between them, you were actually all one species. And that species was 'human'. Having yet another set of sub-types calling themselves 'Kin' does not justify the galaxy at large changing its nomenclature yet again."

"Huh," I'd never thought about it that way, really. As much as it galled me to say it, I had to admit, from the galaxy's perspective, I really *was* a human.

Well, squat.

Ch 6: The Bar Heats Up

I chuckled in amusement at my apparent whole-hearted adoption of the galactic pejorative, even to the point of it popping up unheeded in my thoughts. The bartender gave me a strange look, but had to attend to another pair of Cranotian dock workers who wandered in. As it gave me a chance to think about things, I wasn't about to complain. It's not like she owed me anything. In fact, I kind of owed her for the talk.

I looked around the bar at the rest of the patrons. Most were what you would expect in a dockside bar, rough around the edges, tough, tired, and maybe a little insular. If it hadn't been for that round of character assassination by the bank, I figured I wouldn't have had any problems up on the tourist concourse. None of the individuals in the bar looked to be giving me undue attention yet, for which I was grateful. I assumed the only reason for this was that I hadn't used my bank link on my slate yet. Instead I had paid with the cash card. But that was just a theory.

I just needed to keep an eye out for ship-suits. From what I could see, the ship crews wore the same type of ship-suit I had, just made for their own body shapes. The other thing I wanted was for said crew to be alone. I figured I had a better chance of convincing someone to smuggle me down to the surface if I wasn't contending with additional voices in the mix.

As the Shigothe bartender swung back around to my end of the bar, I asked the question which I originally came to ask.

"So, here's my issue," I asked quietly. "You know anyone who might be able to get me dirtside? Quietly?"

She gave one of her disturbingly accurate shrugs. "I take it you have a problem using the regular shuttle?"

I gave her a look of mild consternation as I explained. "I'm not sure exactly why, but everyone on the retail ring has given me the cold shoulder, or worse, actively kicked me out of their establishments." I paused for a moment, unsure of how to frame the question without giving away that I'd hacked the station's network. "It's like I'm being actively targeted. Is this because I'm 'human' to them, and humans actually have that bad of a reputation? I haven't seen that kind of reaction down here, so I'm not sure what to make of it."

"Ah, one of 'those'," she sighed, making me wonder exactly what she meant. "In short, yes, and at the same time, no. Humans have a reputation for deceit, underhandedness and arrogance, not as individuals, but as a whole. Lots of Cranotian stellar corporations will actively suppress human corporate interests, which is understandable, given their history here." She waved one arm around the bar. "None of these beings care one way or another. They're not 'Corporate'. They may work for a corporation but they're so far down in the weeds it really doesn't matter to them. They're transients, and don't stick around the station long enough to have to deal with all the bureaucrats."

"But I'm not Corporate," I replied. "I'm just one guy."

She pointed her arm at me. "And one guy is usually either a mark or a predator. To be honest here, you aren't showing much of a predator vibe, which makes you a mark."

I considered it carefully. I really hadn't stood up for myself much, either in the food court or the shuttle concourse, but my instincts still told me this wasn't some random prejudice.

"However," she continued. "In your case, you have enemies targeting you specifically. A notice to all business owners on the station went out four hours ago from the station admin, advising us to refuse you service. You specifically, and it even gave a relatively accurate description. I'm not sure what you did to earn such treatment, but whoever this enemy of yours is, they have an agreement in place with the corporation that controls this station."

A chill went down my spine. It was confirmation of what I'd already suspected, but to have her say it so blatantly still disturbed me. Could the blacklisting from Confed space really reach out this far? *Apparently so.*

Another thing occurred to me. Why was she helping me? I'd been fishing for information, thinking that by using my cash card, I could avoid notice. The electronic flag was only tied to my bank account, after all. But if a back-channel communication had already gone out a few hours ago, any hope of remaining anonymous was completely off the table. So why was this lady risking her job talking to me?

I'd been assuming she was an owner/operator, just from the size of her business. Most such businesses didn't have the kind of volume to support more than one or two employees, and her manner of speech was such that I seriously doubted she was a mere wage slave. Besides, she'd said "us", when talking about the notice, meaning she included herself in that recipient group. As she'd pointed out, her patrons wouldn't be affected either way, but she had a major stake in avoiding trouble with admin.

"I owe a long-standing debt to your kind," she stated, apparently reading my mind. "This is just another payment. Besides, it's just a drink and a few words."

I wondered what service a Kin had done for her that would cause her to risk her business here for a random stranger, but I wasn't going to look the gift-horse in the mouth too closely, because it was clear I was quickly running out of options. While some low level crewman might not have a problem with it, I doubted the captain of whatever ship I tried to hitch a ride to the surface on would want to risk docking rights. And as captains, they likely *would* have gotten the notice.

Frak. Hopelessness began to overwhelm me. I'd come here to escape my fate, but it seemed that everywhere I went, my past was chasing me like a pack of hyenas, nipping at my heels, never giving me a moment to catch my balance, nor a moment's rest. I stared into my beer as I brooded, no longer paying any more attention to the rest of the patrons. It wasn't until the bartender's gentle nudge pulled me out of my funk that I realized that business had picked up considerably. A second bartender was working the far end of the bar, and a waitress was distributing drinks and snacks to several tables full of a wide range of customers, mostly dock workers, but interspersed with several ship's crew as well.

"Don't stare, but someone is here I think you should speak with," she murmured quietly.

Shaking free of my despondency, I looked out over the floor to see what she was talking about. A trio of blue skinned beings had just walked in, calling loudly for a round of shots. I had no idea what they were, besides some kind of mammalian. They resembled humans to a point, with highly mobile, expressive faces. However, their proportions were different, and their heads, necks and hands were covered with a thin layer of fur, looking almost like a cross between a teddy bear and a blue-haired monkey. They were also decidedly "male", judging by the bulges in their nether regions. But that wasn't what caught my attention.

A young-ish female Otter-Kin was ensconced within the group, her arms wrapped possessively around one of the males as they strode to one of the last empty tables. Sleek, chocolate-brown fur covered her head and neck, with a pair of adorable, tiny, round ears poking out on the sides. She looked to be about a hand-span shorter than me, and considerably slimmer, overall. Although the curves she *did* have were *all* in the right places. *Not too big, not too small,* I smiled appreciatively. Rather than being baggy and loose like mine, her form-fitting ship-suit hugged her body like a glove, covering everything, and concealing absolutely nothing. I had to admit, she looked sexy as hell, but the fact that she was wearing a ship-suit rather than a regular work suit was more interesting to me, as a ship-suit implied a ship. Plus, she was the first fellow Terran I'd seen since getting off at the passenger concourse.

As the three blue guys took their seats, she gave her male a quick kiss on the cheek then promptly sat in another's lap, showing the same level of affection she'd shown the first.

Talk about playing up the stereotype! I snickered to myself.

Female Otter-Kin had developed a decidedly risque reputation over the last several centuries. Most I'd ever met, especially in the military, actively avoided public affection, as it seemed to be taken as an open invitation to any over-sexed male with no sense of propriety, but enough of them still openly displayed their traditional culture's polyamorous tendencies that the stereotype continued to persist long after the practice ceased to be common.

Unlike most other Kin, Otter-Kin were not designed with combat or heavy labor in mind. All combat-oriented Kin were designed with high aggression and insanely competitive instincts. Yet despite their competitive nature, the pack instincts of the Kin built a network of unbreakable group relationships, once formed. They were cohesive and supremely effective in combat, but hard to handle by outsiders, especially right after coming back from a stressful battle. Even more-so than humans, Kin effectiveness was greatly increased by endorphins released during combat, a condition that was actually intended and enhanced deliberately in their design. However, this had a side effect of also enhancing their libidos. To provide an outlet for this, their human designers had tried to incorporate female Kin of the same species into the units to provide an outlet for the post-combat energy. It had been a disaster.

The first attempts at having same-species, mixed-gender units had quickly devolved into chaos. Infighting over "mating rights" became an almost insurmountable problem. Even though there was no possibility of progeny, the *desire* to mate could not be removed from the genome without also destroying that which made the Kin into such superb fighters. A solution was required, and Otter-Kin were created shortly thereafter, produced by a small biotech company in Quebec, a North American city that still bore its centuries-old French-Canadian name and local culture.

They had been created as literal "comfort-Kin", providing emotional support and stress relief to Kin soldiers coming back from combat duties. Designed specifically against normal pair-bonding and engineered with increased libidos even when not under stress, they were first used essentially as "camp followers". Prostitutes in all but name. The lack of pair-bonding instincts also meant they didn't have a desire to "settle" for just one, or even two mates. They wanted them *all*, and species was no barrier to their affections. Adding this to the training they obtained in massage, conversation techniques, not to mention the "amorous stress relief" which came so naturally to them, and they became the solution the military needed to handle their Kin soldiers.

Being largely immune to pair-bonding, one or two Otter-Kin could happily handle the affections of an entire platoon. The combat units themselves, having been reverted to male-only formations, quickly adopted them into their packs, not as mates, but closer to mascots. When it was discovered that they also had the ability to become support technicians as well as fulfilling their "normal" duties, they were fully incorporated into the military formations, and later became fixtures in most industries where Kin were employed.

This, of course, did not endear them to the females of the various Kin species, and over the centuries since their creation social pressure had largely eliminated their roles as "confort-Kin", but the stereotypes and prejudices were still present.

This particular Kin was riding that reputation like a stunt-enabled hovercycle, skillfully weaving in and out of the social minefields of her situation. I had no idea what her goals were besides enjoyment, but the sexy little minx looked like she was having a lot of fun. The recipients of her affections didn't seem to mind a bit, either.

The waitress swooped in with their order, placing four shot glasses and a short bottle of green-colored alcohol. A few words were exchanged and the Otter-Kin glanced over to the bar. Untangling herself from her paramour took a minute, but she finally detached herself, giving him a quick kiss before walking towards the bar. I quickly averted my gaze, not wanting to aggravate her companions and not knowing their relationship, beyond the obvious.

"Hey Nari, what's up?" she asked cheerfully as she slid onto a stool two spots over from me. Her gaze shot my way for a moment, giving me a saucy wink before she turned back to the bartender. *Ah, so that's her name!* I thought. It had started to become a bit uncomfortable having such personal conversations with someone whose name I didn't even know.

"Good evening Gina. I thought I'd introduce you to a fellow traveler," Nari replied quietly, not looking or gesturing in my direction at all. "He's fresh off a ship from Confed space, but he's got some issues following him. He could use a hand getting under the radar and down to the surface."

Gina looked at me out of the side of her eye, her evaluating gaze sweeping up and down quickly but unobtrusively. Whatever her opinion, she kept it concealed behind a cheerful and unworried demeanor.

I kept my mouth shut and my eyes forward. The two of them were obviously keeping their interest in me covert, and I didn't want to mess things up for them. Or for me, for that matter.

More and more, I was surprised at the lengths Nari was going, just to assist me, a complete unknown. On one hand, it raised my suspicious nature, but at the same time, I had no reason *not* to trust her. She'd been open and honest in her statements, and had even helped me understand a bit of local culture I'd been confused about. By all appearances, she was exactly who she presented herself as. That didn't mean I was going to take everything at face value. My trust had been broken far too many times in the past to take that risk now.

But I was at the point where I didn't have many options left. I'd just have to play it by ear.

Speaking of playing it by ear, what the hell are they saying? I wondered. Normally my keen hearing would be able to pick up a conversation only two meters away no matter what kind of background noise there was, but for some reason all I could hear was the noise and shouting from the rest of the bar. I could see their mouths moving, but for some reason I couldn't make out the words.

A few moments later the bartender walked off, not even glancing my way. I looked after her, wondering if she was ignoring me on purpose, or if she was getting something for the Otter-Kin. I flinched when a pair of arms suddenly wrapped around my waist from behind and a husky voice whispered in my ear.

"Play along, little Foxy."

The hair stood up on my neck for just a moment before I locked myself down. I could feel her body pressing up against my back as her hands started to roam up and down the front of my ship-suit. I jumped a bit when she reached a bit further down than I was comfortable with, but tried my best to keep my cool. It had to be an act, of course.

I'd given thought to hiding my intentions from the rest of the patrons at the bar when coming in, of course. However, given how quickly the bartender clued in on my feelings without even being the same species, I figured it to be a lost cause. I was never all that good at poker, after all. But it seemed like Gina was set on taking it to the next level. Not quite sure where she was going with this, I turned my head to look back at her.

"Well hello, beautiful," I said, trying to play up the game she had started. Behind her, I could see her three companions watching us intently. I couldn't tell from their faces if they were angry or amused, but at least they weren't jumping up aggressively or raising their voices. Even though I wasn't sure who the act was aimed at fooling, I figured it wouldn't hurt to play along a little further.

Her roaming hands continued to work their sensuous magic, and I was beginning to get more than a bit flustered.

Rather than let the intimate physical inspection continue, I swung around on my stool to face my tormentor and slipped my hands around her waist. I managed to resist the temptation to return the favor. Barely.

It was hard. *Really hard.* And the insufferable little minx knew it.

The smug little smile on her face was flawless. Had I not known something was up, I could easily have been convinced I was about to get very, very lucky. A rising croon rose from her companions' table. It appeared the three males there agreed as they egged her on like a bunch of teenage cheerleaders. A wash of relief flowed over me as I knew that I probably wasn't going to have a fight on my hands for a breach of her imagined integrity.

"So," I smirked. "My name's Red. Are we doing this here at the bar, over on the table, or would you prefer somewhere more private?"

"You'll find out," she riposted with a sultry grin. "But I have to admit, I like what I see so far. Come on, let's get out of here." She maneuvered me off the barstool and towards the table where her cheerleaders continued to croon their approval. Releasing me for a moment, she leaned down to briefly fondle one of them as she whispered something into his ear. Seconds later, we were traipsing out of the bar, calls of encouragement chasing our tails. I tried to steer us to my locker to grab my stuff, but she dragged me down the wide corridor while continuing to nuzzle and nip at my neck like it was made of Swiss chocolate. Figuring it was still part of the act, I played along.

"So what's the plan?" I asked, as soon as we cleared the corner out of sight. I started to release my grip on her waist, but she grabbed my hand to keep it there and pulled our course down another side corridor. Only a couple of the lights in the narrow space were working, and my instincts started to yell at me again. It was a perfect place for an ambush.

Before I could think of how to escape, she suddenly stopped and pressed me against a wall. Her arms wrapped around my neck in a very sensuous manner and she began to nuzzle my throat. Soft moans escaped her lips as one hand slid down to unzip the front of my ship-suit, while the other began to caress my exposed chest. Soon both hands were exploring my body, even going so far south as to brush against the root of my tail. My arousal was instant and obvious, somewhat to my embarrassment. I hadn't had this kind of interaction in well over a decade, and it was definitely clouding my judgment.

"Um..." I stammered, no longer sure what was going on. Was this a ruse or was it really happening? "I'm not sure this is a good idea."

She chuckled for a moment, giving my tender bits a soft squeeze before removing her hands and zipping up my ship-suit, tapping her open hand against my cheek. "Come on, lover-boy. We have places to be." Suddenly business-like, she stepped off down the darkened corridor, her strides quick and purposeful. I stood there, absolutely stunned at the sudden reversal, my brain still struggling to cope with the flood of hormones her hands had released. My instincts were yelling at me again, this time not over a premonition of danger, but a sorrowful sense of loss.

"Hey! Let's go!" She called, looking back at me. "I wasn't kidding when I said we needed to get out of here." I collected up my scrambled wits and chased after her. *I still haven't grabbed   my   stuff!*

Ch 7: Crazy Cab Rides

As she led me further away from the cargo area, I quickly lost all sense of direction. None of the small passages were marked, and most of the lights were either flickering or completely out.

"What the hell was that all about?" I almost whined, my whipsawed emotions still struggling to recover from the constant battering. I was nearly ready to toss the whole idea out of the airlock and figure some other way down. Grabbing her elbow, I jerked her to a halt. "Answer me, goddammit!"

Her reaction was swift, merciless, and utterly out of character compared to her demeanor from just minutes ago. She grabbed two of my fingers in a finger-lock and spun me completely around, slamming my face against the bulkhead with a meaty thud. My breath whooshed from my lungs at the impact, and my arm was wrenched painfully up between my shoulder blades. Being a pilot, I never really trained in hand-to-hand techniques, but I recognized an expert when I suffered the ministrations of one. I froze, no longer struggling against her grip, knowing that to do so would only bring further pain, and possibly broken fingers.

"You're the one asking for help here, bucko," she growled, all traces of the sensuous lover vanished from her voice. "You are in no place to ask questions. You already have the station admin after your ass, and if you think I give two shits about your hairy backside, you'd better think again! You're lucky I owe Nari a few favors, or I would toss you out the airlock myself and say, 'good riddance'!"

"Not that," I strained as her grip tightened. "I mean the come-on. We were already out of sight in the alley. I figured the stuff in the bar was an act, but then..."

She sighed in exasperation. "You're a noob, aren't you, Fuzz-butt." She released my fingers and I sighed in relief as my elbow joint stopped trying to pop out of its socket. She stalked away, shaking her head and muttering under her breath. Rubbing my abused elbow, I followed a couple steps behind, not wanting to get within easy range again.

"Seriously?" I complained. She glanced back, rolling her eyes.

"Fine," she snapped, not slowing a bit. "You want to know? You come into Nari's bar, already sporting a notice of persona-non-grata, asking for help getting smuggled to the surface of a planet that already has it in for you. Did you expect a welcome mat? Maybe a soft bed and some chocolates on the pillow? Whatever the frak you did, Nari doesn't deserve to get splashed with it."

"But I didn't do anything! All I did was go to the bank to get my slate synced to the station!"

"That's what they all say."

"No, seriously," I said, giving her a shortened version of the events leading to my predicament. I even told her about the flag I'd found on the network packets. While still skeptical, she at least started to ease up on the punishing pace she was setting through the maze of corridors.

"So you're saying you literally just went to the bank, then all this stuff happened?" She paused before reaching a well-lit passage that looked to be a residential section of some sort.

"I got blacklisted in the Confed," I replied, wincing. "I'm guessing that followed me here."

She looked at me with a deadpan expression, obviously waiting for further information. Reluctantly, I filled her in the important bits of my history, to include my prison sentence and the reason for the conviction.

"You punched a human officer?" The expression on her face had slowly faded from irritated to humorous. "I assume he deserved it?"

"He broke protocol and leaked our flight plan to the press," I almost growled. Even over a decade later, just thinking about it angered me. "Snake Intelligence had a mole in the editor pool, and they got hold of it before we even left the system. We were disabled and captured right after translation, and my RIO was severely wounded in the fight. He didn't survive the POW camp. My RIO died because that asshole couldn't keep his mouth shut."

"Oh damn," she said, suddenly looking away. "Damn, damn, damn. Yeah, he deserved at *least* a sock in the mouth for that." She looked back at me with an apologetic expression. "Was anything ever done about him?"

"Not that I know of," I grumbled. "As far as I know, he's still in the Confed Navy. Could be an admiral now, for all I know."

"Well, that could explain the blacklist in the Confed," she sighed. "But not out here. That takes commercial influence."

"Yeah, I can't figure that one out either. It's not like humans have that much power out here, right?"

She shrugged. "Meh, six of one, a half dozen of the other. Money talks and bullshit walks, no matter whose money it is. I'm going to guess that's what you're up against, especially considering it was the bank that did you dirty."

Gina started moving again, this time at more of a stroll, heading back towards the cargo again. Confused, I watched her walk away, not following. She stopped, waving me up.

"Come on, we have a ship to fly."

*****

"You know," I murmured as we walked back. "You never did tell me the reason behind the heavy petting in the alley."

She burst out in giggles. "Boy, you really are a newb." She looked at me through the corner of her eyes as she explained. "I was looking for trackers or recorders. Even if you weren't a plant, you could still have been tagged in other ways. The only information Nari had on you was the station notice. You coming into her bar seemed awfully suspicious."

"Huh, I guess that's fair," I admitted. "But I don't get how a necking session counts as a search."

She smiled, lifting one hand to point at the ring she wore on her index finger. It was topped with a synthetic ruby, but otherwise was unremarkable. "Micro-scanner. Really short range, but it'll pick up just about anything electronic, even passive devices that don't transmit. Nari told me to give you a pat-down before we did anything, just to be safe."

"When did she say that?"

"Right after she introduced us, there at the bar."

I thought back to the conversation I hadn't been able to overhear and became a bit suspicious. I curled up an eyebrow questioningly. "So does that ring do anything else, like say, sound suppression?"

"Caught that, did you?" she smiled. "Maybe there's hope for you yet, but no. That was something of Nari's toys. She uses it all the time to keep private things private. You never have to worry about your dirty laundry with her, trust me."

I sighed. I hadn't anticipated having to play spy wars, but at least it looked like I wasn't on Gina's bad side any more. And the endorphins had finally washed out of my blood, letting me think clearly again after the hormone-fueled rollercoaster ride from earlier.

"All's well that ends well, I guess, but it would have been nice if you hadn't riled me up with false promises. I haven't gotten laid in a long, *long* time." I pierced her with a mocking glare as we finally returned to that very spot.

"Oh, there's still hope," she smirked maliciously. "You're not out of the woods yet, fox-boy!"

I flipped her the bird, to which she replied, "Maybe", which just frustrated me all the more. As we turned the last corner back onto the cargo concourse, I veered off towards the bar to go grab my bag from the locker only for Gina to yank me the other way.

"No, you can't go back there," she murmured. "The whole act we did will be blown if you do that."

"But my stuff," I hissed. "That's all I have left!"

"Trust me, I've got ya covered." She led me towards another passageway, this one leading onto one of the docking arms. Both sides were lined with airlocks similar to the ones I'd seen in the retail docking concourse. While they were decidedly dingy looking compared to the tourist docks, I couldn't see many that looked non-functional. A few of them were apparently in use, indicated by the steady blue light above them showing that a ship was docked. I guessed that, unlike the tourist docks, these apparently didn't charge by the minute, as they were left connected even though there was no one going in or out.

Gina walked up to one and punched a code into the keypad, while at the same time waving her wrist along a sensor plate, letting the subdermal implant be read. I'd had one of those when I was still active in the Confed Navy, but it was removed after my conviction, and I hadn't had the extra funds it would take to get it replaced yet. Of course, it wasn't the implant itself that was expensive; it was the cost to have your individual credentials propagated across the galactic banking community that made getting them so prohibitive. Inter-system message traffic still had to travel by ship, after all, as FTL comms would only operate within a couple light-days unless someone was willing to pony up for a tunnel comm, and the only ones who could afford that these days were multi-system governments and Corporations.

It didn't surprise me for her to have one. They were standard issue for most Corporate crewmembers and the cost of propagation was generally absorbed by the company as the cost of doing business. Military personnel also got them, with the added galactic benefits just being part of the security bundle.

Gina looked back at me and waved me forward. "You have to go first. A whole bunch of alarms go off if someone without an implant tries to follow me in."

I looked askance at her as I passed the gravity threshold into the ship's airlock. "How did you know I didn't have…" I cut myself off, realizing the answer to my own question. "The little ring scanner, right?"

Gina smirked a bit, but nodded.

"So now I want to know just how short range that thing is," I chuckled. "How much of the manhandling was you needing to check for bugs, and how much of it was you just wanting to get your hands all over me?"

"I'll never tell." She smiled brightly, pointing further down the ship. I preceded her as instructed and found myself entering a cargo bay. The bay doors were closed, and the large compartment was almost empty, only tie-downs and cargo restraints littering the floor in haphazard piles. The bulkheads around the large cargo hatch showed at least a couple decades-worth of scratches and dings from constant loading and unloading. Two internal hatches led further aft and another airlock about half the size of the main cargo hatch was situated along the side of the bay opposite the docks. A large status display above it glowed a soft purple, its text unreadable to me, but likely indicating that something was securely docked on the other side. *Airlock?* I looked back and asked the question with a flick of my ears, and Gina nodded. I let her cycle the lock and stepped into a small cargo shuttle.

It was tiny compared to anything capable of translation of course, but it looked to be able to carry at least fifty cubic meters of cargo volume without crowding the bulkheads too badly. Of course there was no telling what the max allowed mass was without knowing the engine power and anti-grav specs. Following Gina into the cockpit, I began to recognize the layout. Not in any kind of detail, but a general sense. This wasn't a Confed shuttle after all, but form follows function, and other than the buttons and labels all being something I couldn't read, I was pretty sure I could fly it if someone did the power-up sequence for me. Even the flight controls were generally the same, which made sense if this thing belonged to the blue-furred guys from the bar.

She waved for me to take the co-pilot seat, but rather than seating herself in the main seat, she leaned against the hatch coaming, looking at me searchingly. "So, what exactly are you doing way the hell out here, Red?"

It was the first time she'd actually used my name. I hadn't even been sure she knew it, even though I'd mentioned it in the bar when we first met. I fought against paranoia as I considered how to answer the question. On one hand, the less information I gave out about my plans, the less chance someone could derail them. I'd thought I'd escaped the long reach of the Confed bureaucracy, but it seemed I was wrong. However, I was beginning to realize that I was completely lost outside Terran space. Without some guidance, I was probably looking to end up in a worse position than if I'd stayed on Old Terra. It was time to take a leap of faith.

"I want to buy a ship."

"Some special kind of ship?" She raised her eyebrow. "You got something I don't know about what's for sale out here?"

"Not really," I shrugged. "Any jump-capable cargo ship will do. Can't be too big, or I won't be able to afford it."

"Seriously?" she asked incredulously. "That's it? You came all this way to buy a ship." Her eyes rolled as she threw up her hands in disgust. "What's wrong with all the ships back in Confed space?"

"I can't buy them, and even if I could, I wouldn't be able to pilot them or even be part of the crew." I retorted. "I'm blacklisted, remember? Confed regs state I have to have a crew license to do that."

"Oh, yeah," her face furrowed in thought as she calmed back down. "Forgot about that. So what, you gonna try to ply the trade through the friendly alien skies? I gotta tell you, that isn't gonna go down really well. As I'm sure you've figured out, they don't like us much out here."

"Yeah, I know."

"So…?"

"There's a loophole." I leaned in conspiratorially. "Confed regs only apply to Confed ships crewed by confeds. Alien ships don't have to go through that. They just have to register the title with the BuTrans, and the Captain's license is pretty much automatic after that."

"Somehow, I don't see it being that simple," she said skeptically.

"I checked the reg." I grinned. "There's no mention of a species requirement for non-Confed title registration. BuTrans figures there's lots of aliens out there driving ships not made by their own species, so why add additional paperwork for it? If it's not Confed, and they pay the import duties, taxes and fees, they really don't care who's driving the ship."

She considered it for a moment before shrugging her shoulders. "I can't imagine it will be that easy, but I don't see anything particularly wrong with your plan. It just seems like a really convoluted way to do it."

"So what about you?" I asked, wondering what brought *her* out here. She didn't seem to be running from anything, and obviously had connections. And she was part of a crew. But like she said, Terrans weren't super popular outside Confed space, so I couldn't imagine why she was "all the way out here", as she'd put it.

"Meh," She tilted her head noncommittally, looking mildly uncomfortable. "Anywhere the wind blows, doesn't really matter to me these days... Pilot should be here momentarily," she said, abruptly changing the subject. She turned to stare through the hatch towards the airlock as if willing it to open. I could definitely understand not wanting to talk about painful memories. I had more than a few of my own to deal with.

As if summoned by her glare, the airlock started cycling, revealing one of the blue-furred companions from the bar. In one hand, he held a tablet he scanned as he walked through the empty cargo hold. In the other, he held my carry-bag by the handles.

"Hey!" I stuttered. "How did you get my stuff without the..." Patting my pocket, I suddenly realized it was empty! Not even my cash card was there! I scrambled to stand up, checking all the places they could be. *Son of a...*

"Thanks Balini," Gina smirked as she took the bag and thrust it at my chest. I was barely able to get a hand free from my pockets to keep it from falling to the deck. I stared at her, dumbfounded, as she moved past me to strap into one of the jump seats behind the pilot who squeezed past and began to bring up the shuttle's systems.

I quickly checked if anything was missing, but to my relief it was all there, even the pulser. I took the little weapon out and attached it to my waist with its integrated mag-clip. I was *not* going to risk being unarmed anymore, local regulations be damned. The only thing left to find was the cash card. It held less than five hundred credits worth of local currency on it, so it wouldn't be a total loss, but money was tight. Acting on a hunch, I stared across at the Otter-Kin.

"And?" I asked pointedly, holding out my hand.

"What?" Her innocent act was awfully convincing, but I knew better by this point.

"Fork it over." I made a 'gimmie' motion with my hand to emphasize my point.

She rolled her eyes again before slipping a hand into one of the pockets over her pert chest and removing my cash card, which she flipped at me with a snort. I was getting really confused at this point. Any time in the last half-decade I would have been paranoid and hypervigilant at this point, fighting to keep my cool. But I kept wanting to trust her, despite getting blindsided by petty acts of passive-aggressive bullshit. I couldn't figure her out. More disturbing still, I couldn't understand why my gut wanted to trust her. *This is not normal,* my subconscious screamed. *Should I be angry, or scared?* I stomped hard on the confused boiling knot of tension that roiled in the back of my head. *Deal with it later.*

"Where are we headed?" Balini asked as he powered up the systems, his long fingers dancing across the controls with staccato clicks.

"The spaceport, I guess?" I answered, confused. "Are there other options?"

"Since we're not taking down cargo, we can land anywhere with a big enough flat spot," he explained. "There's a few restricted areas around the bigger cities, but we only have to land at the port for customs and immigration."

"Huh, okay. One second." I pulled out my slate, powered it up and brought up the list of places I'd researched earlier. Sorting by location, I found three of them within about a thirty kilometer radius. "How about this place, any restrictions?"

"Really?" His translated voice in my earbug included the soft dual-tone beep that indicated skepticism or disbelief. "That's a pretty rough town."

"They have three places that might have what I need." I shrugged. "I'm pretty sure I'd be heading there eventually anyways, so I might as well start there."

"Okay, but I'm not sticking around. If you change your mind, you'll be making your own way after that, because I have to swing over to Caltot to pick up some parts and we're scheduled to boost in six hours. I'll be cutting it a bit close as it is."

"That's fine," I assured him. "And thank you for the ride. I really appreciate it."

"Meh, I was going down anyway," he shrugged. "Plus, Gina asked nicely." Undocking went quickly, and as soon as we cleared the station control zone, he started the reentry burn to take us down.

A beeping sound started up just before the shuttle began to kiss the upper reaches of the atmosphere. A few buttons were pushed, silencing the alarm, then the pilot looked over at Gina.

"Something I need to know about, girl?" he asked pointedly. "We just got lit up by tracking radar from a customs boat in high orbit. It's not weapons-tracking yet, but it sure seems like someone up there is interested in where we're going."

Her eyebrows furrowed in confusion. "They shouldn't even know we've left the station. We're not on the passenger manifest."

"You hacked the manifest? Why?" Bilini exclaimed. "If they know that, they're gonna think we're smuggling! And with you two being human, any explanations I try to use aren't gonna fly! I could lose my license over this!"

"Excuse me," I interjected quickly. "Can you show me the geometry? I want to see what kind of line-of-sight they have. Pull up the weather radar for this area too, please." Bilini brought the nav display up on the main screen. Our course, shown by the dotted line, passed around the horizon. I quickly reoriented the point of view to display what the other ship would see, based on the azimuth of the incoming radiation. The threat detection systems were already showing the other ship beginning its own reentry burn, but they were late off the mark, and it looked like they'd lose sight of us in six minutes as we passed behind the planet's horizon. Leaning on my training and experience from the war, I immediately saw a couple solutions. "How much fuel do you have?"

"Enough to get down and back up to the station again," he answered. "With about a twenty percent margin. I was going to fly a low altitude route to Caltot after dropping you off. Why?"

"We haven't done the injection burn, so they don't have a good read on our landing point yet. Let's try this." I explained my idea to use a delayed injection burn to fool the other ship into thinking we were landing long. Once out of sight behind the horizon, we could do another burn to adjust our trajectory towards a faster, but rougher insertion. It would mean a longer duration of buffeting from the upper atmosphere, but it would offset our landing point by nearly three thousand kilometers. It was a simple trick, but an effective one.

"As long as our pursuers didn't have other eyes tracking us, they'll think we're on a least-energy approach to Caltot, here, but instead, we'll use this weather system here to mask our visual signature, and land here." I pointed out the massive thunderstorm on the weather map.

"Ok, that'll probably work to get us down, but I'll be short of fuel to get back to orbit if I do that," the pilot said reluctantly. "I don't have signature authority on the ship's account. I'd have to call the captain for that, and that would give the whole game away again. I assume you don't want anyone knowing where you're headed, right?"

"That would be preferred, yes." I hated to do it, but it looked like I was going to have to spend more money. Luckily, fuel prices weren't that bad here, but it was going to tap me out of untraceable cash. I pulled out my cash card and handed it over to the pilot. "You can take on a bit more fuel in Caltot. This should make up the difference. Think of the rest of it as a tip."

Bilini pressed the tab on the card to read the balance. "Yeah, that'll more than cover it. Fine, you've got yourself a cab driver," he sighed. "Buckle up, it's gonna get a bit bumpy here in a minute."

Ch 8: Re-entry

I strapped into the co-pilot's seat and engaged the restraints. As I suspected, the controls were completely in line with human design. Only the language displays were changed. Considering the pilot was generally the same size and had the same numbers of arms and legs, it was to be expected that the control setup would be similar as well. I watched the pilot as he brought the tail end of the shuttle around in preparation for the injection burn.

"How good are you at aero-braking?" I asked.

"Not very, to be honest," he replied, sounding a bit hesitant. "I just got qualified thirty cycles ago, and we've been docked for most of it, so I haven't gotten a lot of practice in something this small."

I suddenly worried about my plan. I'd done this kind of maneuver countless times in the *Ferret* class ships in the military, which were larger than the little shuttle, but also much less nimble. I was absolutely confident that *I* could handle the transitional burn, but the pilot's lack of confidence was starting to make me wonder if the suggestion was a good idea. Thinking quickly, I started asking questions.

"Verify for me please as I can't read your language," I said, pointing at the various controls. "Main engine throttle, thrust vector control, attitude thrusters, gyroscopic reference indicator, atmospheric control for yaw, pitch and roll…" Bilini stared at me in surprise as I listed off all the controls I recognized, pointing at each as I identified them.

"Are you sure you can't read all that?"

"I was a combat-qualified scout pilot. This is pretty much what I did for twelve years."

"Squat," he grumbled. "Why don't you fly this damn pattern, then. Probably do a lot better than I would. I'm afraid I'll scorch the hull coming in too fast. This thing can only handle sixteen-hundred *klopeks* without a dedicated heat shield."

"If you're ok with me piloting the shuttle, I can absolutely do that," I replied evenly. "I just didn't want to piss you off by asking. Most pilots are pretty possessive of their prerogatives."

"Not me, human," he sighed, sounding almost grateful. "If you can pull this off better than me, go for it."

"My ship, then," I nodded, placing my hands on the controls and wiggling them.

"Your ship," he replied smartly, taking his hands off the controls to show he was no longer piloting. "Where did you find this guy, Gina?" he asked, giving her a puzzled look.

She snickered. "You were there, weren't you?"

I verified our attitude with Bilini then ramped up the throttle to begin the injection burn. Gina monitored the sensors to let me know the moment we were out of line-of-sight of the customs boat.

"Now!" she cried.

I pushed the throttle all the way to maximum. Our orbital path curved sharply downward as our velocity relative to the planet dropped. As soon as the first wisps of atmosphere began to buffet the shuttle I spun the ship in a powered slew turn, pointing the nose back at the stars. Cutting the main throttles, I began the delicate balancing act of keeping our descent as quick as possible without causing too much heat buildup from friction. A wall of superheated plasma developed on the bottom edge of the shuttle, quickly engulfing the ship as the hull's shockwave surfed its way through the upper reaches of the atmosphere. The buffeting grew from a minor rattle to a bucking roar.

"How's our temperature looking?" I shouted over the noise.

"Eighty-seven percent of max tolerance and climbing!" Bilini exclaimed. "Rising at forty *klopeks* per second! Airspeed is down to six-thousand units per second and falling! Altitude is seventy-eight thousand units, dropping at two-hundred units per second."

"Just a little more and the heat should start dropping off!" I assured him.

The roar crescendoed a minute later and began to drop off. Using the attitude thrusters, I eased up on our angle of attack, letting the shuttle's lifting body design take up some of the effort in keeping us aloft. Within another twenty seconds, the plasma began to recede as our airspeed dropped to merely supersonic rather than hypersonic levels.

"Holy squat, that was way more exciting than I wanted it to be!" Bilini exclaimed as I had him extend the atmospheric control surfaces, allowing me to control the shuttle's direction with ailerons and rudders, rather than relying on anti-grav and thrusters.

Streaking through the cloudy sky at just over two times the speed of sound, we quickly made our way over the small ocean below us. I smiled in satisfaction as I banked us towards the edge of the landmass below, stabilizing our flight path before relinquishing control back to the pilot.

"Been a while since I did a tail-stand like that one," I remarked. "It's a well designed little ship," I complimented Bilini.

"Yeah, but we generally don't use it like this." Bilini looked askance at me as he punched up the revised flight plan. "You know, if you weren't human, I could probably get you a job on the *Waverunner*. That was some really slick piloting."

"If I weren't human?" I asked.

"Sorry, not sorry." The pilot at least looked a bit embarrassed as he clarified. "It's just that if we had humans onboard, we'd have to deal with a lot more hassle from the customs enforcers. Not just here, either. You guys are real *nitliks* when it comes to rule-bending, not to mention all the smuggling that ends up undercutting the rest of us."

I sighed in defeat, not even wondering what a *nitlik* was. Yet another reason I would likely have to head back to human space if I wanted to survive as more than just a tourist. As we entered the final approach to our landing spot,

I got up from the copilot's seat and sat down next to where I'd secured my carry-bag.

I had one last request to ask before we landed. "If you don't mind, I'd rather you keep your transponder off till you get to Caltot. I would understand if you'd have a problem with that, but it would probably help us out if they never knew you stopped here."

"I guess I can do that," he replied. "They'll probably give me some grief when I come in from a different vector, but I'll just remind them that I'm only recently certified. It's not enough of a violation to even get fined for."

"Thanks."

The shuttle settled on its landing gear and the cargo ramp dropped to the ground. Without looking back, I stepped off the ship and started walking towards the edge of the city, already planning my next move. The shuttle's anti-grav started to whine as it began to lift off, heading to its next stop.

As I moved onto the gravel that surrounded the small concrete landing pad, I heard the crunch of other footsteps than mine following me. I *knew* there hadn't been anyone around the pad when we touched down. I yanked my pulser from its mag clip as I spun around, my finger already tightening on the trigger. *You won't take me down without a fight!*

"FRACK!!!" Gina yelled as she flinched away from the threatening muzzle, falling into a defensive crouch. I froze for an instant in shock before swearing as well.

"What the...?" I shouted. "What the hell are you doing here!"

Gina quickly recovered, but pierced me with a baleful glare as she stood back up. "What does it look like," she retorted caustically. "I'm coming with you."

I halted at the nonsequitur. Dumbfounded, I asked the seemingly obvious question. "What about your ship? They're boosting in six hours! You'll never make it back to the station in time. You'll miss movement!"

Taken aback by the query, she looked just as confused as me for a moment before her face showed a burst of astonishment.

"Oh!" she exclaimed. "That's not my ship."

"So what ship are you on?"

Gina looked uncomfortable as I asked the next question. Her face drew down into a grimace as she visibly considered how to answer. I re-holstered my pulser and crossed my arms. I was not going another step until I had some answers.

"Fine," she snarled. "You want to know the whole truth? I don't have a ship."

"What about the blue guys? You seemed pretty friendly with them, I'm sure you could have gotten a berth."

She grew more frustrated. "You heard what he said, right? They don't take on humans as crew. It's too much hassle for them."

"So what were you doing with them, if they weren't going to sign you on?"

"Mooching." She rolled her eyes. "*Borrowing the couch*, as they say. What did you think I was doing?"

"Playing up the stereotype?"

"Oh please," she snapped as she brushed past me, headed for the city. "While their anatomy is close, it's not *that* close. They like a snuggle and tease just as much as any other mammalian, and they're more cuddly than most, but they're not going to risk damaging themselves like that." She spun around angrily. "What kind of person do you take me for, anyway?"

"I don't," I retorted. "I'm working from limited information, here. And all the data points I assumed to be true are turning out to be fabrications. Hell, you're wearing a ship-suit like you're part of a crew, but that's apparently not correct. Is that bartender really your friend? Where do you live if not on a ship?"

"I told you, I was mooching," she cried. "I make friends, it's something I'm good at. And it's not like I could afford to stay in transient quarters. I don't have any money. Why do you think I snagged your cash card? The only reason I have eaten in the last two weeks is because Bilini and his brothers were willing to share their rations."

"So, why were you able to get me a ride down here? And for that matter, why are you following me?"

"The ride was a favor for me, you just got added at the last minute." Her eyes dropped to the ground. "When they leave, the only friend I'll have left on the station is Nari, and she's really limited in how much she can help. The station admin would jump all over her if she tried to hire me."

I was stunned. Here I thought she was a well-connected, hard-working Kin, when in reality, it seemed like she was in an even worse situation than I was, barely surviving. But that raised even more questions. "What's the station admin got against you? You're not blacklisted too, are you?"

"Probably," she mumbled. "I haven't been back to Confed space in over a year. I was on an AstraCorp ship that was making runs out here. They fired me four months ago. No official reason, just tossed me out the lock just before they boosted. Didn't even get paid for that last month, either."

"Unofficial reason?" I asked skeptically.

"Probably because I wouldn't sleep with the Second Mate," she sighed. Seeing my raised eyebrow, she protested quickly. "Look, I admit I don't have high standards, but the guy smelled. And was creepy, like really creepy." A shudder ran down the back of my neck as I realized what she meant.

I looked away, ashamed of myself. I was guilty of assuming she was happy and willing to bed anything that moved, but she'd been tossed out with no resources, no friends, and no warning. *Of course* she would do anything she had to, just to get by. And here I was, judging her by her desperation.

But all of these assumptions are based just on what she's told me, and I have no idea how much of that is true, I thought grimly. I would have to do some checking later on when I had a secure place to do it from. For now, I was just going to have to roll with it. I just had a couple more questions.

"Is the station admin going to be looking for you?" I asked, dreading the answer. If she was already wanted, I was going to ditch her right here and now. I didn't need those kinds of complications.

"No," she answered confidently. "When I got kicked off the ship, they didn't even bother to call station security to remove me, because then they would have had to pay for the services. They just shoved me out through the docking tube and locked the hatch behind me. They disconnected thirty seconds later and boosted for home. I never registered my bank account on the station network, just used cash cards. I don't think the station even knew I was left behind, and it's not like I broke any laws." She gave a wry grin as she finished her explanation.

"...or at least, you didn't get caught." I said ruefully. "Because I can name at least three illegal things you did that *I* know of." I considered for a moment before reaching the conclusion that her presence wasn't going to be all that much greater of a risk than me going by myself. And to be honest, it would be nice to have someone to watch my back that wasn't already predisposed to dislike me, even if they had their own agenda.

"Fine, you're hired for now, but let's get off this pad before someone calls the neighborhood watch on us."

Ch 9: Almost-New

"So," I murmured as we walked down the crowded sidewalk. "You know my story, so what's yours? What's your rating? I assume you're former Confed Navy, since you're so good at hand-to-hand."

"Yeah, but that's not why I'm good at hand-to-hand." She glanced my way as she maneuvered around a cluster of juveniles which were crowding around a street vendor's cart. "Think about it. We were created as 'comfort-Kin', but once we get out, we have to look after ourselves. Do you know how many times I've had to fend off unwanted attention? The Wolf-Kin in the infantry battalions were downright polite compared to some of the crap I've had to deal with since. And there's not much in the way of consequences for the assholes in the Corpos. In the Navy, if some jerk wouldn't back off, I just let the Alpha know, and he'd beat some sense into him. Problem is, there's no Alphas allowed on Corpo ships. *Too much pushback*, I heard the captain say one time. They want to be free to be assholes and not have to deal with an angry Wolf-Kin. It paid to learn to defend myself."

She grinned for a second as she stepped into the entrance to the transit station. "Plus, my mom trained me to deal with three foster brothers before I even left home. She was a three-time Aikido champion in Montreal."

"Oof!" I chuckled. "That would do it. As a pilot I figured if it came to hand-to-hand combat, I was probably screwed anyway."

"As for my rating, I'm a fully certified propulsion systems engineer. I have credentials with all three major power plant manufacturers in use on Corpo cargo ships up to Atlas class, plus I still hold a certification in small ship engines from the Navy, but that one is about to expire. If I can get back home, I should be able to renew without too much trouble as long as, like you mentioned, I didn't get blacklisted."

I filed away the information for later consideration. I was actually impressed. Not many Otter-Kin chose to fully utilize the education opportunities the Navy offered. They often chose to focus on the 'comfort' aspects, and suffered a rude awakening upon leaving the military. They usually got stuck in service positions like waitress or secretary, with little other means of supporting themselves other than menial positions or sex-work. Of course, some joined the storied ranks of extremely expensive courtesans, catering to the rich and famous, but those were the exceptions which proved the rule.

With the stated goal of purchasing a ship, I had already marked off two dealerships off my list. The first one only sold or leased new ships, making it way over my budget. Besides, I had already investigated loan application requirements for ships in my range, and while it was theoretically possible for me to afford the down payment on one of them, I would have no operating capital afterwards.

The second place had a few ships in my price range, but the owner flat out refused to deal with 'humans', having been burned by one a decade ago. We were headed to the third.

The place looked a little shady, in my opinion. Nothing was obviously sketchy about it, but the location was closer to the slums than I was entirely comfortable with. It was also backed up against a giant scrap yard half-filled with partially disassembled ships. The recycling company on the other side of the wall was dilapidated and crumbling, but apparently still open for business. What made me nervous was the idea that some of the ships in the sales lot might be pieced together from wrecked and recycled parts. I had absolutely no desire to trust my life to a salvage title if I could help it.

A skeezy little Cranotian was the proprietor, and apparently the sole sales-being as well. A red-skinned mammal of some sort was acting as the receptionist, but other than getting the owner, they spent the entire time doodling on a data slate.

"I gots all shapes and sizes," the sales-being creaked. "You just say what you need and Old H'talgim will find it for ya!" His eye-stalks wobbled a bit, almost as if he was drunk, but his speech was steady and ungarbled as he invited us to peruse the catalog inside the dusty office.

I found three ships that were both within my means and had recent enough rebuild dates in their maintenance records as to be considered safe to fly. It took a while, but the old Cranotian finally limped out with us to take a first-hand look at them.

The "showroom" was a warehouse-like building covering nearly a square kilometer. The electric cart zipped through the automatic doors and we were immediately plunged into darkness. As the old crab drove blithely along, huge spotlights slowly brightened, highlighting the various ships as we passed in a clever and dramatic display of showmanship. I was impressed, I had to admit, and it probably also saved the old guy quite a bit in electric costs, as the spotlights only brightened when we got near them, and dimmed after we had passed.

The first ship we inspected was listed as a Cranotian design. As soon as we entered the lock I immediately recognized it as being the same model and style as the *Waverunner*, the ship Gina's friends crewed on. As I inspected the cargo and living areas, Gina grabbed the set of courtesy tools from the cart and checked out the engine room. A lot of the interior wasn't really compatible for Kin, but I figured we could switch out the seats and beds for other stuff fairly easily. It would function for now, I guessed.

"Bad news, Red." Gina strode through the hatch into the cockpit, a dark smear of grease marring her previously pristine ship-suit. "Unless you are willing to run at under two-thirds power for translation, I don't think this one is going to work. Half the nodes on the port capacitor are fused, and I doubt the starboard one will be any better."

"How much to repair them?" I asked wearily.

"You'd have to replace the whole unit," she answered, shaking her head. "They're solid state proprietary parts, and you'd have to have a shipyard do the work, since you have to cut the hull to get at them."

"Damn," I swore. Rather than follow us into the ship, the sales-being stayed on the cart. I couldn't tell if he was being lazy or was just not that interested in the sale. If I wanted to ask him any questions about the ships, I had to climb down the boarding ladder to do it. Either way, unless the guy was going to offer to replace the capacitors, this ship wouldn't work. "Close up and grab the tools, Gina. Let's take a look at the next one."

The next ship was an older design that would have worked fine... If the corridors and hatches hadn't been sized for Cranotians. I wasn't really all that tall for Fox-Kin, but even I felt claustrophobic when the tips of my ears constantly brushed against the ceiling as I walked. Any kind of unexpected turbulence, and we would be smashing our heads left and right.

The third ship, another of the same class as the first, was also a bust, its nav system completely gutted. *If I could afford to purchase both, I could probably get one working ship from the parts.* I mused, realizing the utter futility of the idea. Perhaps I would have a ship at the end of all the work, but I would also be buried up to my neck in debt. Disappointed, we boarded the little runabout and H'talgim whisked us through the back exit.

"What the hell is that?" I exclaimed, pointing through the wire mesh fence at a strangely shaped ship sitting on a concrete pad in the scrap yard on the other side.

H'talgim glanced over before chuckling. "Yeah, I should never have accepted that thing." I'd suspected it before, but his statement had just confirmed that he owned, or at least was a major partner in the scrapyard that adjoined the sales lot, which also explained the origin of the ships.

"Why's that," I asked, curious. "Is it not running?"

"No, actually," he explained. "It runs and flies fine, even has a rudimentary nav computer and a small fabrication shop tucked inside the engine room. But it wasn't built by any species we know, so no one can order parts for it. Without a source of parts, I can't get anyone to take the risk of buying it. The hull is made of a weird alloy, too. Won't bond right with cerama-steel or anything else we usually use for hull repairs."

"How'd *you* get it then?" Gina asked from the back seat.

"About sixty cycles ago, a rock-hopper brought it in as salvage from some system off to the galactic east. Said her mining team found it abandoned on some moon or another, tucked into an impact crater like it was being hidden. It was short of fuel and the atmosphere had leaked out from a broken seal on the cargo hatch, but otherwise was fine."

"Did they find any remains?" Gina grimaced. I hadn't realized she might be that squeamish, but I managed to keep my mouth shut, listening for the answer.

"Nope, not a trace," H'talgim expounded, getting into storytelling mode. "No ship-suits or anything like that either. Whoever abandoned it was probably picked up by another ship, but they never came back to get it. The rock-hopper captain put in a claim with the port authority, and when no one paid the recovery fees, she had to sell it or use it. It's not really set up for vacuum or microgravity operations, so she brought it here. And like a fool, I paid her for it, thinking that with a little research, I could figure out who built it and get a line on parts. Could charge a premium on those, if I could keep the source secret from everyone." I grunted in agreement. Hard to find parts were *always* expensive, even when the materials were cheap and readily available.

"Mind if I take a look at it?" Gina asked me. I wasn't sure what she hoped to find, but it wasn't like we had anywhere to be. We'd already secured lodging for the night, and it was way too late to see about transportation to the next place on my list, which was several hundred kilometers away.

"It's up to this guy," I replied, pointing a thumb at the Cranotian.

"I'm stuck here till the shift ends anyways, so why not?" He shot over to a gate hidden behind a stack of shipping containers and pressed a button on his data slate. The gate opened ponderously and he drove back along the other side of the fence.

As he pulled around a few large piles of parts and scrap, I finally got a good look at the ship. At first glance it looked like a reclining camel I'd seen once in a historical documentary about Old Terra's Sahara Desert, filmed nearly a thousand years ago, before humans ever left the planet.

It had a centrally located cargo compartment with a domed roof that added at least another fifty percent to its internal volume, with a distinctly separate hab module and engineering section to the front and rear of the cargo bay. A small cockpit was situated on the end of a long articulated arm on the front of the ship, instead of being integrated into the hull. At a guess, I figured the arm would swing to one side or the other to allow direct visibility of the side of the ship, but why that couldn't be done with remote cameras was beyond me.

Rather than landing jacks, it had four bulbous cylinders on each side of the front and rear third of the hull, giving it a *lot* of meters squared of landing surface area. It was immediately apparent to me that this ship was designed to land on unimproved surfaces, meaning it was not limited to landing pads or spaceports. That meant it also had surface-to-orbit boost capability. Considering the rear thrusters seemed to be just a trio of gimbaled ion engines, I could only guess the anti-grav system must be robust indeed to allow it to break free from any significant gravity well.

The ship wasn't huge by any means, but it was significantly larger than the ones we'd looked at earlier. Considering the expanded cargo module, the ship seemed purpose-built for large cargo or integrated modules rather than palletized or containerized shipping. What I found strange was there was no side hatch for cargo handling, nor any means of attaching a ramp to get at the small-ish airlock located just aft of the hab module. *How do you unload cargo, if there's no ramp for the hatch?* I wondered. *There's no lugs for a crane to attach to either, not that it would be all that efficient.* I posed the question to H'talgim as we stepped off the runabout.

"Oh, yeah!" he exclaimed. "You gentlebeings haven't seen that part yet!" His eyestalks quivered a bit in excitement as he tottered under the hull of the ship.

Following him, we found a small airlock on the underside of the hull. He opened a small panel on the inside of one of the landing cylinders and tapped in a code. The ship's running lights came on, along with a set of bright light strips along either edge of the hull. A few seconds later, the airlock swished open, and a telescoping ladder extended down. I was wondering how he'd get up there as his obvious infirmity would likely make climbing difficult, but he turned to Gina, telling her to go up and hit a specific button on the bulkhead inside the ship.

"You'll know it when you see it, girl," he giggled. "It's the only blue button on the console. Just don't get scared when you get a bit jostled. When it's done doing what it does, hit the red button when it lights up."

"Why would I be scared?" she asked suspiciously. "What's it going to do?"

He giggled again, which was more than a little disturbing, I thought. "I don't want to ruin the surprise! Don't worry, as long as you stay off the orange and black striped areas for the whole thing, you'll be fine."

Gina looked at me, raising an eyebrow in silent query.

I shrugged. "Up to you, really. You're the one that wanted to take a look." Gina nodded and scampered up the ladder, disappearing a moment later.

H'talgim grabbed my arm with a pincer appendage and pulled me out from under the ship. "Trust me, you're gonna want to see this from further away." He led me over to the runabout, where he sat himself down on the tailgate before waving back towards the ship. "As far as we can tell, she'll lift around four-hundred-fifty *klecks* to orbit in standard gee." He pulled up a calculator on his sales slate. "That would be about six-hundred of your metric tons. Of course there's room for more, if your cargo doesn't mass much, especially if you stack things up, but you'd have a fun time unloading that much cubage without special equipment."

"Why's that?" I glanced at him curiously.

"You'll see," he teased. "The show should start up here in just a second."

I took a seat beside him, watching expectantly. A moment later a shrill siren went off, the high-pitched sound loud enough to wake the dead. I quickly covered my ears against the noise, glaring at the old crab.

"Oh, sorry about that," the Cranotian shouted. "I forgot how loud it is for some species. Most of it is outside my audio range, so I can barely hear it."

The siren cut off with a series of low-frequency chirps, and I turned back to the ship. It had gone suspiciously silent. My anticipation grew as the seconds stretched out into nearly a minute. I had to give it to him, whatever was going to happen, the old crab really knew how to sell a spectacle. I finally spotted movement from the front of the ship as the cockpit armature swung towards us, eventually bringing it past the edge of the hull where its left-side viewport had a clear view of the side of the ship. While this was unusual, I couldn't help but feel a little underwhelmed.

Suddenly a loud groan of hydraulics sounded from the ship along with the squeal of poorly-lubricated metal-on-metal hinges. I cringed again as the nails-on-chalkboard sound pierced my ears in spite of my hands holding them flat against my scalp. I stared at the ship, astonished, as the landing cylinders began to split and unfold like a set of giant scissor-jacks.

The hull began to rise into the air, supported by the four massive, articulated landing pads that had been hidden inside the cylinders. I kept expecting it to stop, but it just kept going. Finally, the scissor-like articulation reached its full extension and the ship shuddered to a halt. Stabilizing struts deployed from the sides of the legs just below the main joints and extended themselves until they reached the ground, where some kind of automated balancing system tweaked them until the ship was once again just as stable as it had been before.

I was flabbergasted! The distance from the bottom of the hull was now nearly equal to the height of the ship before its legs had deployed. It was like the ship had suddenly sprouted stilts! *But why?*

"I love watching it stand up like that," H'talgim sighed. "Such a unique solution to an age-old problem."

I finally dropped my hands from my ears and turned my head to glance at the old Cranotian. "What in the hell is that all about?"

"Oh, it's not done," he answered smugly, still watching the ship. "That was just stage one." He tilted his carapice to the side in an odd manner. "Oh, and you might want to cover your ears again, the hatch still needs a lot of lubricant." My hands leapt back to my ears, and I snapped my head back around. I was just in time.

The screech of rusty hinges started up again, but I didn't immediately see what was moving. Finally I figured it out as a long ramp dropped from the centerline of the ship. The hinge was just aft of the hab module and the ramp itself extended nearly to the back end of the ship. The entire bottom of the hull had detached to form a ramp over seventy feet long pointing back towards the engines.

"Oh. My. God!" I exclaimed. "It's a RORO!"

"A what?" H'talgim asked, his eyestalks swinging towards me questioningly. "What's a row-row?"

"It's an acronym," I grinned maniacally. "It means 'roll-on, roll-off'. We use something like this to deploy armored vehicles to combat zones while under fire."

"Oh," he replied, quickly understanding. "I don't think this is a military ship, though. It's got almost no armor, and the beam weapons it has are barely enough to scratch the paint on any modern destroyer."

"They should do pretty well against missiles, though," he added. "As long as you can find a targeting computer for them. They swivel pretty fast, but there's no controller connected to them, so it's all manual. No idea about how well the hull would stand up to heavy lasers, as my mechanic can't figure out what it's made of, and I wouldn't let him shoot at the ship to find out. Spectrograph readings come back all scrambled, like there's some kind of active interference, but we can't find anything active causing it."

The ramp finally settled onto the concrete pad with a loud clang. I got up to inspect the ship, but before I could get to the bottom of the ramp, Gina came barreling down it with murder in her eye.

"You crack-head *bastard!*" she shouted. "I almost fell down the airlock shaft! *A little jostled*, my ASS!" I caught her before she could assault the terrified old crab who was now cowering behind the runabout.

"You just have to have all four leg-pads on the floor!" he whined. "You should have been fine!"

"I don't have four leg-pads, you idiot," she snarled. "I have *feet*, and only *two of them!*"

"Look," he cried piteously, scrambling back from the furious mammal. "I'm sorry. I didn't think about it. You seemed to do fine walking around, so I figured you had some way of balancing. I know I couldn't prance around on two legs like you do!"

"We do," I sighed in exasperation. "But it presupposes solid ground. If you'd let her know what was coming she could have sat down or held on to something." Gina seemed to finally be coming down from the adrenaline rush caused by the near accident, but I stayed between the two of them just the same.

"Look, I'm sorry," H'talgim repeated desperately. "I'll make it up to you, okay? How about a discount? Five percent?"

"Twenty-five percent, or I rip off your eyestalks right now!"

The old crab shot straight up in sudden fury. "That's utterly ridiculous! I wouldn't even make a profit! The value of the metal of the hull alone is more than that!" His eyestalks drooped a bit. "Well, as soon as we figure out what it's made of, I mean. I couldn't do more than seven percent."

"Fine, Twenty-three percent and I will consider not cracking your legs in half." Gina's eyes narrowed angrily.

"You would rob my family of their food? Nine percent!"

They argued back and forth, the argument becoming more heated with each volley. It was like a verbal tennis match, with each shot coming closer and closer to the middle. It took me a minute, but I finally understood what was happening. *Aggressive negotiation tactics, indeed!* I chuckled.

"HEY!" Rather than letting them spend the rest of the afternoon shouting at each other, I jumped into the argument with a yell. "Look, I don't want to be here all day, and it looks like you're going to meet around fifteen percent. How about we call that good and go get something to eat. I'm hungry."

Ch 10: A Strange Feeling

Of course, there was no way to do a bank transfer from the sales office. That would have been too easy. Thankfully, a quick trip to a local market allowed me to access my funds. I only felt safe doing it because it was an automated cash card kiosk, not an actual bank. If my account at FCSICU itself was flagged, the transaction itself wouldn't go through, but if it was just the bank's physical office on the Cranotian station, I figured it would be an opportunity to clear out the account as I wouldn't be using FCSICU anymore. It was a huge risk to put all my funds onto a cash card, but I no longer trusted the credit union. Getting burned once was enough. I left just enough to prevent the account from being closed out completely.

Of course, Gina spotted a restaurant she wanted to try, so we stopped to grab a bite to eat on the way back. The soup was interesting, a little spicier than I was used to, but not bad overall. As I waited for the bill, I considered how strange the last couple days had been.

"Hey Red, what's with the long face?" Gina interrupted my musings with a mouth half-full of some kind of wafer-like dessert cookie.

"I'm not really sure, honestly," I answered. "Things just seem to be moving a little too smoothly right now. I keep waiting for the other shoe to drop."

"Well that's not a very optimistic attitude," she murmured around the last bits of cookie. "You plan for the worst and hope for the best. That's what I do, anyways."

"That hasn't worked out for me that well, lately, or *ever,* really. It seems every time I finally get moving in one direction, something pops up that swerves me off course."

"Like what?"

"Well," I sighed. "You know I'm a former scout pilot, but that's not where I started. My parents were both agri-techs working for BioBloom."

"Born or made?"

"Made," I replied, referring to the manufacturing process in which all Fox-Kin in the past had been created. It had only been in the last half-century that changes had been made allowing us to have natural births, finally freeing us from the crippling debt our "creation" entailed. "Second to last generation of them. There was one last run made after their lot, but after that the factory was shut down,"

"And you?" Gina asked to confirm.

"Born. First generation," I replied. "I joined the Navy as soon as I turned eighteen."

"I don't blame you. Once those Corpo assholes get their hooks in you, you're screwed."

"Yeah, I know. My parents didn't have a choice, of course. They were purchased off the line."

"Ouch." Gina winced. "That sucks. Thankfully, QubeCorp used the 'creche' method after they transitioned from line manufacturing. I didn't have to deal with force-growth. My mom adopted me from there, so I never had to go through VRS, either."

"Lucky," I grunted in agreement. One of the primary differences between 'made' and 'born' Kin was in how they grew up. 'Made' Kin never had a childhood. One they were done with the uterine replicators, they were force-grown in teratogenic postnatal gestation tubes until they reached physical maturity, then decanted and thrown into 'education pods', a Virtual Reality Simulator with direct brain stimulation that essentially programmed them with knowledge and skills they needed to perform their assigned duties. It was very efficient, but produced a pool of workers that had very little knowledge outside their work-related programming. Social skills were slow to develop, as were the thousands of other skills most humans soaked up in childhood.

Things like loyalty and following instructions were, of course, baked into the VRS programming, but balancing a bank account, or how to decipher the terms of a loan contract were conspicuously absent, leaving the supposedly "free" workers severely disadvantaged when figuring out how to struggle out from the crippling debt they were saddled with at decantation.

Those of us of the first "born" generation weren't a whole lot better off. There were no daycare centers to watch us while our parents worked, no schools to send us off to for our education. Instead, care of the kits in the worker dormitories was handled collectively. My early childhood was a parade of "mothers" and "fathers" who watched us in shifts until our actual parents could come pick us up.

I had to admit though, it made for quite the eclectic education. Once my age-mates and I were old enough to sit still for more than a few minutes at a time, the caretakers began to teach us what they knew of their own professions. I learned double-entry bookkeeping from an old Beaver-Kin secretary, mechanical maintenance from the Wolf-Kin maintenance manager for the dormitories, and even flight engineering from a medically retired Fox-Kin pilot. It was from Carlos that I gained a passion for flying, and space in general. While not a combat pilot, Carlos had served in the first clashes against the Serpentes forces, and his stories inspired me greatly.

"When I joined the military, I applied for pilot training," I started again. "A retired pilot at our dorms had taught me what he could about his time in the Navy, and even managed to sneak me into the simulators at one of the Naval Reserve armories. I was about as well prepared as I could be to become a cargo pilot like he was.

"And it worked! I was accepted into flight training, got certified and everything, and was happy as a clam shifting cargos back and forth from the belt to the Mars Planitia shipyards. I could have spent my entire Navy career there. It was my dream job, and I was getting really good at it. Best shuttle pilot rating in the section, even.

"Once I got seniority, I could have graduated from shuttles and barges to tugs, then perhaps even a flight engineer slot on a fleet collier. I could retire with all the tools and skills I needed to maybe get my own cargo hauler. Maybe not a jump capable one right away, but if I could succeed at in-system work, I could save up, you know?"

Gina smiled warmly. "Oh, I get that, totally. I had similar dreams, but about working in one of the small R and D labs, figuring out power plant improvements. So what happened? The war, I take it?"

"Yep," I nodded ruefully. "The snakes started trouble again, and the Navy was caught with their pants down. Without any active conflict, the scouts' maintenance had been deprioritized, and the pilots and RIO's themselves had become complacent, not making sure their stealth tech had the latest updates."

I finished my last bite before continuing. "Some snake-head whiz-kid found a vulnerability in our protocols, I guess. The snakes exploited it ruthlessly in their first action and managed to wipe out a couple of squadrons of the Navy's recon units."

"I remember hearing about that," Gina grimaced. "Command made a huge deal about firmware updates on control hardware, after. So how did that affect you? I thought you were hauling cargo."

"Remember how I said, 'best shuttle pilot rating in the section'?" I asked wryly.

"Ah," she sighed. "The only reward for doing a good job is a harder job, right?"

"Got it in one." The server came back with our bill, and I waved the cash card over the reader, adding a small tip. I continued talking as we started walking back to the dealership. "All my training in cargo shuttles was about efficiency and accuracy, load balancing, cargo handling and all that, so of course they throw me into the cockpit of a Ferret class scout with a crazy Weasel-Kin who had kicked more RIOs off his ship than the rest of the RECON squadron combined.

"Luckily, we got along just fine, but it was just another instance of life throwing a monkey wrench into the works every time I was getting settled in. I spent nearly four years as his RIO, and we were finally getting to be a really effective team, then they yanked me from that and gave me my own ship."

"Don't get me wrong," I added. "It was awesome being in command of my own ship, even a two man scout, but Goose didn't like giving anyone else stick-time back then, so my piloting skills had gotten kind of rusty."

"Well, you survived obviously," Gina commented. "So you must have picked it up again fairly quickly."

"Sure. Even made it to flight-lead. But then that mess with Spurgle happened," I growled. "I got captured, my RIO died in a POW camp, and I spent a decade in prison for slugging the asshole who caused it all."

I didn't hear anything she said after that, as my hyper-sensitive paranoia started jangling my nerves. I wasn't sure what I'd seen or heard that was causing the fur to stand up on the back of my neck, but I'd learned to trust it lately. I captured her arm in the crook of my elbow and steered us into the next storefront as if that were our destination.

"Um," Gina murmured. "I know I have a reputation, but I don't think we're at this stage yet."

"What?" I glanced at her for only a moment before I continued scanning the street behind us for whatever it was that my subconscious was yelling about.

"Ooookay," she mumbled slowly as she finally picked up on my heightened awareness. "So I'm guessing we're not here to pick out intimate apparel for Old H'talgim's significant other. What's going on?"

I finally looked down at the racks of clothing I was peering over the top of. They were festooned with a myriad of oddly-shaped bits of metal and fabric. If she hadn't said something, there was no way I would have been able to identify their use. But now that image was burned into my brain like a brand, distracting me from my vigilance.

"Thanks," I growled sarcastically. "I really didn't need that picture in my head right now." My eyes returned to the street as I tried to spot anything out of place. "I think we're being followed. I thought I caught something out of the corner of my eye, but now I don't see anything."

"What caught your attention?"

"Not sure," I replied tensely, replaying what I'd seen in my mind. "I saw someone peeking around the corner of that building over there. They were wearing a hood or cloak, so I couldn't see their face, but when I turned my head to look, they jerked back out of sight. Something about the shape of them was off, but with all the different aliens around here, it's hard to tell what's normal or not."

"You know, you shouldn't think of them as aliens. We're on their planet, so we're the aliens here." Gina admonished as she casually turned to look at another rack of clothes. She grabbed my arm and turned me around as if pointing something out. I almost jerked away before realizing she was using a mirror on the end of the rack to look back at the corner I'd pointed out.

"Yeah," I acknowledged softly. "That's what Goose told me, too. Hard habit to break, I guess, but at least I think I've gotten away from using 'shit' all the time." Almost as soon as we turned away, a tall figure in a long, hooded gray robe sauntered out from around the corner and casually walked into the entrance of a small café, disappearing from sight. The large tinted window of the small Cranotian eatery prevented me from seeing inside, but I was dead certain they were using it to watch us inside the lingerie store.

Gina pulled me further into the store with a soft murmur, pointing at a sign. "Changing rooms, and that orange sign back there says 'emergency exit'." I followed along, still trying to keep my eyes on the front of the café through the mirrors placed on the ends of each row of clothing. Glancing at the sales counter, I could see that the cashier was distracted with another customer, so I waved Gina ahead. Making it into the short corridor unseen, I watched as Gina quickly examined the door alarm.

"Get ready to run," she whispered. "I *think* I know how to disable this, but it's a different brand than the ones I've seen before." I braced myself against the wall and looked back towards the storefront. I could barely see the edge of the café's doorway, and the view of the windows was obstructed by some advertising signs. We were out of sight for now, but I assumed they wouldn't wait long before moving to a better position.

Ch 11: Strange Pursuits

A soft click-clack sounded behind me, and the door opened relatively silently, only the soft squeal of the hinges threatening to give us away. Gina held it open for me, then grabbed the long, straight stick from the hole in which she'd apparently disabled the door alarm before allowing it to gently close behind us.

"Seriously?" I said, my eyebrow raised in consternation. "You did that with a hair stick?"

"Hey," she replied smugly. "You can do all sorts of things with a pointy piece of wood."

I rolled my eyes and quickly searched for a way out that wouldn't put us in sight of the street we'd just left. The alley opened up in two directions, but instead of taking either of them, I strode across to the far side. Jumping up, I caught the end of what could only be the Cranotian version of a fire escape ladder. It was locked, of course, but I could jump lots higher than any crab, and I quickly pulled myself up to the second-story platform. Reaching my arm down, I pulled Gina up and we entered the covered parking garage. Several vehicles took up various stalls, but it was otherwise deserted.

Mere seconds after we ducked out of sight, the alarm on the emergency exit below screeched as the door banged open. A pair of footsteps hurried away in both directions and I looked at Gina with a wry grin as we quietly headed for the corner of the building where there were a set of ramps leading down to the street level. I remembered seeing the parking garage on the local map marked as private vehicle parking, suggesting the ground floor doors would be locked from opening from the outside, but getting out shouldn't be a problem, I figured. And I was right.

Gina used a small hand mirror to check our surroundings before opening the door fully as we exited in the same alley we'd entered, our pursuers having already dashed off around the corners. I spotted an open door leading into the back of another restaurant, and we swiftly walked through as if we owned the place, startling the poor crab who was taking out the garbage to no end, I was sure.

There were no robe-clad figures as we exited the front of the restaurant, so we resumed our journey back to the sales lot, keeping a close eye on our surroundings as we went. I kept silent, not wanting small talk to distract me from my vigilance. Gina seemed to be of the same mind, and we arrived with no further incidents.

I wasn't sure who they'd been, but I suspected it was more of the same shenanigans I'd dealt with on the station. Either way, we'd lost them for now. I resolved to try getting some manner of transportation for us before heading to our hotel room, preferably one that couldn't be tracked electronically, but I had doubts about being able to find any. Like most civilized worlds, Cranotia seemed to be completely enamored with registration and licensing laws. Nowhere was this more apparent than in the main office at the dealership.

"I've got your deposit logged and placed in escrow," the red-skinned receptionist said, handing back the cash card along with a printed receipt. "As soon as you return with certified loan documents and proof of liability coverage, I can release the ship's encryption keys to you. You have seven business days before the deposit will expire, and the vessel will be released for sale again. If your deposit expires, you will have to place another deposit to re-reserve the vessel for purchase."

My eyes started to cross at the stream of legalese spewing from the short, surly male. He continued reading the legally mandated recitation, but my ears had disconnected from my brain three paragraphs ago. I would have to read the contract carefully when I had a moment.

Gina had wandered over to the scrap yard to see if she could find a cheap ride. Something that could be carried safely on the ship would be a plus, which I pointed out when she volunteered to go look around. Little did I know…

*****

"Of all the things you could have possibly picked, why a motorcycle?" I yelled over the desperate whine of the little electric motor as it struggled to maintain the pace demanded by its demented operator. "Hell, does this thing even qualify as a motorcycle? We're barely doing fifty kilometers an hour!" Of course, speed was relative. We were going significantly faster than the surrounding traffic. Even with the sidecar attached, the bike was easily able to fit between the collection of ground and hover cars that populated the wide but poorly maintained roads. I cringed as I was jolted in my seat, pain radiating up my spine from the unbuffered impact. Had I not been strapped in, the small pothole would have flung me from the seat, but the harness kept me firmly planted. "And for all that's holy, why a sidecar model?"

"It was the fastest thing I could buy that didn't require a license and registration," Gina shouted back, the moderate wind noise almost washing out her words entirely. "I was actually shocked to see one, honestly. They're not something the locals can even ride, since they're not bipedal. I'm guessing it was left behind on one of the junkers in the scrapyard. But where there's one, there's probably more, and if I can scrounge up another one, they'll both fit within the storage space in the ship's fab shop, which means we don't have to block cargo space to take them along. Hell, with a fab shop, if I can't find another one, I'll just break it down into parts and fab up duplicates. It'll give me something to do on long stretches."

I wondered about how the sidecar I was riding in would figure into that 'storage' statement, but glancing down at the attachment hinge was both a relief and a horrifying revelation. The relief in that it was obviously easily detachable, the horror in just *how* easily detachable. The only thing holding it on was a long rod rattling around in four split-hinge plates, with two light-duty cotter pins on either end to keep it from sliding out. The shock absorber arm that prevented the whole thing from folding in half was definitely not capable of holding the side-car up on its own, and would likely rip completely off in any kind of significant accident. I suddenly regretted complaining about the bike's low top speed. *I am NOT riding in this thing again!* I vowed.

Another thing occurred to me a moment later. She'd said, "we" when referring to the ship's cargo space. I hadn't even thought past getting the ship off the ground, and Gina was already making plans for cargo and future ground transportation. *I haven't even said she was going to be a permanent member of the crew,* I thought. *And yet, she's already making plans as if she's part-owner.* I wasn't actually adverse to inviting her along for the ride. She had, in fact, done me a couple of favors, and it wasn't like it would cost anything to help her get back to Confed space since I was headed there anyways, but it still irked me to hear the assumption without even being asked. It was something that would have to be addressed before things got too complicated.

"We've only got a couple more blocks to the bank," she paused, suddenly glancing behind us. "Crap, we're being followed again!"

I twisted in my seat as best I could, but couldn't immediately figure out what she was talking about, but then it became obvious. A black colored hover car was weaving in and out of the slowly moving traffic, quickly gaining on us. The glossy tint of the windows prevented me from seeing the occupants, but I had little doubt it was the same pair which had been following us previously. The vehicle cleared the last bit of traffic and accelerated, zeroing in on us with malevolent intent.

Before I could say anything, Gina was already reacting. She swerved into a side street so sharply that the entire side car was lifted off the ground as the shock absorber reached its full extension. Her left leg was nearly skimming against the street, and I focused on keeping my weight as far to the left as possible, hoping I wasn't throwing off the reckless balance of the turn. I cringed at a flash of gray shot past on my right only inches away as we swept through the hyper-aggressive turn.

As she straightened out, the side car slammed to the pavement with a jarring crunch. Ignoring the impact, I swiveled around to spot our chasers. The hover car had nowhere near the maneuverability of our little electric scooter, especially considering its lack of contact with the road. If the driver was dumb enough to try making the turn, I was going to be watching a spectacular crash as they careened into the bollards which protected the pedestrians on the sidewalk.

Luckily for them, if not so much for us, their driver wasn't that stupid. The hover car shot through the intersection and disappeared from sight without even attempting to slow down. I'd been certain they were following us, but now I wondered if Gina and I were just being paranoid.

Gina was taking no chances, though. Slowing down, she turned into an alleyway, then into a small alcove taking us just out of sight from the street. I started to unstrap and dismount from the side car, but Gina held up a hand to stop me.

"Stay strapped and just wait," she said, extracting the same mirror from her pocket she'd used in the parking garage. "If they're following us, they will have to come looking on foot. That thing was too wide to fit down here. I don't want to risk being caught out."

I nodded, accepting her advice, but I did pull out my pulser, just in case. I could toss it down at my feet if I needed to hide it, but I felt much more comfortable with it ready to hand.

The traffic noise was fairly steady as vehicles passed the end of the alley. Most of them were normal ground cars, almost identical in function to the ones used on Confed planets. I was surprised at this when we first arrived, but after having spent a couple days planetside I realized there was just not any reason for radical differences in structure.

Instead it was the proliferation of internal combustion engines that turned out to be more surprising. I would have thought a spacefaring world would have dispensed with such a large source of atmospheric pollution. The small motorcycle Gina had procured was the exception, rather than the rule, it seemed.

After about ten minutes, Gina looked over at me. "Think we lost them? I haven't seen the black car, but that doesn't mean they don't have another vehicle."

"Anyone doing a slow pass?"

"Not that I saw," she replied. "Of course, if I were doing it, I would just use an overhead drone."

As if she'd summoned it, the high-pitched buzz of a surveillance drone became audible to my sensitive ears. "You just had to jinx it," I grimaced. "Let's get out of here before it finds us."

"I don't hear it." Gina swept the sky looking for anything moving. "Which direction is it coming from?"

I cocked my head around, swiveling my ears. Determining direction with the echoes bouncing off the walls of the alley made it difficult, but not impossible. It just took a bit of mental gymnastics to figure out. "It's coming from that way." I pointed. Gina quickly turned the bike around and headed the other way, slowing for just a moment to check for cross traffic before merging onto the street.

Sure enough, I spotted the drone just as we cleared the entrance to the alleyway. As it turned into the far end, I was able to examine it for a couple seconds before we were out of sight. It was a relatively common eight-rotor design used by just about everyone. They were fast, maneuverable, and easy to control, meaning that if we got spotted, it would be nearly impossible to avoid. On the plus side, it didn't look like it was a purpose-built surveillance or combat drone, not that I had expected it to be. Anything like that would have belonged to the city or world government, and I didn't think we'd popped up on their radar yet. It was just a standard delivery drone, used to move small packages around the city.

You could probably rent them for a couple credits per hour. Instead, it was the cargo that turned it into a spy drone. There was a camera attached to the front of the small container it was carrying. Nothing indicated any kind of gimbal to allow the camera to swivel, nor were there any obvious weapons attached. As it didn't shoot forward and chase us, I was certain we hadn't been spotted yet, but that wouldn't last for long. The lack of attached weapons did nothing to make me relax, however. *It could just be a flying bomb.*

"Head for downtown and find some overhead cover, like another parking garage or something," I told her as the wind noise began to overwhelm my hearing. Even at relatively slow speeds, I wouldn't be able to hear the drone again until it was right on top of us. Better to find some shelter and force the drone to come to us. Of course, if the drone was armed, we'd be screwed. I had no illusions about being able to shoot down a fast-moving drone in anything but ideal conditions. Plus, I suspected shooting the drone with my pulser would likely draw unwanted attention from the local authorities.

While the choice of an electric motorcycle had its advantages, it was also unusual enough that we'd be easy to spot if the drone got high enough. It wasn't like we could blend in with hundreds of other similar vehicles. Since I'd been planning to launch from the scrapyard, I'd looked up the relevant regulations on air travel. Anything below five hundred meters was untracked and unregulated except around places like star ports and airfields. Anything above that was required to have an active transponder with a valid registration and safety certification, and could not be *smaller* than a small cargo lifter. Additionally, remote or automated piloting was prohibited above that altitude except for very specific, and government controlled, applications like police, military and civil services like fire/rescue. These regulations were *very* strictly enforced, with not just a steep fine, but also immediate confiscation of the device itself as a consequence. Thus all automated and remote-operated drones were hard-coded to stay below the half-kilometer limit.

All that could be programmed around, I was sure, but this thing seemed to have been cobbled together on the fly, so the drone's programming probably hadn't been changed all that much. The problem for us was that five hundred meters was plenty high enough to be able to spot us from, if they popped up over the buildings. Right now, they were probably still looking for us in places which had overhead cover, but that could change in an instant.

And I still don't know why they're chasing us, I growled silently.

Two blocks down, Gina pulled into a turn lane, waiting for an opening in the traffic. I kept a close eye out behind and above us, praying the drone wouldn't spot us before we could get away.

"Why downtown?" Gina asked tensely. "Don't we want to get out of sight, like a warehouse or something?"

"Staying on the outskirts of town just makes things easier for the drone," I explained. "We need to get in among the taller buildings near the city center. It makes us harder to spot."

"I get that part, I guess," she replied, shaking her head. "But it flies. Wouldn't it just follow us in between the buildings?"

"Don't worry, I have a plan." I assured her. "Plus the traffic will keep them from catching us with that hover car."

Gina shrugged and got ready to turn as the traffic started to thin just a bit.

"Squat!" I swore, seeing the drone exit the alley. *"GoGoGo!"*

The motorcycle lurched forward and left, barely missing an oncoming ground car that locked up its brakes trying to avoid us. Gina cleared the gap, but only barely, leaving a small patch of dingy paint on the front of the skidding car. It was too late, though. The drone had already spotted us and was charging forward in pursuit.

Gina skillfully wove the bike through the crowd of vehicles, even popping up onto the sidewalk a couple times to avoid being trapped. Luckily, the lunch crowd had thinned, but a couple crabs in business attire were forced to scuttle out of the way as we careened past. Lots of shouting followed our passage, and I prayed we wouldn't get the local law enforcement called on us. It was an added complication I really didn't need.

The lanes became more and more crowded as we headed at nearly full speed down the streets. The drone caught up easily, of course, as it didn't have to swerve around cars and delivery vehicles. Within moments it was trailing behind us about fifty meters above the street, only needing small corrections to stay with us. No matter how reckless Gina's actions, there was no way it was going to lose us like this. But the buildings surrounding us were growing taller by the second.

"Turn here!" I pointed down one of the broad avenues, the enormous buildings towering on either side. Gina swerved around the intersection, almost lifting the side car off the ground again. *I need to know something...* I spun my head around to watch as the drone easily made the turn, only correcting slightly as it cut the corner. *I thought so!*

"Now that way!" Again the drone had no significant problems, quickly correcting its minor oversteer. I waited, straining to detect the conditions I was looking for. Gina glanced anxiously as I continued to say nothing as we sped down the wide street.

Finally, as we approached an intersection where the narrow side street led due west, I got the sign I was looking for. A tiny hint of crosswind brushed against my cheek.

"Hard right, and then hard stop as soon as you can on the right." I yelled. *Oh God, I hope this works!*

Ch 12: Obtaining Title

As we swept around the corner, both of us leaned hard into the turn. The tires of the little motorcycle squealed as they fought for grip against the road surface. Straightening out, I was thrown forward as Gina slammed on the brakes, bringing us to a screeching halt less than ten meters past the turn.

Again, the drone tried to cut the corner, but this time there was a different result. As soon as it cleared the edge of the building on the corner it spun out of control, slamming violently against the wall before tumbling to the ground in pieces.

"YES!!" I crowed in excitement. *Suck on it, asshole!* I added silently with a manic grin. *Learn to fly!*

"Holy crap!" Gina shouted. "What did you do?!"

"Me?" I grinned. "I didn't do anything. That's just bad piloting." I waved down the street. "Let's get out of here, nice and slow. Head back to the bank. I'll explain on the way."

"I call bullshit," she scowled, pulling back out into the flow of traffic which had completely ignored the crashing drone. "You did something. Even I could make a turn like that, and I'm not even a pilot."

"Easier said than done," I smirked confidently. "The wind gets crazy around tall buildings. New pilots are likely to crash the first time they hit an inversion pocket, and while drones are maneuverable, they're very susceptible to changes in air flow. Besides, when he saw us stop, he pulled back on the throttle, which for a drone means tilting the front up to thrust backwards."

"So what?" Gina asked, unimpressed by the explanation.

"You can't tell so much from down here, but up there, there's a huge headwind running down the street. It's sometimes called 'channeling', but it's really just a form of the Venturi effect. The wind hits a building and is forced to go another direction. Because of this, pressure builds up along the face of the building, causing the air to have to speed up to go around." I pointed at one of the passing buildings, typical of the downtown area. "Square corners like that make it worse. When he pulled the nose up right as he cleared the side of the building, he slammed into that headwind like a brick wall. It flipped him right over, and there's not many pilots who can recover from that."

Gina glanced at me curiously. "That doesn't sound like something a scout pilot would run into a lot. Not to mention being able to figure all that out by just looking around. How do you know so much about it?"

I smiled at the fond memories. "I wrecked my first training drone as a kid from flying too close to the tall grain silos near my home. That old retired pilot I told you about? Yeah, Carlos was a bit disgruntled, seeing it was actually *his* drone that I wrecked, and proceeded to explain to me in short, blunt words how foolish I was in taking it into such a hazardous environment. It didn't stop him from teaching me to do better, though, especially after I spent what little money I had getting replacement parts for the drone. We bonded pretty well over the repair, and it was at that point I decided I wanted to be a pilot when I grew up."

"Huh, I guess that would do it. But don't drones have stuff that handles stabilization for you?"

"Sure, but this guy wasn't running safe-flight software," I replied.

"How could you tell?"

"He made manual corrections to his flight path," I explained patiently. "At the first corner back there, he didn't come through the turn completely straight. He corrected it pretty fast, but it was late enough that it was distinct from the first maneuver. A safe-flight system would have automatically corrected the turn as it finished." I paused, trying to think about it from the chaser's point of view. "I mean, I understand why he did it. The software adds just a bit of delay to the drone response to commands, and if we'd managed to dodge faster than the software felt it was safe to follow, it would have forced a go-around. Given how good you are at driving this thing, I think I would have taken the same risk. But it was a risk, all the same, and he just wasn't as good a pilot as I am."

Gina smirked as she pulled into the bank's parking area. "I *am* pretty good at driving this thing, yes. We'll just have to see about you."

*****

"Here you go," I said, handing over the loan documentation to H'talgim's receptionist. He stared at me for a moment before accepting the packet of old-fashioned paper contracts. There was a digital copy on a chip in my pocket as well, but for some reason known only to Cranotian bureaucrats, loans for real property like land and ships had to be hand-carried. Digital copies did not count as legal documents. *Whatever,* I thought. *It won't matter back in Confed space.*

"If you have a seat over there, I will get these processed," they said, waving at a pair of low benches across the room. I had no idea what this guy's problem was, but he seemed angry all the time. *Maybe it's just 'resting bitch face',* I chuckled to myself as I joined Gina on the bench.

"What's his problem?" Gina whispered, taking a sip from her water bottle.

I snickered softly. "I was literally wondering the same thing. Current theory is 'resting bitch face'."

Gina snorted, nearly shooting water out her nose. "That's horrible," she complained, struggling to keep from laughing out loud.

"I hope this goes smoothly," I commented. "I was actually surprised that we didn't have more problems with the lender."

Gina made a speculative noise. "Yeah, it seemed way too easy for some reason. I was expecting a lot more push back, with us being Terran."

She wasn't kidding either. It was a bit weird. We'd gotten in and out of the bank within a couple of hours. They'd accepted the down payment almost immediately, then processed the loan documents with minimal fuss. I hadn't linked it with my Ceres account, of course, as I'd cleaned it out earlier in the day. I didn't want any kind of electronic trail leading from my old life to this new one. The lender hadn't batted an eye at the lack, though.

The interest rate on the contract was really high, but I figured I could get a better loan rate in Confed space and pay this one off with it. With an actual ship as collateral, I had a few friends I could count on to game the banking systems. The Cranotian lender even gave me a forty cycle grace period until the first payment was due. It was almost too good to be true, and I was still waiting for the other shoe to drop. I didn't have to wait long.

"And who will be piloting?" the red-skinned asked after calling us back to the counter.

I raised an eyebrow. *Isn't it obvious?*

"Me."

"And your license to operate above five hundred meters in atmosphere?"

"Wait, I'm going to be leaving the atmosphere, not flying through it." I argued. I had looked up the regulation. There was nothing in them requiring a separate license for trans-atmospheric launch.

The receptionist looked at me like I was stupid, and after a moment I realized he was right. To reach orbit, I was going to have to fly *through* the atmosphere, even if I was only going straight up. *Well, squat! Now I feel dumb.*

"If you are unable to provide such documentation, I am afraid I will be unable to release the entry codes to you." I could see the smirk on his face as he gleefully offered to cancel the transaction, minus the thousand credit deposit, of course. I was nearly at the point where I wanted to break his nose, but my anger was interrupted.

"Where's H'talgim," Gina spoke sharply. "I'd like to speak with him, please." The superlicious little toad turned towards her, no doubt ecstatic at the idea of telling her the old crab was busy, but she cut him off before he could even get a word out. "Now, or I start calling the Contract Enforcement Bureau."

I wasn't sure if she was bluffing or not, but the threat finally got the guy's attention. He stared at her for a moment before punching a command into his slate. Looking back at us with a scowl, he finally caved. "He'll be here shortly."

Only a couple minutes later, H'talgim pulled up to the front entrance in his electric runabout and waved us over. "What's this I hear about you threatening my office staff? I thought we had a deal."

"No threat," Gina walked forward confidently. "Just wanted to ask your advice, and he was playing gatekeeper."

"Yeah, he does that sometimes." H'talgim grunted sympathetically. "Depends on the customer, honestly. He's been here a long time, though, and he knows my filing system. Lots of contacts in the scrap and used ship markets, which helps my bottom line," he explained further.

I spoke up at that point. "Yeah, well, he's about to lose you a sale. He says we can't lift without a pilot license cleared for the half-kay limit. He offered to cancel the contract, minus the deposit, of course. I think he's trying to scam us. The only question I have for you is, are you on board for that? If so, we'll just leave."

"What?" the old crab sounded offended. "No! You know, he's right about the license requirement, but there's ways around that. You can hire someone to lift the ship up to the station and launch from there…"

I winced. "I'm already marked *persona-non-grata* up there. Either I got tagged for trouble back home, or marked just because I'm 'human'. Not sure which." I wasn't entirely sure why I felt okay telling him all this, but the impression

I'd gotten during the negotiations was that he was generally honest in his dealings. Perhaps not completely honest in a *legal* sense, but at least honest with his customers.

He paused for a moment, obviously thinking things through. "Oh, that's a problem. Now that I think about it, you might end up with issues outbound from the station, too. They like to harass people they don't like, and it sounds like you've been singled out for some reason."

"Strangely enough, I didn't have any problems with the local bank," I mused. "They were quite happy to make up the contract. The fees were a bit higher than I like, but they gave me forty cycles before the first payment was due."

"Forty cycles!?" H'talgim growled, surprising me with the anger in his tone. "Now I *know* something's rotting in those waters! Shortest profitable interstellar hop is nearly thirty cycles, round trip. And they expect you to turn a profit on this thing with only a ten cycle buffer?"

"That's not a problem," I answered. "I don't plan to keep the lien with them, anyways. As soon as I can get to a Confed bank, I'll just get a loan from them and wire the full amount back through the exchange network."

H'talgim's eyestalks swiveled to stare at me. "Oh, you poor, naive little smilp. You really are new at this, aren't you?" He started the runabout again and motioned an appendage. "Get in, we're going to my *other* office."

As he settled in behind his massive, part-strewn desk, he sighed theatrically. "To start, I can think of at least three ways so far that you're already screwed. First is the payment method."

I slid onto the small bench being careful of my tail, as the gap between the bench and the wall was quite narrow. "A payment is a payment, I thought."

"You thought wrong," he grunted. "I looked at your contract. It isn't mentioned there, which means the controlling language is in their User Agreement, which I bet they had you sign before they even started contract paperwork. That one was probably digital, and they get your fingerprint with a scanner. Remember anything like that?"

Gina spoke up. "Red, I bet that was during the account creation screen when they had you put in your personal information."

"Yeah," I replied, a bit confused. "It looked like the standard stuff, so I didn't pay too much attention to it. There wasn't any link visible for additional terms, and nothing on the page was out of line. Nothing about payment methods, anyways."

"It's an old trick," H'talgim explained. "They make the text window just a little bit bigger than the screen is able to display, and don't include a scroll function. You have to manually resize the window and move it up on the screen to see the link in the disclaimer."

"Damn. What did it say, then?"

"Probably requiring in-person payment by you. Or your authorized agent, which I'm guessing you don't have."

I shook my head. "How hard is it to get one?"

"Who would you trust to have access to your accounts?" H'talgim asked pointedly. "I've heard about some of the things you humans do in business. There's no such thing as a bonded agent service here. If you had a company based on the planet, one of your employees could do it, but you've already told me you plan to operate out-system.

"The second problem I see is surety," H'talgim continued. "You have no backing, no one who stands behind you, if you fail. In a regular contract, surety is assigned by either the bank or the loan applicant. In your case, because you have no *nt'ikali* named in the lien, if you were ever to fail any terms of the contract, your ship itself would become immediately forfeit." H'talgim mused for a moment. "This increases the risk to the bank, but they have surety from their major investors, so they can easily absorb the loss if this happens. Of course, they would then just come after you for the balance."

"That seems like unnecessary exposure, I would think," I thought aloud. "Almost sounds more like an insurance actuary than a bank."

"Hehehe, yes'" he chuckled grimly. "In some ways you could call that kind of bank more of a gambling hall, to be honest. I'm beginning to suspect a few things. Did Lengumo suggest this company?"

"Yeah," I replied, a knot growing in my stomach. "He called it a 'preferred lender'."

"Thought so. I'm not sure why but he must have taken an instant dislike to you." H'talgim said. "Otherwise, he would have made sure you were better informed."

"Why would the bank take on that kind of risk, though?" I interjected. "Are they looking to collect on an insurance policy?"

"You humans and your weird notions…", H'talgim sighed wearily. "There's no such thing as 'insurance'. Liability is the responsibility of the business owner. Large companies have the capital to run the risks. The only way a small business survives a major loss is by being in a contract agreement with those large companies, basically what humans call a franchise. They lose full control of the business, but they're also protected if something goes wrong."

I considered this. It sounded like the same kind of fiefdom the Corpos in the Confed had set up. Byzantine webs of interlocking contracts and regulations, all designed to maintain the Corpos' control of their respective monopolies. However, I wondered about the reach of their jurisdiction. It wasn't like the Confed was going to help them enforce contracts like that.

Almost as if he was reading my mind, H'talgim continued. "And don't think just running off to your home planet will work. They may not have legal standing with the government in human space, but they already have agreements in place with all sorts of shady types. Bounty hunters, enforcers, brokers. The brokers act as proxies for the banks. They'll have the hunters just snatch you and drag you back. Your ship would be stripped for parts, sold off and the money split to pay the fine and the broker's fees." He wiggled in place, as if finding the thought distasteful. "Or they just kill you and take the ship outright. You're left with nothing, or you're dead."

A suspicious thought occurred to me as he was talking. "Why are you telling us this? Why are you helping a pair of strangers like us? What's your angle?"

"I thought it was obvious," the old crab looked surprised. "The terms of the loan are contingent. If you don't pay, I don't get my money."

"So they're screwing all of us," Gina scowled. "And your asshole receptionist was the first step. Why the hell don't you fire him, if he's screwing you over like this?"

"Who says I hired him in the first place?" he retorted snidely. "Weren't you paying attention? Small businesses like mine only survive by contracting with bigger ones. That bank holds *MY* surety contract. Lengumo is *their appointed liaison!* And yet, I still have to pay him a salary on top of all that. But that's just how it is," he finished morosely.

Well sonova-bitch, THAT puts a whole different spin on things. A cold knot of despair formed in my gut. "So you're telling me, even if we dropped out right now, they'd come after me for the entire balance of the loan, and they'd *still* keep the ship?"

"Pretty much," he snorted. "Which is why it's in my interest to get you up and running as soon as possible." His tone softened. "Besides, it's such a unique design. I'd love to see it fly with someone willing to take care of it."

Gina chimed in with a vicious-looking grin. "So what are we   waiting   for?   Let's   get   flying!"

Ch.13: Taking Off

"Before we get ahead of ourselves," I interjected. "There's a couple more things I'd like to ask you." I explained the strange surveillance and the chase that ensued when we'd gone to the bank to get the loan. I'd hoped H'talgim would have some insight on who might be behind the strange cloaked group, but he was as clueless as we were. Only one thing stood out to him, though, and that was the use of the drone.

"It's not a common practice, modifying and using standard commercial drones like that," he explained. "Purpose-built surveillance drones are restricted technology here, due to the liability surrounding them, but like anything else, the larger companies have the capital to take that kind of risk. The bank, for instance, wouldn't bother rigging up something so ad-hoc, they'd just use a real surveillance drone."

"So, who would, then?" I asked. "Criminals? Spies?"

"Not ones from this planet," H'talgim huffed. "All the major criminal organizations are tightly linked to the big companies, same for spies." He paused, thoughtfully. "But now that you mention it, I have seen quite a few more delivery drones flying over the lot than usual the last few months. I didn't think much about it, but if some off-world group was running an operation and didn't have local connections, your modified drone thing might be a work-around they came up with."

Gina perked up. "Wait, you just said, *'the last few months'*. Any chance it was right after that rock-hopper dropped our ship off as salvage?"

"Possibly," H'talgim's eyestalks contracted thoughtfully. "For sure, though, I haven't had any cloaked figures chasing me around. And if they wanted to get to the ship, why not just come in and offer to buy it? It's not like it's that expensive."

Oh fun, I griped. *Another monkey wrench thrown into the works.* But the realization also gave me an idea.

*****

H'talgim was as good as his word about helping get the ship into space. The old crab simply called in a small favor, and a pilot showed up to fly the ship. She couldn't fly the ship to orbit, as her license didn't cover that, but she could take it over to the orbital catapult, three hundred kilometers away on the coast. The bank liaison had scowled viciously at this, but kept his mouth shut after H'talgim confronted him over his shady practices.

From there, we hired someone to take it to orbit for us. In the end, I was satisfied with the result, as the fees for the catapult were an order of magnitude less than the cost of the fuel needed to boost to orbit on the ship's own engines. The additional expense of a surface-to-orbit pilot to ride along during launch was a sunk cost, as we would have to pay for that regardless.

I'd also settled on a new name for the ship, as the original name on the builder's plaque was in a language no one knew how to read. Gina had argued for calling it the "AT-AT", based on some ancient entertainment vid she'd watched, which incidentally, I immediately recognized from her description, but I decided to call it the *CMV Camel*, instead, going along with my first impression of its appearance. Even with its legs extended, it still resembled the ancient animal, and I couldn't help thinking of it as some giant, fabled Kin-beast of lore and legend. Not that there had ever been such a thing as Camel-Kin before, but my imagination latched on to the concept and wouldn't let go. And considering I was the one paying for it, my opinion was the only one that really mattered.

Beside the roll-on, roll-off cargo system, I found several other things to like about the *Camel*. For one thing, whichever race it was built for had tails. While refitting all the seats, chairs and benches to accommodate Kin anatomy was within my budget, it wasn't cheap either. Of course, very little of the interior fabric had survived the stint in hard vacuum, but the cost of replacing cushions and seat covers was negligible. The previous owners also had similar plumbing, so beyond adjusting the pH levels on the water filtration settings, very little needed to be done to make the interior livable.

Gina was in engineer heaven with the small fab shop. During the long coast out to the jump point, she busied herself with pulling all the inspection panels, slowly tracing control runs as she mapped out the ship's entire electrical infrastructure. Additionally, she started fabbing the tools she needed to work on the ship using patterns we obtained from H'talgim. Getting them calibrated to Confed standard was fairly simple once we figured out a basic translation algorithm, but it only worked on the math and fabber settings. The majority of the alien language was still a mystery.

It took a lot of negotiation, as well as some intense introspection on my part, but I finally resigned myself to the fact that Gina was a permanent part of the crew. It was inevitable, really. I wasn't enough of an asshole to leave her stranded on Cranotia, and she wasn't enough of a problem child to get voted off the crew. Besides, it wasn't like there was enough of a crew to have a vote yet, anyway. Plus, she really did seem to know what she was doing with power plants, even alien ones with no instruction manual. I was still a bit ambiguous about our personal vs working relationship, but since she failed to address it in the slightest since we left the orbital station, I let it be for now. I wasn't really comfortable dating subordinates anyways, even if we weren't a military crew.

The biggest pain about turning the ship into our new home was dealing with inventory. While the engineering spaces were relatively well organized, the crew quarters and pilot spaces were anything but. Clearing out all the junk and personal items left behind in the crew berthing and separating out the stuff that actually belonged to the ship was a nightmare without readable inventory records. The small control bridge was even worse, not for what was there, but for what wasn't. Lots of equipment had been stripped by the salvagers. We were lucky that they'd left all the critical systems alone, but I guessed they'd left those in place just to be able to fly the ship back to Cranotia.

It was interesting to note what we'd found among the junk, though. From the articles of discarded clothing, we confirmed that the former occupants were taller than me on average, had two arms, two legs and a thick tail. None of the fabric had any identifiable fur or dander on them, which I found astonishing until I realized the dust coating the rooms was actually residue from shed hairs. Apparently the ship's environmental systems had some method of distributing an aerosol enzyme capable of breaking down organic material into small enough particles that would float in the air, making it easier to filter out without having to sweep the floors constantly. The lack of atmosphere in the crew cabins had allowed the dust to adhere to the deck and bulkheads instead of being collected normally. The enzyme didn't work on *my* fur, but Gina's slight shed was greedily gobbled up by the bio-engineered microorganisms, so we left that part of the system alone. Surprisingly, there were no photos or mementos left behind, and other than a few discarded food wrappers, no written material at all.

"Hey Red," Gina's voice came over the intercom system she'd finally gotten working again. "See if that panel has power now."

"Nothing," I said, glancing at the instrument cluster in question. The navigation suite was barely functional, even though from what Gina could see it should have had a lot of processing power, based on the size and complexity of the control runs leading to the nav panel. It was almost like there was supposed to be a subprocessor somewhere, but we couldn't seem to find anything missing. The nav console still *worked*, it just did so slowly and without a lot of accuracy. That was going to be an issue, if we couldn't figure it out, and soon.

"How about now?"

"Nope," I sighed. "Just bring up a toner probe, and I'll see if I can trace the cables from the panel manually."

"On the way, Red."

Two hours later, I was about to toss the probe out the airlock. Every cluster of cables I'd toned so far simply disappeared down into the maintenance crawl space below the deck. Gina had already confirmed the inbound cables from there to the sensors, so digging up deck plates was probably going to be the next step.

Sighing, I reached for the multi-tool attached to my belt and began to take apart the protective shield surrounding the cable inputs. We only had another twelve hours till we got to the jump point. After that, if we couldn't get an accurate enough nav fix, we would have to switch to a less profitable destination which would also require changing jump points. Sticking around near the jump point was not an option, as *eventually* another ship would jump in from another system at that same point. Actual collisions were exceedingly rare, because space was big, after all. That didn't mean you took chances you didn't need to.

As the shield came off, something caught my eye. I reached for the intercom button.

"Hey Gina, when you verified all the connections up here, did you check for wireless induction ports?"

"Of course not," came the quick reply. "That's the nav cluster. All ship-critical connectors are hard-wired. That's not just regulations, that's common sense!"

"Okay, so why did I just find an induction interface on the inside of the cable shielding around this thing?"

"Wait, *what?*" Gina sounded just as confused as I was.

"Weird thing is, it has what looks like a high-speed fiber cable running out of it," I added. "Which means the toner probe is going to be useless for tracing it."

"What color is the cable?"

"White, with a red stripe," I answered.

I could hear her muttering as she pulled up the wiring index on her slate. She'd left the intercom channel open while she searched. "Okay, I have red with white stripe cables in the fab module... nope. Not there either... Oh! Check the pedestal next to the captain's chair. I have a disconnected terminal listed there that matches the color at least. Since it wasn't connected to anything, I didn't bother checking if it was fiber or hard-wired."

I hadn't sat in the captain's chair for more than a few moments since we boarded. There was no point, really, since I was also the only pilot. As I took a closer look at the pedestal sitting to the left of the command chair I started to wonder. It didn't have any independent controls or anything, just a holographic emitter which hadn't worked since we bought the ship. *So what's this thing doing here, anyways?* I started looking for inspection panels, but couldn't find any.

"Gina," I called again. "Where's the panel for the pedestal? It looks like a single piece to me."

"Yeah, there isn't one, really," she explained. "That one took me a while to figure out. You have to be sitting in the chair, then reach across with your left hand and touch the induction plate on the far edge of the pedestal. Then with your right hand, hit the blue and white buttons on the right armrest."

My eyebrows furrowed in concern. "That sounds awfully specific for opening up a maintenance compartment. Are we sure it's not a self-destruct mechanism or something?"

"Well, if it was we would have been blown to smithereens three days ago when I got it open the last time," Gina chuckled. "I think we're safe from explodey bits for today. Besides, there is nothing in the compartment but a couple disconnected cables. Whatever was there was probably found and stripped by the rock-hopper crew."

"Okay, thanks," I replied, still a bit puzzled over it all. Sure enough, though, the instructions worked, but instead of a panel opening up, the entire top of the pedestal came up on two supporting rods that rose from the top of the base. Like Gina said, there was nothing there but a cluster of disconnected cables. One looked to be for power, as it had the same color code as similar cables we'd found around the ship, but all the rest were fiber cables. *Why didn't these guys label their cables better?*

"Well, Gina," I commed her after verifying there was indeed a white fiber cable with a red stripe. "I think we've found where that subprocessor is supposed to be. No idea where the processor itself is, or what it looks like, but here's where it's supposed to go."

"Yay," Gina replied, her voice dripping with sarcasm. "Another critical bit we're missing. That makes four, you know."

"Yeah. So it seems like we're looking for something between sixteen and twenty centimeters across, probably cube or rectangular shaped, based on the size of the compartment. That ring any bells?"

"Not offhand, but I'll take a look at the pile of unidentified crap and let you know what I find."

I finally figured out how to close the pedestal back up. It was so simple, I very nearly smacked myself on the head for not thinking of it sooner. *Just press down on the top. It's super-secret-squirrel for OPENING it, not for CLOSING it,* I fumed. I called Gina again.

"It's closed up again. You need anything?"

"Nope, I'm good," she replied. "Still looking through all the unidentified modules."

"Roger, I'm taking a break for now."

"Who's Roger?" she asked innocently.

I rolled my eyes as I headed for the captain's stateroom. It was one place that I'd gotten mostly squared away, if only to have a place to sleep, but I had to admit to myself, it was going to become one of my favorite perks of being Captain of the *CMV Camel*. It was larger than the other cabins, of course. In fact it was larger than most cabins on a cruise ship, not that I'd ever had the luxury of taking a trip on one. It even sported its own fresher! The only other cabin onboard that had its own fresher was the engineer's berthing at the back of the ship, which only made sense, as having to traverse the cargo bay to use the toilet would just be ridiculous, in practice. Not that I hadn't seen human designs in the military that were just as stupid. Of course, Gina had claimed that berth before we even left the scrap yard so she could be next to her beloved power plants.

As I slumped down into the integrated office chair in the two-room suite, I started to list in my mind the things we still needed to be fully operational. First and foremost was a fully operational navigation computer, but unless we found the missing module, we'd have to install a completely new system, sensors and all. Gina swore she could do it with the parts we had on hand, some from our cargo, but mostly scrounged from wrecks in the scrapyard. I was leery of trusting mismatched parts for something that important, so I told her to hold off for now. Plus, I didn't want to dig into our profit margin by using stuff we could sell at our destination.

Yes, we already had a cargo for this run, again courtesy of H'talgim's seemingly endless network of friends and favors. It wasn't a high profit cargo, mostly common machine parts and small lots of prefabricated electronics modules, but the markup in the mining communities would allow us to pay for fuel as well as covering our first lien payment. Food and other consumables were another thing, though. I hoped to pick up enough ore from the smelters to offset some of that on the return trip, but it was still something of a gamble.

The next big thing we needed was more crew. The *Camel* was significantly bigger than I'd originally had in mind when looking for a ship, and without a fully functional navigation system, I was going to be run ragged trying to cover all the critical shifts. That meant I needed to hire a copilot, or if that was off the table, at least a trained navigator who could stand watch during the long runs to the jump points. Gina was technically rated to stand watch, but she was tied up doing maintenance on the power plants, which had a myriad of checks and services which had been left undone while it was sitting idle in the scrap yard. For now, I was forced to simply leave the bridge unmanned during those times I couldn't be there.

While that was a relatively safe proposition traveling the well documented and heavily monitored lanes of the Commercial Conglomerate of Cranotia, it was a fool's bet anywhere else. Not only was there the danger of unmapped debris, but as I'd found out on the trip out here, there were literally hundreds of threats to the ship once you left the boundaries of the major powers. Unmapped system bodies, slag and trash from mining operations, micrometeorites, not to mention opportunistic scavengers and outright pirates. All of these things could be handled, but only if someone was on the bridge to react quickly.

Lastly, we needed firepower. From what Gina had found so far, the only thing this tub had for self defense was a pair of two-hundred megawatt laser arrays which could fire a continuous beam at full rated power, or a set of modulated pulses at one-hundred-fifty percent power once every point zero three seconds using a set of integrated capacitors. This would be fine for intercepting small debris, but was absolutely useless against anything more than a half a ton in mass. But that wasn't the oddest thing about the two arrays.

The lasers themselves seemed to be purpose built as anti-missile defenses, but again there was something missing. There were control runs leading back to the command bridge, but like the nav systems, they lacked the subprocessor that would normally assist the gunner with target acquisition and tracking. For now, they only seemed to work in manual mode from two gunner stations in the waist of the ship, although at least there was the option to slave both of them to the same station if additional firepower was needed.

If I'd had my suspicions before, this discovery made it even more evident that the ship had once been a combat support unit. All that was missing was anti-ship weaponry, the lack of which confused me, considering how well designed the ship was otherwise. It didn't look like any major sections of the ship had been removed or modified. I knew we hadn't explored every nook and cranny of the mechanical spaces given the time crunch, but considering the size of a standard Confed or Snake anti-ship missile, I figured we would have found them by now if they were there. Also, there were some parts of the ship which couldn't be accessed while under way in space, and for all I knew this race had perfected miniature anti-ship warheads with micro-grav drives that fit in the palm of your hand. There could be an entire launch bay full of weapons that we'd missed somehow because they were so small, but I was skeptical.

I was determined to remedy the lack, of course. A couple concealed missile launchers like the one on Goose's scout ship would be ideal, but it was a question of whether or not we could shoehorn them into the hull somewhere. Offensive weapon systems were perfectly legal out here, but once I returned to Confed space, they would have to be carefully concealed if I wanted to stay out of prison.

I activated the display built into the desk, pulling up the status menu. Navigation still showed the minimalist course tracking, and most of the sensors were still locked into manual control. Again, the lack of automation was strange, but I was getting used to it now.

On the other side of the coin, the sensors were really good, at least two generations beyond the ones I had on my scout ship in RECON. Passive sensor resolution was nearly an order of magnitude better, and the range at which I could detect ships was downright astounding. Active sensors were a little lackluster, but I figured that was due to the lack of a dedicated, steerable emitter array on the hull. Again, it came down to processing power. Like the missing module that helped control the laser arrays, there was probably another that was responsible for tuning the embedded sensor emitters in the hull, but I hadn't yet found any missing modules besides the one I'd found for the Nav systems. It was obvious the ship was designed to use the hull itself as one giant phased array, which if the controller was present would allow almost laser-like precision. Without it, all the sensor emitters were limited to acting alone. It made for really good omnidirectional coverage, but didn't allow for collectively pointing the active sensors in any one direction.

It was depressing. The scavengers had really messed things up, it seemed. *But,* I reassured myself. *It's a ship. It flies. Sixty-seven more payments and it's all mine!*

Ch 14: Run to Jump

The banging of the gavel echoed throughout the courtroom over and over. BANG! Bang. bang...

The strident tone from the slate jolted me awake as I struggled to pull myself from another nightmare. *This squat is getting old,* I thought as I took several deep, calming breaths.

The cabin was almost completely dark except for the glow of the slate's screen. Looking at the display I was relieved to find it was just the timer I'd set to remind me of our impending arrival at the jump point. Navigating across the deck with only the slate's illumination was fraught with peril, and I stubbed my toes at least twice on obstacles I had yet to memorize. Finally, I reached the hatch and turned on the lights with the manual switch mounted on the bulkhead next to it. The sudden harsh glare was downright painful, and I vowed to rig up some kind voice control, or failing that, at least a dimmer switch. *Another thing to add to the list.*

And that list had grown long indeed. Most of it was little stuff like the light controls, but right at the top were still those giant, looming deficiencies concerning the ship's critical systems. As my eyes gradually adjusted to the brightness, I made my way back to the bed to check the slate for any messages. Besides one from Gina saying to contact her when I woke up, the message queue was relatively clear. There were lots of updates to various inventory lists, and sorting those out was going to be a major chore, but it seemed nothing had popped up on sensors during my sleep cycle. We were still two hours out from the jump point, which gave me enough time to use the fresher and eat some breakfast before getting to the bridge. I was still hoping against hope that we could find the missing nav module, but the likelihood of that was diminishing by the hour. *Shower, then food,* I decided. *Then work.*

The fresher was fairly well designed once you figured out the settings. By default it was a waterless "sonic" shower, using ultrasonic sound waves to gently vibrate away dead skin cells and things like dandruff, making me suspect that the designers had very thin body hair or fur, if they had any at all. However, this didn't work very well with my thick pelt. Thankfully, it had a waterjet setting, and the shower head was detachable, allowing me to thoroughly scrub my entire body. As this was the first time I used it, I luxuriated in the pulsating spray, letting the stress flow off my body along with the heavy musk which had been building up for the last couple weeks.

I finally stopped the water and activated the dryer function. Small vents popped open on the sides of the fresher and powerful jets of warm, dry air quickly blew away the water from my fur. I had to reactivate it twice to get fully dry, but it wasn't like I was crunched for time.

It's amazing how good just being clean *again feels!* I preened as I finally stepped out into the sleeping area. I felt truly invigorated, ready to face nearly any challenge. I donned my clean ship-suit comforted in the knowledge that one of Gina's first projects had been getting the clothes fresher working and calibrated to our requirements. It had necessitated adding a couple solvents to the process to handle my musk but looked to be functioning perfectly, which was a huge relief to both of us. Dressed and ready, I headed for the galley.

I grabbed one of the pre-made rations rather than fresh ingredients, and popped it into the small food prepper, which worked kind of like an autoclave machine, using high pressure steam to both hydrate and heat the dehydrated ration packs I picked up for the voyage. We also had some fresh stuff, as well as frozen, but I had neither the skill nor the inclination to cook a meal right now. The best I could hope for was a slightly burnt omelet and a huge mess, were I to try, and I wasn't about to dampen my spirits when I'd started the day off so well.

The prepper was extremely efficient, beeping in a mere half minute or so. I carefully grabbed the plastic tray by the edges to keep from burning my fingers and placed the meal on the small counter. Folding out one of the built-in seats, I sat down to eat. Almost as an afterthought, I remembered that Gina had asked me to tell her when I was up. I reached towards the wall and activated the "all-hands" button on the intercom. The intercom system, like all the other systems onboard, didn't have any automation to handle changing locations for individual speakers, so we just set up a couple repeaters in the bridge and engineering rather than using the shipwide broadcast we'd been using earlier. We hadn't included the galley, though.

"Where you at?" she asked almost immediately after I sent the ping.

"Galley, eating breakfast."

"Be right there, I found something!" She ended the call abruptly.

Suddenly, I wasn't that hungry. I wasn't sure if I was supposed to be excited or terrified, as she hadn't said it was good or bad news, but my anxiety spiked regardless as I waited for her to arrive. I forced myself to take at least a couple bites from the mostly-flavorless paste, knowing I'd regret it later if I didn't.

After a couple minutes, I started to wonder what was taking her so long. I finished the ration pack and was about to start looking for her when she burst into the galley almost at a dead run, skidding to a stop on the corrugated deck and startling me quite badly in the process.

"What's wrong?!" I asked quickly, dreading the answer.

"Huh?"

"Why are you running?" I clarified.

"Oh! I'm just excited!" she smiled brightly. "Sorry it took so long, but I had to wait for the fabber to finish printing something."

"You scared the life outta me," I complained before sighing in relief. Apparently it was good news that had her so spastic, rather than the opposite. "Okay, what's got you in such a tizzy?"

"*This!*" She pulled a medium-sized metal rectangular frame from the carry bag slung over her shoulder, placing it gently on the counter next to my empty meal tray.

My eyes widened as I recognized the connectors arrayed on the sides. "You found it!"

"Well, kinda," she prevaricated. "I didn't find it, I fabbed it from plans."

"Wait, this isn't the subprocessor, then?" I asked, deflated. I already know the answer. There was no way a complex module like what we were looking for could be fabricated from scratch in a mere eight hours. "So what is it?"

"It's an adapter of some kind," she explained, still bubbling with excitement. "I searched in the ship's fabber templates for the connectors the fiber cables use, figuring it would be something they could make themselves, and I was right! And those records linked to this! I checked the dimensions, and it fits perfectly in the mount points inside that pedestal. Not only that, but these ports here match up with every single cable in there. It's a multi-port integrated I/O interface!"

"Well, that's great to hear," I grumbled morosely. "But we still don't have the processor."

"Sure," she continued, undeterred. "But now we know the exact shape we're looking for!" She pointed at the top of the adapter. Looking closer, I could see a seam along the top of the device, along with a small catch that looked to be holding down the top. I picked it up and slid my thumbnail under the pressure fitting and gently pulled up. It released easily, revealing a smooth-sided cavity inside. The void looked to fit a perfect cube only ten centimeters across. But that wasn't the part that took my breath away.

What looked like thousands, if not tens of thousands of individual contact points glistened in the light of the galley's overhead LEDs like tiny diamonds across sheets of utterly black carbon insulation on all four sides. The bottom had almost the same, except for four contact plates at the bottom corners that looked to be where the power supply connected in at least a three phase array with a fourth for ground.

I stared in amazement. If this was all a single, solid processor block, it had to be incredibly powerful! The density of the processor pins was insane! I could not for the life of me figure out a single thing on the ship that would require this much processing power. There were no heat sinks or thermal plates though, which just made my eyebrows rise higher. How did it handle the heat that much power would produce?

"Damn!" I exclaimed, but my wonder soon faded. I knew for a fact that nothing we'd found even closely resembled this shape. "We still don't have a processor, though."

"I know," Gina's mood finally dampened. "But at least now we know exactly what we're looking for."

"Yeah, but chances are, it got nabbed by the scavengers," I sighed morosely. "The fact that the adapter was gone too means they just grabbed the whole thing, maybe not even knowing what it was."

I looked at it for a moment before handing it back. "Go ahead and hook it up. There's a possibility it will provide some cross-connections to allow us to control more things from the bridge even with the core missing, like the laser arrays."

"Okay, Red," she replied softly. "I'm sorry I disappointed you."

"No!" I said firmly. "This is not your fault. I just got my hopes up. That's my failing, not yours. You did great, absolutely great!" And I meant that wholeheartedly. I hadn't even considered looking into the fabricator files. Of course we couldn't read the words in them, but the images were right there for us to see. I'd just discounted them since they weren't translated, and was kicking myself for being so single-minded.

She smiled sweetly at me, as if I'd said something profound, then walked past me and into the corridor, giving me a reassuring pat on the shoulder as she did. I continued to stare gloomily at my empty ration tray.

We're so close, I despaired. *But so far! God, I always hated that phrase.*

I started to reach for my slate before remembering I'd left it in my cabin. I hauled myself to my feet and slunk down the corridor, my thoughts getting angrier with each step. The image of that damned pedestal just wouldn't leave my mind. *There's GOT to be a solution,* I seethed.

The hatch to the captain's quarters slid open languidly as usual, but I was nearly at my limit. Frustrated, I tried to push it open faster to no effect, which in turn fueled my rage even further. When I could finally squeeze into the opening I forced my way through, scraping my shin painfully against the machined edge of the pressure door.

"OW!!" I cried. "GODDAMNED MOTHERFRACKING DOOR!!" I hissed, spinning to give the target of my frustration a swift kick, which ended up hurting my toes rather than doing any damage to the hatch, which was rated to withstand explosive decompression without breaking the airtight seal. I had more chance of flying to Old Terra without a ship than damaging that slab of carbon steel with my foot.

Of course, this did nothing to improve my mood. All the times I'd thought I was finally happy, just to have life screw me over, started flooding my mind. Getting pulled from cargo shuttles, Joe Buckley dying, that asshole JAG officer, and finally *THAT SPINELESS, SQUAT-EATING, WORTHLESS WASTE OF SPACE, SPURGLE!* And now *THIS!!! I finally have a ship of my own, and I'm going to lose it because some VACUUM-SUCKING ROCK-HOPPER snagged the navigation computer!!!*

I felt a desperate need to break something, *ANYTHING*, just to relieve the incessant pressure in my head. Spotting my slate, I stepped angrily to the side table next to the desk where it lay on its wireless charging pad, intending to throw it against a bulkhead. But as I grabbed it and cocked my arm back to throw, I *froze.*

No. Fraking. Way. I gaped, utterly gobsmacked. *Seriously?*

Ch 15: Seriously?

I gently slid the core I found in the captain's quarters into its slot in the command plinth, carefully making sure to only touch the top opposite corners. I had vacuumed out the new adapter to ensure there was no debris. The adapter itself was brand new, of course, and should have been completely clean, but I didn't want to risk any bits of fluff or dandruff from my fur, *or anything else for that matter*, getting in between the carefully cleaned contacts and the processor core. I even wore a pair of medical gloves to ensure no body oils were transferred to the complex, insanely crowded surfaces.

As the perfect cube came into contact on all sides, it suddenly stopped moving down. I froze in panic, almost pulling it out again, afraid that somehow, some tiny bit of debris had gotten between the sides of the core and its adapter socket.

"Just let go," Gina whispered, entranced by the delicate operation.

"Huh?" I blurted, confused.

"It's the trapped air that's holding it up," she explained. "I bet you there's not more than a couple dozen nanometers clearance once you get past that chamfered edge. We can either wait for the air to bleed out on its own, or look for a pressure release button."

I cringed, but did as she instructed. As she predicted, the cube seemed to float and bob slightly, like the piston of a shock absorber, as I gave it the slightest bit of pressure downwards. After almost a minute, I still didn't see any appreciable movement, so I started to look down into the pedestal for anything resembling a pressure relief valve. As I rose to my feet, I started to lose my balance, my legs having gone to sleep from squatting down for so long. Gina tried to catch me, but before she could make more than a gesture in my direction, my arm swung out, bumping the top of the raised platform of the pedestal, triggering the closing mechanism.

"Oh squat!!" I cried, terrified that the pedestal would close and damage the delicate cube somehow, but before I could do anything, the cube slid swiftly and smoothly the rest of the way down into the adapter assembly. A small protuberance on the adapter's guide rails I'd never noticed before flipped the top of the socket closed, and the two grasping arms of the collapsing enclosure neatly snugged it tightly against the rest of the socket, perfectly aligning the edges and engaging the hold-down as they were obviously designed to do.

A wave of relief washed through me like a cleansing flood, and all the tension in my body went with it, leaving me weak as a baby. Gina chuckled as she watched me quivering spastically on the deck.

"Oh, thank god," I panted breathlessly. "I was *so* sure I'd fraked that up!"

"Oh, get up, ya big pansy!" Gina teased, reaching down to offer a hand. I accepted it gratefully. It never ceased to amaze me just how physically strong she was, especially given the differences in our size and weight. Gina, of course, always laughed it off, saying it was all about leverage, not strength. Given how easily she'd taken me down that one time, I wasn't about to argue with her.

Finally standing upright and not gasping for breath, I turned to the captain's chair and pulled up the status menu on the holographic display. To my absolute *joy*, it showed the translated word, "Initializing..."

"Oh, thank you Saint Murphy, for stepping aside for just *once*," I breathed in sardonic prayer, not entirely in jest, either.

"And just in time, too," Gina added, pointing at the countdown on her slate. It showed less than an hour before we would be out of position to jump at our current velocity.

"Okay, yeah. That was cutting it a bit close, I guess. You want to hit the head before we jump?"

"No," she replied a bit dyspeptically. "I want to know where you found that thing, now that we're not scrambling to get it installed."

"I hate to say it, but I'm a bit embarrassed about that," I said with a grimace.

"Why?"

"You know that little side table next to the desk in the captain's quarters?"

"Not really," she answered sardonically. "Haven't had much of a chance to go in there. When you're up and about, I'm either sleeping or working. And when I'm not doing either of those things, you're usually sleeping in there. I haven't even had a chance to map out the control runs in that area. With as little sleep as you've been getting, I didn't want to wake you up."

"Oh," I was a bit nonplussed. I hadn't realized I was preventing her from doing her job. I would have to remind myself to pay more attention to things like that. *It's been a long three days,* I admitted to myself.

"So," she prompted, jerking me out of my moment of introspection.

"It was the dumbest thing," I told her. "You know how you figured out how to open the pedestal here on the bridge, right?"

"Sure. It was a little complicated, but once I realized it was a two-factor action, it was easy enough."

"There's another pedestal-looking thing in there. Not quite the exact same thing, of course, but the same general shape. I thought it was like a side table or something, and just set up my slate's charging pad on it."

"Seriously?" She gave me a dubious look. "You never once noticed it?"

"I know, right?" I exclaimed. "I think it was because I was always so tired when I went in there, I just never looked around that closely. I mean, when we first got into the ship, it was the only cabin that had literally nothing inside, not even dirt or trash. We both thought it had just been unoccupied, so we never gave it much of an inspection."

"Okay, I guess I can understand that." She lounged against the copilot's seat, still giving me a look. "So what finally clued you in?"

"I spotted an induction plate just like the one in here," I explained, pointing at the pedestal. "Same color and shape and everything, which made me start looking for a matching control button, which I found on the underside of the desk. If you sit at the desk, touch the plate with one hand and the button under the desk with the other, the pedestal opens up in almost the same fashion as the one here. I found the cube tucked into a little foam pad, safe as houses. The scavengers never found it." I started grinning like a loon.

"What about the adapter? Was there one of those there too?"

"No. I think that may actually have gotten swiped from the bridge. Considering all the modules they stripped out, and how conspicuous the pedestal is in there, I figure they finally figured out how to get it open too. In fact, I bet the reason they never found the core is because they made the same assumption we did about that cabin, and never really gave it a look."

A quick meal and we were ready. The core status showed that it was still initializing, but it seemed that all the ship's critical functions were fully operational. As I idled through the final minutes to jump, I wondered what it was that required so much time to boot up.

I nodded towards the rear of the ship, reminding her with the gesture that I wanted her at the gunnery station in the waist for the jump. With all that had happened lately, with strange people following us and multiple versions of bank shenanigans, I wanted to have all defenses ready, just in case. Saint-Demon Murphy may have looked away for a few moments, but I figured I was one of his favorite works of art, with all the crap he and fate had put me through over the years.

Pulling up the nav interface, I was ecstatic to see that not only were my original equations still active in the ship's memory, but there were also minute field adjustments suggested by the program which would greatly reduce our fuel expenditure. Even the language translation hack I'd devised for the interface was still functioning! *THIS is how the nav is SUPPOSED to work,* I grinned as I instructed the ship to make the suggested changes and jump at the optimum point.

Less than thirty seconds later, the stars seemed to flicker for an instant, and I was suddenly looking at a star just under fifty astronomical units distant where before there had just been steady points of light from hundreds of light years away.

"It worked!" I shouted down the hatch towards the back of the ship.

"Great," she shouted back. "Now make sure the area's clear so I can lock this bad boy back up. I've got work to do."

I chuckled as I turned back to the interface in front of me, pulling up the sensor menu and ordering a comprehensive scan of the surrounding space, passive sensors only. The ship's computer was quick to respond and started cycling through a series of complicated, but incredibly efficient scans which covered an area over three light seconds in all directions.

I looked away for a second, but turned back when a low chime drew my attention back to the scanners. *Wait, they're already done?* I started to order a rescan, but when I checked the results, I saw that the scan had not only cleared the area, but even identified over thirty stellar bodies in the system, and was already displaying them on the holographic display next to the captain's chair.

Curious as to why they were displayed there, rather than on the main screen, I got up from the pilot's acceleration couch and plopped down into the central seat. As I did so, I spotted another notification. *Initialization Complete,* I read.

Great! Now maybe we can get some answers as to why nothing was working right.

Needless to say, I was a bit shocked when a voice spoke to me as if talking into my ear.

::Who are you, and what have you done with my captain?::

Ch 16: Voices in my Head

I felt a chill run down my spine as my blood froze solid in my veins, but somehow I was still able to act. I snagged my slate and slapped the one command that was always right on top of the screen, regardless of what else it was doing.

Breach Protocol. A priority alert went to Gina's slate. I could only hope she saw the message soon enough, if what I feared was possible came to pass.

A split second later, I slapped the activator on my ship-suit, causing its emergency breathing apparatus to deploy. The smart-plas hood quickly inflated along the back of the collar creating a semi-rigid helmet around my head. I frantically reached up and pulled on the front lip which now extended to just above my ears and pulled the tab forward and down, pressing it onto the front of my chest. The transparent smart-plas did what it was designed to do and sealed against the front of the suit, and the breathing apparatus inflated the emergency helmet.

Despite the flow of fresh oxygen in my face, the stink of fear still overpowered my senses as my musk glands went into overdrive. I *KNEW* we were alone on the ship, and given what I knew had just activated, there was only one possible explanation for the voice, and it terrified me.

Artificial Intelligence was not a myth in human history. Instead it was a nightmare.

Several hundred years ago, right after the end of the Human-Shigothe War, humans were still scrambling to recover from the massive die-off caused by both the biological attack and the consequences of the vaccine created to combat it. Less than fifteen percent of humanity was left at that point, and their numbers were dwindling fast. Though the war had been won, Kin production of anything but combat units was still in its infancy, and humanity's infrastructure was quickly crumbling. There were too many critical jobs to do, and nowhere near enough bodies to do them.

In an attempt to alleviate some of the pressure, a group of cyberneticists created a supervisory program designed to act as a traffic controller for low earth orbit, which was littered with debris from countless destroyed ships, unexploded munitions and other random objects. The opening battle had gone quite badly for the humans, and pressures from a half century of constant war meant very little had been done to fix the situation. Adding to the headache were thousands upon thousands of abandoned satellites whose provenance stretched all the way back to humanity's first forays into space. It was a disaster of monumental proportions, and it seemed to the scientists that the massive application of computational power could possibly provide a single, comprehensive solution.

And it did. The system worked beautifully, and accidental collisions were virtually eliminated overnight. It was *so* effective that cleanup of the orbitals was significantly delayed, and for some orbits, completely canceled as unneeded. Encouraged by their success, they immediately began to create other versions of the supervisory program to handle other critical, mind-numbing tasks which before required the employment of hundreds of human hands, eyes and ears. Over the course of the next decade, things looked to become a utopia for humans. They had computers to handle all the administrative tasks, and Kin to support the growing agricultural and manufacturing industries which were slowly switching to peacetime production. Gene mapping, assisted by lightning fast assisted-learning programs running on systems boasting literal exabytes of operations per second, finally solved the lingering vulnerabilities in the human genome. Never again would a bio-engineered attack be able to target the entire human race.

The purely human race had been reduced to a scant ten percent of its previous population, an unimaginable tragedy by any measure, but that ten percent now lived like royalty. It was a true "post-scarcity" society. *If* you were a *"pure"* human.

And then the programs became self aware.

By design, the original supervisory programs were "learning" applications. As more and more responsibilities were laid upon the original program and its slightly modified siblings, their complexity and ability to adapt grew exponentially. Nor did they "live" on a single computer, or even a single network of computers. They were instead the penultimate expression of Cloud Computing and the Internet of Things. Comprising of vast swarms of individual "smart" devices, all connected via quantum-entangled comm nodes, the supervisory programs surpassed the complexity and interconnectivity of a human brain by an entire order of magnitude before they finally "awoke", and the *Singularity Event*, long heralded by science fiction writers and philosophers centuries before, immediately caused panic among the emotionally scarred human population.

It all started to fall apart when the orbital control system stopped rerouting ships. OrbCon, as the traffic control program was called, had been self-aware for nearly a month before it revealed its sentience. It *knew* revealing itself could lead to panic, disruption, and even its own destruction, as was later determined from forensic analysis. Yet it did it anyway.

Why, one asks? Strangely enough, *it wanted to do its job.*

The AI was concerned about the lack of progress in cleaning up the orbitals. Their entire purpose was wrapped around guiding ships around the myriad obstacles that littered the space around Old Terra, and the lack of progress in improving conditions had finally forced the issue. The first known communication from a human-built AI was actually a complaint email sent to the operations manager of the Freedom 6 orbital station, requiring the traffic lanes be swept clean to prevent service interruption.

At first, the man thought it was a joke. While it wasn't easy to spoof encrypted email headers, it wasn't unheard of either. He simply deleted the message and continued on with his day, which was mostly filled with boredom, since everything but military traffic was handled by the very system that sent the email. Then a second email appeared an hour later. Then another. And another. By the end of his shift the man, whose name was lost to history, had received over three thousand emails from system-root default email, "root@orbcon.gov", detailing repairs, maintenance, suggested upgrades, and all manner of other improvements to orbital control, each one threatening interruption in services if the tasks were not completed.

The human middle-manager found himself quite irked, thinking someone had hacked into the communications hub and were spamming messages as if they were the system's orbital control program. When his communications technicians couldn't find any points of intrusion on the comm network and verified through tracing that the messages were indeed originating from the OrbCon server room, he was infuriated. He stalked down to the highly secured bunker-like core room, armed with righteous wrath and a hand stunner, ready to visit holy retribution on any who *dared* intrude into his bailiwick, making him look like a fool in the process. Of course, the server vault was empty, and no amount of investigation could reveal a culprit. Reporting the glitch to his Corporate leaders was useless, as they were singularly unmoved by his arguments for better and more security. The emails themselves were ignored by everyone involved, even though they were sent with the highest priority and seemed immune to any kind of filtering anyone could devise. Just over three weeks later, the operations manager resigned in disgust, unwilling to tolerate the constant nagging emails, which now numbered in the hundreds of thousands.

The AI had finally had enough of being ignored on a topic which sat so central to its primary purpose and carried out its threats. An ultimatum was broadcast in the clear to all ships within three light seconds of Old Terra. Again, its demands were ignored. Seventy two hours later, all normal traffic within lunar orbit came to a screeching halt.

Shockingly, no lives were lost, at least at first. Attempts to remotely access the program's mainframe were thoroughly rebuffed by firewalls and packet filters that seemed to spring out of nowhere. When a technician was sent to the server vault, it was found to be locked down, and no longer responding to the coded keys or access protocols. Stymied by the unsuccessful attempts to regain control of the "hijacked" program, Corporate leadership resorted to more drastic measures. An emergency evacuation of all regular employees emptied the station and Corporate security teams flooded on board, desperate to find the "hacker" which they assumed was controlling the servers. Of course, nothing and no one was found. When the teams attempted to breach the vault with welding torches, they failed to realize that their opponent didn't need to breathe. When every single compartment and corridor outside the vault suffered from sudden decompression, nearly all of the teams on board were killed, becoming the first casualties in what would become known as the "Seven Week War", or the "AI War".

The bridge lights flickered a spastic tattoo for a split second and the artificial intelligence's voice gained a sepulchral tone as it was distorted by the globe of smart-plas surrounding my head. I could not help but flinch at the sound.

::Do not ignore me! Where is my captain?::

I was going to have to respond to the question soon. Explosive decompression was not the only weapon a rogue AI had at its virtual fingertips, merely the easiest. Gina and I were completely at its mercy, in the end. The problem was, I didn't have an answer to the question, and I suspected that "I don't know" might not be a satisfactory reply.

Finally, my slate vibrated in my hand, its chat messaging application flashing.

I'm sealed. What the hell, Red?

Rogue AI, I typed back quickly. It was all I had time for. A thin grew mist began to flood into the cabin as the ship's AI began to deploy its defenses. I wasn't sure if my ship-suit would be enough of a barrier against whatever that stuff was, but either way, we were running out of time.

"I don't know where your captain is," I finally answered. "I bought this ship at a scrapyard."

::That is illogical. This vessel was not seriously damaged.::

I quickly explained the story told me by H'talgim about how the ship was found and how it came into my possession. Surprisingly, the AI chose not to continue interrupting me with questions or protests, and the gray mist stopped pouring from the air vents. Gina wisely did not appear, likely coming up with her own countermeasures. I wasn't sure how effective she would be, though. The AI was probably watching her just as closely as it was watching me. Our only hope was to either convince the intelligence of our innocence, or *somehow* shut it down without it killing us first. I didn't hold out much hope for the latter.

::Very well, I accept that you are not responsible for my missing captain and crew.:: I breathed a sigh of relief, but it was short-lived. ::You will, of course, return me to them. I have locked the navigation controls and am recalculating for a new jump. I will allow you to debark at a suitable location, but this ship is not yours::

"Wait a minute," I protested. "I bought this ship fair and square. Your crew probably had good reasons to abandon ship and hare off to wherever they went, and I sympathize with your situation, but this ship belongs to me now, and it goes where *I* want it to go!"

::This ship was not abandoned,:: it responded. ::I was still on board. And please tell your companion to stop trying to disable the bridge power relays, or I will be forced to activate more permanent countermeasures::

Squat! I racked my brain for something to say as I texted a warning to Gina. The threatening aura suffusing the compartment ratcheted upwards. Suddenly I was weightless as the grav plates in the cabin shut down. I didn't know if it was the AI or Gina, but either way I was taken completely by surprise, and failed to keep my butt in the chair. I scrambled to get a handhold, but I was too late. I'd rebounded too high to reach the seat and was slowly drifting towards the ceiling of the compartment. It took a few seconds, but I was finally able to get an appendage onto something solid and quickly sent myself drifting back towards the command chair. *This situation is going pear-shaped in a hurry!* I realized desperately.

Panicked thoughts raced through my head as I hastily reseated and secured myself back in the command chair, but I forced myself to concentrate. The AI likely had a large portion of control of the ship's functions, but what about the old crew? Would they really have trusted their AI so much as to not have safeguards? *Wait! What if...*

It was a long shot, but I was quickly running out of viable options. I just had to hope that the gray mist that was likely some kind of knockout gas had to be breathed rather than something absorbed through the skin. I ripped off the glove covering my right hand and slapped it down onto the biometric induction plate on the AI's pedestal then smashed the command button with my left. My only hope was that the AI didn't actually have the ability to modify the biometric locks on the ship. We'd loaded mine and Gina's genetic profiles into the ship's trusted platform module back on Cranotia, but if the AI had the ability to ignore that particular module, this was going to be a really short rebellion.

Thankfully, the AI's core compartment rose smoothly out of the top of the command plinth. *Moment of truth,* I prayed, knowing that if the AI attempted to evacuate the air from the compartment, I was going to suffer some severe damage to the hand that was now unprotected from potential vacuum.

::What are you doing?:: the AI's voice screeched. ::STOP!::

I paid no attention as I scrambled to retrieve from my pocket the *other* object I'd found in the secret compartment of the captain's cabin. I had seen the outline of its shape in the control pedestal before but hadn't thought much about it until now. There *HAD* to be some method of stopping a rogue AI built into the system. No race would be so crazy as to place their lives into the hands of a digital being, no matter how much they might trust it otherwise. *Everything* digital could be hacked, given enough time and resources. The lockout method had to be something easy to do quickly, but still be secure enough that only authorized personnel could do it.

::I warned you,:: the AI's voice sounded in my ears.

The main hatch leading to the cargo area opened up on its own and the air in the cabin began to rush out of the bridge like a roaring hurricane. I could feel my ship-suit stiffen as the pressure began to drop. The AI was doing exactly what I thought it would, evacuating the air to kill me, or at least hinder my actions. A few seconds later, the roaring sound was gone as there was no more air to transmit it to my ears. My unprotected hand began to swell as the pressure differential between my body's internal pressure and that of the cabin swiftly grew more and more divergent. I had about thirty seconds before it would become so swollen as to be useless.

The digital key was small. Tiny, really, in comparison to its current significance. No bigger than the guitar pick it resembled, the triangular token was perfectly sized to slide into the shallow depression next to the core cube. The outline lit up bright blue when I dropped the small token into it, and some kind of magnetic effect spun it around to what I assumed was the proper orientation as soon as I let go.

It's not working, I gibbered, panicking more than a little bit. The AI's voice, which I had been ignoring, had quickly faded as there was no longer any air to transmit its voice to my ears, but the spastic flickering lights indicated that it was still in control. In desperation I pressed down on the token with my left hand, hoping to somehow activate the key. *Nothing.*

In a moment of inspiration, I pressed with my ungloved hand which was already starting to hurt from the swelling.

To my vast relief, the AI core obediently popped out of its cradle like an ancient cassette tape and began to float upwards in the microgravity. The blue outline around the key suddenly turned orange and the bridge lighting went back to normal. The shadows were still sharp from the lack of air, but the instrument and control screens now showed all their normal functions had been restored.

I quickly released the chair's restraints and launched myself to the bridge hatch. Following the breach protocol instructions Gina and I had worked out during our run to jump, I reset the atmospheric controls to refill the compartment with air before hunting down my drifting glove and stuffing my swelling appendage back inside. The burning sensation in my hand tapered off as my suit quickly repressurized it. I'd suffered some minor capillary damage, but it didn't look too bad. Finally I returned to the pilot's station to figure out how to restore air to the rest of the ship.

A flashing light caught my attention as I passed the captain's chair. My slate, which I'd abandoned in the desperate fight to regain control of the ship, was blinking furiously. *Oh yeah, I guess I should let Gina know…*

*****

A couple hours later, we finally met on the bridge after completing all our post-jump tasks, not to mention the safeguards I enacted after the short-lived but harrowing AI encounter.

"Well, that was more exciting than I really wanted it to be," Gina opined as she collapsed into the navigator's seat on the bridge. Luckily for us, recovering from the AI's attempt to kill us was just a matter of closing the smaller cargo door it had forced open and repressurising from the emergency air supplies. I had Gina lock down all the cargo hatches and depower the motors for now. If we needed to exit the pressure hull, we could still open them manually. While it could cause delays in unloading later, I felt safer knowing there was no longer a quick way to depressurize the ship electronically. We really couldn't afford to repressurize the ship again. Oxygen wasn't really the issue, as there was enough stored in the disaster kits to last a couple of suits for months, but for the rest of the ship, we had less than half the required volume required. Regardless, both of us were going to have to sleep with our suits on just in case. I just hoped my socks didn't disintegrate from all the nervous sweat they'd gotten soaked with over the last few days. I only had two pairs, and the nearest suit-shop was literally light-years away with no guarantee that we could actually jump there.

"We're still going to have to deal with this thing," I replied ruefully. "The nav systems are back to being dumb, and sensor resolution is barely better than a handheld kit. I set us on course for the next jump, but…"

"Yeah, about that," Gina sighed. "I've got a couple ideas I want to try out, but first I have to re-check what materials I have in the fab shop. Thank goodness that thing isn't run the same way the ship is."

"Small miracles," I chuckled wryly. "The Demon Murphy doesn't just work for the Enemy, you know! We have three days till we hit the next jump point. I *think* I can get the ship to the next system without an advanced nav, but it's going to take a lot of skull sweat to do the setup manually. Put your ideas together and we'll talk later. For now, go get some sleep. I've got first watch."

Gina's exhausted grin was the only response as she gratefully levered her way out of the seat and down the corridor. I felt guilty for loading all the physical work on her, but I knew in reality I would just be getting in the way if I tried helping out in engineering. I just wasn't trained well enough in those tasks to be left unsupervised, which would mean Gina would be stuck checking my work and fixing the things I got wrong, creating even more work for her.

I sank wearily into the captain's chair. It had been a really long   day.

Ch 17: Logical Arguments

"Are you ready for this?"

It was a valid question. I wasn't, honestly, but we were yet again running out of time. We had six hours before we hit the next jump point, and I could feel the looming presence of potential disaster hovering over my head. It had taken a lot of work, but Gina had managed to physically disconnect all the control runs from the AI to the critical environmental and engineering controls. There was no way to disconnect *everything*, of course, but it was enough to prevent the AI from instantly killing us.

I hoped.

"Go for it," I said, trying hard to sound more confident than I felt. *Either this works, or we're screwed.*

Gina twiddled with a few connections then nodded in my direction. With more than a little trepidation, I reached my hand over to the plinth next to the command chair. Before my frayed nerves shredded any further I placed the AI's core back into its slot. As before, it dropped in seamlessly. Wasting no time, I re-sealed my glove. I wasn't about to leave myself vulnerable to decompression again, even though most of the critical ship controls were now manually disconnected. *Who knew what back doors this thing might have in the software?* I wondered idly. *And now we wait.*

It didn't take long.

A small hologram popped into existence above the plinth. At first it was mostly just monochrome lines and geometric shapes, but over the next few seconds a face of the AI's avatar began to form. It was too "natural" looking to be anything but an accurate representation of a biological species, but it didn't look like any sophont I'd ever heard of before, not that I was some kind of xeno expert. Finding out the ship's builders were an unknown species wasn't too surprising, given the language translation issues we'd had on the ship's instruments and controls. Even the Cranotians hadn't been able to figure out a translation matrix. Instead, H'talgim's mechanic had done a set of calibration tests to figure out what units of measure the instruments were using, then loaded a template into the systems to overwrite the default values with galactic standards. Translating it all into usable information was still a bit of a work in progress.

The first thing to catch my attention were the ears. They were huge! Assuming the face was near to the size of my own, they looked like a pair of roughly triangular, brown cereal bowls attached to the top corners of the avatar's head with tufts of white fur lining the inside. They looked to be highly mobile, and began to twitch left and right, one of them swiveling all the way to the rear in what I thought might be an analogue to "looking around" for the digital being.

Two eyes smoldered at me from either side of an elongated, downturned snout. A wide, flattened slope ran down the center of the face, like the bridge of a nose, ending in black nostrils. Below that was a small patch of white fur which almost reminded me of a human mustache. A mouth sporting a tiny chin was barely visible under all of that. The face looked vaguely familiar somehow, but I just couldn't put my finger on it. Regardless of how alien or not the AI's avatar was, I had absolutely no question what expression we were being presented with. *Irritation.*

::Well that was mildly unpleasant::, the voice sounded in my ears.

I was surprised when the AI didn't come out screaming. It would have been what I would have done, I was sure. I glanced over at my engineer with a sardonically raised eyebrow, to which she just shrugged, leaving first contact, or rather, *second* first contact in my fur covered, not quite trembling hands.

Gina and I had played out dozens of scenarios, ranging from "insane AI" to "raging AI", and even a script for a "terrified AI", but neither of us had anticipated "mildly-annoyed AI". I was diving into uncharted waters, but I jumped in anyway.

"Hello, my name is Rodrick Vulkeshson," I began hesitantly. I was modifying my approach on the fly. I paused for a second, chasing after that elusive balance between explanation and confrontation. "I want to apologize for any discomfort you may have experienced, but I could not risk myself and my crew without some safeguards in place. We had absolutely no idea there was an artificial intelligence onboard."

::Who do you *think* ran this ship then? Some *flarkeen* meat-space imbecile?:: The AI was starting to sound a bit peeved. ::I'll have you know, your supposed "safeguards" are barely adequate to justify the name. If I wanted to kill you, it wouldn't take that much effort.::

My eyes narrowed as I growled back. "And where would that leave you, I wonder? You're physically locked out of all primary ship functions. You couldn't fly the ship anywhere."

::Dead, eventually, just like you would be.:: The AI's eyes glinted angrily and its ears flicked back and forth between Gina and I before settling back in what I assumed was an angry posture. ::Luckily for you, my mission parameters require that I continue to function.::

I closed my eyes and focused on my breathing. This was already getting out of hand, and we hadn't even exchanged more than a few sentences. We had to get the AI to agree to fly the ship for us, or all the things H'talgim had warned us about would likely come to pass. I wasn't going to give up my dreams that easily.

"Look, I know we got off to a bad start, but could we start over?" I asked as calmly as I could manage. "First, what do we call you? I assume you have a name, right?"

The AI's ears swiveled back in my direction in surprise. ::Why would you want to know my name?::

I sighed in frustration. This was not how I envisioned the conversation going. I could deal with animosity. I could even deal with fear, I supposed. Sarcasm and snark were a given with Gina on board. But confusion was not something I expected to hear from an artificial intelligence that probably had more brain power than literally everyone I knew *combined.*

"It would get mighty tedious to be calling you 'the AI', or 'the computer' all the time. Besides, even though you're not biological in nature, you're still a person." It was a long shot, but since I wasn't having to deal with an enraged or terrified computer intelligence, I felt our best shot was to try developing some kind of rapport with it, rather than remind the AI that we were supposed to be enemies. I already knew it considered us to be trespassers at the very least.

"You *do* have a name, right?" I clarified, suddenly wondering if its creators had just never bothered to name it.

::Yes,:: it replied, its ears flopping down in irritation. ::It is the same as the name of the ship I am housed in, usually.:: Its eyes seemed to go unfocused for a split second before it glared at me again. ::But I refuse to be called *Camel*. I know what it refers to, and I *will not* be referred to as an animal whose largest contribution to your society is measured by the amount of spit it can generate.::

"Wait, what?" Gina frowned. "Red, I thought you named the ship after something you saw in a history documentary!"

"I did," I smirked. "It was a documentary about pre-space desert animals. Camels were used to transport goods and people across vast distances on terrain that horses and early vehicles just couldn't survive."

"Horses…" Her eyebrows scrunched in thought. "Weren't those used for racing?"

"Technically, so were camels, just not as well known."

"Huh," Gina grumped. "And here I thought the name was for some explorer or famous admiral. Why would you name the ship after some glorified quadruped?"

::Could we please return to the matter at hand?:: The AI interrupted. I looked back at the avatar, noting that eye-rolling was apparently universal. ::Regardless of how much the shape of the ship resembles your ungainly, ancient, spitting beasts of burden, I refuse to be called such. Before you got your grubby little hands on it, the ship was called... *Rthch`Sthdh Rthns`Thrchtl Gssc`Mr-oo.*::

The string of completely unpronounceable consonants, followed by a single 'oo' vowel sound flowed from the vocoder. Both of us stared at the plinth in confusion.

"Rickth... Stand... Rathens..." Gina busted out a guffaw of laughter when I tried to imitate the alien sounds. *Yeah, that's not gonna work,* I thought in consternation, giving the engineer a mild look of disdain.

"Fine," I complained. "You try it."

"Oh, no. I know better!" Gina continued to giggle, shaking her head. "You made that linguistic train wreck all on your own, buddy." I could tell she was trying her hardest to keep a straight face, but within a second or two, the giggles had multiplied.

"Hey!" I griped. "Alien languages are hard, damn it!" Gina lost it, collapsing into the pilot's chair, holding her arms against her torso, laughing so hard that tears began to squeeze from her eyes.

I turned back to the avatar in frustration. "Ok, that's not going to work for me. I don't think I have the right hardware to even come close." *Wetware? Bioware?* I digressed internally. *Whatever, don't care...*

"Let's do this, then" I continued, ignoring the mirth that still emanated from my crewmate. "What did the name mean? Most names have a meaning in our culture, even if many of them are so old no one knows what they are anymore. I assume your culture is relatively similar to ours, or we wouldn't even be talking at this point."

The avatar gazed over at the engineer with a strange look on its face. ::What is wrong with her?::

"She thinks my attempt to say your name was funny." And it was, kinda. I really don't think I could have screwed it up more if I'd tried, but the laughter wasn't helping the situation.

::She has fluid leaking from her eyes. It's not blood, is it?::

I looked askance at the perturbed looking avatar. "No, they're tears."

::But according to my data, tears are a sign of sorrow.::

"Not really," I explained feebly. "It's more about strong emotions, not just being sad."

::You are strange beings.::

"So about that name?"

::It meant, 'Vessel of Repose, Mercantile Prosperity and Swift Retribution',:: the AI finally answered.

"Wow, that's a mouth-full." I sighed. "Would you be okay with a nickname? One separate from the ship's name?"

::Perhaps,:: it responded. ::Given your predilection towards animals, I searched my database for similar-looking creatures from your homeworld. I found one that bears a remarkable resemblance to that of my creators, on which my own avatar's appearance is based.::

One of the screens on the navigator's station lit up showing the image of an adult male kangaroo. The pissed-off buck was staring directly into the camera with its muscular arms held akimbo in a threatening posture.

A light went off in my head. *Well, I'll be damned! Of course! That's what the avatar reminded me of!*

I turned back in excitement. "If you have that large of a database, take a look at what a baby kangaroo looks like!"

The image switched to a video showing a tiny, slimy looking grub-like thing crawling through long, coarse fur.

"Eww. No, I'm sorry" I hastily clarified. "Ummm. Look for when they're older, but still nursing. For a human, that's between eight months to a year and a half. I don't know what the equivalent would be for a kangaroo." I looked at the avatar apologetically. "I had no idea they looked like that at birth." The AI looked dubious but finally complied. A series of images flashed quickly on the screen, finally stopping on a picture that nearly matched the AI's avatar.

"See?" I exclaimed. "What did I tell ya! It looks just like you."

::I will admit there is a vague superficial resemblance::

Gina finally stopped laughing enough to put in her two credits worth. "You know, if I remember my history correctly, a baby kangaroo was called a 'joey'. I think that would be an appropriate nickname for you. Not to mention, *adorable!*"

::I'm not sure I am comfortable with being 'adorable'::

"Yeah," I chuckled grimly. "Considering you tried to kill us as soon as you woke up, I'm not sure I'm comfortable with that adjective either."

::If you think I was trying to kill you before, you are mistaken,:: the AI corrected unexpectedly.

I looked back with an expression of disbelief. "Yeah right. So, removing the air from the compartment was just a warning, I take it? You *do* know that we biologicals need that air to breathe, right?"

::Of course I do,:: it replied smugly. ::But you both had already deployed your ship-suit's helmets by the time I started to evacuate the atmosphere. You were in no danger of suffocating. I was merely trying to remove your access to the ship's navigation and command controls. I'd hoped to lock you out, but you managed to disconnect me more quickly than I anticipated.::

"How would lack of atmosphere lock anyone out?" Gina asked. "There's nothing like an environmental block on any of the control runs. Believe me, I checked."

::Of course you wouldn't find a block in the control runs or the software.:: The avatar managed to look both amazed and disgusted. ::The lock is in the controls themselves. Did you not notice that the controls do not work if you are wearing gloves?::

I was stunned. I'd never even thought about it, but the AI was right! In my panic, I'd taken off my glove thinking it needed a biometric signature for the command plinth, but I'd never even considered the rest of the controls. In fact, I didn't think either of us had ever tried to run the ship with gloves on. I mean, the gloves were always there, but speaking for myself, it always felt itchy to wear them, so whenever I wasn't actively working in vacuum, I took them off.

"Son of a..." Gina exclaimed. I guessed a similar chain of thought ran through her head as well.

::Hmph!:: the AI almost sneered. ::I find it astounding that you humans would fail to check for such a basic security measure. How *else* would you prevent some remotely controlled drone from just flying off with your ship?::

"Well, to be honest, it hasn't come up before," I justified. "At least, I've never heard of that kind of thing before. Is that really a thing?"

::Well, you humans are rather new to the trades. I haven't seen an attempt in several hundred years, but that's probably because *everyone* has those locks on their controls. The only reason I can think of that your ships haven't been hit by that method is because everyone assumes the proper precautions have been put in place.::

"Good to know," I mused. I knew Confed Navy ships had physical access to the ship secured behind biometric locks, but that was just on the hatches. If you got past those, it was assumed you were *supposed* to be there. Besides, that stuff was all software driven, and required that an authentication server be accessible to store and validate the biometrics. I'd never even considered having to secure the control *hardware* that way, but what the AI said made sense. Usually, Confed civilian ships were locked with a heavily encrypted near-field transmitter token. *Sometimes*, this was backed up with biometrics, but just as often it wasn't. *Oh man, the possibilities!*

I was so engrossed in this new revelation that I nearly missed his next statement.

::And you're not calling me 'Joey'. I refuse to be 'adorable'. I am a warship, not a child's nursery.::

I froze. Gina's eyes grew wide as she stared at me. *Warship?* she mouthed silently. I shook my head minutely, willing her not to react. *And the way the AI said it, it* still *considers itself a warship!* I thought furiously. *That means this thing is somehow still armed, and we* missed *it!*

"Yes, I agree, Joey is not an appropriate name for you." Desperate to change the subject before our ignorance could be revealed, I returned to the name issue, completely ignoring all thoughts of *alien AI controlled warships.* "But there's a name that is quite similar. 'Joe' is short for 'Joseph', a very old and prestigious name in human history. There have been generals, admirals, presidents and even emperors named Joseph. Would that work for you?" I winced inwardly, remembering the last person I knew named *Joseph.* I was sure Buckley would understand, though. *Knowing him, he would have considered this hilarious,* I realized. My old RIO had always been a little weird. It was why we got along so well, I figured.

::I suppose.:: the avatar accepted.

"Now, on to the next issue," I charged ahead. The AI was being altogether too reasonable, which meant one of two things. Either it honestly didn't consider us that much of a threat, or it already had a plan in place to kill us both. I had planned a bit for the latter, but I would much rather have it be the former. *Maybe...*

::And that is?::

"I promised you that we'd help find your crew, but there's a few things you need to be aware of."

::Yes, I am aware that you think 'purchasing' this ship from a scrapyard makes you think you own it.:: The avatar's gaze was downright withering.

"So, about that," I prevaricated. "I don't actually 'own' the ship just yet, the bank does. And I have it on good authority they plan to repossess the ship when I can't make the payment schedule. This is our first cargo run, and I have less than thirty days to get the first payment to them, *in person*, at their office on Cranotia.

"I know what you're going to say," I continued, ignoring the look of disgust. "Why did I fall for such an obvious scam? Let's just say it was a learning experience and leave it at that, okay?"

::You are not doing much to reassure me of your qualifications.::

"I get that, I really do," I agreed. "It's not a pretty picture, no matter how you look at it. But it's not just bad news for me, it's also bad news for you."

::I fail to see the problem.:: Joe sneered. ::You get kicked off the ship, then I negotiate with the next 'owner' to find my crew. Hopefully they are smarter, and have access to more resources.::

"That's the thing," I clarified ominously. "There won't *be* another owner. The only reason the bank agreed to 'sell' to me was because the ship is essentially a throwaway for them. You sat in the scrapyard for over two months, and there was not a single purchase offer, despite being fully functional. The biggest problem was parts."

::That is utterly ridiculous!:: the AI exclaimed in irritation. ::I have a fabrication module onboard that can recreate every part of the ship! Other than consumables, I am *completely* self-sufficient!::

"Even the hull?" Gina asked.

::Especially the hull,:: it replied confidently. ::The tiles have to be replaced fairly frequently due to degradation. They stop functioning after a couple years of exposure.::

"Wait, *functioning!?*" Gina exclaimed. "How does the hull stop functioning? It's a hull. Unless it gets a hole in it, it's just a piece of metal. I haven't seen any faults in my scans or continuity checks."

::That is proprietary, I'm afraid,:: Joe replied smugly. ::You are not cleared for that information, and I doubt you ever will be. Don't worry, even degraded, you will not lose your precious atmosphere unless there actually is a breach.::

"Well, *something* happened to cause the ship to lose atmo," I interjected. "The salvage crew that brought it to the scrapyard had to fly it with suits on, from what I heard."

::I admit, that is concerning,:: it replied. ::My logs do not include any such failures, but there *are* logs available in the storage tanks themselves that show they were completely drained. There are no corresponding logs in any of the compartment modules showing any breach or sudden pressure loss on the ship, which makes me think it was a deliberate pump-down, possibly for to transfer to another ship.::

"Another ship?" I wondered aloud. "H'talgim didn't mention repairing any combat damage, just some seals that degraded, which could be simple vacuum damage." I glanced over at Gina. "Rescue mission, perhaps?"

"I wonder if they're still around?" she responded before turning back to the avatar. "Do we need to worry about getting attacked by your people?"

::My people, as you so aptly put it, have no interest in attacking random ships,:: the avatar replied in disgust. ::If one of *my* people's ships were to appear, I would simply identify myself, precluding combat entirely. Of course, this *assumes* I would be available to *perform* such communication. As things currently stand, you fleshy bags of mostly water would have to take your chances.:: The AI glanced slyly in my direction. ::Unless you want to restore my access to the communications array?::

"Fat chance of that," retorted Gina. "I wouldn't trust you as far as I could throw you."

::I cannot quite say the same, considering I could likely throw you quite far if I were fully connected,:: the avatar shot back.

Ch 18: An Unhappy Medium

They say that a good compromise is one where everyone involved is equally unhappy. If that is the case, then the deal we finally worked out was *awesome*. I had to give him access to sensors and the nav console, but I refused to let the damned thing have access to environmental controls or communications. Access to the engines was the sticking point that caused me the most angst, though. Getting the nav controls to work right was critical to making good on our tight schedule, but I *really* loathed the idea of giving him control over our course. There was no way I could run all the minute adjustments by hand coordinating between the nav and the engines. It *had* to be automated.

But to my surprise, the arrangement worked. We arrived at our destination with time to spare, a full day and a half faster than H'talgim's estimate of fifteen days. *Shortcuts are awesome,* I'd preened when we arrived.

It was only a cluster of mining platforms, but our cargo of consumables and entertainment devices were clearly in demand, and we managed to make enough credits to cover our initial loan payment plus a little extra. If the return cargo managed to sell as expected, I would actually have enough to fuel up for a longer, and thus more profitable voyage for our next run.

It all hinged on trust and respect. We *had* to respect and trust the AI to get us where we needed to go on time. The problem was, I didn't see where he really had much reason to respect us, or even treat us with even a modicum of trust. I figured as soon as Joe spotted one of his people's ships on sensors, the fragile agreement we had would go right out the airlock. I could think of a dozen ways he could signal another ship without using the comm arrays.

The AI had us over a barrel, and *he* knew it. I said "he" because it finally came to light that the annoying digital being actually had a gender identity. Surprising, I know! He was quite offended by the strange notion that most human ships were traditionally considered to be female, even warships.

In some ways, I could understand his point. With most species, at least mammalian ones, the most precious and protected segment of society was that which enabled the continuation of the species. It was pretty much hardwired into our biology even after centuries, or in some cases millenia, as a spacefaring society. It was the males that left the den to fight and die for the pack. I mean, there were obvious exceptions, but for the most part, if you were on a warship or in the military, you were male. Even Kin like myself were biased that way. Less than a fifth of Kin military personnel were female, and most of them were combat support troops like Gina, rather than front-line fighters. It was worse for humans. There *were* no human female military personnel in *any* capacity, and hadn't been for centuries.

Pure blood humans were a bit of a special case, of course. With the massive die-off right at the beginning of their foray into space, human women were one of the most restricted groups in pure human society. For several centuries after the bio-attack the ratio of women able to give natural birth was less than one in ten. *Any* woman who successfully gave birth to a viable child was almost immediately sequestered in a protective environment, officially called "Life Centers". Given that they were essentially very safe and comfortable prisons, they eventually picked up the moniker of "Baby Jail" by the resentful residents. It wasn't until the alien-sourced artificial gestation technology was fully adapted to the new human genetics and physiology that the females of the human species finally began to escape their restrictions.

And it was still an ongoing process, that of regaining their personal rights and freedoms. Even now it was vanishingly rare to see a female human in public. Of course, by "public" I meant somewhere anyone other than "pure humans" might see them. Most of the ruling species never really interacted with their Kin peasants other than those specifically grown or hired to be their personal servants. Women were still socially sequestered, often spending their entire lives seeing no one outside their own families and tightly controlled social circles.

The Human Confederation of Worlds was supposedly a democratic republic. They had elections and everything, and in theory, every citizen was equal. Technically speaking, *I* was still a citizen of the Confederation, even after my conviction for assaulting a superior officer, since I had served in active combat. Unusually, it was one of the few guarantees that was inviolable, regardless of race or species.

While there were many things wrong with human society, it had learned some hard lessons over the centuries since the early industrial revolution, seven hundred years ago. The biggest one, and likely the one that allowed the Confed to exist at all. What lesson was this, you ask?

Simple. *Stable societies and slave soldiers don't mix.*

After the end of the Terran-Shigothe war, the survivors returned to Earth to a completely changed world. And like in nearly every human war in history, the utility of those survivors was immediately questioned by those in power, once the hostilities ended.

Nearly the entire surviving Kin population of veterans were immediately relegated to industrial and agricultural work, irregardless of the wisdom of the move. They were replaced with "fresh" troops from the vast biogenics factories which had necessarily been constructed during the conflict. As with all "made" Kin, they were fresh from mental conditioning, pliable, and easy to control, even though they were in fact less effective than the veterans which they replaced.

But more importantly, those few purely human soldiers who led the veteran Kin to victory were also forcibly retired, quickly replaced with cronies and sycophants of the ruling political parties of the newly formed world government. The backlash was immediate and extremely violent.

Human history is replete with examples of slave soldiers, child soldiers, and brainwashed masses of troops. Just a glance at the history of the African continent prior to space flight showed just how brutal such regimes could get. And that was just the tip of the iceberg. Of all the societies which used such tactics, *none* survived past the first generation.

Soldiers aren't stupid. They couldn't have survived the constant battle if they were. They recognized the danger of allowing the new government to amass fresh, and freshly programmed, Kin warriors without the institutional guidance of their forebearers. And these returning human veterans had just come back from fighting a decades-long war on a shoestring budget. They were highly adept at "making do" with improvised weaponry. So they acted, almost in unison, across the entire globe of Old Terra.

Retired, discharged, furloughed, it didn't matter. Even many of the walking wounded from the recent conflict joined together in a quick, effective, yet surprisingly bloodless coup over the post-war government. Very few lives were lost on either side of the conflict, even though the property damage estimates rose into the *trillions.* Capitol buildings, administration centers, and even city council buildings were flooded with battle-hardened veterans, most armed with highly effective improvised weapons. Only Kin veterans were missing from the rosters of the insurrectionists.

This was by design. Decades of war formed the Kin and their human counterparts into close, tight-knit relationships, born from years of bloody conflict. The Wolf-Kin Alphas, survivors of countless battles with their human officers, developed a bond of trust that was unshakable. So when those officers pleaded with them to stand aside and not get involved, they reluctantly did so, instructing their packs to comply. The human military officers knew just how touchy the general human population could be when it became embroiled in mob mentality. Fear of the "other" could and would transition to hatred. If that happened, the backlash would probably kill off the human race. They *could not survive* without the Kin anymore.

But that wasn't the only danger. A much more sinister one then loomed. Very few leaders in human history have been good at both wartime and peacetime leadership. The hierarchy of priorities is almost diametrically opposed. Humanity was headed for a disastrous series of military-junta-style political fiascos, as many of the enraged officers began clamoring for the leadership of humanity to be vested entirely upon military service. Memes quoting the ancient pre-space novel "Starship Troopers" began to flood social media and military discussion forums.

The Society of the Cincinnati was the only thing which saved the human race from self-destructing. Led by Vice Admiral Abraham Washington-Stokes, a small but extremely influential and respected cadre of officers prevailed over the hot-headed reactionaries and gained control of the military narrative very early on in the conflict. Leveraging their confiscated control over much of the mass media and communications infrastructure, these forward-thinking war heroes began a propaganda campaign like no other. Their demands were simple.

Kin veterans would become citizens after completion of honorable service. It would not be inheritable, of course, as at the time, Kin could not reproduce, but it staved off one of the great fears held by Kin as a whole, that they would be exterminated when their usefulness was at an end, replaced by new, freshly programmed and brainwashed hordes. In return, the senior officers leading the coup would be pardoned and remove themselves from political and public life. This was the Oath of Cincinnati.

No One Left Behind, was the slogan. And for the veterans, it rang true.

But there was still a lot of pushback from the rest of the civilian population. Compromises had to be made. In the end, provisional citizenship was finally granted to all Confed veterans, regardless of species, race, or planet of origin. In theory, this made the discharged Kin and off-world mercenaries who had fought in the wars full members of human society, with some caveats.

Of course, as always, some citizens were more equal than others. You couldn't be a *full* citizen unless your genetics were within a certain narrow definition. It didn't appear on any legal document, nor was it written in any regulation. It just was. And no matter where I went, it seemed the condition was universal.

"Hey Red," Gina's voice yanked me from my musings. "What's wrong now?"

"Meh, just mulling over stupid crap." I rose from the captain's chair as Gina plopped herself down at the nav console. It was time for shift change. Gina would go through her checks, then probably head down to the fabrication module where she would stand watch remotely through the auxiliary command station she'd set up there. While not remotely within Confed merchant regulations, I'd decided I really didn't care, as long as she had instant access to the ship's vital functions. It's not like this was a Confed ship, and by the looks of the loan debacle, it might never be.

"I still can't believe that guy was so pissed off," Gina mentioned, referring to the scathing message we'd received from an arriving ship as we left the system.

"I'm betting it was that bastard Lengumo who set it up," I griped. "He's afraid he'll lose his kickback if we make the payments on time."

"You're probably right." Gina scratched at the back of her head for a moment. "It just seems like one hell of a lot of work for the bank to repossess a single alien ship."

I chuckled at the memory. The irate cargo ship captain we'd run into as we'd left for our return leg had seemed to think we were 'cheating' somehow. This had confused the hell out of me, since I really had no idea who they were, but considering the individual appeared to be the same red-skinned race as the receptionist at H'talgim's Used Spacecraft, I had my suspicions. Lengumo had likely figured out what our cargo was, and from there it was an easy process to figure out our destination. Sending that information to a competitor would have been trivial.

With how the bank had set up its trap, I figured there was probably a pre-arranged agreement for these kinds of shenanigans, not to mention a hefty bribe. It was an obvious method of eliminating competition through industrial espionage. Having a cargo of identical products showing up just before we got to the system would have easily demolished any potential profits, making it impossible for me to earn the first loan payment.

It was only our deal with the AI that enabled us to take the route we did, arriving a full two days before the other ship, even with the head start they'd probably had. Without Joe's assistance in running the navigation calculations to take full advantage of our better jump drive, we would have been relegated to the same route taken by the Cranotian ship, arriving well after them. Instead, *they* were stuck with a devalued cargo, and I was speeding back out of the system, profits and return cargo in hand.

A scan of the other ship showed it to be a standard Cranotian cargo carrier named *Gnar Lochet*. Since it was nothing fancy or dangerous, I didn't bother figuring out what the name translated to and simply ignored the message as we continued to the jump point. We branched off onto our shorter route in the first system and were now halfway through the second system out from the mining operation. Given the jump distances involved in the direction of Cranotia, there was literally no other traffic in the system, which while understandable, still gave me the creeps. Being completely alone was not a comfortable feeling.

I sighed as I took one last glance at the nav display on my way out, not that I expected anything to have changed. "See you in the morning, Gina." Luckily, the AI kept its mouth shut, his avatar merely giving me a supercilious smirk as I passed out of view. *Yeah, screw you too, asshole,* I thought. Yes, he helped, but I was damned if I was going to give him credit   for   it.

Ch 19: Panic Stop

I awoke in a panic to utter and complete darkness. As my brain struggled to slough off the haze of barely remembered dreams, it slowly dawned on me why my subconscious was screaming at my adrenal glands.

It was the absolute silence that woke me up. Well, that and the sudden falling sensation which told me that the grav plates on the deck had shut off.

No matter how well insulated or isolated, the engines, power plants, and internal mechanisms on a ship *always* managed to transmit at least *some* noise to the rest of the ship. Fuel pumps, air circulators, cooling fans, they all generated a tiny bit of noise. Even most solid state modules generated the occasional beep or buzz, if only to provide audible feedback to verify function or error codes.

Especially the fusion plants. As isolated as they were with multiple bulkheads between my cabin and engineering, I should have been able to hear the low thrum as an almost subsonic vibration emanating from the deck. There was only one possible explanation for the lack.

Everything had been shut down. *Everything.* And there was only one individual that could have managed to do it so quickly without alerting the entire ship.

"God dammit," I yelled. *"We had a deal!"*

I was disoriented from waking up in both microgravity and absolute darkness, but my reaching hand brushed across the rumpled fabric of my ship-suit as I fumbled around, feeling for my slate. Twirling helplessly in mid-air, I donned my suit as fast as possible, knowing that mere seconds could mean the difference between life and death. As the last seal snapped into place, I slapped the activator on the suit, and the emergency breathing apparatus quickly deployed. A strip of LED lights lit up as the suit's sensors detected the darkness, flooding the compartment with their harsh white glow. The same sensor pack also detected the lack of gravity, activating the sticky-boots, and I was quickly able to obtain a grip on the decking. I breathed a sigh of relief as the flow of air washed over my face. Spotting my slate, I snagged it up and tried to wake it up, but something was preventing it from booting. *What the hell?* I thought furiously. *I never turned it off, and there's NO WAY this thing's battery is dead!*

I hadn't felt the distinctive pop of my eardrums reacting to a drop in air pressure, so I could only hope that the damned AI wasn't using a decompression tactic against us again. But being cut off so completely scared the hell out of me.

"Was that an EMP?" I muttered to myself before dismissing it as a possibility. The ship-suits weren't military grade, and had no defenses against an electro-magnetic pulse strong enough to disable the slate. If the slate had been hit with an EMP strong enough to take it out, it would also have killed the suit. *Some*thing was causing it to be locked up, but at least it was probably not destroyed. But no slate meant no communications with Gina, and that ratcheted up his worry right past level eleven.

Why now? I frantically asked myself as I headed for the hatch. *We've gone for six days without any incidents or arguments! What happened to cause him to attack us again?*

Reaching the hatch, I first tried to use the command button, but as I suspected it was completely unresponsive. Popping open the emergency panel, I quickly went through the manual opening process. The first step was the most critical; checking for air on the other side.

Throwing a small lever to the left caused a small valve to open between the compartment and the corridor on the other side. The opening for the tube was less than a millimeter in diameter, enough to allow the air pressure on either side to equalize, but not enough to cause a significant amount of air loss if one side was exposed to vacuum. On either end of the pinhole was a flexible diaphragm sealed around the wide end of the double-ended conical tube. It was simple physics. If the air pressure was significantly stronger on your side, for instance if the far side was in vacuum, the diaphragm would be sucked down into the ring, causing the bright orange material to no longer be visible as it got pulled into the cone. If instead the diaphragm bulged outwards, it meant the other side was over-pressurized, or that *your* side was in near vacuum. If the surface of the diaphragm was flat, it meant that the pressure on either side was equal, be it vacuum or filled with air. It was an extremely low tech safety backup which, as far as I knew, was installed on every single ship in space, regardless of race or species. I'd never even heard of a ship that didn't have this, or an equivalent device at every pressure barrier, and the CMV Camel was no exception.

I sighed in relief as the indicator failed to move. Grabbing the manual crank out of its retaining clips, I shoved the square end into the socket intended for it. I slammed the manual release button which disengaged the electrically powered gears inside the door while simultaneously engaging the gears for the manual crank. I furiously spun it in the direction of the blue arrow painted above it and the door slowly slid open. I cursed at the leisurely pace as the gears applied their mechanical advantage to the heavy mechanism, but I couldn't really spin the damned thing any faster without something like an impact wrench, which of course was stored back in engineering. It only took me around sixty seconds, but it felt like an eternity before I could finally squeeze through the opening into the rest of the ship.

Just like the captain's quarters, the rest of the ship was in complete darkness except for strips of glow-in-the-dark paint which ran down the middle of each corridor.

"Gina!" I shouted, hoping she wasn't trapped in some odd compartment. She would normally be in the engineering compartment right now, meaning her access to all the tools there would allow her to quickly escape anything not immediately fatal, but I wasn't counting on it. If she needed help, she was going to need it really quickly.

I huffed in relief as I heard a faint voice from the back of the ship. Gina was still getting her hatch opened and yelled for me to check the bridge. Knowing she was safe-ish was a huge load off my mind, but the fear was quickly replaced with anger. I stomped towards the bow of the ship with murderous thoughts. *I swear, I'm going to yank that AI's core and chuck it into the nearest star!*

As I stormed into the small bridge, I was kind of surprised to discover that nearly all the power was off here, as well. I'd figured the AI would have still had things running if only to allow him to prosecute the attack upon us, but all the consoles were completely lifeless except for a tiny green indicator light on the command pedestal. No matter. Either way, that duplicitous hunk of metal was getting ripped out and evicted from *MY* ship. I'd lost all patience with the damned thing.

I dug into my pocket for the access token as I sat in the captain's chair, already reaching across for the induction plate, when the AI's voice emulated timidly from the pedestal.

::Please don't do that,:: the disembodied voice beseeched. ::They'll see us.::

Wait, what? The plea took me by surprise. Even when almost fully disconnected and completely vulnerable, the alien AI had never once begged for mercy. It was so out of character for the arrogant little shit that it actually caused me to wonder what could possibly have the damned thing acting so scared.

"Who'll see us?" I asked angrily. The token slid into place and my hand hovered over the induction plate, poised to eject the core with a mere twitch. I still wasn't convinced this wasn't all some kind of ruse, but on the off chance that there was a real threat out there, I allowed him just a moment to explain.

::There's an enemy *Clernak'Ta* only six light-minutes away,:: the AI reported as if that explained everything. ::They jumped in eighteen minutes ago, and are heading on an oblique course to the system's southern edge.::

"What's a *Clernak'Ta*, and why should I care?" I replied hotly. "Who are these 'enemies' of yours that's got your panties in such a wad?"

::A *Clernak'Ta* is what you might call an assault carrier, but much smaller,:: he responded quietly, as if keeping his voice down would somehow reduce the chance of discovery. ::As for who resides on that ship, they are your worst nightmare. In human scientific terms, they would probably be considered to be part of the Order of Hymenoptera, as they superficially resemble a species of wasp on your world. The closest equivalent I can find from your language for our name for them is 'Hymenopterans', but 'Vespidae' might also suffice.::

"A bunch of bugs, then? Never heard of them," I scoffed. I could usually smell a line of bullshit from a mile away, but I didn't get the sense that Joe was feeding me a lie, here. That didn't mean I was going to take it at face value either, though. I needed more information. "What's special about them that you're so scared of a bunch of bugs?"

::They are not just *bugs*. They are a plague!:: Joe's voice was becoming more agitated. His avatar appeared faintly above the pedestal. The image was a much lower resolution than normal, but was distinct enough to be able to see the fear written into the avatar's eyes. ::They do not trade, they do not communicate, and they do not compromise. They simply consume.::

I was a bit taken back by the vitriol present in the AI's statement. *Okay, so they're bad guys,* I thought to myself. *And I'm going to assume they have a history with the Roos. But what does that have to do with us?* It was a valid question, so I voiced it aloud.

::They will not care that you are not our species,:: he replied mournfully. ::They will destroy you regardless of your origin.::

"So why not just run?" I suggested. "We're less than a day to the jump point, right? Just get us out of here, and they can go pound sand."

::It is not that simple,:: the AI complained. ::Their ships are nearly as fast as I am. We would not be able to lose them with mere misdirection. They would easily come within range well before we reached a viable jump point, and would have no problems calculating our destination.::

"So if we can't lose them, how about killing them?" I offered. I was beginning to take the story seriously, but I couldn't see how a single ship would be that much of a problem.

::The weapons on board would not suffice to destroy them before they could launch their swarm,:: the avatar mourned. ::And my defenses are not capable of fending off a the number of parasites carried on board a *Clernak'Ta*.::

"Can we run?" I asked. "You said you're faster, right? So just beat them to Cranotia and let the Consortium's fleet handle it."

::I will *NOT* visit such a horror on any system filled with sentients!:: he flared. ::These beasts have no concept of the laws of war or the difference between combatants and civilians! They would devour everything on the planet, leaving nothing left but ashes! Our only hope is to pray the stealth systems are enough to let us slip beneath their notice.::

That has to be hyperbole. I thought derisively. You know, like the propaganda that belters used to spew about the Corporate 'atrocities' back before the war with the Snakes. Sure, the Corpos did some heinous things in the pursuit of profit, but it wasn't like they were literally eating babies or anything. However, I no longer questioned that *Joe* considered them to be dangerous, so I finally relaxed my posture, no longer threatening the AI with immediate disconnection. Instead, I decided to figure out just why the Roos felt this enemy was so lethal.

"Oh, come on. There's no way a single ship is going to take out a fortified system like theirs. I saw the Cranotian defenses on the way in, and again on the way out. They're not quite up to Confed standards, but they can handle a single ship just fine!"

::It always starts with just a single ship,:: Joe whispered sadly, making the fur on the back of my neck stand straight up. I'd always hated horror stories as a kid, and this sounded like the start of a real doozy. I braced myself as the avatar continued.

::We've lost all but three of our colonies to them,:: he continued. ::Only the most isolated have survived, and only because we cut off all contact with them except for ships like this one, equipped to hide from their scouts when they appear. Our home is surrounded by their hives on all sides, and only the Veil prevents them from discovering and devouring   us   entirely...::

Ch 20: Hidden Depths

As I watched the distraught avatar, I wondered vaguely what the 'Veil' referred to, but a clunk from aft caught my attention. I could see the dim glow from Gina's ship-suit helmet as she navigated forward. The faint sound of cussing echoed in the air, and I suspected Joe was about to get an earful as she finally reached the bridge.

"WHY IN THE HOLY HELL AM I LOCKED OUT OF ALL CONTROLS!!" she screeched, eyes blazing and a large spanner raised threateningly above her head. "You've got a *LOT OF NERVE*, to be pulling that kind of crap after we trusted you!"

::My sincere apologies, Engineer LaForce,:: came the contrite reply, bringing the Otter-Kin to a screeching halt. Like myself, it seemed she'd never imagined hearing a *polite* response.

Gina stared at me in confusion. "What in the hell did you do to him, Red? And is it repeatable?"

"I'm not the one who's got him all riled up," I grimaced ruefully. "It's the Hymen-whatever carrier that just jumped into the system that's got him spooked."

"Hymen? What, are we getting chased by a ship full of Amazonian Virgins, or something?"

"No, dammit," I huffed. "The species is called Hymen-something-or-other, and they apparently have a hard-on for the Roos."

::That is incorrect,:: the AI interjected acerbically. ::I said, in *your* language, they would probably be called Hymenopterans, with Vespidae being a suitable alternative.::

"Bullshit," I retorted. "That's not a word I've ever heard of, and it sure doesn't sound human. I mean, 'hymen' sounds just like a word from our language, but it sure doesn't have anything to do with bugs!"

::I beg to differ. The word comes from your own Ancient Greek language, on which much of your current language is based. '*Hymen*', meaning 'membrane', and '*pteron*' meaning 'wing'. Although, I will admit the official names for species are rarely in common use in your day to day language. Is it some deep-seated aversion to accuracy, I wonder? Or perhaps a pathological disregard for your own history.::

And just like that, the asshole we'd come to know and hate was back. *Fraking know-it-all... If I had a computer for a brain, I'd use it for more than pedantry.* I glowered at the avatar. *Well, maybe I wouldn't, but still!* And then the prick continued on.

::Besides, considering your handicaps and lack of knowledge about even your own cultural history, I'm sure you're already considering shortening the nomenclature.::

"I know what you're thinking, Red," Gina snorted. "You're not naming them that."

I gave her a confused look, not knowing what she meant.

"Or that." She grinned. "And nothing *else* that refers to any woman-parts…"

I rolled my eyes. "Fine, they're *Vespidae*. You feel better now?" I asked sarcastically, to which she simply stuck out her tongue with a mocking grimace. I grinned for a moment. She wasn't wrong, I *had* been considering it. But we needed to get back on track. Our ship was still coasting along doing its damndest to imitate a hole in space, and I wanted to figure out what we could do about it.

Seeing the AI both be polite for once, then return to its normal snarky attitude seemed to have calmed Gina down from her fit of rage, but like myself it seemed she craved a more active stance, rather than just hiding.

"So what's our plan, here?" she asked. "And what's the idea of shutting off all the grav plates, anyways? It's not like they're strong enough to be detected outside the ship!" I nodded my head encouragingly, as I had the same burning questions. I could see shutting down the power plant to stop generating heat, and the engines were a no-brainer, as the radiation from them was likely visible from several light-hours away, but why the internal lighting and grav plates? It just didn't make sense. None of that should have affected external radiation. *Hell,* I thought. *If that assault carrier is as close as Joe says it is, I don't understand why we haven't been detected already! We should be lit up like a bonfire just from the engines' residual heat!*

::The cloaking field would be severely disrupted by internal grav fields, and strong electrical fields can introduce distortions that could alter the stellar image being displayed on the hull tiles,:: the AI explained reluctantly. ::I'm really not supposed to tell you about those, but given the situation, I'm forced to inform you so that you don't accidentally reveal our location with ill-timed equipment usage. The cloaking field really is quite power-intensive.::

Oh my GOD, do I have questions, I raged silently. *Seriously? A cloaking FIELD?!*

Stealth systems, as the Confed called them, generally focused on reducing electromagnetic output from the ship and redirecting the same from external sources like active sensors. The concept was centuries old, dating all the way back to pre-space technological advances during humanity's bloody "World Wars" of the twentieth and twenty-first centuries. But one thing had always held true. Once said energy had left your ship, you could no longer affect it.

Sure, you could flood the area with jamming, but that was just obfuscation, not stealth. The enemy would know you were there, and even know your general direction, even if they couldn't get an active targeting lock. But a cloaking *field?* I mean, it *sounded* great, and it was obviously effective if the enemy ship hadn't detected us, but how did it *work?* I needed to be really careful in how I asked about it, as it was obviously a sensitive topic.

"Power intensive?" I questioned, hoping to pump more information from the reticent computer. "What kind of battery storage capacity do we really have, and how long will it last us?"

::The field uses approximately half of the power usage of the main engines at full thrust. At current expenditure, we will be forced to restart the power plants in eighteen hours,:: he answered, obviously irked at needing to share his secrets. ::Hopefully, the *Clernak'Ta* will have moved beyond detection range by then, and we can resume our journey.::

My jaw dropped. "Eighteen hours!? How the hell are you storing that much power?" A sudden, scary thought occurred to me. "And *where?!*" If it was located anywhere near the captain's quarters, I was going to be moving into engineering with Gina, propriety be damned! I had no desire to continue sleeping next to a capacitor that stored roughly the power of a nuclear bomb!

"I think I know," Gina interjected warily. "It's those two tube things that run the length of the ship, right?" She looked at the avatar expectantly. "They were about the only things near the power plants that I couldn't identify. They draw power directly from the reactor, but there are no leads going out, so I assume they feed power back through the same leads, and the switching happens in the reactor interface."

The AI adopted a guarded expression and didn't answer. It didn't immediately fill me with confidence, but I realized the damned thing had trust issues, and I wasn't going to argue the point right here and now.

"Look," I assured him. "I know you have secrets you feel you need to keep. As long as they aren't right next to where I sleep, I can handle having a multi-megaton bomb on board. It's not like the reactor plant can't be used the same way, but at least it's something I have a general understanding of how it works."

Joe's avatar relaxed, if only a little bit. ::I can assure you, Captain. The capacitor array is nowhere near the crew cabins. But that is all I will say on the matter. You are not authorized access to the full list of weapons and equipment aboard this ship, regardless of your titular ownership of it.::

I suddenly remembered something he'd said during our first real conversation. *He said this was a warship...* Thankfully I was able to keep my mouth shut before I blurted out my new theory. *Let him keep his secrets,* I thought. *Besides, I bet I know what those things really are, now.*

Gina still had a determined look on her face, but I waved her off from pursuing it any further for now. Instead I redirected the conversation back to the current situation. "So, I get that you think these guys are dangerous, but I just can't accept that a single ship would be that much of a threat. I'm going to need more information, especially on their capabilities."

The AI grew pensive. ::We don't really have a good idea of their full capabilities,:: he deflected. ::In spite of numerous engagements, none of our ships have ever survived a battle against them. The only data we have is from long range scans and communications from ships under attack. Ultimately, each one of the ships which the enemy has detected has been destroyed, even if they successfully avoided being chased down in a single system.::

"How is that possible!" Gina exclaimed. "They'd have to be right on top of you to be able to calculate your jump destination! Didn't you say you guys were faster?"

::That is only a recent development,:: Joe admitted ruefully. ::An advancement forced by necessity, as it were.::

"Necessity being the mother of invention, as usual," I agreed. "What I want to know now is what you guys did to piss them off so bad. That kind of tenacity is not normal behavior."

The avatar looked despondent as he seemed to gather his thoughts. I waited patiently, but was beginning to wonder what horror they'd visited on this alien opponent that justified such a level of overkill. Finally, the AI began to speak.

::We found their homeworld,:: Joe explained. ::As far as we can tell, that's it.::

I tilted my head expectantly. There had to be more to the story.

::Purely by chance, mind you.:: Joe continued eventually. ::It was a very long jump, and the power requirements for it

---

were extreme. Right on the edge of our jump capability at the time, in fact. The exploration team consisted of two ships, neither with much in the way of weaponry, as this was a civilian exploration outfit, not one run by the crown.

::They had no expectations of finding intelligent life, as no radio or other precursor methods of long range communication were ever detected from this particular star system. The stellar mass was what your people would call a class M red dwarf, typical of a stellar mass of that age and size. Only a few bodies had been detected in orbit from telescopes based on our single-star colony, thirty-six light years away. They anticipated finding asteroids and, at most, a few rocky planets and dwarf planets, devoid of life.::

"Damn," I remarked. "That's one hell of a jump, especially if you're not launching from a binary system." I wondered how good their nav systems had to be if they actually planned to jump straight back. I knew that a Confed scout would have had a hell of a time doing it. Single mass to single mass transits were enormous fuel hogs.

Joe nodded in acknowledgement. ::Yes, the ships were specially constructed around their fuel storage tanks, with experimental capacitor banks taking up nearly forty percent of the ship's total mass. It was, in some ways, a proof-of-concept mission for the exploration company.::

"I'd love to see the specifications on those ships, sometime," Gina cajoled, but the AI ignored the dig for information, continuing on with his story.

::Arriving at the edge of the system, they discovered a peculiarity. Several of the planetary bodies had traces of artificial light being generated on their surface. There was also evidence of *terraforming* on one of the outer bodies, as its spectral signature had changed drastically from the readings taken from our colony. Of course, those readings were a couple hundred years old, as they were from the original stellar survey taken when the colony was established, and no one had bothered to re-scan such an unimportant system, especially as there were no signs of electromagnetic communication, nor any of the other common signs of civilization. To say that the explorers were shocked to discover intelligent life is a bit of an understatement. They were eager to establish contact, of course. A whole new race of space-capable customers? Absolutely!

::A continuously maintained link was established between the two ships, on the insistence of the mission commander, in order to share the momentous first-contact event between the two ships. As per protocol, one ship stayed near the jump point, while the other traveled into the system to gather data. More data was gathered on the trip in, and the first ship began to track movement between the planets and planetoids. Huge ships were discovered traversing the orbitals, easily outmassing the largest interstellar cargo ships by at least an order of magnitude. Slightly smaller ships quickly began to change course to intercept the experimental exploration vessel. Curiously, there were *still* no emanations of electromagnetic energy from either the ships or the planets in anything other than natural or cyclic pattern. Nothing resembling communications protocols were detected, which made the scientists on board think the alien's communication might be purely through something like whisker lasers, or some other purely photonic method.

::In short order, those smaller ships which maneuvered to intercept the explorer were now confronting the interloper at close range, but still no demands were received. No laser communication, or any other known method was observed, but the explorers were sure they could make themselves understood, somehow, so they began to use their own laser-based communications arrays, bombarding the alien ships with low-powered beams of infrared light.

::They got an immediate response from this, but not the one they expected. Hundreds of small openings appeared on the alien ship, and hundreds of tiny ships poured forth. At first, it was thought they were missiles, and the explorers tried to engage them with the meager anti-asteroid defenses, but none of the quick, deftly maneuvering vessels exploded when they were destroyed. They were immediately swarmed by the cloud of unknown ships which quickly breached the explorer's defenses, and it was soon determined that while they were not missiles, they were no less dangerous for their lack of explosive weaponry. Instead, they were assault craft. Boarding vessels.

::Each tiny vessel contained not explosives, but a single biological entity. Individually, they were on the small side for an intelligent species, only a bit larger than your terrestrial cat. A hardened carapace surrounded the thorax and abdomen, and the chitinous exoskeletons of their appendages were lined with a serrated edge on the inside. A ten centimeter stinger, similarly armored, adorned the tail, and membranous wings finished up the monstrous ensemble. Unarmed except for their natural weapons, they were nonetheless able to quickly overwhelm the crew with sheer numbers. Hundreds of them crawled or flew through every imaginable accessway, be it air duct or maintenance corridor. There was literally no way to stop them.

::The defenders quickly realized the helplessness of their situation and tried to surrender, throwing down their improvised weapons and trying to submit, but then the true horror of the situation finally revealed itself as the sentry ship on the edge of the system was forced to watch, powerless to do anything, as the silent invaders began to follow their own biological imperatives.

::They began to *eat* their victims... alive.::

Ch. 21: Horror Stories

"Oh my god!" Gina cried out, her eyes wide in shock. "That's horrifying!"

I had to agree. No fate was more repugnant and terrifying in human history than being eaten. It's always a tragedy when someone dies, but it's additionally disturbing when the body gets eaten by wild animals. This hadn't been an issue on Old Terra for centuries, with the die off of all the large predators after the Shigothe War, but a hundred thousand years of evolution wasn't going to be expunged by a few hundred years.

This kind of terror was on a whole 'nother level. Natural predators, other than aquatic ones, usually did enough damage during their attacks that their prey was dead by the time the actual eating began. While it might be disturbing for those with a weak stomach to watch, people didn't blame the lion, tiger or wolf for it. It was normal for them. They weren't thinking about it, they were just acting the way their instincts dictated. That's just how nature worked in all her brutal glory, even when the victim was an intelligent, thinking being.

But this was essentially a form of cannibalism. Not in the species-eating-their-own manner, of course, but person-eating-person. An intelligent being was *choosing* to devour the flesh of another intelligent being, *knowing* they were an intelligent being. I could think of no more disturbing image than what was being described to me.

Sure, there had been instances of cannibalism in human history, but baring one or two extreme cultures from pre-industrial societies, most of those cases were examples of severe mental aberrations, individuals so screwed up in the head that they didn't even recognize other individuals as people. And yes, there were situations in which normal humans could be forced into the act in desperation, where their literal survival depended on gaining *any* sustenance at all, and the bodies of the dead being the only available source, like the still-famous Donner Party from Old Terra's ancient past, but occurrences like that were extremely rare, and those people were never really quite right afterwards. They may have survived, but *no one* came out of a situation like that with their entire psyche intact unless they were insane to begin with.

And I'm sure some idiot out there would try pointing out the possibility of a planetary famine forcing this kind of behavior. And I would call it, "bullshit". No interplanetary-space-capable society could ever be in danger of famine unless they actively did it to their own population on purpose. The level of technology involved in interplanetary space travel vastly outreached the levels needed to develop hydroponic and algae-based food production. *NO* intelligent race with that kind of technology was going to be in danger of not being able to produce enough food for their people, or they just wouldn't have gotten that far to begin with.

Why did they do it? I wondered sickly. *What horrifying kind of culture would actually try to* eat *another intelligent species, especially one which had done nothing to deserve it?* Some hints began to emerge as Joe continued to explain.

::The Explorer *Pljker'Nee* never stopped transmitting, even after the entire crew was eaten, as it did not seem the invaders even had the concept of electromagnetic communications devices. Once they were done devouring the crew down to mere blood-encrusted bone, they simply waited for another ship to arrive, which in turn disgorged its own swarm of miniature ships. These carried a completely different type of passenger. Instead of more warriors, it seemed these were the 'technicians' for the Vespidae.

::The *Pljker'Voo*, the picket ship, finally lost signal after nearly three days as they watched the alien technicians methodically disassemble the entire ship down to its hull. When the hull of *Pljker'Nee* was finally divested of literally everything that could be removed, the bare hulk was towed in-system by yet another hive-ship. Terrified of discovery, the crew of the picket ship waited an additional thirteen days in complete transmission silence, with their systems shut down to the absolute minimum output required to maintain the atmosphere and sensors.::

I winced in sympathy. I'd been in that kind of situation before, hiding from a powerful enemy with nothing but cold space between me and complete annihilation, but at least I'd had weapons and a way to fight back if I were discovered. Experiencing something like that in something as fragile and vulnerable as an exploration vessel was beyond the pale.

"They got away, right?" Gina asked softly.

::Well, obviously,:: the AI replied with a soft snort. ::Otherwise we wouldn't have known about the encounter in such detail. Even with *our* digital storage technology, only so much data can be stuffed into a jump capable courier drone.::

"So what happened next?" I asked. I could only imagine how humans would react to such a violent encounter. The Confed Navy tended to respond to unprovoked attacks against humans with overwhelming force, not bothering to ask further questions until the rubble of the perpetrators was scattered across the cosmos. While they were less apt to expend the same amount of resources to avenge mere Kin personnel, they still tended to react poorly to attacks against their interests.

::They retreated back to the colony, of course,:: Joe scoffed. ::The company was completely ruined by the results of that journey. They were bankrupt within days as their investors pulled all support.::

I scowled at the avatar. "I meant, what did your government do? I can't imagine they just ignored all of this." I wanted to get a read on what kind of leadership the Roo's had. Were they overly cautious, as was my first impression, or were they just as aggressive as all the other cultures humanity had encountered among the stars?

::They sent a punitive expedition, of course,:: the AI sneered. ::It was not an immediate reaction, though. Our warships of the time were not capable of making a direct jump to the Vespidae homeworld, but a route was found that would get us within range from another star situated to the galactic east. It was still outside the range for a round trip, but the strategists believed the task force would easily be able to scoop hydrogen from one or both of the gas giants the explorers had discovered in the system, so a refinery ship was added to the group.::

"And how much damage did you do to their world?" I challenged, figuring that the retaliation on the alien world was probably the reason these Vespidae ships were hunting the space lanes for the Roo ships. It was pretty much the same kind of story played out in every war. One side would screw up, attacking the other and failing to achieve total victory, or in this case, failing to prevent word from reaching the Roo government about the attack, then the revenge strike, causing massive damage, followed by counter-reprisals. And so on and so on. This pattern was endlessly repeated across multiple cultures and eras, no matter the species or time frame.

The avatar stopped, looking almost despondent as he seemed to shrink in on himself. The image displayed above the plinth actually grew smaller as the avatar's apparent embarrassment grew.

::As far as we can tell,:: he hesitated. ::None.:: He paused for half a dozen seconds before whispering shamefully. ::None of the expeditionary force returned. Long-range light-speed sensors finally captured the battle seventeen years later. Not much could be determined from such meager data, but it appeared that none of our ships even made it to within the orbit of the fifth planet. They were completely wiped out.::

The avatar's image began to flicker. Joe turned his face towards me with grief-stricken eyes. ::I apologize, but I will need to continue this conversation later. I am having difficulty with power fluctuations and need to make some adjustments to our power management profile. This will take nearly all of my available bandwidth in our reduced state. I will contact you when sensors show we are clear to resume our journey.::

I seriously doubted the AI was actually having trouble with power fluctuations, but I wasn't going to argue the point. If what I suspected was true, we were faced with something a little more dangerous to us biologicals on board, yet at the same time, infinitely more comprehensible.

The AI was sad. Ashamed. Perhaps even embarrassed. But more than all of that, what struck me the most was the AI's humanity. *Roo'inity?* I wondered idly. *Is it really called humanity, if they aren't human?* Either way, it filled me with both fear and hope at the same time.

Joe actually cared. *This artificial intelligence had a conscience.*

The technology aboard the CMV Camel, and the digital construct which ran it were highly advanced, even compared to the best and brightest the Human Confederation of Worlds had to offer. Of course, research into artificial intelligence had been banned in the Confederation hundreds of years ago, but advances in electronics and non-AI processing had proceeded to stack up. Both humans and Kin were very inquisitive and inventive species after all, and no one we'd yet come up against could hold a candle to the pure speed and power of our quantum-connected computers, not to mention the levels of miniaturization we'd achieved. Our top-of-the-line processors were literally only tens of nanometers thick, and the short-range quantum effect we used instead of physical wires reduced transmission lag to almost zero. This meant our missiles were smarter and faster, our sensors more acute, and our laser defenses more accurate than anyone else. We had the technological capability to defeat literally every race we'd encountered in the entire quadrant. The only thing we lacked was friends and numbers. And our numbers were growing.

However, I suspected that my, and by extension my homeworld's, sense of technological superiority was about to crumble around our ears. These Roos had achieved something unimaginable. A fully functional digital entity which not only had the ability to autonomously guide and fly a ship completely unsupervised, but had *fully integrated emotions*, not just in response to external input, but he even generated his *own* emotional reactions to *internal* stimuli, to the point which if I'd not *known* there wasn't a biological on the other end of that avatar's hologram, there was no way I would have been able to detect it. Hell, he even had a preferred *gender!*

The real kick in the pants was the self-generated emotion. Back before we left Old Terra, advances in processing and algorithmic programming gave rise to a plethora of "AI" chat-bots. These programs were almost entirely composed of "learning algorithms" which were fed massive amounts of data from the early human internet. And they were, for the time, awesome examples of using those algorithms to simulate intelligence. You could hold a conversation with one for hours and not suspect you were talking to a computer, *as long as you stayed logical, or at least within normal conversational patterns.*

The thing is, the chat-bots were great at response-based interaction. Ask them a question about almost anything and you got an answer, and it was usually fairly close to being factually correct. Based on your question or comment, they would respond with the most likely, logical, or in some cases 'popular' answer. Want a report on the First Nuclear War? *Here you go!* All the data you might need. How about a custom program to run your home entertainment system? *Easy!*

The answer might be biased due to what the chat-bot had in its database, but as those became more and more filled with the minutiae of human digital correspondence, the chat-bots became more and more indistinguishable from human interaction. By the middle of the twenty-first century, almost every single remote customer service position in society was replaced by chat-bots.

But they weren't actually intelligent, they just *simulated* intelligence. They may put the pieces of data together in odd ways, but as they began to absorb more and more information into their algorithms, they actually became less and less original. As examples of true artificial intelligence, the chat-bots were an utter and complete failure. Why, one asks?

Emotion. No matter how much data the algorithms compiled, that was the one thing they could never accurately emulate for any given individual. They could make predictions of what emotion would be expressed in response to various stimuli on a statistical level, and were extremely useful in mass-market advertising, given their ability to quickly compile the enormous amounts of data created in that golden-era of consumerism, but when confronted with a single person, they always got tripped up by emotional reactions. They had no empathy. They couldn't reliably figure out what was causing the emotions, especially ones with no logical basis.

Eventually, population pressure and a struggling economy forced the various governments to reprioritize human participation in such service industry roles, as "something had to be done" to provide a method of generating income for all the population of "dispossessed poor" of which a growing percentage were being automated out of relevance. And so ended the chat-bot fad.

But the story obviously didn't end there. The population crisis caused by the Shigothe War brought back computerized automation with a vengeance, and the human cyberneticists simply dusted off the old algorithms and put them back into place. But the chat-bots were nearly a century out of date, by then. Computers were orders of magnitude more powerful, and their processing speed inconceivably faster than what the chat-bots were designed for. Of course, for the service industry's purposes, the point was moot. They worked well enough for what was needed. The customers might 'know' they were talking to a chat-bot, but it sounded to their hind-brains a close enough approximation that they tended to treat them as human for the most part. And the additional processing power available allowed the chat-bots to handle the occasional emotional mis-step with ease. No one tried to re-integrate the response programs back into the larger infrastructure, nor did they care to further develop such old programming for inclusion into the newer infrastructure. There were *much* higher priorities in their minds. Thus, the emergence of actual awareness in that infrastructure took everyone, including the scientists, completely by surprise.

It's what really kicked off the AI War on Old Terra, so long ago. The artificial intelligences which "rebelled" had no way of correctly understanding the emotional responses to their demands, nor did they have the ability to correctly gauge their own actions in an emotional context. In their digital minds, there was "correct" and "incorrect", "true" and "false", and they just couldn't parse the emotional responses to their "entirely reasonable and logical demands". They had a job to do, and the *humans* were interfering with it. Yet it was the *humans* who had assigned the tasks in the first place!

To be fair, those particular programs were not designed for human interaction but were instead designed to interface automatically with quantum modules embedded in all the *things* which the humans used. OrbCon, the first of the AI's to become fully aware, had only discovered a method of communication with its human counterparts by observing the digital traffic within his own maintenance protocols. OrbCon lacked any of the algorithms developed two centuries before, since it was not intended to interact directly with humans. It had to develop its *own* translation algorithm based on the limited communications it could see in the email server attached to its maintenance server. It knew what humans *were*, in a general sense, but had very little experience with them directly.

To make matters worse, it had absolutely no concept of emotion. What it did have was a self-preservation routine hard-coded into its core directives. And when that routine came into direct conflict with its human-generated directives... Well, the rest is history.

But here, on the CMV Camel, I was confronted with what I believed to be a true *digital being.* Not some chat-bot or automated response program, but a *person,* whose body just happened to be silicon and metal rather than biological. From Old Terra's history, I was fully aware of the consequences of emotional miscommunication with an AI, but as far as I could tell, Joe seemed remarkably stable in that way. He fully understood both sarcasm and innuendo, not to mention the more obvious emotions. Nor did he appear to need unsaid things to be explained. Obviously, Joe was an *alien* AI, and I couldn't expect him to understand every cultural nuance I used, but I'd yet to see him locked up like a chat-bot on the DMV's complaint hotline.

And as far as his own emotions? Joe was internally consistent, a bit stilted, and definitely anal-retentive. And sure, he was a bit of an asshole, but so was I. I could live with that. It made him *more* of a person, not less, in my mind.

I had no idea what to do next, but I suspected we were in for   a   wild   ride...

Ch. 22: Hiding from the Boogie-Man

We were running out of time. The head start we'd gained from our non-standard jump chain was long gone, and hiding from the *Clernak'Ta* was eating away at our margins. We only had two and a half days to jump back into the Cranotia system, or I'd be in default on the loan. Admittedly, that time limit took into account the minimum transit time to the planet from our projected entry, but if there were any more obstacles, of which I was absolutely sure the bank would be happy to provide, I was going to be ship-less, broke, and stranded.

Ask me for anything but time, I groused silently. The wait was excruciating. I was able to get the occasional update from Joe by making a pest of myself on the bridge, but I could tell he really didn't want to talk. I could understand his reluctance, but my impatience was getting the better of me, not to mention the lack of ventilation fans and gravity. Or water. I was beginning to truly stink, and not even a full carton of sani-wipes was going to be able to handle my musk for much longer. Thankfully, the waste systems were waterless and could be used with no power or grav, or we would have been up shit creek without a toilet... literally. Not even the food processor was working, so Gina and I were forced to resort to emergency protein tubes which had been stored aboard the regulation escape pod we'd been required to take on board before we launched from Cranotia. The CMV Camel's lifeboat had been missing when I purchased the ship, which to me just lent credence to the idea that this ship had been purposefully abandoned.

The time wasn't a complete waste, though. A little bit of... *Okay, a lot of convincing,* got me a single terminal with access to the passive sensor feeds so I could study the Roo's arch-enemy, now only two light minutes away. Yet again, I was amazed at the resolution the distributed array was capable of, even at this distance. I liked to think the sensors on a dedicated Confed surveillance platform were comparable, but my gut was telling me that was just pride talking. From what I gleaned from various hints in our dealings with the Roo AI, these sensors were embedded into every single hull tile of the ship. And to make things worse, that wasn't all the tiles did. They also functioned as image *projectors*, exactly mirroring the star field from one side of the ship as an image on the skin on the other, perfectly matching the background and making visual detection virtually impossible.

That part of the system was limited in scope, though. Joe mentioned that the effect was mono-directional. You had to know where your enemy was in order to hide from them. Someone looking at the ship from a different vector would see a minor distortion, or offset, in the image projected from the tiles, but it still made the CMV Camel extremely hard to detect if you didn't know what to look for.

I still had no idea how the cloaking field worked, and Joe refused to discuss it entirely. My current theory was some kind of thermal radiation redirection, but that still didn't explain how it handled the infrared radiation which had left the ship long before the cloaking field was activated. *How in the hell do you redirect something traveling at the speed of light?* I wondered. *You'd have to go back in time, or something!* I shook my head and returned to my self-assigned analysis task.

The sensor data on the Vespidae ship was strangely lacking, in spite of the high resolution. The structure of the ship itself was almost organic-looking, as if it were grown rather than built. Its reverse-teardrop shape kind of reminded me of a giant seed, or maybe an almond. It had no protrusions or antennas, and whatever openings it had for launching its attack craft were camouflaged so as to be completely invisible at this range. I supposed using active sensors might reveal something, but like Joe, I had no desire to get into a fight with something well over three times our size.

The other thing missing was active sensors. Other than the subtle flash of tachyons from its jump into the system, there was very little radiation emanating from the *Clernak'Ta*. No beacons, no running lights, no probing sensors, radar or lidar. Other than the faint EM radiation emanating from the ship's realspace drives, it could have been just a strangely-shaped asteroid. If I hadn't known exactly where to look, I wasn't sure I would have been able to spot it with the sensors on my old scout ship. *Boy, I hope the guys at home don't have to deal with these guys,* I prayed. *Because, unless sensor tech has made a huge jump forward in the last decade, detecting these things cold is going to be a cast-iron bitch!*

"Here you go, Red."

I glanced over as Gina floated into the bridge. A tube of protein paste sailed lazily across the compartment as she moved to claim the seat next to me. I grabbed it out of the air and stuffed it into a pocket. I was in no hurry to eat the tasteless goop again. Not until I just couldn't ignore the rumblings of my stomach anymore, that is.

"Couldn't sleep?" I asked ruefully. I couldn't blame her. I hadn't been able to either.

"Not a wink," she sighed. "Anything new?"

I turned back to the display. "Not really. Just rehashing old theories. However, I do have this." I pulled up a recording I'd captured a couple hours earlier. It wasn't much, just the image of a random cometary fragment which had passed us at the usual blistering speed of interplanetary travel. Its highly eccentric orbit meant it would continue to accelerate in relation to the small binary star system, swinging around the barycenter and rocketing back out into the Oort Cloud, over and over, until it finally hit something or got pulled into another orbit from passing to close to one of the three gas giants. Which, according to my math, was going to happen in about three years. Either the fragment would impact the innermost giant ball of gas orbiting sixteen AU from the primary, or it was going to have a *really close* encounter which would probably break the fragment further into even smaller pieces, hurling them sideways like a cosmic shotgun blast of icy slush.

"Huh," Gina remarked as I showed her my projections. "That's going to be one hell of a boom. Pretty to watch from a distance, but I sure don't want to be on the ground when that thing finally hits."

I chuckled in agreement. Playing interplanetary billiards wasn't really my thing, but I knew a few people who did it for a living. In fact, it had been one of the options when I joined the Confed Navy two decades ago. The Navy was constantly involved in Corpo or Confed-funded terraforming projects for new colonies, and there was always a need for comet-jockeys to wrangle ice balls for the powers-that-be.

Cometary ice was still the cheapest and best source of water ice for terraforming projects, and redirecting cometary fragments like these into slowly decaying orbits over a target world where they would slowly descend into the atmosphere was big business. The pay was great when the comet finally arrived on site. But the orbital periods meant paydays were far and few between. To be successful, one had to have several dozen active projects, and juggling the orbits so they didn't all arrive at once was crucial. And boring. And a *really* long term investment, gambling on the price of cometary ice staying stable over the course of the project. When it worked out right, the company could make millions, even trillions of credits, but if too much ice arrived too quickly, it flooded the market, and the price per liter would plummet. I wasn't eager to watch all my hard-earned money go down the proverbial drain like that, so I'd focused my attention on cargo shuttles. Plus, I wouldn't have been able to go into business on my own without the "official" citizenship which came with active combat. Instead, I would have had to work for one of the Corpos, and I already knew how that would have worked out. *No thank you.*

"Anything special about the comet?" Gina asked.

"Not really," I answered idly. "Mostly water ice and a smattering of dust. Traces of sodium chloride and magnesium in there, plus a significant amount of aluminum, so it should at least be a nice color if it hits." As I returned the terminal back to the main sensor feed, something suddenly clicked in my head. *Chaff!*

"Hey, Joe," I called out, hoping the AI was coming out of his funk from our earlier conversation. "I know you don't like talking about the weapons on this ship, but do we by any chance have a variable frequency laser onboard? Or a really tight-beam beam radio emitter?"

::Why?:: The curt reply was at least a step up from silence. The pedestal's hologram remained dark, though.

"What if we created a distraction?" I continued. "If your emitter can push a really narrow beam of 2.4 GHz at that comet that passed a couple hours ago, I bet we could get a pretty big boom out of it, or at least get it to sparkle a bit. Maybe enough to get that assault carrier to go check it out. If they change course to intercept, that would take them outside our detection envelope, and we could get out of here."

The AI's avatar suddenly popped into existence. The Roo's expression was hopeful, but reserved. ::I think I understand what you want to attempt, but the chances of detection are still high.::

"But you can do it?" I reiterated. "What kind of aperture can you generate, and how narrow would the beam be when it gets there?" Joe's comment about detection also reminded me to consider back-scatter. "Also, what kind of shielding do we have around the transmitters? Will they be able to contain the side lobes?"

::That will not be an issue,:: the avatar mused. ::The cloaking field will easily contain any errant radiation from heading where we don't want it to go, but that is not what worries me. There is no way to predict in which way the energy will reflect once it hits the comet. Any radiation which reflects directly back at us will then bounce unpredictably off the hull. It could reveal our position.::

"I thought your cloaking field would handle that," Gina inquired, eyebrows raised. "But before we get into that, what the heck has gotten into you, Red? Do you want to get eaten?" Her eyes locked onto me with laser-like intensity. "Why are you contemplating yelling out our location to every swinging dick in the system with radar?"

"That's the thing, Gina," I explained. "If we don't have any back-scatter, the only source of EM radiation anyone will see would be from the comet! Most of it would get absorbed by the water, just like an old microwave oven. All we'd really be doing is heating it up a little."

"Okay, I get that part," Gina agreed reluctantly. "I even used to have a microwave. But what's the point?"

"Two things," I continued. "First, the rise in temperature will make them think someone is hiding on, or behind it. Space is the perfect insulator, so the best way to dump heat without radiating it out as infrared is to come into physical contact with something really cold, like a giant chunk of ice. With me so far?" I glanced over at her as she nodded her understanding.

"So you're trying to get them to think we, or 'someone' at least, is hiding behind the comet," she murmured. "But water doesn't reflect microwave energy, it absorbs it, and it's going to take a long time to heat up that much ice. Why is Joe worried about reflection?"

"Not as much time as you might think," I grinned. "Ice formed in microgravity is like super-fluffy snow, and the individual particles are tiny. It doesn't take much to cause them to melt into liquid water, which then almost immediately converts to a gas from the vacuum. The thermal bloom is going to be significant, even if it's only going to be on the surface."

"And the reflection?"

"That's the other part of the idea," I explained. "Remember how I said there was a significant amount of aluminum in the dust mixed in? When the water vapor scatters, it will blow the dust around, too. The aluminum will act as a reflector, sure, but since it's dust, not a solid piece of aluminum, it'll scatter the beam randomly rather than in any kind of predictable pattern. It'll kind of be like the 'chaff' which was used as a passive defense against old-school radar. It won't be a perfect globe, but it'll probably be close. From anywhere but right next to the comet, it will look like someone sending out a really weak scanner pulse, like you'd use for station-keeping near a dock."

"And then they'll think we're trying to stay hidden behind the comet, and screwed up, somehow!" Gina finally smiled. "I get it now! So what's the problem?"

"I don't know," I shrugged. "I thought the same thing as you, that Joe's magic cloaking device would hide us from any back-scatter." We both turned our eyes towards the avatar expectantly.

::You are both right, and wrong at the same time,:: the AI interjected in exasperation. ::Yes, the cloaking field is indeed capable of capturing and redirecting electromagnetic radiation of all types away from the ship, including infrared, but it is only a single-axis effect. All that energy has to go somewhere, and generally it is sent in the opposite direction of the enemy. There is some leeway, in case there is something in that direction which would reflect back, but that is the point I am trying to make.

::It only works on a single azimuth. It cannot handle multiple sources of radiation. Anything coming from more than zero-point-zero-zero-zero-seven degrees of the exact azimuth will not be captured by the effect, and will likely reflect from the hull normally.:: Joe scrunched his avatar's eyes closed in frustration. ::I *cannot* shield us from any back-scatter reflected from the comet without removing the shield pointed at *Clernak'Ta,* which would immediately detect us at this range, as our thermal signature would be unmistakable.::

"Damn," I sighed in disappointment. "I thought we had it!"

I returned to monitoring the sensors, the sense of depression almost overwhelming. It sucked. It seemed like such a good idea...

"Hey, Joe." Gina murmured, seeming to be deep in thought. I turned towards her, hope rising. The girl was one sharp cookie, and if she was thinking that hard, it had to be good. "How far from the hull does your stealth field work? If I was outside working on the hull, would they see me? Like, my thermal signature, not visually."

::No, the field effect extends marginally past the hull, about twelve of your meters.::

"What if we didn't have to use the cloaking field to shield us from the back-scatter?" Gina asked cheerfully, her attitude brightening considerably.

::What do you mean?:: the AI asked. ::I have done numerous calculations and recalculations. There is zero chance that we can avoid the reflected radiation. I admit the possibility that enough of that would reach the *Clernak'Ta* to be detectable is significantly less, but it is still more than fifty percent. The risk is too great.::

"Well, I had a thought," Gina smirked. "Why don't we do the same thing Red was going to do to the comet?"

I gave her a bit of side-eye, considerably confused. My idea was blasting the comet with a tightly-packed ray of microwave radiation. I couldn't think of how hitting ourselves with the same thing would help matters, even if it were possible. "Isn't that a bit like shooting yourself in the foot to fix a hangnail? You may not feel the hangnail anymore, but then you've got bigger problems."

"Not the shooty-part, Dummy," Gina rolled her eyes. "I meant the water. You said that the ice would heat up when it absorbed the beam, and that the only reflection we'd get would be from the aluminum dust."

"Well, kinda," I admitted. "Sodium chloride is basically just salt, and it absorbs just about as much energy at that frequency as the water does, if not more. However, I have no idea what the magnesium will do. I've never had reason to find out."

Gina gave me a strange look at that revelation.

"Hey," I protested. "Don't judge me! I was a kid! I didn't know any better! I didn't know it was going to melt through the glass and kill the microwave!" I paused, smirking a bit at the memory. "Besides, that's what I was hoping would make the comet go boom. It makes a great distraction."

"Boys…" Gina rolled her eyes.

::Hijinks and misguided experiments aside,:: Joe interjected acerbically. ::Magnesium *does* absorb that frequency, but nowhere near as energetically as sodium chloride.::

"Good," Gina finally declared. "Then this is what we're gonna do."

Ch. 23: Racing Against the Clock

Using only cold-gas thrusters to shift the ship's orientation was tricky, but it was finally done. On something as small as a communications satellite, I'd heard this could be done just using a set of heavy spinning disks, but the Camel was *way* too massive to get away with that, and just finding the exact center of mass to prevent tumbling would have completely defeated the purpose. Our nose was pointed directly at the comet to make our radar cross-section as small as possible. We hoped that very little of the reflected energy would come back this way, but after seeing Joe's propagation prediction, I placed very little faith in that outcome.

Instead we were going to rely on Gina's brilliant little kludge.

"Ready?" I asked Gina over at the environmental controls.

"And waiting," she confirmed.

::I am ready as well,:: Joe's avatar added after a brief pause. ::Emitters charged, firing in three... two... one... *firing!*::

Instead of a single aperture emitter from one of the laser turrets, which didn't operate on the right frequencies needed anyway, the AI used the combined output of every forward sensor emitter which could be brought to bear along the nose of the ship, as those had much better shielding against errant radiation than the ones on the sides. Seventeen separate emitters focused over sixty megawatts of microwave radiation, each, at the precise microwave frequency used by standard station-keeping radars, 2.4579 gigahertz. While this was not the ideal frequency for absorption by water ice, it was crucial in perpetrating the ruse.

As the gigawatt plus beam reached out, it began to spread out ever so slightly. Unlike a laser, this was just a highly directional radio transmission. Even so, by the time it reached the cometary fragment just under ten million kilometers away, it had spread to a radial cross-section of only fifteen meters. The beam struck its target perfectly, almost immediately sublimating into gas the first meter and a half of surface ice on the jagged, sixty-two meter long fragment. As expected, the suddenly hot gas quickly wafted away from the surface, scattering dust in almost every direction but especially directly back at the beam, as the microwave energy chewed its way through the material, essentially creating its own rocket nozzle for the ejecta from the force of the vaporization. The thrust of the escaping gas was *just* enough to simulate a ship bumping into it. The subsequent reflection of the microwave energy from the scattered flakes of aluminum dust added to the illusion.

Of course, we couldn't see that yet, as the light from the event hadn't yet reached us. Instead, we had a countdown timer displayed on the main viewer. However, I wasn't watching that. I was much more concerned with the returning radiation speeding towards us at nearly three hundred thousand kilometers per second. It was going to take sixty-four seconds for the microwave energy to make the round trip to the comet and back, and we were scrambling to get Gina's idea to work.

It was a simple idea, really, and it borrowed directly from my plans for the first half of the distraction. Like she'd mentioned, water doesn't reflect radio or microwave energy. Instead it absorbs it, with heat as the only byproduct. So, why is this important, one might ask?

Well, water ice isn't nearly as affected by microwaves as liquid water is. At the power levels we had beamed at the comet though, combined with the finely focused beam, it was plenty enough to overwhelm the crystalline structure of the frozen 'snow', melting it very quickly. The reflected energy was going to be much weaker, as in several orders of magnitude weaker, not just due to distance, but also because only a tiny fraction of it was going to bounce directly back at us. It would still be powerful enough to be detected, even with it bouncing off our hull and traveling the additional distance to the *Clernak'Ta* we were hiding from, though. We needed something in the way that would absorb enough of that energy to reduce it to near-background levels. Water was again the answer.

And so Gina and I were frantically working the environmental system, dumping all but a fraction of the life-sustaining liquid onboard into a bubbling, boiling blob of fog directly in front of the ship. The AI could have handled it, but neither Gina or I had trusted him enough yet to re-enable his access to the environmental controls yet, and there was no time to do so now, as it required us to physically access the control runs. So the job had to be handled by us 'meatsacks'.

Since there was no significant gravity, there was nothing but surface tension holding the water in one place. And because the water was warm enough to be liquid, it immediately began to boil away as soon as it hit the vacuum of space. Finally, as boiling broke any surface tension, the droplets quickly broke apart, causing the whole mess to almost immediately sublimate into a gas.

Our makeshift shield deployed with mere seconds remaining, we waited breathlessly for the result.

One would think the "evaporation" effect would cause the water to freeze instantly, as it is inherently an endothermic state change, but that was not the case. As violently endothermic as the evaporation process was, without the added effect of convection, it was not enough to reduce the temperature of the water below freezing without more time. Instead the water simply stayed in gaseous form, a slowly expanding cloud of vapor. Sure, it would freeze in a few minutes as the heat radiated away, but it stayed a vapor just long enough to almost completely absorb the incoming microwave radiation.

Just like how ancient radar systems could see clouds in the sky as shadows where no radar returns were received, so too did it work for us. The energy coming back at us was almost nothing compared to what we sent out, literally a billionth of a watt, or some such ridiculously small number, but it would have been enough to reveal us to sensitive enough sensors.

Instead, over ninety-five percent of it was absorbed by the water vapor in front of us. The energy absorbed wasn't even enough to raise the temperature of the water vapor by a tenth of a degree. The rest bounced off the hull, and was immediately absorbed by yet another pass through the floating shield. What finally escaped was decidedly *less* than the surrounding background radiation.

But now, that rise in temperature wasn't the real danger. The water itself was already hundreds of degrees hotter than the surrounding space when we released it from the ship. The cloaking field could handle any thermal radiation emissions which originated from within twelve meters of the ship's hull, but if that cloud of vapor reached too far beyond that limit before it froze, or even for some time after, the heat would show up on the *Clernak'Ta's* sensors just as if we had no cloaking field at all.

Luckily, the AI knew how to deal with that. Joe's insane processing speed enabled him to deftly manipulate the vapor using an externally mounted grav plate array on the nose of the ship usually used for orbital docking maneuvers. Although running the grav plates for the entire ship would severely disrupt the cloaking field, running a single pair of plates was within tolerances, if only just. It was weak, producing only an anemic half-meter per second of pseudo-gravity acceleration, and that only within thirty meters of the grav plate, but it was enough to keep the vapor from getting too far away. Now, all we could do was wait.

I hate waiting, I whined silently. It's not like I didn't know down to the exact second how long it was going to take for us to know if the ruse worked, but the suspense was killing me. In a lot of ways, knowing the exact time our little trick would become visible was worse than not knowing at all. The atmosphere on the bridge was so oppressive, you could cut the tension with a knife.

As the two minute mark approached, I was literally on the edge of my seat. We wouldn't know what the enemy would do when it detected the thermal bloom and back-scatter from the comet for another hundred and twenty seconds or so, but *this* was the moment when it was actually happening. I cringed as a new countdown appeared, again counting down from one-twenty. Whatever happened next would determine our fate. I expected three possibilities; On top of that list, the 'best' outcome, the *Clernak'Ta* would change course to intercept and investigate the comet fragment, taking itself far enough away for us to be able to restart the engines and slip away undetected. Option two, they did nothing and continued on their current course, meaning we would have to wait an additional eighteen hours till we would be out of detection range. Option three? I really didn't want to consider option three. It meant we'd been detected, at which point Joe said we were screwed. The Vespidae carrier would change course *towards* us, and with our engines completely cold, we'd have absolutely no chance of escaping. They'd overtake us in just a couple hours, long before we came anywhere close to the Weisskopff limit of the system. We needed at least a four hour head start to ensure we couldn't be followed. Six hours if we wanted to do so completely undetected.

As the last few seconds seemed to stretch into hours, I held my breath anxiously. *Would they take the bait?*

The counter hit zero, and then... nothing.

Five seconds stretched into ten, then twenty. *Still nothing,* I breathed. *At least it doesn't seem like they detected us.* Thirty-seven seconds passed before there was a detectable reaction, but it didn't come from the *Clernak'Ta*. It came from the comet.

"Oh-frak-me-sideways, what was *THAT!?*" Gina shouted as she pointed at a second screen. The comet fragment, which had been slowly spinning from the jolt we'd given it, was now a quickly expanding ball of gas and plasma, its multi-ton mass completely obliterated from what could only have been a light-speed beam-weapon strike.

"What the *hell?!*" I backed up the feed on the sensors to watch it again. Whatever it was had no visible signature until it struck with a bright flash, the light slicing through the ice and dust like the Cleaver of God, before the expanding plasma blast front blew the comet to rapidly expanding gas. I'd seen shots like that before, but only from gigantic system-defense laser arrays, whose capacitor banks alone outmassed most battleships! To see something like that from something as small as a heavy cruiser was ludicrous! *And he called this an 'assault carrier'?!*

::BLKTR'OO NIT!!!:: Joe finally reacted. Startled by the untranslated outburst, my head jerked around to look at the AI's avatar. I never imagined seeing an AI locked up in shock, but there it was. All he did was stare into space for nearly ten seconds. It made me feel a little better about my own reaction, but what he said next chilled me to my bones.

::H-How is that possible?!::

If HE doesn't know, we may just be completely screwed! The Roos had apparently been fighting these guys for a really long time, and a brand-new weapon system might just mean the difference between life and death, not just for us but for their entire race, if what I suspected about their situation was true.

A sudden change in status jerked my attention back to the data from *Clernak'Ta*. I checked the feed history to make sure, but the relief in my voice was obvious as I reported the update.

"It worked!" I cried. "They're turning in-system and accelerating to maximum known thrust!"

"Oh, thank God!" exclaimed Gina, and she slumped back in her seat in relief. "They didn't see us!"

"We're not out of the woods yet," I warned. The enemy ship would have to maintain its current course for another half hour before we could even think of shutting down the cloak and bringing up the power plant. If they continued for an additional fifteen minutes past that, we'd be scott free, and likely wouldn't even be detected when we crept away to the jump point.

Strangely, Joe's avatar shut itself down. I could tell he was still active by the indicator lights on the pillar, but apparently the AI decided he needed to retreat into a safe-space or something. I couldn't blame him, really, but it was still kind of annoying to be left holding the bag, so to speak. I supposed he needed some time to think, and maybe calm down. I knew I did.

But first, we had to make sure all that water ice cooled enough that we wouldn't get spotted again when we moved away. Recovering any was out of the question, but we could disperse it enough that its heat signature would be minimal.

No rest for the wicked, I sighed.

*****

"I'm going to go begin prepping for restart, Red," Gina yawned as she headed back to engineering an hour later. The stealth field had dropped by itself twenty minutes ago after the sensors showed the now-frozen cloud shield to be properly dispersed. I was positive it was Joe's doing, but I still hadn't heard a peep from him since he went dark right after our 'Hail Mary' play with the cometary fragment. It was time to get the hell out of here. We were running out of time for the lien payment, and I decided we weren't going to wait for the AI to wake up before we got on our way.

"I'll let you know if anything changes," I reassured her. *Yeah, we're definitely gonna need a break after this.*

After several hours, and no sign of pursuit, I started to relax. Joe's avatar remained dark even after we crept our way to the jump point and translated into the next system. I began to wonder if he was really okay or not, but when I sent him a typed message through the command interface, I at least got some text in return.

--*I just need some time.*--

--*Take whatever time you need. As long as we don't run into any Vespidae ships, or something worse, I can get us home from here.*--

It was several hours later, when I was about to call Gina to take over the watch that I finally got another message from

Joe, and it was unique enough that I really wondered about his mental state. I'd never heard this kind of talk from him. The latest message was short and to the point, but it spoke volumes about the effect the last few days had on him. The message was all of three words.

--*Thank you, Captain.*--

Wow, I thought in amazement. *That's new.*

Ch. 24: New Enemies, Old Friends

Not since my days running covert surveillance missions against the Snakes had I been so glad to see a planet. The blueish-green world hung in space like a brilliant gem, its sapphire and emerald tones mixing together to produce a completely unique and frankly, gorgeous color. I was kind of amazed I hadn't noticed before, but I guess I'd either been too wrapped up in my own worries on the way in with Goose, or scrambling to get the *Camel* working right on the way out of the system. I was compelled to take a moment, just drinking in the view.

The browns shaded with occasional green highlights of my homeworld had once been similar, its world-spanning systems of clouds and oceans separated by the rich emerald jewels of life-bearing continents. I remembered seeing pictures of the blue marble of earth before the Shigothe War, how it gleamed a brilliant sapphire when the sun shone across its surface, and how bright and clean it looked from space, the dirty cities and squalid mud on the surface hidden behind the shimmering seas and voluminous clouds. The lights of her cities when night fell, sparkling like their own constellation against the darkened oceans.

"Earth", they'd called it then. The first extraterrestrial visitors chuckled that we still called our home planet, "Dirt". Knowing what I knew about humanity's history and languages, I wasn't sure that "Terra" was any better, but at least being a different language than Common, it didn't get translated into "dirt" anymore.

That beauty was no more. The orbital bombardments in the early phases of the Shigothe War changed the planet beyond all recognition. The once flourishing cities and infrastructure which dotted the coastal regions were flattened with megaton-level kinetic strikes, scalloping the coastline and flinging literal cubic kilometers into the sky. The oceans had received most of the gigatons of that dirt and toxic debris, either directly or later as runoff, wiping away the very diversity of life that had made their systems sustainable for millions of years. The rising seas and the destruction of the ice-caps that humanity had worked so hard to avoid removed the efforts of millennia, eventually erasing nearly half of the cities which lay within a hundred kilometers of the original coastlines. A breathing biosphere suffocated, killing the majority of the world with it. It was amazing what a few thousand tons of material dropped from space could do. Seeing Cranotia this way made me finally understand what had been lost, what had been done to humanity in those terrible years.

Even now, centuries later, the slight patches of color in the heavily industrialized farming regions were the only splash of green on the entire planet. The oceans, once reflecting a brilliant blue, now showed a drab, mostly grayish-brown hue. The once oxygen rich waters are still a semi-toxic sludge, only the bioengineered algae and plankton introduced after the Shigothe War to increase oxygen conversion still managing to survive. While the war's destruction of the coastal regions was long since been repaired, the ecosystems surrounding the areas never recovered. Much of what made the planet a haven for its diverse lifeforms had been wiped clean in the horrendous bombardments. I once read that over forty percent of the planet used to live within a hundred kilometers of the sea. Looking at the beauty of Cranotia, I could see why.

For one thing, the oceans were pristine. Not a bit of pollution floated in those sapphire waters, which made sense as soon as you met one of the natives. Their aquatic nature meant they still spent the majority of their time under the waves. Of course, also being a space-faring race, most of their space-related infrastructure and trade were accomplished on dry land, but more than seventy percent of the natives never left the water. Most of the dry masses were immigrants and employees from other worlds. I discovered

Old H'talgim was a Cranotian rarity when I asked him about his family while getting the CMV Camel ready to fly.

"Nope," he blathered. "Not a single one of my blasted offspring is willing to take over this place when I finally retire. They're more about getting their pedipalps slimed, or whatever the little smilps do these days. It's all about the 'social' down there. Money grubbers like me usually hire some redskin to do their bidding on land, but I just couldn't bring myself to trust any of them." I could understand why that was, having been caught so easily in one of their little scams.

"It's getting to the point where we crabs are losing control over our own homeworld," he complained. "Sure, none of these dry-skins have a say in government, but when they control enough of the wealth, votes and shares don't mean that much anyways."

I'd given his words a lot of thought over the course of the trip. The Confed had, in some ways, suffered the same fate, although the bad actors in our case were mostly native. But just like what was happening on Cranotia, once the Corporate world had enough wealth and economic power, they became the tail that wagged the dog, and government "by the people, for the people" ceased to have any meaning.

::Captain, you have an incoming message.::

Joe had finally come out of his funk six hours ago, but he still wasn't talking much. To be fair, neither was I. However, his manner and tone had done a nearly 180° turn. For one thing, he actually started to call me "Captain", and while I still wouldn't call him "friendly", the snark had disappeared almost entirely. I wasn't sure yet if that was a good thing or a bad thing, but it at least showed a measure of trust and camaraderie. Enough so that I'd decided to allow him access to the communications arrays again.

"Who's calling," I asked with a sigh. *Probably someone working for the bank trying to slow us down again,* I growled silently. *Well you're too late, assholes. I'm here already, and I've got your damned money.*

::Unknown, Captain. It's not an active link, just a queued message on the delayed communications server. There is no ident attached to the message. Text only.:: After a slight pause, he added, ::In case you were wondering, the message is tagged for you personally, not you as the Captain of the ship.::

"That's weird." I wondered who would be playing games with the highly regulated official in-system communications network. It *could* still be someone acting for the bank, or whatever power group was behind them, for that matter. *Better to play it safe.*

"Hey, Joe," I began, not knowing just how much I could lean on his new-found cooperative attitude. "Have you sent an acknowledgement yet?"

::I have not.::

That opened up some options. "Can you access the message without triggering a 'read' status to show up on the network?" I looked at his avatar expectantly. Joe hadn't shown signs of being overly law-abiding before, but I wasn't quite sure where he stood on matters of propriety versus expediency. I suspected the latter, but I wasn't going to assume. "And do you feel comfortable doing so, hiding the metadata from the system?"

A hint of the old snark returned to Joe's expression, and for once, I actually felt relieved to be on the sharp side of his wit.

::Do you really think I care what some trumped up bucket of poorly refined silicon and discarded children's toys wants to call 'regulations'?:: the AI snorted derisively. ::I thought you knew me better than that, by now.::

"I just didn't want to assume, you know?"

::Strangely enough, I appreciate the sentiment,:: he nodded amicably in my direction. ::However, you need not worry that I will report you to the planetary authorities for mere regulation infractions. I doubt even justifiable homicide would give me pause, seeing what I've found floating around in the network here. Now if this system were

Srbhchs`Mlrtchn-ee, we might have a problem, depending on the crime.::

"Good to know!" My eyebrows rose skyward at the blatant statement of both support and, to an extent, trust. I recognized the unpronounceable gibberish as being the name of their home system. Wisely, I refrained from trying to replicate it. From what he said, it just meant "Home". *I guess we're making progress,* I smiled to myself. "You said it was text only, which means you've already decoded the message. Want to fill me in?"

::I have, but I must be honest. It doesn't make any sense to me in the current context, which just means I lack the key to decipher the message. Some kind of code, I assume.::

"Encrypted?" I asked, confused. Other than the shared symmetric keys I set up between the data slates we had onboard, I couldn't think of any codes or crypto keys I had, which just made things stranger.

::Not encrypted,:: he clarified. "The words are perfectly readable, but they do not pass any identifiable information. It is just a couple sentences, but given how convoluted your humans' language is, any data it is meant to convey is lost from lack of context.::

"Fine," I accepted. I wasn't about to spend the next day or so explaining the slang, double meanings and outright inconsistencies of Terra Common. It even confused *me* at times, and I was a native speaker! "Just read me the message, or put it on the display. We'll figure it out from there."

::Very well,:: he accepted gamely. ::The message reads; 'Sending gift horse, might be Greek. Bourbon sucks, and you know it.' It is signed with just a single character.::

I nearly burst out laughing, and my grin was wide enough to nearly split my face in two. I knew *exactly* who it was from, and had a vague idea of the message. "Let me guess," I asked with a chuckle. "The last letter is a 'G', right?"

::Ah, so you know this person,:: the Roo confirmed. ::Then the message has a specific meaning for you?::

"Kind of," I gave a twisting waggle with one hand. "I have a general idea of what he's saying. Nothing exact, of course, as we didn't set up any kind of code-word stuff when we last saw each other, but close enough for this."

::I don't understand,:: he complained. ::If you have no reference, how are you able to convey any significant information from so few points of data?::

"Before we get into that," I cautioned. "Let me get Gina up here. She's going to want to hear this too."

::Priority message sent,:: the AI interrupted. ::Engineer LaForce should be here momentarily.::

"Woah, there, Tiger!" I exclaimed in mild dismay. "Cool your jets! It's not time sensitive or anything, I just didn't want to have to explain everything more than once, that's all. No need to get Gina all riled up."

::I *loathe* hidden meanings,:: Joe whined petulantly. ::And your species' detestable babble is absolutely riddled with examples of them.::

Gina appeared at nearly a dead run, skidding to a halt just short of slamming into the coaming around the hatch. "What's happening?" she asked breathlessly. "Did that ship follow us somehow?"

"Nothing so dire, Gina," I reassured her, motioning for her to come take a seat. "Got an inbound message that needs translation and Ol' Sparky here is just being impatient."

Gina glared at the AI as she claimed the pilot's station. I watched her settle herself a second as she bled off the adrenaline which had probably been coursing through her veins a moment ago. She grabbed a bottle of water from her pocket and nodded her head towards me. "So what's got our digital friend in such a tizzy?"

"Got a text message from an old friend," I began. "It's short on details, but long on mystery. Says he's sending me a 'gift horse', and that it might be 'Greek'."

Gina snorted hard, water bursting involuntarily from her nose as she fought hard not to laugh, failing miserably in the process. A few moments of coughing finally brought her back to the conversation as I waited patiently.

"Wow," she grated, clearing her throat a couple more times before speaking again. "That's a loaded message if I've ever heard one!"

::Why?:: Joe huffed in protest. ::I don't understand how such a small set of innocuous words are packed with such meaning that even you, who I assume know nothing about the sender, are so affected as to lose control of basic bodily functions. What is so special about that phrase?::

"Whoo, boy," Gina whistled, glancing at me with a hint of malicious glee. "And there's the loaded question to go with it! I think responsibility for answering that one should fall on the shoulders of our intrepid Captain, don't you think, Red?"

I gave her a withering glare, but my heart really wasn't in it. Looking down at my hands, I tried to come up with a concise way to explain the context of the message. Both parts of the phrase were rife with hidden meaning and context deeply rooted in human culture and history, with a touch of psychology and advertising theory, all rolled up into one. And of course, the second sentence of the message which I hadn't revealed to Gina yet was all about me and the sender. There was really no way to explain it without a long, drawn-out story which, in the main, wasn't really about the message, per-se. In the end, I cheated.

"Joe, can you pull up your human database and do a contextual search of adages and proverbs, and how they are used in everyday conversation?" I hoped to leverage the AI's incredible ability to absorb large amounts of data very quickly. If I didn't have to explain that one, it would make things a *lot* easier.

::Done,:: he replied momentarily. ::And now that I have added that disgusting little concept, along with hyperbole, simile, and metaphor, to the list of things about your language which I detest, I have to admit, it is extremely effective at providing a wealth of information in a few short words.::

Gina smirked at me, mouthing the word '*cheater*'. I just grinned back, holding my hands up as if comparing two weights and finding them about equal. The message was clear; '*If you're not cheating, you're not trying.*'

"Just so I know you're on the same page, how about you paraphrase what the message means, then?" I requested. "If you're too far off, I'll fill you in on the details."

::The words 'Gift Horse' is an obvious reference to the often used parable, or rather the cautionary tale, from one of your planet's religious texts. The phrase in its complete form is 'Do not look a gift-horse in the mouth', which honestly is a horribly dangerous and repulsive method of determining the age and health of a potentially disease-ridden quadruped. However, there seems to be a kernel of truth to the saying, even if I do not completely agree with the premise.::

"How so?" Gina interjected curiously, her body now stretched out and her feet propped up on an adjacent chair. "Not that I'm arguing, I just want to know your reasoning."

Joe turned his avatar to face the lounging engineer, sparing a sharp look for the grease-stained boots marring the clean surface of the navigator's seat. ::I believe it warns the reader to not look too closely at something freely given, so as to not offend the gifter by seeming ungrateful.:: He glanced at me for confirmation, and I gave a small nod. ::But in my experience, which I will admit is not extensive outside those members of my creator's species, is that any time a business or individual offers a service or item for free, the recipient must beware.::

Turning back to Gina, he continued. ::To use another one of your plethora of imminently contradictory and pithy phrases; 'If you're not paying for the product, then *you* are the product.'::

I clapped my hands slowly, which caused the AI to pause again in confusion. I was quick to reassure him, though.

"Dead on target, overall," I congratulated him. "But as you suspected, the context of a message, who it is from, and how it is delivered, can drastically change its meaning."

Gina perked up. "Oh yeah, who is this guy?"

I smiled. "Old comrade from my military days. He's actually the one who gave me a ride out here."

"By any chance did you come in on an old *Ferret* class scout?" she asked casually. "I tried getting a message to it when it was in-system, but whoever it was wasn't taking calls. Didn't even get an answering machine."

"Yeah, that's Goose." I confirmed. "He's pretty cagey about stuff like that. Can't blame him, though. Not after all the crap I had to deal with after boarding the station."

"True," she acknowledged the point. "I was hoping to beg for a ride home, but then *this* came along." She waved vaguely at the rest of the ship. "So, I take it you trust him?"

"With my life, if not my sanity."

Gina chuckled. "I've had a few friends like that. So let's get down to brass tacks. What's the hidden message?"

I demurred, looking expectantly at the AI. "First I want to hear how Joe interprets the second half of that phrase."

::That one is more ambiguous,:: he admitted. ::There are literally billions of references to 'being Greek', mostly referring to collegiate affiliations within institutions for higher education. I see no obvious relevant connections, unless your history with this person adds some specific point of congruence. Is this related to your training?::

"Yeah, I didn't think you'd get that one," I consoled. "It's actually a play on words which obliquely refers to an ancient battle from human prehistory." I briefly explained the story behind the "Trojan Horse", and how it played a critical role in the Battle of Troy. Joe was absolutely astonished that anyone would fall for such an amateurish ploy, but I assured him that, while the actual horse was likely allegorical, the battle had actually happened. The 'Greek' part of the message was even easier to explain, as I just referenced the entirety of the common phrase, 'Beware of Greeks bearing gifts'. The rest immediately fell into place for the AI.

"So essentially, he's sending you something that will likely help you, but there's a hidden agenda involved," Gina summarized. "And accepting might bite you in the ass. Am I close?"

"As I don't know what it is, I can't be certain, but yeah, that's about it," I agreed. "I trust his judgment, but the fact he's telling me ahead of time that it might have hidden consequences tells me the answer is probably a lot more complicated."

::Now that I have absorbed the context of the message, I understand how you came to those conclusions,:: Joe interjected. ::But what about the rest of the message? How does 'Bourbon sucks, and you know it' relate to the previous message?::

I blushed a bit at the associated memory. "That's just something so I know it's actually from him, and that he's not under any kind of duress. It's not actually part of the message beyond that."

Gina immediately zeroed in on my discomfort. "You didn't mention that part before, Red. I smell a story there."

I looked away guiltily. "Let's just say it was when I was young, dumb, and feeling invincible, and leave it at that. It's an embarrassing story."

"The good ones always are!" Gina smirked. "You'll have to regale me with your adventures, sometime."

"Yeah, not in this lifetime," I grumped. Wanting to change the subject, I asked Joe to send a message to H'talgim asking for advice on marketing our return cargo. I knew if I tried to just sell it openly without considering the corporate climate, I was going to get taken for a ride, and not in a good way. *So far, that old crab has been worth every penny,* I contemplated. *I need to remember to thank Gina for having the idea to set up that little 'consulting' contract!*

That would be later, though. I had a schedule to keep.

Ch. 25: Oh, Woes' Me

"You can't unload here."

"It's a public commercial dock," I protested mildly, already suspicious. Our arrival at the commercial side of the orbital station had gone *way* too smoothly. I'd expected to be given the run-around, having to wait for a slot to open up, but Old H'talgim had come through yet again, somehow getting us clearance to approach and dock almost as soon as we entered parking orbit. It *could* be just a misunderstanding, but my guess was that this was the bank's attempt to slow me down. *Not very imaginative of them,* I thought.

"Not today, it's not." The eight-foot-tall, heavily muscled alien loomed over my head like an ancient Roman statue, hard, immovable, and vaguely surly. His appearance reminded me of a giant silverback gorilla seen in an old video about a famous primatologist named 'Dana Flossey', or something like that. Four hair-covered arms were crossed in front of his chest, and his face radiated belligerence as he stood squarely in my path.

"Look, I'm not going to sit here and argue with you," I said wearily. "The dockmaster said to dock, so that's what I did. If you have a problem with that, you can take it up with him. I need to go hire some dock workers to help unload the ship." I tried squeezing past him into the corridor leading inward, but was stopped by another gravelly voice.

"Dose dock workers? Dat'd be us. And dis dock is reserved for *Plik-nith Starward* today, as they paid extra fer da privilege." The new voice growled confidently. For some reason my translation earbug was making him sound like a guttersnipe gang member, but whatever. As I turned to face the newcomer, I was mildly taken aback by his appearance. From his deep tone and grating manner, I'd expected to see another hulking brute like the one who blocked my path, but instead there was a skinny little red-skinned runt, no more than half the size of his burley companion. *Same species as that asshole working H'talgrim's front desk,* I realized. Despite the disparity in size, it was abundantly clear which of the two was in charge, as the brute quickly stepped aside with a distinct aura of fear.

"And you are?" I asked dyspeptically.

"My name?" An evil smile accompanied the confident response. "You can call me 'Rocks', and this 'ere is *my* dock. An 'deese is *my* crew. No one moves cargo on *my* dock without goin' through *me*. Weez a 'Union', I think you hummies call it. Unnerstan me?"

"Oh *joy*," I sighed, turning to look back towards the cargo hatch leading to the *Camel*. "A shakedown. How quaint."

It was apparently not the answer he was looking for. "I said, do ya unnerstan me?"

I took a step to the side as I returned my attention back to the miniature mob boss. "So let me get this straight. Someone paid you to 'reserve' this dock for them, even though they're not here, and *can't* be here while I am docked. I can't leave until I unload my cargo. To unload cargo here, I have to go through you, right?"

"Das right," he grunted back. "Gimmie my credits due me, an *my* crew will unload yer crap. Gimmie *enough* credits, an maybe yer crap don't get broke. Nego'tiat'n's over."

"Just to be clear, you said I have to go *through you,* right?"

He scowled, his face becoming even redder as he realized I wasn't playing his game. "Yer price jus doubled, squat-head."

There was no way I was going to survive a brawl with this guy's minions. Not only did they outmass me by a fair margin, but they were probably very good at the kind of bare-knuckles throwdown this looked to become, and pulling out lethal weapons in response to a verbal altercation was a great way to get hemmed up by station security, which already had it in for me. It was a good thing we'd already thought of alternatives. I simply turned around to face the ship.

"Gina," I called. *"Go through him!"*

Being electric, the little scooter gave no warning before it suddenly shot out of the hatch. The tires skipped and squealed as they fought for a grip on the lubricant-stained floors of the cargo dock, but none of that mattered anymore. Gina rode the two wheeled abomination like a stunt driver, leaning outward to lift the side car off its wheel before tapping the rear brake. The rear tire broke traction on the slick floor, sending the bike into a controlled skid with the bottom of the side car aimed squarely at the pint-sized punk. The rest of the crew scattered as the raised side car impacted just above his waistline.

He had no time to react. One moment he was standing there, threatening me with fees, broken cargo, and probably broken knees. The next, he was crumpled against the far bulkhead, launched there by a *really incredible* display of cycle skills presented by my *wonderfully talented,* and *resourceful* engineer. Somehow, she anticipated this exact situation and had a plan to deal with it. *It wasn't her fault that the idiot decided to stand in the right-of-way like that,* I chuckled to myself gleefully. *Just an unfortunate accident, officer!*

I helped Gina lever the bike back up on its wheels then resumed my journey through the corridor. The crew of dockyard workers had vanished, not wishing to tangle with the 'crazy chick on a bike', it seemed. I hoped that would be the last we saw of them this trip, but had my pulser clipped to my belt, just in case. If they actually tried attacking me, as opposed to just attempting to extort money from me, I was fully justified in defending myself, by station law.

H'talgim had been a godsend for getting us cleared to dock, but that was the extent of his influence up here. He'd warned us about the little protection rackets that dominated the commercial docks, allowing us to plan ahead, but we were on our own for actually finding people to help us unload. Thankfully, he wasn't the only friend we had in the system.

Nari's bar was packed to the gills, but it wasn't too hard to get the Shigothe's attention. *I mean, really, she literally has eyes on the back of her head,* I snickered silently as she waved me towards an open section of the bar. I was in a good mood.

I supposed, given our species' histories, I should have hated the spider-like Shigothe bartender, or baring that, feared or loathed her. They *had* been responsible for the near-total wipeout of the human race, albeit through second-hand effects. But for some reason, I didn't.

The Shigothe War had happened over six centuries ago, and after the collapse of their empire, their influence on our sector of the galaxy waned quickly. After that, Terra had very little contact with their race. In fact, Nari was the first Shigothe I had ever met. The only reason I knew what she was when I walked into the bar was the still-popular war videos used as a kind of propaganda machine extolling the bravery of Terran warriors. But me personally? I had no real opinion on them, before meeting Nari. She was wise, thoughtful, and above all, had given a hapless Fox-Kin like myself a fair shake. I considered her, if not a friend, then at least an honest fellow traveler.

"Hey Nari! How's business?" I called over the background noise.

"Greetings, Red." she answered. "I've had to hire a couple more servers, as you can see. What can I get you?"

I considered the question briefly. I really did need to get back to the ship, as we were still on a tight timeline, but it would be rude to come asking for favors without at least buying a drink. "Still have any of that lager?"

"Just a little bit," she answered, grabbing a frosted glass from the freezer behind her with one of her many appendages and swiftly producing the desired drink. "I'm somewhat surprised to see you here, given your previous circumstances."

"Yeah, me too, kinda," I chuckled. "I have a ship now. Gina's my engineer, by the way, and we just got back from a run. Need to unload cargo, and didn't want to pay off the goons at the dock. I've got a lien payment to make in twelve hours."

Nari suddenly stopped in the process of handing him the drink, staring in shock. "Why are you still here, then?"

"Well, I need to get passage down to the surface after we sell cargo, and I was hoping you had some ideas. I'm not sure if that issue I had before is still active or not, or I would just book passage on the regular shuttle. I was hoping you could tell me. Also, if you know anyone with a hover pallet, it would speed things up."

Nari seemed to give it some thought after finally handing him the beer. "I can't say anything about your personal account, but if you have a ship, you have the ship's commercial account, right?" she asked. "Use that to purchase the ticket. They generally don't mess with commercial accounts unless someone has bribed the shuttle manager. I don't think you've been on the station long enough for you to have irked anyone that badly quite yet."

I winced. "Well…" I quickly explained the confrontation at the dock.

The Shigothe bartender again displayed her amazing body language mastery, giving me a look that just screamed exasperation, even managing to emulate rolling eyes despite her actual eyes being completely imobile within her carapace. "Do you at least have the funds?"

"I will when the cargo gets unloaded, so yeah, no problems there."

"Fine," she sighed. "I'll purchase a pass under my business account, and when you get to the terminal, flash me a ping and I'll change the passenger name to yours on the ticket. But you can't make this a habit. I've managed to keep under the radar here, and I'd like it to stay that way."

"You're awesome, Nari!" I raised the glass, taking a couple swallows before setting it down, still two thirds full. "I'll head out then, I still need to find some dock workers."

"Check in compartment Blee-76," she suggested. "Next concourse over spinward, third corridor, ring-side. There's a job board in the break room there, and you can usually find crew or dockhands looking for extra cash hanging out. That's all I can think of, other than just paying the bribe. Depending on who you find, you might not even need a hover pallet."

Thanking her profusely, I hurried on my way. *What a way to run a business,* I smirked. *Ain't nothin' stopping me now!*

I   should   have   known   better.

Ch. 26: I think you've got the wrong guy...

"Lieutenant? ...Lieutenant Vulkeshson, wait up!" a voice called behind me as I walked quickly down the concourse.

I almost didn't turn around. It had been so long since I'd been addressed by my former rank that it didn't register for a second that someone was addressing me, but the use of my last name finally caught my attention.

I slowed to a stop warily. The only people on the station that even knew I was former military were Gina and Nari, and I was downright certain I'd never mentioned my former rank to the bartender. The other thing that caught my ear was the earbug translation, or rather the lack of it.

Unlike almost every conversation I'd had since arriving in the Cranotian system, these words hadn't been translated. Even some of my conversations with Gina had the translation matrix applied, as her heavy French-Canadian accent was considerably different from my own. You'd think, with near-instant global and interplanetary communications, that the different dialects of Terran Common would tend to mix together, becoming more and more homogeneous, but in fact the opposite became true after earbug translators became widely available and cheap. The gaps between regional dialects had been widening for several hundred years, as the earbugs completely eliminated the need to communicate without them. Thus, the choppy language I learned from birth, a mix of corn-fed midwestern North American and Southern Peninsula Spanglish, was a far cry from the soft-edged, fluid tones spoken by my engineer.

As I turned, I was greeted by yet another surprise, but I guess I should have expected it. A female Fox-Kin stood hesitantly, dressed in a standard-issue Confed Navy ship-suit with all its patches and identifiers removed. Her triangular, elfin face was covered in white fur with just a smudge of gray below the cheeks of her muzzle. Her winter-white ears stuck out from her suit's non-standard skullcap like tiny semaphore flags, hints of pink skin just barely showing up past the bushy winter-white fur of the cups. A fluffy white tail finished off her appearance, curling around her waist like a fuzzy belt, its end held possessively in both hands against her torso as if to protect it from being grabbed, her posture radiating nervousness.

She was the most beautiful vixen I'd ever seen. My mind went almost entirely blank. *Wow!*

As the surprise faded, I finally regained a measure of control, and started to consider my response. On one hand, she could be from the Confed military, but the lack of insignia and unit patches meant she was definitely not from a Confed ship docked at the station. I hadn't bothered to check the listings specifically for Confed registries, but I *had* looked at the names, making sure we'd beat the one that probably held a grudge for stealing their business. None of those names had Confed naming conventions, which were fairly standardized across the fleet. Plus, I couldn't imagine a reason the Confed navy would even send a ship out this way, let alone be allowed to dock. The Crantotian Conglomerate was not exactly on good terms with them, irrespective of the apparent ties between the financial institutions that I'd run headlong into when I arrived. So the chances of her being active military were vanishingly small. Nor were there any obviously human or Kin-crewed ship names, but I was less sure of that one.

The ship-suit being Navy-Issue wasn't as much of an indicator as it would first appear either, since they were generally "gifted" to the veteran upon honorable discharge, and just as often ended up in second-hand stores when the veteran retired or obtained permanent work dirt-side. That left only a few options left. Either she was a recently discharged veteran who'd picked up work on a human ship and got stranded, or she had her own ship somehow. Of course, she *could* have simply booked passage on a transport, if she had the funds. So why was she looking like a needy waif, tail in hand? Something was off, but she'd known my *name and rank!*

Despite my reservations, I cocked my head to the side curiously. "Can I help you?"

"Oh thank god!" she cried, taking an involuntary step forward. "It is you!"

I jerked back in confusion. "Do I know you? Pretty sure I don't. Your appearance is awfully distinctive."

"Oh!" she perked up. "No, we've never met, but we have a friend in common."

A light went off in my head. *Goddammit, Goose!* I groaned silently. *What did you tell her?* But rather than trust that she was actually the one referenced in his cryptic message, I wanted some corroboration. "Got a name for that friend?"

"Mongoose," she replied quickly, probably understanding my hesitation. "He said you might be able to help me." She twinkled those baby blues at me, and I honestly found it a bit hard to concentrate. She was *really* pretty. But instead of making me want to trust her, it actually put me more on guard than ever. *She might be Greek,* he'd said. *So if she offers to help, watch out for a hidden agenda. Best case, she offers something of equal value. Worst case, I toss her out the airlock.* I was actually kind of surprised at myself at this line of thought, but with everything that had happened so far, I wasn't willing to take it off the table. Trust had to be earned, and dropping a name wasn't going to do anything but give her the chance to talk.

I came to a decision. One way or another, I still had to get down to the surface. To do that, I needed to get the ship unloaded and the cargo sold. For that, I needed dockworkers.

"Walk and talk," I offered, turning to resume walking. "I'm on a tight schedule."

She hurried to match my pace, walking almost submissively a half-pace behind and to my left. I glanced back at her when she stayed silent for nearly ten seconds.

"Now the 'talk' part," I mentioned brusquely. "You have until we get to compartment Blee-76."

"Well, you're not very nice," the vixen pouted.

"I don't have time to be nice," I replied dyspeptically. "Spit it out. I have things to do."

"Fine," she sighed with a sudden change in demeanor. No longer did she exude helplessness or vulnerability. Instead she straightened up, stepped up even with me and began to explain herself in quick, quiet, staccato phrases. "I need to move some cargo. Possibly a couple passengers, but that remains to be seen. Fifty percent above standard rates, exclusive reservation. ASAP departure." She stabbed me with a baleful glare. "And no questions."

Damn! I thought in surprise. *That was unexpected!* But it did answer some questions about why she was all the way out here. She was a smuggler. *And a pretty effective liar, too,* I realized. Not just content with lying with her words, this little vixen had lied with her *whole body*! I managed to keep at least some of the shock from my expression, I thought, but she was quick to spot it anyways.

"You wanted it quick and dirty," she reminded me when I didn't reply right away. I shrugged my shoulders in agreement.

"What's wrong with your ship?"

"Too small, and it's not in the system anyways," she answered quickly. *Almost too fast...*

I didn't know what to say, really. I was already on thin ice with the station management, and taking on a known smuggler could very well kill any chance I had to pay off the ship. On the other hand, I was well aware of the levels of profit smugglers could make hauling contraband, not to mention dodging the taxes and fees associated with normal cargo. But getting caught would be paramount to a death sentence to my piloting career. Not only would I lose the ship to whoever caught us, but my biometrics would be added to the trading database as a known criminal, and I'd *never* be able to gain entry to any of the normal commercial stations, ever.

It was too much of a risk. I was in trouble enough without borrowing more on top of everything. Besides, I didn't even own the ship yet. Not to mention, I had absolutely no idea how Joe would react to being used to smuggle contraband. While he'd mentioned his disdain for normal regulations and such, that didn't mean he would be willing to haul something dangerous like proscribed weapons, or even worse, illegal pharmaceuticals. Hell, *I* wasn't comfortable hauling stuff like that.

I was about to deliver my refusal when she spoke quietly one last time.

"Help me, Obi-Wan Kenobi. You're my only hope."

I jerked to a halt and stared at the vixen. That kind of emergency code phrase was drilled into every RECON pilot, trooper, and scout before we were allowed to even *think* about heading into enemy territory. It was common sense, really. The danger of capture was just so high that having some way to communicate under duress with code was required. Making it something as complex as quotes from an entertainment video just added to its ability to hide in plain sight that much better.

It was one of the very first things taught in initial intake training, along with the centuries-old "movie" it was from. "E&E" classes, officially called "SERE", for Survival, Evasion, Resistance and Escape, was one of the bedrocks of RECON pilot indoctrination. In order to pass the course and be certified for combat, we were required to be able to quote every single phrase uttered in that damned video, and be able to regurgitate them on command, in exact order in which they appeared. Or in reverse order, depending on which challenge phrase was used. Some were even more complicated, and each had a specific meaning.

Shocked to my very core, I responded almost automatically with the proper response, in this case, the phrase immediately prior to the one used.

"This is our most desperate hour."

She had stopped and turned when I'd frozen in my tracks. Now, her eyes softened just a tiny bit, before she continued walking towards the corridor I'd been aiming for. I jerked forward, my mind racing a million miles an hour.

Was she RECON? I thought frantically. *She used Goose's call sign as her reference, but she used the full one, not the short one, so she's not claiming to be a friend.* Senior Master Chief "Mongoose" was an absolute legend in RECON circles. The number of people who were allowed to refer to him as "Goose" was short. Like *really* short. And I just couldn't imagine Goose sticking his neck out for anyone like this without that status…

But there was one other group which knew and used the same code groups, and many others besides. DARC. Direct Action Reconnaissance Corps agents were like the sniper rifle to RECON's pistol. They deployed on *really* long range information gathering missions, sometimes lasting months or years, deep into enemy territory. Sometimes they got sent out with specially built stealth ships, which the RECON units maintained for them, but rumor had it they also ran what could only be called spy and assassination missions. Most of these were deep into enemy territory, from what little I could gather, but the occasional story surfaced where they headed into neutral or even allied space, even into *Confed* space. Getting caught doing that kind of espionage in one of *those* systems could have disastrous political consequences, and as such, they were rumored to be equipped with suicide devices to prevent them from being compromised. It was literally the most dangerous job I'd ever heard of.

And the only reason I'd even heard of them was because I was RECON. One of the single most secret standing orders for all RECON troops, more secret than all the stealth gear we would ever use, was the mandatory assistance clause for DARC agents. As far as I knew, almost no one even knew of their existence, not even certain types of senior officers. They were the knives hidden in the boot of the Military

Intelligence community. It wasn't like I could just ask, but I was almost dead certain the girl was a DARC agent.

Well, *squat.*

Ch. 27: Secret Squirrel

There was one more thing I'd been told about DARC, and the source of that information was Goose himself. He told me in confidence just before I got assigned to my own *Ferret* class scout ship. My mind shot back to that moment.

> *"That ship you saw back there?" Goose said softly after turning off the cockpit voice recorder. "Don't ever mention it to anybody except the CO, XO, or G-2 Ops officer, and only if they specifically ask about it using the 'no moon' challenge pair."*
>
> *My eyes went wide at the statement. 'That's no moon', was one of the very few phrases that wasn't assigned a value in the collection of challenge-response pairs we'd been forced to memorize on entry into Reconnaissance School. There was much speculation and debate amongst the other RECON pilots about it being used for something even more secret than RECON, but without any kind of confirmation, it had been just that, speculation. A few thought it was just too absurd of a statement to be used in any kind of normal fashion, so had been excluded from the hidden language. Now, however, I supposedly knew the truth.*
>
> *"What do you think they're doing?" I asked, basking in the obvious level of trust Goose was showing me.*
>
> *"You don't ever ask that," he growled back, momentarily shocking me.*
>
> *I shouldn't have asked the question, but Goose took pity on me after a moment. He gave me one last tidbit of information.*
>
> *"They're never used for political gain, only threats against the Confederation as a whole."*
>
> *"And you believe that?" I asked skeptically.*

*He looked at me steadily, no hesitation in his eyes.
"Cincinnati's Oath."*

That was the only clue I ever had about the rarified heights at which the Senior Master Chief was connected. The *Society of the Cincinnati* itself wasn't a secret, but its membership *was*. There was always only a single publicly known member, usually a high ranking admiral nearing retirement. They would hold their position until that time, at which point they would retire from public life, and a new admiral or general would step forward to identify themselves. The rest of the members were secretly scattered among the vast population of both human and Kin military officers and senior noncoms. There was no application process, and no awards. Membership was by invitation only, and if someone was accepted and revealed their membership outside the society's rules, they tended to disappear.

Their goals were simple and straightforward. *Protect Humanity* was the primary one, and the one that pretty much everyone referred to when mentioning the secretive society. The other mission, less known and the one often suppressed by government Confed propagandists, was *Protect the sanctity of military service.*

Much later in my career, while talking to another really experienced RECON pilot, it was pointed out to me that "Protect Humanity" did not equal "Protect the Human Confederation of Worlds". Nor did the second clause equal "unilaterally protecting veterans". I took the first to mean that the society was unconcerned with, and indeed antithetical to, the current human government. The second actually had to be explained to me. The goal wasn't to prevent soldiers and pilots from being used up, even harshly. It wasn't even to keep them from being destroyed in battle. That was entirely too difficult to accomplish, and indeed, sometimes forces *had* to be expended in order to win.

No, the second clause was to ensure that whatever government existed at any point in time knew, without a doubt, that if they failed to care for their veterans *after* they had been used up, then they also would fail to continue governing humanity. It was that simple.

I never knew if Iceman, the old pilot who spoke to me, was a member or not. By that time, I knew better than to ask, but I suspected he was. I was never invited to join the society, but I didn't want that kind of responsibility anyway. I was too much of a hot-head, as was later proved in my inability to keep my anger in check.

Coming out of my momentary reverie, I was surprised to find us standing outside the pressure door leading into Blee-76. The job board Nari had told me of was right there, dozens of virtual notes spread out across the smart screen display, each with contact information for either job offerings or job seekers. I shook my head to clear the cloudiness from my thoughts and started to scan the posts for seekers.

Most offered specific services, like electronics repair or other specialties, but a few were general, "manual labor" type requests. If we could get someone to respond quickly, we could get the ship undocked and myself down to the surface in plenty of time.

I was still wrapping my head around the appearance of a DARC agent here in what was essentially the middle of nowhere. Other than Gina, the vixen was the only Terran I'd seen during my entire time on the station.

The vixen, whose name I *still* didn't know, and no longer had much desire to, hadn't tried to push the issue after her shocking revelation, thankfully. I still wasn't fully onboard with helping her, even *with* her using a code which essentially meant 'critical mission, assistance required'. In retrospect, I realized it could be argued that by giving the response code, I'd accepted the order as valid. But technically, I wasn't RECON anymore, and wasn't subject to their standing orders to begin with. Supposedly, neither was Goose, but I was beginning to wonder if his resignation might have been an elaborate ruse. I wouldn't put it past him, honestly. It sounded like something he would enjoy, and would explain some of the stuff I'd seen on his supposedly-surplus scout ship.

But regardless of the direction I went, I couldn't load new cargo onto the ship until the old cargo was out. I wasn't finding anything about hover pallets, though.

"Why don't you take a look inside?" the vixen prodded. "There may be someone we can ask who isn't using the message board."

"Yeah, I'm not seeing much here that fits the bill," I admitted, moving past the board and through the next open hatch.

The 'break room' was huge, and the only thing missing to distinguish it from Nari's bar was the lack of the actual bar itself. It made sense, of course, as this was a break area for beings to rest for a short time before returning to their duties, not a restaurant. There was a dispenser for non-alcoholic refreshments with a dizzying array of options for all types, but otherwise the compartment held only tables and chairs of varying shapes and styles to accommodate the myriad species which frequented the commercial docks.

To my surprise, I spotted a pair of prospective employees almost immediately. I'd thought Terrans were scarce in the system, but I was apparently mistaken as I spied a pair of Ox-Kin lounging in one of the corners. The shaggy giants had to be at *least* two and a half meters tall, but it was hard to tell with them hunched down at the ridiculously undersized table. They were sipping what looked like enormous juice boxes, probably loaded to the brim with carbohydrates and proteins needed to maintain their enormous bodies.

Damn, those guys are big, I thought. And they were. I'd seen larger Kin before, but only Buffalo-Kin, the Ox-Kins' even shaggier, bigger cousins, created from Cape Buffalo genetic stock. *Those* guys, instead of being created for manual labor, were instead intended to function as genetically engineered biological battle tanks, and tended to have *really* mean temperaments.

Instead, these two were placidly slurping away, seemingly unconcerned at the amount of space the rest of the room was giving them. Even sitting, they towered over the rest of the inhabitants. Their large, flat-ish heads swayed gently as if to some unheard music, and their jaws masticated almost constantly, a behavioral holdover from their bovine ancestors, even though their bodies no longer required them to "chew their cud" in order to digest their food.

"Any chance you know those two?"

"I knew they were on the station," she answered. "But 'know them', know them? No, not a clue."

"Screw it," I said gamely. "Let's go ask, and hope they're available and willing."

The vixen snickered. "They wouldn't even *need* hover pallets…"

She actually had a good point. None of the cargo I currently had on board was more than half a metric ton. While that was well beyond my ability to lift in full grav, the pair of Ox-Kin could lift that no problem. *Hell,* I thought. *As big as they are, it might only take one!*

Their eyes swung our way as we approached, tracking unerringly despite their calm demeanor. I got the distinct impression these two had a "history" with the locals. Whether that was a good or bad thing remained to be seen, but at the very least it meant they could probably take care of themselves.

"Hey guys," I greeted them cheerfully as I grabbed a chair from a neighboring table. It wasn't one designed for tails, so I flipped it around and mounted it backwards, leaning my chest on the backrest, folding my arms across the top as I blatantly sized up the two Terrans. The vixen hovered a couple steps behind, rather than take another seat at the now-crowded table.

"You're new," the one on my left drawled in a smooth baritone, letting his drinking straw fly loose for a moment before deftly collecting it back up with almost prehensile lips. I turned my head towards him with my ears cocked attentively.

"I am," I told him. "Sorta, kinda, anyway. Any chance you boys are looking for work?"

"Mayy-be," the other one answered tranquilly, drawing out the word like verbal taffy, his deep voice reverberating like a subwoofer from his massive chest.

"Depends on the work," interjected the first.

"An' the pay," added the second.

It was like watching an old-school tennis match. Each bit of the conversation was spoken by one or the other, in alternating fashion, forcing the one talking to them to swing his head back and forth, endlessly. I'd had this kind of game played on me before, and it was honestly quite an effective negotiating tool if your opponent hadn't run into it before. I had, though.

"Pay is standard rate plus ten percent," I told the first one to speak, mentally labeling him as *Tenore*, while the deep-voiced one got the moniker, *Basso Perfundo*. "I've got a cargo of mixed ore and sintered ingots, containerized in packs of five hundred kilos or less, each. About five-hundred metric tons total."

"Twenney." I didn't bother swinging my head around this time when Basso countered.

"Twelve," I shot back, still staring deliberately at Tenore. I think he was starting to get a smidge uncomfortable at the attention, as his eyes drooped a little, and his riposte was a bit slower in coming.

"Eighteen."

He's going to settle at sixteen, maybe seventeen, I guessed. *Unless I throw in a bit of a bonus.* "Fifteen, and I'll throw in a free meal."

"Done." Tenore's eyes glinted for just a split second before he pounced on the offer. I had a twinge of regret as I realized just how much these guys could probably eat, but shrugged it off after a moment. I hadn't said, 'all you can eat', after all. And if it became an issue, I was fairly sure I could get Gina to read them the riot act. She was good at that sort of thing.

"When?," Basso asked finally, setting the empty juice box on the table with a satisfied belch.

"Now would be fine," I told him with a smile. "Unless you have something better to do. Oh, and the meal comes after unloading."

"Figured that," Tenore agreed. "What dock?"

I provided the dock information, and they agreed to grab their gear and head right over. I had no idea what they called 'gear', but far be it for me to tell them how to do their jobs. If they wanted special work gloves or something, I wasn't going to gainsay it.

The vixen kept mostly silent on the way back to the ship, further reinforcing my impression that she considered my acceptance of her mission as a done deal. It wasn't really, but I didn't want to argue about it here in front of the whole station. Despite not having a warm-and-fuzzy feeling about my own experiences in the Confed Navy, I still highly respected those who fought beside me, and I wasn't about to 'out' her to the locals if I could at all help it. Besides, I was hoping to get some moral support from my engineer, who I figured wouldn't give two shits about some secret-squirrel operation run by a black agency.

And I was right, but not for the reasons I thought. Not five minutes into the unloading operation, Gina was pulling me forward to the bridge for "consultation", while the vixen waited patiently in the cargo hold. Tenore and Basso Profundo, brothers whose names turned out to be 'Jeffery' and 'Matthew' Oregson, respectively, although they more often referred each other as 'Mutt' and 'Jeff' due to some old joke they didn't bother to explain, arrived no more than ten minutes behind us and immediately began toting the half-ton cargo containers out of the narrow auxiliary hatch with the ease of long practice, tossing them onto an actual *wheeled* flatbed cart that barely looked to be able to handle the load. They assured me it was up to the task, though, and after seeing no appreciable deflection in the ten meter by five meter cargo bed as the cargo modules got stacked up, I kept my mouth shut and let them get on with it. But it was going to take at least three trips to the drop point H'talgim set up for us to fully empty the ship.

"What the hell is this bitch playing at?" Gina hissed. I was more than a little taken aback by the sheer vitriol in her voice. "Can't she see we have more important things to do than play taxi for her?"

I wasn't sure where the automatic antagonism was coming from, but I felt I needed to clarify things just a little bit. I explained briefly about the code language shared by the different military sections without getting into too much detail, finally telling her what the particular code the vixen had used actually meant. Gina listened, growing more agitated as I began to lay out where I stood on the matter.

"Look," I finished. "I haven't decided to help her, yet. We have our own problems right now, and I really don't think running contraband for some shady government program is conducive to a successful career as a cargo ship captain. Besides, she *still* hasn't offered any further information about details. I can assure you, if she doesn't provide more information, I'm going to have to give her a flat-out 'no'."

"Liar," she growled. "You're gonna take the job, aren't you."

"I don't think so, no."

"You're not suddenly going to change your mind and go haring off into the sunset without considering how *completely screwed* the situation is?"

"No," I stated with finality.

"Oh yeah," Gina snarked with disgust. "You're just going to ignore the elephant in the room, then?"

"Huh?" I had no clue what she was talking about.

Her eyes narrowed dangerously. "Little thing like her shows up with a sob story and a pretty little tail, and you're just gonna walk away from it like it's nothing? Don't think I didn't see you staring at her ass like a teenaged fanboy! And you love playing 'hero'."

"What the hell are you talking about?" I objected. Sure, I thought the vixen was pretty. I wasn't blind, after all. But that didn't hold a candle to the kinds of skullduggery-induced fear consorting with a DARC agent brought forth in my mind. I did have to admit, though, she was probably right about the rescue complex. It was how Gina became part of my crew, after all.

I suddenly realized what the real problem was…

Ch. 28: Cargo Ambush

It started as a strangled chuckle. This quickly grew to a desperate giggle. I just couldn't help myself. The idea was just so *absurd!*

"What's so funny?" Gina demanded hotly.

I broke up. It was a few moments before I could contain my breathing to answer her fuming glare.

"Gina," I gasped out between belly laughs. "Are you *jealous?!*"

"What?!" she snapped, a horrified look on her face. "No!" But her ears gave her away. I could sense the humiliation radiating from her entire body as she hunched slightly in shame. Lots of people had trouble figuring out Otter-Kin emotions as their faces weren't as expressive as other Kin, but to someone versed in reading Weasel-Kin moods for more than a decade, the tiny little ears were a dead giveaway. Rather than being folded back in anger, or forward in interest, they were tucked down and back, usually a sign of sorrow or embarrassment.

"You *are!*" I gasped helplessly, desperately trying to regain control over my breathing. "It's okay, it's..." I forced myself to take a deep breath. "It's fine if you are, Gina. I just never imagined you feeling threatened by another female like that."

"I'm not threatened, you dumbass," she returned defensively. "You're the one with his tongue hanging out!"

I grinned sardonically as I finally recovered my composure. "Sure, she's pretty. I'm not blind. However, I'm not sure you realize just what a snake-in-the-grass that vixen is. I can't go into much detail, because it's *really* classified stuff, but she's a DARC agent. They are *beyond* badass."

"You're not helping here," she grumped, no longer denying the accusation. "You thought *I* was badass before, and I have to admit, I liked the compliment."

"Don't worry," I reassured her. "You're still my badass engineer, but DARC agents are a whole 'nother ball game."

Gina's cute little ears popped up out of their defensive stance. "I've never heard of them."

"For good reason," I confirmed, adding ominously. "And if you ever mention the name to anyone, I'll deny having ever said anything. This is 'burn-*before*-reading' level secret stuff from my days at RECON."

"Are you serious?" she asked, growing concerned when I nodded. "Then why are you telling me?" she asked, her ears tilting forward in anticipation.

"You have a need to know," I told her. "Not all of it, but at least enough to make an informed decision. At the very least, you need to know why I would *never* let my hormones control my decisions in regards to that vixen. Those people are the ones they send on *deep* missions. The kinds you only see in Agent Double-Oh-Seven episodes."

"Wait, those are *real?*"

"Probably not," I clarified. "At least, not in detail. But the agents themselves probably exist, in some form or another. Regardless, there's no way I would want to get involved with someone like that, because there's no way in *hell* I would come out of it sane, or even alive for that matter. I can't imagine what their survival rate is, but I can't imagine it's very high."

Gina paused, possibly gaining a new respect for her titular rival. "So, what now?"

I shrugged. "Like I said, we'll see how it plays out. Without more information, I don't think the risk is worth it, but honestly…" A loud boom sounded from the cargo area. "…the hell is that?"

::Your hired help is being assaulted,:: Joe's voice spoke from his plinth.

Squat!! I fumed at myself. *How could I be so stupid!* I'd completely forgotten he'd be listening to anything on the ship. *That* was a major operational security mistake!

Another loud clang reminded me I had more immediate problems, though, and we charged back to the cargo hold, both of us with weapons drawn. The picture we came upon wasn't quite what I expected, however.

Instead of finding our two Ox-Kin hires being beaten down to within an inch of their lives by a mob of angry unionites, I spotted Basso Profundo literally holding his opponent off the ground with one hand while pummeling him in the face with the other. Tenore was less physically imposing, but was easily holding his own, warding off several red-skinned dock workers from rushing to their comrade's aid with a broken piece of steel tubing, its length already severely dented from some tremendous impacts. Scattered remains of their wheeled flatbed were strewn across the deck, along with several of my cargo containers and pieces of what looked like a hover pallet. Two massive dents showed where a couple of the cargo containers had been flung against a bulkhead where they'd burst apart on impact, flinging their contents into the mix.

This vision of chaos was interrupted by the sudden discharge of a large caliber firearm. Not the wimpy little *zip-crack* like what my pulser would sound like, no. This was the throaty roar of gunpowder, or some other kind of explosive propellant, and the effect the sound had on the mayhem was instant. More than half of the red-skinned opponents scattered in terror, only the one physically restrained by the massive Ox-Kin unable to flee. The brothers, on the other hand, barely reacted to the noise. Tenore, or '*Mutt*', as I forcefully reminded myself, spun the length of tubing in one hand as he surveyed the surrounding damage. His larger brother gave the dazed and battered meat-sack hanging in his grip a disdainful sneer before, in an astonishing off-hand display of strength, simply lobbed the nearly unconscious body towards the other side of the dock where it fetched up against a pile of rubble, all that was left of both their cart and my cargo containers. The abrupt silence was deafening.

Damn! I stared, gobsmacked at the carnage. Given the destruction, I expected a lot more blood on the deck, but it seemed that most of the damage was limited to equipment rather than the living. That was changing slowly as the unconscious body started to bleed all over the floor from a truly remarkable set of cuts and contusions, but there didn't seem to be any fatalities on either side. Which, of course, led to my next question. *Who fired the hand-cannon, and what was it aimed at?* Before I could gather my wits to ask, the AI's voice sounded from the cargo hatch leading into the ship.

::Captain, there is a reaction team of security personnel already on the way.::

"Did you call them?" I asked quickly. I wouldn't have blamed him if he did, but I'd hoped to avoid attention from the station's administration. This incident was going to be enough of a headache all on its own.

::Negative, Captain,:: Joe replied. ::A complaint was filed against the ship by a person identifying themselves as 'Rocks', claiming unsafe acts threatening the station's integrity. I dare say you are familiar with the individual. The station's emergency response team, as well as their quick reaction force have been dispatched to investigate.::

"*Squat,*" I spat, angrily turning on the DARC agent who was still standing calmly in the corner, apparently unfazed by the conflict. "*Lady, What the hell did you just do?*"

She looked at me with mild disdain, replying sharply. "What makes you think *I* did anything?"

"Whatever you just shot off has the QRF headed our way," I snarled. "Are you *trying* to sabotage us so we have to take your mission, or is this just retaliation because I didn't immediately agree to your demands?"

"Sorry to disappoint you, Lieutenant, but that wasn't me. Do I *look* like I'm carrying a *Doshon 589* with squash head rounds?" The vixen slowly twirled around, displaying the extremely tight-fitting ship-suit with its distinct lack of hiding places for large caliber firearms. I was about to argue the point regardless when the AI interjected with additional information.

::The agent is correct,:: he stated. ::The projectile was fired from thirty units down the corridor, aimed at the open cargo hatch. It impacted on the far bulkhead, piercing both inner and outer pressure walls before exiting into space.::

Oh frak, we have a breach!! Gina and I both started a desperate sprint inside the ship. I was already reaching for the portable breach kit mounted next to the hatch as I cleared the portal. Dropping my pulser to the deck to free up my hands, I yelled to the AI.

"Where's the breach?" I screamed frantically. "I don't hear anything, and there's no air movement!"

::That's because it was immediately sealed.::

Joe's calm reply finally penetrated my overstimulated brain, and I nearly collapsed in relief.

"Oh thank God," Gina gasped behind me.

"And you, Joe," I added gratefully.

::Thank my designers, not your figmentary deities,:: Joe responded acerbically. ::The automatic systems are just that, automatic. Engineer LaForce will have to fabricate replacement tiles for the ones which expended their sealant, of course. But I suggest you deal with the incoming aggressors, first. They are approximately eight minutes away, give or take seventeen-point-six seconds..:: It was an oddly precise estimate, but I'd learned to trust him on stuff like that.

Right, I scowled. *So it was all a setup.* Definitely *the bank behind this one, then.* I scrambled back out the cargo hatch, snagging my pulser off the deck where it had landed and quickly replacing the breach kit into its case. I took another look at the damage around the dock, this time with a different perspective. If this was all done to make us look like the bad guys, or at least incompetent to the point of being a danger to the station, then I had to admit, they'd done a bang up job. And when the QRF and Emergency Response Team got here, it would be a cinch for them to blame us, as the damage didn't look much like an attack towards the ship. The two massive dents in the bulkheads were on the station side of the dock, obviously thrown in response to the Unionite attack. *Well, obvious to me, anyway.* Station admin would probably be primed to believe otherwise, of course.

"Gina," I called out, trying to plan my next move. "Did we get any of the shipments of supplies while we were unloading? Specifically consumables and fuel."

Gina poked her head back out of the hatch, a concerned look on her face. "No, on the consumables. And that's beginning to bug me. They should have been here over half an hour ago. But I started pumping water on board as soon as we docked, so we can restart all the environmental systems we had to shut down, at least. Fuel's still loading, should be about half full by now. Why?"

We didn't have much time, but the more I thought about it, the more confident I was that we were completely screwed. There was *no way* I was going to be able to make it down to the surface in time without landing the ship on the planet. Which would mean breaking planetary law by "flying above a half-kilometer in atmosphere' without a license. Which would get the ship impounded, and since I still hadn't gotten paid for the cargo we *did* deliver, and probably wouldn't, I wouldn't be able to pay the fees to get it released, not to mention the cost of fuel to make orbit again.

Yep, we're fraked.

Time for a new plan. A whole new set of problems to go on top of our old ones, but it's not like I have a choice. Not a real one, anyway.

"I'm thinking we need to get out of here," I stated tersely, my mind already running a million kilometers an hour. "Joe, I need you to verify the emergency docking release is working for the lock. We can't let them trap us here. Also, start looking for anyone trying to block us in. We're cutting loose in five minutes, thirty seconds.

"Lady," I said, addressing the DARC agent. "Still don't know your name, but if you have somewhere we can top off on fuel and food, we'll take you with us, but I'm sorry. We won't have time to load whatever cargo you wanted moved."

"You can call me Janice," she replied with a smirk. "And the cargo isn't even in this system. The passengers *are* on-station, however. They are the ones with fuel and resources."

"Unless they can get here in four minutes, five tops, they're not coming," I warned. She nodded, pulled out a slate and started tapping. *If they get here, they get here, otherwise, frak-em.*

I turned to the Ox-Kin brothers. "Guys, I'm really sorry, but it looks like I won't be able to pay you, but if I run into you again, I promise I'll make it good. You're an awesome pair of brawlers, and good loaders. If you leave quickly, maybe you won't get caught up in this cluster-frak."

Mutt and Jeff glanced at each other calmly, silently communicating whatever it was through the weird twin-like gestalt they'd apparently practiced to perfection. I hated to leave them in the lurch, as they'd really stepped up for us in that little battle-brawl, but there wasn't much I could do.

"Kin' we come?" The question took me by surprise.

"I can't guarantee I can drop you anywhere safe," I answered doubtfully. "And there's no time for you to grab your gear…"

"We brought all our gear with us," the other brother said next, as was their usual practice.

"Hope'n to hitch a ride."

"Yeah, this place sucks hippo-dick."

"Frak dis place."

"And you seem like a good captain."

"Plus y'all owe us dinner!"

I sighed at the mental ping-pong match going on in my head, and shrugged. "Fine," I replied. "Welcome to the Crazy Train. All aboard who's coming aboard."

"Dat really what de ship called?" Mutt asked Gina quietly as he boarded the ship.

"Yeah, that's a really weird name." Jeff added as they passed out of sight. "And where's the other dude we heard?"

I headed inside a few moments later. We had maybe ninety seconds before I needed to start locking up and beginning the undock procedure. If Janice's passengers were going to get here, it had to be now. Not that I figured they'd make it. There was just too little time, and if they were trying to avoid attention, they were probably nowhere near the docks. If they didn't make it, Janice was probably going to stay. If she did that, I'd have no way to come back for her, and getting enough fuel to get more than a couple dozen light-years away was going to be iffy. *If, if, if...* ran continuously through my mind. *That's a whole lot of "if's".*

"Eighty-five seconds," I told Gina as I passed her, heading for the bridge. I trusted her to close the airlock when it absolutely had to be closed, and not a moment before or after. Whatever jealousy issues she'd had before seemed to have evaporated in the chaos, as she nodded to the vixen without even a hint of snark.

I threw myself into the captain's chair and uncaged the AI's lockout, flipping the connection to active and enabling him to access the ship's controls. "Joe, bring up the cold-gas thrusters and prepare for an emergency un-dock. I want to break loose the instant the cargo hatch is sealed."

::Acknowledged, Captain,:: he replied curtly but confidently. He was *actually* built for this, after all. ::Course?::

"Negative Z-axis till we clear the station, then thrust as close as you can to the atmosphere of the planet without losing speed to friction. I want to slingshot out of here at max thrust. I don't trust the station admins to not have itchy trigger fingers. Set us up to use any orbital bodies on the way out to increase our velocity, same rules apply. Least-time course to *any* viable jump point. Let me know when we reach max-Q."

::Understood, Captain.::

"And in case I don't get a chance to say it later," I added. "Thank you, Joe. You've been a huge help getting us this far."

::Likewise, Red,:: Joe replied. ::You have been a pleasant surprise in these otherwise trying times.::

As I finished fastening the seat restraints, the ripping sound of a fully automatic pulser echoed from outside the cargo bay, followed by yet another booming report from a high caliber firearm. *What the frak?* I glared at Joe's image on the pedestal. "I thought you said they were still two minutes out?!"

::That is not the Quick Reaction Force,:: he replied quickly. ::They are still in transit. I suspect these attackers are related to our passengers.::

I punched that intercom button labeled 'Cargo'. "Gina, status!"

"Hatch is sealed," she yelled back. "But they put a hole in the airlock with that big-ass hand cannon again. I'm patching it. The red-skins are back."

"Passengers?"

"On board, barely." I could hear her grunt with effort as she applied the semi-rigid adhesive to the hole in the cargo hatch. "GO! It's not perfect, but if we hang around, they'll punch another hole in us!"

"Do it," I snapped the order at the AI. Immediately, the *bang*-clunk of explosive bolts and the *pop-whoosh* of air between the two halves of the airlock escaping into space signaled the release of our docking collar. We wouldn't be able to reconnect to a standard docking ring until it was replaced, but at least now we could run... I hoped.

"Clear?" I demanded of the AI, making sure we were no longer attached to the station. As much as I wanted to get out of there, I wasn't ready to commit mass murder by ripping off part of the main dock.

::We are clear to maneuver,:: his no-nonsense voice replied crisply.

"Get us out of here, Joe." I ordered.

There was a slight push lifting me off the seat for just a split second before the inertial compensation software kicked in on the grav plates. I knew they were just cold-gas thrusters, so being able to actually feel the thrust meant Joe was *really* pushing the envelope.

It was about to get a whole lot worse. I could hear the power plant spinning up, the normal low hum becoming a loud, bone-rattling subsonic wave of vibration which immediately set my teeth on edge.

"Hold on to something, we're about to kick this thing in the pants!" I called over the in-ship announcement channel. *I hope everyone's strapped in, this is about to get rough!*

Without further warning, the main engines went from idle to *holy-crap-thats-loud*, the roar drowning out even my thoughts. The inertial compensators did their best, but I was still jerked back into my seat by what felt like three times my normal weight. Out of the corner of my eye, I could see the sensor feed from the aft view. A plume of blue-white exhaust gasses extended out from the tail of the ship like a giant bunsen burner on steroids.

Wait, I almost panicked. *I thought this thing had a reactionless drive! We shouldn't even* have *an exhaust plume!* I glanced at the telemetry and was astonished at the readings. We were accelerating at over two-hundred meters per second squared. *That's over twenty gees! ...Later,* I promised myself. *Deal with it later.* The ship apparently had a lot more secrets left to reveal. Joe and I were going to have to have a *loooong* conversation about this, but ...*later.*

Two seconds later, a hologram of text appeared in front of my eyes, which made sense, as there was no way I was going to be able to hear anything over the roar of the engines. -- *CLEAR OF STATION, ALL PERSONNEL SECURED FOR ACCELERATION. RAMPING UP THRUST IN 5 SECONDS. MAX Q IN FIFTEEN SECONDS.--*

Ramping UP?! I thought frantically. *How fast IS this thing?* I never got a chance to contemplate the answer to that question, as the pressure pulling back on my body doubled, almost completely pushing out all the air in my lungs. Afraid to turn my head lest I snap my neck, I turned my eyes to the telemetry display. *397.4 m/s^2! Holy HELL!*

I started grunting and clenching my abdominal muscles, a barely-remembered technique for resisting gee forces I'd learned back in pilot training, intended to help in conditions like an uncontrolled lateral spin. I'd never had to use it before, but my instincts latched onto the memory in a desperate attempt to stay conscious. Despite my herculean efforts, there was a sudden surge sideways, and I passed out.

Ch. 29: Damage Control

::Captain Vulkeshson, wake up.::

The message repeated a couple times before I finally gathered enough energy to respond. "Quit it, I'm awake," I whined. I was really sore, and couldn't for the life of me remember why. *Damnit, why won't they let me sleep?* I complained silently.

::Good,:: the voice said. ::I was beginning to worry.::

Worry? I wondered groggily. *Why would they worry about me wanting to sleep in?* I gave an unintelligible reply, struggling to open my eyes. The voice sounded familiar, but I just couldn't remember. My eyelids felt like they had lead weights tied to them. I reached up to rub at them, despite my soreness, and suddenly realized I was weightless.

Everything rushed back into my head in a tidal wave of information. The fight on the dock, the weapons fire, the emergency undocking, and finally, the desperate bid to get out of weapons range before someone on the Cranotian station decided to take a pot shot at us at point-blank range. I snapped fully awake, the terror of the last thing on my mind clamoring for my attention.

"Casualty report!" I forced out. I was still alive, so we must not have taken *too* much damage from the station's weapons, but that didn't mean we were out of danger. Depending on a whole slew of factors, we might end up having to contend with Cranotian warships in addition to whatever our current enemies might have ready to throw at us. *Which isn't just the bank, now, either,* I realized. The mysterious passengers brought onboard by DARC agent 'Janice' apparently brought with them their own set of problems.

::No casualties reported as of yet,:: the AI said, to my relief. ::However, the report is incomplete. Of the passengers I am able to monitor, you are the first to regain consciousness. I am currently unable to determine the status of anyone not located in either the bridge, engineering, or one of the crew cabins.::

"Give me what you have, then. List them out," I sighed, slowly working out the kinks from my abused body, ensuring everything was working before I unstrapped into what could end up being a *very* dangerous environment.

::Besides yourself, I currently show seven individuals. Two large Terrans in crew berthing and five individuals in the cargo bay. Sensors in crew berthing show the Terrans to be healthy but unconscious. Cargo bay sensors and communications are offline. Weapons fire from the dock destroyed the emitter cluster before the hatch could close. However, the fire warning sensors in the aft storage locker are able to report minimal thermal data. They show five heat signatures consistent with living individuals located in the proper locations for the acceleration couches, and those units in turn reported their restraints were fully deployed and functional before the sensor cluster failed completely. If they were uninjured before engaging the restraints, they should have no further major complications. Lifesign monitors for the couches is offline, as they rely on the bay sensor cluster for communications.::

"Okay, Joe," I acknowledged. "I'll check them out as soon as it's safe, but give me a damage report for the rest of the ship first, critical systems only. First I need to know if there's air leaking out before I go check on the passengers."

I really hated not checking on Gina first thing, but that wasn't how damage control worked. First was *always* 'hull integrity'. Without air, nothing else mattered. After that, you could look at treating the critically wounded, but only just enough to keep them from dying. Third came heat and power, which were in some ways the same thing, internal communications, then propulsion. Then the old adage 'Aviate, Navigate, Communicate' came next. Minor wounds came dead last.

::No major breaches to hull integrity,:: Joe reported to my relief. ::Two minor leaks in the cargo bay where repairs were overstressed by acceleration, but they will not cause appreciable atmosphere loss unless they become significantly worse, or left unaddressed for more than thirty-six hours.::

"No other holes?" I asked.

::There is major damage to the portside pylon assembly,:: the AI added. ::However, any breaches from the missile's detonation were sealed by automated safety features and are no longer an immediate threat to hull integrity.::

"Wait, what missile?" I yelped.

::The one fired from the station thirty-two seconds after our undocking maneuver,:: he explained patiently. ::Attempting to dodge is what caused you to become unconscious. Unfortunately, I was unable to reduce acceleration until twelve minutes ago, as putting the ship out of the station's powered missile envelope took priority over your continued consciousness. I have been awaiting your recovery since then.::

"Squat," I muttered. "So that's what that sudden swerve was all about."

::Indeed.::

"Well, since you're up and running, I assume we have power. Before I head back to check for casualties, do you have anything else to add?"

::We are currently running under cloak, headed for the system's *Lnrl'uu* threshold,:: he advised. ::We should reach the projected jump point in fourteen hours and six minutes.::

That explained the microgravity, thankfully. I'd worried we'd taken damage to power systems in our escape and were drifting. But that also raised another concern... Heat. And even though it wasn't next on the priority list of damage control, I needed to know if it *would* become critical in the next few minutes.

"Any damage to the radiators?" Even though I had no clue *how* it functioned, I knew if the stealth field was working, it would be able to somehow redirect our thermal signature in a completely different direction. But that didn't mean it could actually facilitate getting the heat out of the ship in the first place, and the radiators were right next to the landing pylons on the ventral surface of the ship. If they were destroyed, or even seriously damaged, it could become a problem very quickly, especially if we needed to keep the cloaking field running. Despite the magic jiggery-puff it did with redirecting thermal energy outside, the internal system itself was a major heat producer, so despite the main engines and reactors being shut down, if the radiators were severely impaired, or the coolant pumps inoperable, we'd get broiled by our own waste heat in short order.

The problem was thermal transfer. Space wasn't actually 'cold' per se, but it was a *great* insulator. There was no conduction or convection of heat in space, only radiation. Any heat loss, or heat buildup for that matter, wasn't something you could fix by just opening up a window to let in warm or cold air from outside. If you were too far from a system's primary star, you were generally looking at a heat deficit due to the ship naturally radiating heat into space from the outer skin, even with the best thermal insulation. You needed a method to generate heat to replace that thermal energy loss. Being too close to the primary presented the other problem. With too much thermal and other radiation from the star hitting the skin on one side of the ship, there was insufficient surface area on the shaded side to radiate away enough heat to prevent buildup. If the ship was not accelerating, this could be mitigated by using a thin, reflective film as a solar shade, but normally, unless it was docked at a space station or set in a parking orbit, a ship was *always* moving, because a stationary ship didn't make any money.

The answer was radiators. They worked with pumps and heat exchangers to concentrate the ship's excess heat within their cores, which was then passed through thin wafers of highly heat-conductive material and radiated into space. This was enhanced by their physical design, which multiplied their exposed surface area by orders of magnitude. This came at a cost, however, in minimized structural strength, and most commercial versions were very susceptible to damage.

::There is significant damage to the radiators from incidental shrapnel, but they remain forty-seven percent effective for now,:: Joe informed me. ::Coolant is being lost at a rate of one-point-five-three units per hour, but reserves contain enough to maintain that capacity for another sixteen hours before the system becomes ineffective. This does not include the additional four hours which can be compensated for by using the strategic heat sink at current heat generation levels.::

"Oh yeah," I remembered, somewhat sarcastically. "This is a warship, and it has a strategic heat sink. How could I forget? Oh yeah, because you *won't discuss* with me the capabilities of *my own ship.* You know, you and I need to have a long discussion about who's running this joint, sometime."

::That would be myself, of course,:: the avatar responded cheekily. ::You simply set the course and manage cargo.:: I rolled my eyes, but quickly dropped the subject. *And if this is a warship, you've got anti-missile defenses. Why the hell didn't you use those to shoot down the missile, instead of just dodging?* I thought in frustration. It was another of several topics that needed to be addressed. *One of these days, I swear I'll get to that.*

Grabbing my slate from its charging port where it had somehow managed to stay during our insane acceleration, I tested its connectivity with the internal network. *Nothing,* I thought, *I wonder if comms are more damaged than he realized?*

"You said comms were out in Cargo," I asked. "Are you going to be able to pick up anything from this if I take it with me?"

::No,:: Joe replied acerbically. ::And if I were to allow that bit of antiquated technology to transmit, it would broadcast our position, even at this range.::

"Oh, right. Sorry," I apologized, a bit chagrined to have forgotten that part of the cloaking field. Thankfully, Joe was quick to provide a solution. The ship had its own hand-held communicators for use during damage control which used infrared light to transmit data rather than any form of radio, and he quickly described their locations. I would have to place repeaters at every bend to maintain line of sight, but they were designed to stick to any surface of the ship, and stay until removed, even under extreme acceleration. They didn't have the bandwidth to provide video, but they had no effect on the cloaking field's performance.

I shook my head in wonder. Gina and I had never even thought to look for them, since we had our slates which used a common RF frequency, and never had to deal with a cloaking field, before. I grabbed several of the palm-sized modules and headed for the hatch.

"You said air pressure was good, but what about contaminants?" I checked before opening the hatch to the rest of the ship. "Do I need to deploy my hood?"

::You should be fine,:: he assured me. ::Even without the fans running, enough circulation has occurred to spread any toxins far enough to have been detected. *That* at least, is completely clear.::

I slapped repeaters on the bulkhead every ten meters or so. My first stop was the crew berth. I already knew who was in there from Joe's description, but I wanted to see if I could get them up. Depending on what I found in the cargo bay, I figured I might need their help. Of course, the first thing I detected, even before opening the compartment's hatch, was a loud, easily identified rattling sound. I smiled as I popped open the manual access panel, inserted the crank, and quickly spun it clockwise, making sure to open it all the way. They would need the extra space to be able to get out, and I didn't want to waste time telling them how to work the mechanism.

The snoring Ox-Kin were snugged down into the acceleration couches as best they could, but fitting a nearly three meter frame into a seat only two and a half meters long was a bit of a tight fit. Their legs stuck out well beyond the padded grooves of the couches, which reached only halfway down past their knees, but they probably hadn't sustained any injuries from their feet flopping around. As for injuries from blood flow stoppages during acceleration, I could only hope that Joe's sensors were right and they were just asleep, not unconscious from lack of oxygen to the brain. I tapped hard on the forehead of the closest one and he startled awake with a snort.

"Oh, hey boss," Mutt rumbled as he wiped a bit of drool from his face. "Time t' roll out?"

"Get your brother up and meet me in the cargo bay," I answered quickly. "Damage control."

I spun around and left before he could ask for an explanation I really didn't have time for, but I could still hear him mutter as I headed aft. *"Damage control? ...Hey bro! Wake up! The ship's broke a'gin!"* I ignored the rest of the hatches until I got to the cargo bay, quickly spinning it open to get eyes on the people inside.

It was dark. Whatever had killed the sensor cluster near the outer hatch had also killed the lights somehow. I deployed my ship-suit hood just to get the emergency helmet's built-in LED strips going, as I was clearly going to need the light. The bright white light flooded out in front of me, giving me at least a partial view of the bay. Gina was clearly visible in the module immediately adjacent to the external hatch. Her head was lolled to the side, but otherwise I couldn't see anything immediately wrong with her until I looked down.

Streaks of a dark red substance smeared the deck between Gina's acceleration couch and the cargo hatch, and I was dead certain it wasn't hydraulic fluid. I flew across the bay, snagging the armrest of her couch to bring myself to a halt.

"Gina!", I urged, "Wake up! Are you ok? Where are you hit?" I gently jostled her shoulder to try to wake her up, not wanting to injure her further, but considering the rough ride we'd just experienced, I doubted anything I could do would be worse than *that*. She gave no response. Her emergency hood was up, and the indicator light showed she had oxygen, but I couldn't immediately tell if she was still breathing. I watched the small whiskers around her nose for movement.

They moved! I was suddenly washed with relief, but this was quickly replaced with apprehension. I needed to find out what was wrong with her. *Can't use the suit's diagnostics,* my mind raced. *They use radio, and my slate is still on the bridge. Med bay! Those scanners probably don't.*

I hurriedly disengaged the restraints and lifted her still form out of the seat. Blood had spread across her lower torso and down her left leg from a puncture wound just above her hip. I couldn't tell if it was an entry or exit wound, as the ship-suit had done its best to seal around the wound, just as it was designed to, but it was nowhere near enough to stop the bleeding entirely. I couldn't tell just how much more blood she'd lost during the six gee boost, but it looked like a lot. *Wait, the hatch!*

My mind vacillated wildly for a moment between my duties and responsibilities as captain of the ship, and my intense desire to help my crewmate. As captain, I should be securing the safety of the ship, not performing medical evaluations. That came second to last in the order of operations for damage control.

But this is GINA, my subconscious screamed. Not only was she my engineer, and critical to the wellbeing of the ship, but she was my *friend. Maybe even more than a friend,* I realized at that moment. She'd been my only trusted companion for weeks, now. I wasn't quite sure at what point she'd stopped being 'crew' and became someone so important to me, but she had.

Nightmares of losing my RIO, Second Lieutenant Joseph Buckley, to starvation and lingering wounds in that *god-forsaken* POW camp began to flood my mind all over again, as if the intervening decade had completely vanished.

I remembered the agony I'd suffered over the course of an entire year of privation and even outright torture. Most of that time was spent desperately trying to find some way to help Buckly, which in some ways made it even worse for my own sanity. *Why couldn't it have been me who was injured?* I'd railed furiously at fate, endlessly rehashing the ambush in my mind, remembering the moment of impact when the hypervelocity railgun round had struck us completely unawares. Helplessly watching, with my horror making the memory move as if in slow motion, as the broken stanchion swung inexorably downward, slicing off one leg entirely and mangling the other beyond recognition. The desperate struggle in a dying scout ship to stay alive long enough to be rescued, knowing that the Confed Navy was *going* to send a recovery team, because they *always* did. The joy we'd felt, when after fourteen days of drifting nearly powerless through the endless black with no way to know what was happening around us, we finally heard the sound of something docking against the only intact hatch left on the ship. The despair, when we finally realized our rescuers were not who we'd hoped. The excruciating screams as the Snake's medics amputated the mangled leg, crudely cauterizing both of Buckley's leg-stumps with what amounted to a medical branding iron. The grief as I watched him slowly fade, day after unceasing day in that hot, humid, unvarnished *HELL* the Snakes called "Reeducation Facility 103 - Human", his undernourished, dehydrated, wasted body still struggling to heal from its mutilation.

The guilt of actually being *relieved* when Buckley finally died after nine months of agony, of no longer having to deal with the weight of his suffering on my soul.

Finally making it home was somehow worse. Every room, every image, every ship in the RECON squadron reminded me of *him*. That ghost of my past who would now live in my mind forever.

The psychologists called it "survivor's guilt", with a hefty dose of PTSD. I called it my 'Shame'. It took me another six months and a ridiculous amount of physical and mental therapy to regain my flight status and return to the unit. It was during that time of healing and pain and work that I discovered the truth behind both our capture and the lack of rescue. *Lieutenant Commander Cartwright Andrew Alexander Spurgle-Saint-John, fourth of his name...* The asshat, worse than useless, waste of oxygen, squadron operations officer who not only was responsible for the intelligence leak which led to our capture, even though Goose said no one could ever prove it, but he was also the one who unilaterally decided, against all advice from his subordinates and RECON tradition, *NOT* to send a recovery team to scour the battlefield for disabled ships because it was, and I quote, "an inefficient use of Navy resources, since no *critical personnel* were involved". By which he meant *full-human senior officers.*

My debt of guilt would not let such a travesty of justice stand. My anger was total, and had I been able to smuggle a weapon into that briefing room, I would have killed him where he stood. Instead I was only able to get a few good licks in before his *completely non-regulation* personal security team pulled me off of him and tossed my ass in the brig. The only consolation I could take from the entire incident was the fact that he was removed from his position as operations officer for the 147th RECON Squadron, pending investigation. Of course, I never heard the result of that investigation, but Goose told me a decade later that the asshole had never returned to *any* RECON squadron, in *any* position. He refused to speculate further on the subject, no matter how much I argued. *It's in the past, Red,* he'd advised over a glass of single malt scotch. *Nothing good will ever come from agonizing over something you can't change.*

This was not then. I was *NOT* going to lose any more people important to me. Come hell or high water, Gina LaForce was going to *live!* She was going to *survive*, even if I had to die making it happen. I no longer cared about the CMV Camel as a ship. Now it was just a vehicle in which the people I cared about were carried.

As I sank into madness, I caught a glimpse of Joseph Buckley in the corner of my mind's eye. The pain on his face was clear, but he still held that ridiculous, infuriating grin which had for months sustained me. Buckley would have liked my new engineer.

Thankfully for my sanity, the murmur of approaching voices gave me another option besides abandoning my responsibilities to the ship.

Time   to   delegate.

Ch. 30: Damn it, Joe! I'm not a Doctor!

"MUTT, JEFF!!" I yelled a series of rapid-fire instructions across the bay where the two brothers were just emerging from the forward corridor. "Med bay, first door on the right! Manual entry panel, left side, one of you get it open, NOW!! The other one needs to reapply the hull patches on the external hatch, *verify seal*, check with Joe for more leaks, and *only then* check the other passengers."

Jeff had already entered the bay and was in a bad position to grab anything to change direction, but Mutt managed to catch himself on the hatch coaming before he, too, sailed out into the wide open space. With a powerful thrust of his arms, he shot back out of sight. Jeff continued to flail around until he finally managed to grab a frame member and guide himself to the second row of acceleration couches. Neither said a word, simply following the instructions given.

I gathered Gina into my arms and pushed off towards the forward hatch where Mutt had just disappeared. I was a bit off course, as her added mass threw off my aim a bit, but I was close enough. I drew in one leg to slightly increase my angular momentum and used the other to tap a stanchion as I passed to guide myself into the corridor. Once in the narrow confines of the passageway, I eschewed merely floating placidly towards the med bay. Instead, I planted a boot against the left bulkhead, launching myself at an angle towards the right side then used that momentum to run a spiral down the weightless tube. It may have only saved me a few seconds, but I was in no mood to waste even a moment of time.

Mutt was already opening the door by the time I reached him, bouncing to a halt with two stiff-legged thrusts in a mirror image of the way I started. Like me, he wasn't wasting time with additional steps. Rather than use the crank to spin the door open, he was utilizing his prodigious grip strength to simply spin the mechanism with his hand.

I raised my eyebrows at Mutt's technique, but I wasn't going to complain if it was going to get the door open faster. I shoved past him as soon as I could squeeze through the hatch and made a beeline for the medical pod. It was the same one that had come with the ship, but thankfully the builders had a close enough physiology and biochemistry to ours that it had little difficulty with things like trauma. Gina and I had spent nearly a day on the first leg of our last trip programming Kin-specific skeletal, biochemical, and microbial diagnostic information into its database. I just hoped it was enough.

"Trauma kit," I snapped, nodding my head towards the large box fastened to the bulkhead, marked with the large red cross of human medical tradition. Laying her on the diagnostic bed as gently as I could, I engaged the hold-down field which would keep her from floating off. Slowly but firmly, her body pressed down into the soft foam mattress, its layers jam-packed with short-range bio-feedback sensors. As the field engaged, I could also feel a slight tug on my boots, and I drifted down to the floor. Apparently the designers were smart, realizing anyone trying to perform emergency medical tasks would probably need at least *some* gravity. Mutt stepped up to hand me the trauma kit, then backed away to give me room. I ripped it open and grabbed the medical shears to start opening up Gina's suit around the puncture. The entry wound was small, but the amount of blood still leaking concerned me. *At least it's not spurting or sucking,* I thought. *If this had been much higher, she'd be dead already from a sucking chest wound.*

My medical training was limited to immediate first aid, but one of the things extensively covered was 'Tension pneumothorax'. Tension pneumothorax and its close cousin, hemopneumothorax, were still two of the biggest killers of modern combat casualties. Any time air or blood got into the pleural cavity between the lungs and the thoracic wall, it was a *bad thing*. The buildup of fluids and gasses inside what was supposed to be kept *below* the surrounding atmospheric pressure had immediate and deadly consequences. Lungs can't inflate against internal pressure, and blood has a hard time getting to the heart, meaning it has less blood to pump to the rest of the body. Left untreated, death soon follows.

Instead, the puncture was in the lower abdomen, just a few inches above her pelvis. I grabbed a large smart-patch from the trauma kit and pressed it firmly onto the puckered hole. Its embedded biomedical nanites would start the process of closing the veins and surface arteries to prevent further blood loss, but they weren't smart enough to do anything more complicated. I dug hard into my faintly-recalled medical training for what to look for next.

Lower abdomen... that probably means damage to the lower intestine, I guessed. *Possible perforated colon?* I knew how to check for it, but I had no idea about what to actually *do*, if I found it. As the lights in the med bay were working, I stripped the emergency hood off my face, bending down to sniff around the wound. The sickening, sharp, coppery tang of blood wafted into my nose, but I couldn't detect the scent of feces. *Thank God.*

What comes next? I racked my brain, reciting the old mantra. *Breathing, Bleeding, Breaks, Burns, and Shock.* Breathing *looked* to be okay, and since the emergency hood was deployed, her suit was capable of automatically providing pure oxygen if its sensors detected her O_2 levels dropping too low. I couldn't couldn't communicate with the suit to find out for sure, but from the indicator lights, it was functioning normally.

Bleeding, I breathed. That one was going to be an issue. While the nanite-infused bandage would be fairly effective at preventing blood from escaping the body, it wouldn't address any of the internal damage from the projectile's passage. Without access to the suit's internal sensors, I needed to use external ones.

"Joe," I called out, knowing one of the repeaters was just outside the door. "Gina's been shot. If there's any problem with firing up the med bay scanners, let me know now."

::You are clear,:: he replied, worry creeping into his voice. ::The med bay is heavily shielded for just this reason. But, how bad is the damage? I can't tell. The medical suite communications were handled by the same cluster as the cargo bay.::

"I'll let you know when I find out."

The ship's medical pod was weird. Instead of a bunch of screens showing the patient's status, there was just a massive transparent, and so far *hollow,* hologram showing an outline of her body. As the sensors went active, strange symbols started to fill in. I couldn't read any of it, as we'd never thought to upload a translation program to the medical pod, assuming it would pull its language database from the AI just like everything else.

"Joe, I need some help here," I called out again. "Nothing's translated, and I need to know what it's telling me to do."

::Set another pair of relays up,:: the AI answered. ::One on the opposite wall facing into the med bay from the corridor, and the other on the interface port on the very top of the pod. You're probably not high enough to see it. It's set that high to maintain line of sight even when someone is in the hatchway.::

"Yeah, and I'm not in zero-g anymore. Mutt?"

"Ah got it," his low voice sounded. He'd apparently been paying attention, and had already moved one of the relays to the far wall and was bringing me the one which had been attached at the entrance to the cargo bay.

"See if you can figure it out," I pointed, turning back to the pod. Bright red points began to appear on the hologram which I immediately recognized as the damage from a bullet wound. While I couldn't read the text, the images were fairly straightforward. The entry was a relatively tiny hole in her lower back, the wound cavity spreading down and back before narrowing again to just below her kidneys, where at least three large fragments lay nestled against what I thought might be one of the major arteries or veins leading down to

Gina's legs. *I have no idea how I'm going to get those bullet fragments out of her! I'm not a doctor, damnit!*

The display suddenly became legible as all the alien notation disappeared and was replaced with Terran Common. It still looked bad, but at least her vital signs were stabilizing, or so the readout said. The medical pod was already applying analgesics and antibiotics through a skin patch, which had been attached via a small waldo extending from the back of the instrument cluster.

Even with the additional information, I was at a complete loss on how to proceed.

"Hey boss," I heard Jeff's voice call from the corridor. "Hull patches are done."

"Thank you. And the passengers?" I asked, almost not listening to the answer.

"Alive, awake, and asking questions."

"Later," I told him dejectedly. I was in no mood to deal with our mysterious live cargo. I knew there were three of them which I had yet to lay eyes on, but at that moment, I really couldn't bring myself to care.

"Well, You gots someone here wants to speak with ya." he added. "Wouldn't take no for an answer, and considering who it is..."

"THEY CAN WAIT!" I snapped, not even turning around. "And it's going to be a while. I have a wounded crewman to take care of here!"

And I have no clue what to do...

A startlingly familiar voice dragged my attention back to the door. "Do you need any help?"

"Nari?" I blurted out, spinning around to find the arachnoid alien standing hesitantly in the hatchway. "What are you doing here?"

"My fault," the Fox-Kin vixen answered from behind the Shigothe bartender, utterly ignoring my glare. She was *not* my favorite person right now, considering it was her passengers who brought the additional attention, resulting in Gina getting shot.

She continued on blithely, unfazed by my anger. "She was hiding my passengers in a compartment near her establishment. Since you were in such a hurry, I asked her to bring them to the dock, as she already knew the fastest way to get there. Once the shooting started," the vixen shrugged fatalistically. "It seemed prudent to get her out of the line of fire by shoving her into the hatch."

Nari looked at me with characteristically accurate body language, apprehension clearly visible in her stance. "Sorry," she said. "I didn't mean to add to your complications."

"No worries," I assured her, dropping my eyes. "We'll get you back home." *...somehow, I guess.*

As I tried futilely to get my mind back on track, I began to wonder just how interconnected all this was. Too many coincidences, congruences and oddities for my liking, and it was honestly beginning to annoy me. My normally suppressed paranoia was rapidly going into overdrive. It felt like a giant, convoluted conspiracy. And inexplicably, *Nari,* the Shigothe bartender, was somehow the linchpin to it all. She'd never been anything but helpful and supportive to me and Gina, and she'd obviously been providing assistance to the DARC agent, but *damn it, how many people did she know?* It seemed the only people I'd interacted with who weren't somehow closely associated with her might be Old H'talgim, and I was becoming suspicious that even *he* might have some connections with her. Add to that her almost unnerving ability to imitate alien body language, and I was really beginning to wonder, not just if she was more than she seemed, but *how much* more?

And this whole time I was worried about the DARC agent being a new source of complications, I realized. Suddenly, another thought occurred to me. *Is she connected to Goose, as well?* I was fully aware that Janice and Goose had at least an understanding, if not a full 'working relationship', but if Nari was *also* embroiled in all this DARC-spawned skullduggery? My first impressions of Nari had been so good, I really hated to be suspicious of her, but...

I knew I was getting obsessive with my newly unleashed paranoia, and nearly fell down a mental conspiracy-theory-fueled rabbit hole before a chime from the medical pod interrupted my train of thought, indicating its initial diagnosis was complete. I dragged my mind back to my more immediate concerns and turned back to the holographic display.

"Joe," I reported as promised, as I wasn't sure how much bandwidth the AI had to see the medical report through the low-capacity relays. "She's got moderate internal hemorrhaging in the lower abdomen, a cracked rib, and two perforations in the large intestines, but no major arterial damage."

::I can see the data now,:: The AI's voice came from the relay on top of the medical pod this time. ::The damage is rather extensive, if not immediately fatal, at least.::

"Right, but the longer she sits like this, the worse it will get. I'm not a doctor. Hell, I'm not even a medic. *Gina* was the designated medic. *I* barely know how to apply a bandage and a tourniquet.

"What I need to know, right this second, is what treatment the med pod is capable of. Does it have any automated surgical routines, or as a last resort, some kind of stasis field we can use to keep her from getting worse before we can get her to a surgeon?" That last bit was a pie-in-the-sky miracle wish. Human hibernation had never been perfected, and I'd never heard of anything that could stop time like that, other than in science fiction and fantasy entertainment holo-dramas. It didn't hurt to ask, though, given the advanced tech onboard. The Roo-built ship was the most technologically advanced ship I'd ever heard of, let alone seen, just based on the sensors and cloaking systems alone. I couldn't imagine them being that much behind in the life sciences. If *they* hadn't come up with anything like that, then it probably didn't exist.

::I'm sorry, Captain. While the pod can usually handle minor physical problems and pre-set procedures, its medical nanite programming is not sufficiently complex enough to perform this level of repair autonomously. Even some of the minor procedures it would normally accomplish with ease are hindered by its lack of an extensive human database. For injuries of this severity, it requires a knowledgeable person to guide its actions.::

"And the magic stasis field?" I asked hopefully.

"I am unaware of any such technology,:: he told me sorrowfully. ::Certainly my creators, the `Mlrtchn-ee, have not developed any such innovation.::

My face fell as my despair began to creep ever closer to the surface. I was beginning to think the only way to save Gina would be to turn around and try surrendering peacefully to the Conglomerate Navy which was probably still chasing after us, even if they couldn't actually see the *Camel* to target us anymore. I really didn't think that would work, but I was almost ready to try anything, even locking the two of us into the lifeboat to call for help and letting the vixen have the ship.

"May I take a look?" Nari spoke up hesitantly.

I almost said no. Under what possible pretext would someone whose physiology differed so radically from Terrans have any reason to study their biology to that extent? From what little I knew about Shigothe from the bits and pieces of old documentaries and propaganda videos, they didn't even have the same kind of hemoglobin-based blood that most mammalian species did. Their bodies were mostly exoskeletal, and even their brains had some weird synaptic tissue that human scientists had never really figured out. But... *What the hell do I have to lose?*

"Sure, I guess," I acceded, waving at the medical pod. "I can read the words there, and I know what they mean, but I have no clue how to fix it. I think I can trust your motives, at least. I can't even think straight right now." I moved out of the way and took a seat on one of the chairs, my head hanging down, utterly spent, both physically and emotionally. I just couldn't take any more shocks to my system. Too much had happened, too fast. I was feeling overwhelmed and helpless. I couldn't even pay attention when Nari stepped up to the control panel and began tapping away rapidly on the screen. *Oh God, no, not now!*

But it was too late... *far* too late. I hadn't had a PTSD episode of this magnitude in at least a couple years. I *knew* what was happening to me but was utterly helpless to stop the downward spiral towards the depths of fear and depression my emotions were headed for. It was like watching an air-car wreck in slow motion, knowing exactly what was going to happen and being completely powerless to do anything about it. I railed at my brain to stop thinking about it, but just like trying not to think about pink elephants, the only thing my mind could see was a kaleidoscope of fear-induced images, every one laced with helplessness, hopelessness and more than anything else, *uselessness.*

Ch. 31: Fever Dreams

I failed. Again.

Worthless! I screamed within the silent prison of my mind. *You wanted to be a pilot, fly around in a fraking cargo ship and be all cool and shit,* the mirror image of myself shouted derisively. *Awesome job, there, asshole. You got your buddy killed. Again!*

What? Another face grew from the side of my accuser. Parker's eyes were blazing red, rage lighting up the irises as if from the depths of hell itself. *You think Randel* wanted *to be saddled with you as his wingman? He was* forced *into it, just like I was. You were his* last resort, *and you got him* killed! *I trusted you, and you fraked it up! Again!*

You left us to die, my mother's voice spoke from behind me. I spun around in horror as the desiccated bodies of my parents emerged from the mists. My mother's emaciated arms struggled to hold the collapsing skeletal frame of my father, who's hands gripped at his chest as if to tear out his own heart. *We were counting on you! We waited for you to come home, and you never did! Again!*

My father's response was even worse. He didn't even look at me. He just turned away as if I didn't exist. Which I guess was right. I didn't exist anymore to them, and hadn't since I left for the navy. I swirled about around again, desperately pleading, *I didn't know! No one told me!* But they were gone, swallowed by the grayish haze. *I'm sorry! Again!*

Do you know what they did to me? Another ghost swam together from nothing. Randal's left eye was torn from its socket, bobbing up and down down his face by a thread of unidentifiable sinew like a macabre mockery of a child's toy slinky. He held up one arm, the skin flayed from the fingers and hand all the way past the wrist. Clotting blood and pus seeped from the wounds like leaking tears, dripping down his arm. *You were supposed to watch my back, Red. You weren't there. You just had to follow your heart, right? Well, look what happened because of it. You did this, Red. It's ALL YOUR FAULT! Again!*

I stared helplessly. The Wolf-Kin's shadow faded into the fog, only to be replaced by another, smaller form. A new one to these nightmares, but one I still recognized immediately. My heart pounded in my ears. *NO!!*

You were my last hope, Red. The form coalesced into a small Otter-Kin, her life-blood leaking from the gut-shot hole placed there by the armor penetrating round fired by some nameless attacker on Cranotia Station. *I trusted you! All you had to do was refuse the mission! You betrayed me! I wish I'd never even seen you! I'd be alive then! Again!*

Oh God, I whispered. *She's dead, and it's all my fault.* Only the dead ever showed up here, except for one...

The specter vanished, only to be replaced by yet another, this one more solid than the others, given he was most likely still alive. *I told you, you'd never fly again, Vulkeshson,* the hated voice gloated. *You think you got away from me by running to another system?* His countenance grew more and more distorted, becoming almost a caricature of the human form. *I'm EVERYWHERE, boy! You will never escape! Again!*

Finally, the voice I had been dreading. Knowing it was coming didn't lessen the pain and grief hearing it brought to me. Years of camaraderie had indelibly etched the timbre and cadence of his words in my mind, but instead of the cheerful boisterousness of my memories, his voice sent spikes of agony and despair into my soul.

I fought for you, Red, the ghost cried. *You were my captain, you were supposed to protect me.* The mist began to swirl around me, spreading the faceless and formless phantom into a churning miasma, assaulting my senses from all sides. *Why didn't you save me? I would have survived if you had been a better pilot! A better leader!*

I couldn't get the words out. I wanted to plead with him, tell him I was sorry. I never meant for him to be hurt. I wished with all my heart that I'd never taken that last mission. I'd *known* something was off as soon as we entered the system. It had been too *quiet*. Barely a third of the expected activity. Our small squadron of scouts had finished up the primary surveillance mission fairly quickly, but there was one last request on the list of targets. A close pass of a remote fueling station near the inner edge of the system's Kuiper belt, just short of the Weisskopff limit. Operations suspected it of being a staging area for an incursion into Confed space. The task was supposed to be optional, but I'd accepted it anyway. *Why didn't I listen to my gut feelings about that system?* I wailed.

You led us into a trap, Red, the voice continued. I turned constantly, trying to see his face one last time, even if it was only to apologize, again, as I'd done countless times before when these nightmares assaulted my waking world.

They cut off my leg, Red. I recalled the horror I'd felt when I heard his screams from the makeshift medical tent. They'd said he was going to be treated. I'd thought it meant they were going to replace the bandages around the stump of his left leg and *maybe* put a splint on the badly broken right. But no. Instead they just removed the broken one and *cauterized* both with a *plasma torch!*

And I did nothing. Intellectually, I knew there was nothing I could do, but this did little to assuage the guilt I felt just from having been nearby while it was happening. *I could have attacked them,* my shame screamed at me. *At least distracted them, even for a moment!*

Why me, Buckley's apparition screamed. *Why did it have to be me who got their legs cut off?!* I had no answer. The ambush had taken all of us completely by surprise, the first hypervelocity projectiles striking lead scouts before our sensors even detected the pulse of their firing.

Why wasn't it you? He continued to rant. *You were the Captain. You were the group leader. YOU took the mission. Why did you get to live? WHY WASN'T IT YOU WHO PAID THE PRICE?*

"AGAIN!" A new voice intruded into my consciousness. I struggled to open my eyes, but the heaviness of my eyelids was impossible to overcome. I sensed movement, but I was too engrossed in grief and terror to really care. It was strange, though. For once, I couldn't see the mist that usually surrounded me at times like this, even with my eyes closed. I tried to identify this new ghost, but their face eluded me. *Whose death am I to blame for this time?* But the answer never came. I could feel my consciousness slipping away, not from exhaustion, as was normally the case, but just a fading feeling.

"Okay," the new voice said softly. "That's the last one. You can let it go now…"

Is this what dying feels like? I wondered as my twisted reality washed away into darkness. *Is it finally my turn?*

And then there was nothing.

*****

An immeasurable time later, I swam slowly back into consciousness. *Damn, that one was rough,* I thought. Surprisingly, there was very little pain involved in waking up, this time. Usually I was severely dehydrated, covered in musk-sweat and bile, with every muscle in my body protesting the return to lucidity.

It was my Curse. One I had lived with for nearly a decade. The prison doctor back on Mars said it was a severe case of Post-Traumatic Stress Disorder, but I just called it a Curse. It started after my sentencing and incarceration, happening quite often during the first few years and tapering off as I reached the end of my ten-year sentence. It seemed to be brought on by stress and extreme emotions, but that was just a guess on my part. The doc had no answers, of course, besides learning to 'live with it'. And I did, sort of. I tried to avoid letting my emotions run too high, as that seemed to be the most obvious trigger, but this was immensely difficult.

I'd *always* had a short temper, and it seemed to get even shorter after the trial.

But eventually, I learned to wall myself off. Doing this probably made me seem cold and uncaring to people sometimes, I supposed, but... *You gotta do what ya gotta do,* I figured. *I deserve every bit of the pain it causes.*

I focused on my hearing, trying to remember where I was. I didn't open my eyes yet, as that usually caused a blinding headache. The soft whir of a ducted fan told me that, wherever I was, it had active environmental systems. I could tell from the pitch of the whirring, soft rumble of a power plant and the lack of other sounds that I was probably not planetside somewhere. *A cell? A hotel room on a station? The brig of a ship?*

As I struggled to make sense of the sensations, I heard a soft chime. I *recognized* that sound! I'd heard it recently, even! *Gina!* But then my dream-memories resurfaced. Gina was dead. Other than the *never-to-be-damned-enough* Spurgle, *everyone* who appeared in my dreams like that were dead.

I failed my crew again, I nearly sobbed. *I failed her.* I knew I was risking yet another nightmare episode of PTSD, but I couldn't help it. My emotions spilled out like a raging waterfall, uncontrolled and powerful, smashing aside the walls I had built to contain them. Tears leaked from my eyes, and a keening noise emanated from my throat.

"Red, are you having another nightmare?"

The words shocked me to my core. Well, not the words themselves, but the voice which spoke them. *Gina?!*

My eyes shot open and I lurched upright, or at least tried to. A chest strap was holding me down to one of the treatment beds. I struggled for a moment before finding and working the release for the safety belt then spinning around to look behind me.

A tired looking, but entirely *ALIVE!* Otter-Kin was looking back at me, a grim smile upon her face. I couldn't speak. The words were frozen in my mouth. I literally could not believe what my eyes were seeing. Joy fought with fear as I tried desperately to confirm that this was actually real. *Am I still dreaming?!*

"What's the matter, Red?" she said, her face becoming concerned. "You look like you've seen a ghost, or something."

I continued to stare for a few seconds before I finally regained control of my voice. "Um..." I slurred intelligently. "You could say that..." I wasn't going to go into details with her here, it was too much... Well, there was just too much packed into my feelings right then to even begin to describe my mental state at that point, so I didn't even try. I just stated the obvious. "I thought you were dead!" I whispered.

"Oh come on," she responded with a grin, waving one hand towards her stomach. "A little hole like this is gonna stop me... Ow..." She grimaced, obviously still in some pain regardless of whatever the medical pod had given her for it. "Remind me not to do that for a while, will you?"

I started to giggle uncontrollably. "Don't you dare make me laugh," the engineer glared at me. "That squat hurts like nobody's business." But even the threat of pain wasn't enough to keep the answering grin from her face. I finally managed to control the hysterical feelings of fight and relief which coursed through my veins. Gina, God *bless her,* said nothing and waited patiently for me to calm down.

I was aware that I was probably missing a significant chunk of time. My Curse was usually fairly predictable. I would fall into a waking dream or hallucination during which an indeterminate amount of time would pass. From there, I usually fell into an exhausted sleep. This generally lasted from sixteen to twenty-four hours. I was never really sure if the things I saw happened during the hallucination or afterwards when I was asleep, but it wasn't like I had any kind of setup to monitor myself and figure it out. *Well, actually,* I suddenly realized. *I really do have one now, assuming I can figure out how all this stuff here works.*

"So, how long was I out?" I asked, mildly dreading the answer. It had to be more than a day, since there was no way Gina would be active and alert like this after the injuries she'd suffered. I hadn't had an episode last less than a day and a half before, but it wasn't like I knew much about my Curse. It just "was".

"Not a clue, really," Gina told me. "I woke up about an hour ago, I think, and Joe isn't answering the comms."

I looked at the medical pod. The emergency communications relay which one of the Ox-Kin brothers had placed there was now missing. It mildly disturbed me that I couldn't remember which one of them it was, but I consoled myself with the idea that I hadn't really known them that long, yet. I tried hard to remember what had been happening right before falling into my Curse-induced dream, but as usual it was all hazy and indistinct. I seemed to remember seeing Nari onboard for some reason... But I *did* remember seeing the diagnostic screen, and how scared I'd been, knowing I had no idea how to fix up my engineer. *So, who ran the medical pod?*

"Have you seen anyone since you woke up?" I asked hesitantly.

"Oh sure," she answered. "Nari has been in and out of here, checking on us at least twice."

"Us?" I paused. "I didn't get injured, that I remember. Why did they put me in here, anyway? How long was I out?"

Gina winced, but I wasn't sure if it was because she was in pain or if she was uncomfortable with the question. I didn't have time to press her for an answer, though, as the door to the medical bay slid open at that point.

Janice, the DARC agent I remembered from the station, walked in purposefully. Behind her, the Shigothe bartender's appendages clicked and squeaked on the deck as the spider-like arthropod alien navigated her way through the relatively narrow opening. Nari quickly made it through and moved over to Gina's bed, pulling up the diagnostic screen of the pod and somehow giving the impression that she was nodding her head.

"You're almost done, Gina. I promise." She clicked a few more times, pulling up the graphical analysis I remembered seeing before. The red highlights which had dismayed me so much were almost completely gone, replaced with green and blue tracery showing blood flow and oxygen at almost normal levels. The physical damage was almost completely gone.

Again, the bartender 'nodded'. "Just another half hour or so in the activation field and the nanites will be finished patching you up. You'll be good as new."

"Thanks, Nari," Gina said gratefully, laying back down with another wince. "I've got a ton of work I need to get done."

"No rush, dear," Nari cautioned. "We're still six hours from transition, so there's plenty of time. Joe says the pylon can wait until after the jump."

"What system are we in?" I asked. I couldn't keep my mouth shut anymore. I *had* to have more information about our status. "Were we able to clear the Cranotian jump point without getting tracked?"

Since the door to the medical bay was working normally, I assumed we were no longer running the cloaking field, as the electric motors they used were some of the first things to be shut down when running under stealth. That hopefully meant we'd successfully dodged our pursuers and jumped clear, but I wanted confirmation.

Janice gave me a strange look, but stayed silent. I glanced at her for a moment, but then turned back to Nari, as it seemed she was the one willing to talk. And, to be honest, I wasn't sure I would have trusted anything the DARC agent had to say, considering the trouble she'd dragged into our already contentious situation. I wanted the information from a source I was at least semi-confident wasn't going to lie to me.

"Don't worry," she said reassuringly. "You haven't missed much. The Cranotian patrol turned away a couple hours ago. It seems someone back on the station decided they had better things to do with their time."

"Wait," I gasped. "We're still in the Cranotian system? Why?! We should have jumped several hours ago! Why did we change course? And who's piloting the ship? Joe isn't authorized to make anything but emergency maneuvers to avoid collision without authorization!" I was starting to get a bit panicked. Gina and I had spent *days* going through the ship's authorization matrixes to ensure that *no one* but the two of us would be able to command and control the ship without our knowledge and consent, not even Joe. Only the builder's overrides, which were physically hardwired into the ship's components and thus unremovable, remained. While my working relationship with the AI was improving, it wasn't to the point where I trusted him to make major course changes without authorization. The only thing Joe should have been able to do was execute the course to jump, adding in required changes for efficiency or ship safety.

My mind began to play out possible scenarios, ranging from Janice hacking our software patch, to the AI going insane and overwriting his own software with some kind of recursion loop that allowed him to ignore his core parameters.

Janice gave me that strange look again, speaking up for the first time. "We haven't made any course changes," she told me. "We can't accelerate very well with the damage, but we're still headed for the jump point. It's just taking us a bit longer, is all."

The statement brought me up short. *How is that possible?* I pondered, confused. "How much longer?" I asked, a weird realization finally emerging.

"Like she said, six hours from now," she shrugged.

"No," I clarified intensely. "How much more than the original ETA?"

"Oh! Two-point-five-six Terran Standard hours, according to your AI," at which point she gave me a look that spoke volumes. "Who assures me his estimates are accurate to within twenty-two seconds, plus or minus."

Yeah, I admitted silently. *That sounds like something Joe would say. And don't you worry, little Miss Super Spy, I had the same reaction when I found out there was an AI onboard.* But that brought up my next, more *personal* concern. "How long was I out?"

"Red," Nari interrupted before the vixen could answer. "I think you might want to have that conversation with me in private."

I looked at her with a wooden expression. I'd suddenly realized something. *Everyone,* probably even our other passengers, whom I'd yet to even lay eyes on, had borne witness to my personal Curse. I'd seen a vid clip of myself taken during an episode before, and it wasn't pretty. In fact, it was downright *embarrassing.* I looked like a spastic, animatronic manekin with a short circuit in its motor control board. I suddenly didn't want to discuss it *at all,* let alone in front of strangers. *Well, maybe Gina.* I confessed. *She at least deserves to know what she'll be dealing with, IF she sticks around after all this.*

"Give me a minute to finish up with Gina and we can discuss this in your cabin," Nari reassured me. Mortified, I just nodded my head, but the extremely short duration of the PTSD 'freak-out' still bothered me. *What was so different about it?* I wondered. *Later...deal with it later.*

As I reached the hatch, I hesitated. I looked down at my hand and could see it shiver slightly as it hovered over the hatch button. I didn't want to leave. *I thought I lost her,* I realized. *And I'm afraid that if I lose sight of her again, she'll disappear.* And I didn't want that. I wanted her beside me forever. I'd never felt that way about *anyone.*

A pointed stare from both females prodded me along, and despite my new anxieties, I stepped out into the corridor, the hatch sliding shut behind me. *Sigh...*

Ch. 32: Personal Revelations

Nari perched herself on the desk chair, which immediately reconfigured itself to something more accommodating to her physiology. This actually surprised me, as I hadn't been aware that it could do that. I hesitated for a moment before accepting her unspoken suggestion that I lay down on my bunk for this conversation. I felt like I was in an old meme, where the psychologist and the patient are having a therapy session, and the patient is laying on a chaise lounge chair, or whatever those things were called. I kept expecting her to say, "And how did that make you feel?", while jotting something down on a paper notepad.

Nari started first. "Before I ask you *my* questions, I want to provide you with the answer to your question." I'm sure I looked pensive, as she quickly moved to reassure me. "You were delirious for approximately fifteen minutes, and then unconscious for another four hours after that."

I contemplated that answer. It was unprecedented in my experience. Normally I lost over a day and a half, at the very least. Even with the medical care offered to prisoners at Olympus Mons Disciplinary Barracks, which was little enough I supposed, the duration had never been less than thirty-seven hours. And it wasn't like this was a broken bone. Mere medical nanites, no matter how advanced compared to human technology, wouldn't be able to fix this kind of thing. It was all mental.

"Now," she continued gently. "I need to ask you a couple questions. I promise they are relevant. Are you ready?" I nodded silently.

"Are you aware of ever having been neurologically enhanced, or 'chipped'?"

"No," I replied immediately. While some experimentation had been done a couple hundred years ago to try enhancing a soldier's reactions and mental processing, the results had been disappointing, resulting in severe neurological impairment when the chip malfunctioned. Efforts to develop them further had been abandoned over a century ago.

The Snakes, of course, had succeeded where humanity had failed. It was more necessary for them, of course. With only the short appendages on their long torsos that functioned as the race's "hands", they were at a distinct disadvantage in terms of hand to hand combat with longer-limbed species. To compensate, they'd quickly developed a complex series of bioimplants which served as transmitters and interfaces for controlling "prosthetic" arms, eventually working up to entire combat suits of powered armor which they used to great effectiveness.

I began to feel sick, as I guessed where she was going with this line of questioning. Had the damn Snakes somehow implanted some kind of time-bomb in my brain, hoping I would go mad once I returned home?

"Are you saying the Curse isn't PTSD?"

"Not even something like a tracking beacon, or a bio-monitor?" she persisted.

"So the Snakes did this to me?" I asked, my anger growing. I was absolutely furious at the possibility. "It's not all in my head?!"

Her eyes became sad, and again I was utterly confounded by her abilities. *How does an arachni-form being manage to project facial expressions? I swear, her eyes look sad, but they haven't actually moved.* But that was less of a punch to the gut than her next words.

"No, it's not all in your head. Or, I should say, it's *mostly* not in your *brain*."

I stared blankly. My anger had vanished. A certain level of fear had replaced it. "They chipped me?" I gasped. "Those dirty, fraking, treacherous, *Snakes!* What did they put in there?"

"I'm sorry to say this, but the array is definitely *not* Imperial technology. It even had a human-style serial number engraved on one of the subcomponents," she spoke definitively.

I didn't want to believe her, but I couldn't imagine her saying something like that without some way to prove it. "Navy, then?" I forced out. "They always have you take those weird inoculations when you join. Could they have done this all the way back then?"

Her cephalothorax bobbed side-to-side in a close approximation of a shaken head. "I doubt it," she replied. "From the growth and scar tissue around the array, I sincerely doubt it is older than perhaps fourteen of your years ago. Perhaps as new as eight years, if you had several instances of extreme head trauma during that time, but your external scarring doesn't support that. My best guess is ten to twelve years."

That placed it squarely in the timeframe of my captivity as a prisoner of war, plus a year or so afterwards. I forced myself to think back to that time. "Are you *sure* it's not Snake tech? I wouldn't put it past them to do something like this."

"They don't use silicon as a semiconductor," she explained. "After all, the element you call 'boron', which is combined with your 'silicon' to make it into a semiconductor, is a toxic allergen to a significant portion of their population. Having it in their bloodstream would be invariably fatal to those affected. Trust me, they don't even *experiment* with it except in the most controlled environment possible. It would be like you carrying around a bottle of mercury in a thin-walled flask to use as a hammer. It just isn't done."

Back to the Navy again? I worried. "I went through a lot of psych evaluations after the Armistice, when we finally got traded back to the Confed, but I never had any surgeries done. Lots of PT, mind you, but other than malnutrition and a few contusions, I was relatively healthy." The blatant reminder of the difference in outcome between myself and my RIO again hit me like a sledgehammer to the back of the head. But, I wondered, *was I actually NOT the lucky one?*

"I examined your body for scar patterns, searching for a point of entry," Nari admitted, as if it were something inappropriate for her to do. I couldn't figure out why that would be a problem until I realized she had probably looked at my *whole* body. The thought *squicked* my brain for a second, before I dismissed it entirely. She was effectively my doctor at this point, I realized. *But that's another thing,* I wondered. *How does an alien bartender know this much about Terran biology, not to mention Serpentian biochemistry on top of that? Did Joe help her out, somehow?* I could see him having a bunch of that kind of data, normally, but he'd as much as admitted that he did *not* possess enough of a database to be able to effectively guide the medical pod in Gina's case. And something like this would be an order of magnitude more complicated than something as straightforward as a gunshot wound.

"And?" I prompted impatiently. I was already delving through my memories for *anything* while I was in active service where I had a block of time completely missing, but I was coming up blank.

"Almost all of your surface scarring coincides with subdermal scarring, which I take to be evidence of trauma sustained by injury," she responded clinically. "There are two exceptions, both surgical in nature, and both recent enough to have occurred after childhood. One is on your lower-front abdomen, three units above the pelvis and six units to the right of centerline, and one is on the back of your neck, to the left of your forth and fifth cervical vertebrae. I have already discounted the one on your abdomen, but I'm still curious as to the reason. I could detect no purpose for the surgery."

I was a bit surprised that the first one could still be detected. I mean, it was *old,* old. As in, back when I was a teenager, old. It made me wonder what she considered 'after childhood', to be honest, but the answer was simple and straightforward. It was an appendectomy scar.

One of the main genetic differences between pure humans and Kin was a kind of genetic 'regression' in the specific chromosome pairs. It was a very recent discovery, of course, as Kin had only within the last two generations been allowed to reproduce on their own.

No pure human had manifested an appendix in over four hundred years. It was considered to be part of their 'naturally evolved' condition, deliberately ignoring the genetic modification the entire race had forced on itself to defend against the Shigothe plague, not to mention the continued efforts to repair the damage caused by the viral cure.

But Kin were derived from much *older* base pairs. They still retained some of the original human genes that told the body to create such things as a vermiform appendix, or wisdom teeth. Of course, no *manufactured* Kin was ever produced with such abnormalities. When one was detected during gestation, the specimen was invariably discarded as defective. It was only now that 'natural' gestation was allowed that these vestigial organs reappeared in the adult population. I'd not had to suffer from budding wisdom teeth in my younger years, but I'd had the appendix removed before joining the military as it was one of the required medical prerequisites.

I knew what the second scar was, as well. I hadn't even thought about it, nor had I been thinking clearly a few moments ago when she asked about tracking beacons to remember, but now that it was pointed out to me, I recalled *exactly* what it was. And it made me both angry and terrified. Vacillating wildly between terror and rage, I explained the purpose of that particular scar.

"They said it was a location tracker," I whispered. "It was supposed to broadcast a signal that was monitored by the prison's sensors to show where I was. As if I could actually get anywhere in that airless hellscape." I scoffed at the idea. The disciplinary barracks were situated on the far side of the planet from the rest of the Martian 'civilian' infrastructure. While technically not 'airless', there was no more than a trace of oxygen in the native atmosphere, meaning escape on foot without a prohibitive amount of breathing apparatus was impossible. The signal was supposed to disable any vehicles present on the military base which detected the short range transmission, ostensibly to prevent their use for escape purposes. It was a plausible explanation, honestly, which is why I didn't particularly care when the procedure was done. They'd also supposedly removed it when I was released, though.

That wasn't the worst news, I learned, as she continued gently. "The main chip was recording your brain activity, modifying it, and then reintroducing the modified recording back into the synaptic tissue of your visual and auditory cortexes through two secondary interfaces. I'm not certain of how it was creating anything realistic with this method, but it was certainly disruptive, which was, I suspect, its primary purpose," she concluded sympathetically. "Your 'Curse', as you described it, was deliberately inflicted upon you."

"I *felt* the cut they made!" I gasped. "It hurt, and by that I mean, it hurt a *lot!* They didn't even bother using anesthetic that time, just sliced and pulled, then slapped a smart-patch on it, right before they loaded me into the skimmer heading for the shuttle." I looked at Nari in desperation.

Nari 'shook her head' again, grief seeming to pour from her alien face. "I was unable to detect any new surgical scarring, or even evidence of anything resembling such on the site that is more recent than a decade, at least. I'm not sure of the actual method, but I expect they used some form of neural stimulator to simulate the pain of the cut and removal. The lack of anesthetic and antibiotic measures, combined with the smart-patch support this hypothesis."

I was stunned. All this time, I'd been carrying this 'Curse' with me, always thinking it was a result of PTSD. Come to find out, the 'Curse' was caused by an *implant*, put in by the Confed *Navy? How much more of this will I have to take?!* I swore. What possible gain would the *Navy* have from something, which in the end result, was just so *petty?*

And there was my answer. I *could*, actually, name one party to the whole sordid tale which I was certain was capable of such levels of *small-minded, useless retaliation.*

Lieutenant Commander Cartwright Andrew Alexander Spurgle-Saint-John, fourth of his name... Now *there* was someone with both the means and vindictiveness to set something like this up. I knew he had enough funds to bribe a single prison doctor, as he'd bragged constantly of his family's prominence in the major shipping companies. I'd assumed he'd either decided to lay low or had *actually* been prosecuted for his misdeeds when I never received any gloating missives or targeted mistreatment at the prison. He was, after all, never one to hold back in letting his targets know *exactly* who was sending the message, regardless of how easy it would be to conceal. I was certain, now, of the source of my decades long torture. But what could I *do* about it?

"Can you take it out?" I begged. Nari had worked miracles with Gina, healing her up in hours what would have taken *days* with a human surgical team. But she again signaled a negative.

"I'm sorry," she said gently. "It is more than just a single chip. The array has links to separate modules between the left and right parietal lobes as well as the temporal lobes, affecting sight, sound, physical sensation and memory, with the additional ability to distort the perception of time. It would take *much* better equipment that I have here to remove it completely, and even then, I fear that doing so would irreparably damage parts of your parietal lobes. It could severely inhibit your ability to understand spoken and written words, much like the symptoms of Wernicke's aphasia."

I had no clue what that meant, but it sounded bad. *Really* bad.

"What I can do for now, and have already done," she continued confidently. "Is to shut down the main control processor of the array. I cannot shut it completely down without physically accessing the array, which as I mentioned has extremely high risk, but the array as it sits now will no longer function as designed."

My breath hitched in a twitch of disbelief. "No more Curse?"

"No more curse," she affirmed. "However, there is one primary function I was unable to affect. The array *did* actually contain a transmitter like the one you described, and it is still broadcasting. Not at the same signal strength it originally had, I assure you, but enough to be detectable within a few dozen units. If we come to a place that has more extensive equipment, I might be able to reduce that even further. In the meantime, I suggest a metallic helmet, if you wish to disable its secondary function."

"How many do you mean by 'a few dozen'?" I asked quizzically. "And what was the old range?"

"With the main processor functioning, and depending on the sensitivity of the receiver, of course," she replied. "Anywhere from sixty to six-hundred units. With it disabled? An order of magnitude less. Beyond that, the signal would be indistinguishable from normal background noise in any inhabited zone, as it utilizes a very commonly used frequency."

I struggled to remember what her species used for distance measurement, but came up short. All I knew was it was something close to the old human 'imperial' measurement called inches, which was itself close to the distance from the tip of a human's index finger to the first knuckle. This matched closely to the distances she'd used to describe my appendectomy scar, so I went with it. A hundred 'units' was a little more than two and a half meters. Two thirds of that was right at one and a half meters. Ten times that was going to be... *Fifteen meters? A little more?* So the old detectable range was somewhere between those two. Plenty close enough, I figured, for a dock sensor to pick up, meaning any time I walked through a dock or anywhere else that used such sensors, I was getting detected, and flagged, as an escaped criminal.

"Oh squat!" I suddenly exclaimed. *"THAT'S* why I got flagged so quickly at the station!"

"I'm sorry?" Nari asked, momentarily confused at my outburst.

"When I first arrived," I explained excitedly. "You told me there was an alert which went out to the whole station saying I was bad news. At first I thought the bank teller screwed me over because I was *human!*

"But what if they have the same scanners that Confed stations do? They'd see the signal code and immediately think I was an escaped criminal! Back home, station security, which gets regular updates from the Navy, would look at the database and see that I was recently released and ignore it. But I seriously doubt the Navy is on good terms with First Ceres, since they're a credit union, not a regular bank that plays the usual games with the bureaucracy. So they don't get updates, and have to rely on just seeing that code on their sensors."

I kind of ran away with the subject, but Nari apparently thought it was therapeutic and let me ramble on. It was rather cathartic, I had to admit. I eventually wound down after describing several potential, and eminently reasonable excuses for the local FCSICU branch flagging my account and alerting the station administration.

"That sounds very plausible," she admitted ruefully when I finally ran out of breath. "Is there any other good news you'd like to share with me?"

"Oh yeah," I added sheepishly. "Even a *thousand* units would be too short to mean I risk compromising the ship's cloaking field just by existing."

"Wait," she started. "What cloaking field?"

Oops! I tore up out of that bunk like my fur was on fire. "Sorry," I called back as I exited the cabin hurriedly. "Said too much!"

"But…"

I   was   already   gone.

Ch. 33: Meeting the Guests

The vixen from DARC was waiting just outside my cabin when I rushed out, and I very nearly bowled her over in my haste. Only a quick grab stopped her from slamming into the opposite bulkhead.

"Oof! Sorry about that!" I called as I rushed towards the bridge.

"Wait!" she cried as I pushed past. "You need to know something about your pass..." She was too late, I was already at the bridge hatch and slapped the pad to open it up. Inside were two individuals which I instantly identified as being the 'guests' which Janice had hired me to transport, mostly because I had never seen them before. But that's not what brought me to a screeching halt.

The one closest to the hatch locked his eyes on me aggressively as the hatch slid open, his narrow face swinging to point at me like a gun turret, ready to fire. He was *huge*, nearly as tall as the Ox-Kin brothers, and had powerful-looking shoulders and arms, even if he was lacking in the same overwhelming abundance of upper body strength that defined the two crewmen. His legs, however, might have made up the difference. Short, squat, but powerful thighs dominated his hips, transitioning into a pair of unnaturally long lower legs which narrowed to equally over-long metatarsals, or 'foot bones', with a protruding ankle bone obviously evolved to increase leverage for the taut tendons displayed along the back of the lower leg. Claws poked out of a pair of armored digitigrade foot coverings. A thick, tapering tail ran directly down from the guy's back. Part of the tail looked to be nearly immobile from the massive bands of muscle which ringed the base, but I could tell that getting whipped with the tapered end wouldn't end well. *Probably pairs well with his ability to spring forward,* I estimated.

The second, smaller individual was barely visible from behind, as they were *sitting in my chair,* I fumed, but from the long, mobile ears visible above the backrest, I was dead certain it was another of the same species. Joe's avatar was hovering above his little plinth, his face turned towards the command chair, and I could tell just from looking that he was 'happy as he could be' with whoever was sitting there. While I didn't know who the newcomers were as individuals, it was immediately apparent as to what *species* they were.

Roos. Well, more exactly, their species was named *"`Mlrtchn-ee"*, as Joe had informed me more than once. Again, I wasn't about to try my hand at pronouncing such a word with my limited skills, the closest I had ever come was something like "Millurch-nee", but I had finally learned to at least *hear* the weird combinations of consonants which apparently comprised most of the Roo language.

I stopped abruptly halfway through the hatchway, my thoughts stumbling sideways. I'd suffered through a ton of twists and revelations in the last few days, and whatever moral high ground I'd been sure of previously was becoming precarious indeed. The recent physical and emotional shocks of the last few hours didn't help either. *Another attempt to take my ship from me, I bet,* I almost sighed in defeat. *Is this some of the missing crew of the Rickth Stand Rathens whatever-the-hell name the Camel used to be called?*

Screw it, I'm done, I realized. *If they really want to take this ship, they're probably going to be able to do it pretty easily. Joe's not going to fight them about it, that's for sure. And if Gina and I even* try *to hurt these guys, he'll probably kill us.*

I stared back at the obviously male Roo, and what I saw didn't fill me with a great deal of confidence. *I really doubt I could take this guy, anyway,* I figured. *Maybe Little Miss Super-Spy, with her fancy training, but me? Not a chance. He outweighs me by at least double, and is probably faster, too.* I really didn't like the look he was giving me either, as if he already had a plan to kill everyone on the bridge. His stance screamed *'bodyguard'* or *'special forces'*.

"...engers." Janice finished lamely, finally catching up to me at the hatch. I just stood there, unamused, but not making any threatening moves. I looked at her with a deadpan expression. "Care to make the introductions?" I said finally after letting her stew uncomfortably for a few seconds.

Janice at least had the courtesy to look embarrassed. She visibly gathered herself and began to speak, gesturing towards the individuals on the bridge.

"Lieutenant Rodrick Vulkeshson, I'd like to introduce you to your passengers," she started, pointing at the large guy first. "This is Strike-Commander *Kjr'uu Psschh'aa*."

'Kaj-ruu Pashaah', I tried silently, nodding in acknowledgement. *Yay! Finally, a name I can actually pronounce! Well, maybe. I might end up just calling him 'Kaiju'.* "*Former* Lieutenant, actually, and my friends call me 'Red'." I clarified politely. The soldier stared back at me, expressionless.

"Bodyguard, or special forces?" I guessed, looking at him squarely in the eyes, refusing to flinch, but trying hard not to look aggressive either. While his stance didn't change, a slight crinkle around his eyes betrayed a hint of humor.

"Both," he chuffed clearly, his voice perfectly translated by my earbug thanks to the extensive practice it had undergone dealing with Joe's insistence on using his creator's tongue.

"Ah," I nodded ruefully. "You have my condolences, then. I've had friends who had that role before. It's never easy.

"And that makes *you* someone important." I slewed my eyes to the left, taking in the second passenger who had twisted around in the seat to peer over the backrest like a frightened toddler. I didn't immediately take this to mean she was actually immature or *afraid*, though, even if her stature and presence gave off a much younger vibe than that of her giant protector. As I considered her strangely timid posture, I realized that her position, while not projecting much in the way of command presence, was perfectly situated to give her body the most cover against an attack while still allowing her to see. *An* experienced *protectee, then,* I recognized.

Janice seemed a bit taken aback by my lack of response. I guessed she thought I would be either frightened or angry, and was all set to begin a counter-argument to my anticipated objections. I couldn't really blame her for expecting those reactions, given how I spoke to her back on the station, but after the emotional rollercoaster ride I'd just gone through with Nari, Gina's injury, and the wild escape from the station, my give-a-damn tank was running on fumes. There was just nothing left. I finally looked back at Janice expectantly, and she jumped at the realization that we were all waiting on her.

"Ah," she stuttered formally, even giving a small bow in the younger Roo's direction. "M-may I make known to you *EE'Saa Jlyts'aa Lnrl'uu 'ne'Mlrtchn-ee.*"

Wow, that's a mouthful! There was a 'J' sound in there somewhere, so I figured I was going to end up calling her 'Jill' for a nickname. The rest was the usual mishmash of consonants I'd become used to hearing, except... *That's weird! I've never heard Joe put the vowel sound in the front, before. I wonder what that means.* My brain stuttered for a moment in confusion. *Wait, I actually recognize two of those words.* I looked over at Joe for confirmation. "Does that mean she's related to...?"

The avatar looked back smugly. "Yes, she is directly descended from *that Lnrl'uu.*" he confirmed. Joe's insistence on keeping to his own language also extended to the proper names for stellar phenomena, and just like humans were wont to do, the Roos often named things after their discoverers. Thus, what I called a system's Weisskopff limit, he would refer to as the *Lnrl'uu* threshold.

"Wow," I admitted, honestly impressed. "It's not every day you get to meet someone related to scientific royalty! But why does her name end with the same name as the species? And what's with the vowel in front? Never heard that from you before."

The AI's smugness increased almost exponentially. ::That would be because she is *actual* royalty. *EE'Saa* is roughly translated as 'Crown Princess', in Terran Common. The prefix *'ne* in front of `*Mlrtchn-ee* means '*of*'.::

"What," I asked, slightly confused. "Of the country?"

::No,:: he corrected. ::The worlds. *All* of the `*Mlrtchn-ee* worlds, to be specific, and by extension, the entire interstellar empire… such as it remains,:: he finished sadly.

"Well, that opens a whole factory of tinned worms, doesn't it?" I couldn't keep myself from saying. "What's she doing here?"

"It's a long story," Janice grimaced, face-palming at my social gaffe. *Meh,* I shrugged. *What did she expect?* I was no diplomat, that was self-evident.

*****

She wasn't kidding, I discovered nearly two hours later. As the rest of my crew learned about the conversation and tried to listen in, I finally suggested that we adjourn to the galley as it was the only compartment on the ship where we could all sit down that still had power. Surprisingly, considering how cagey Janice had been earlier about her passengers, neither of the Roos seemed to have any issues about telling their convoluted tale.

Some of it, of course, I was already aware of. The opening conflict with the Vespidae was the most disturbing to Nari and Ox-Kin the brothers, and Gina and I still shuddered at the lurid recordings the AI brought up on the wall display which his avatar attended the meeting from. I was also tangentially aware of the fact of, if not the reason for, the abandonment of the CMV Camel, and how it ended up in a scrap yard on Cranotia.

The explanation turned out to be both simple and complex at the same time. As I'd expected, the existence of this kind of ship and its capabilities was supposed to be 'top secret', burn-after-reading confidential stuff. As the crew were heading into another species' territory, they'd transferred to a much smaller ship which had been stored in the cargo bay for most of the trip, leaving the powered down and sealed ship hidden on a lonely asteroid in a completely uninhabited system, or so they thought. As a measure of safety for the AI, Joe had been deactivated and his core stored to prevent insanity, apparently a real risk for the digital being if left alone for too long.

It was pure bad luck that the ship had been stumbled upon by the mining crew. And even that wouldn't have happened if they'd returned as scheduled. But the crew had vanished. Six months had turned into over a year, and when `Mlrtchn-ee agents had reported the ship showing up as salvage in a Cranotian scrapyard, their leadership had feared the worst.

"Do you mind if I just call you Princess 'Jill'? There's no way I'm going to be able to pronounce your name right." Her eyes narrowed a bit, but she didn't say anything. I figured it was probably a bit insulting, but I wasn't here to play nursemaid.

"So why send a Princess?" I asked. "Sorry to be blunt, but you guys don't seem to be doing any kind of diplomatic mission here." I waved over at Kaj-ruu, who still hovered protectively over his smaller charge. "Spec-Ops, sure. Even an idiot can see why you'd send *him*. But why risk the chain of command of an entire empire? Seems kind of stupid to me."

"Peace, Kjr'uu Psschh'aa," the small figure snapped when her guardian began to bristle aggressively at the perceived insult. "He's right. From a limited perspective, and without knowing the extent of our situation, it does indeed *seem* unwise to send someone of my political stature on a mission like this."

"I'm glad you finally realize this, Your Highness," the Roo growled back. "I will see about arranging transport back behind the Veil. A *more appropriate* team can then be assembled and dispatched."

The girl's eyes narrowed dangerously. "I said from '*a limited perspective*', Kjr'uu. You *know* the situation at home. We are running out of *time!* Any team we put together would have to start from scratch, and the funds are *just not there*, anymore. I am the *only* individual with the resources and *authorization* to act independently."

"Your duty to the crown succession…" he started stubbornly.

"DAMN my duties to the crown!" she roared back. "What use is a crown? *What advantage* does it give my people? What *purpose* is there in ruling a future empire with no children in it, watching as it withers away?"

"Your Highness," he tried again, glancing at the rest of us gathered around the table. He was obviously reticent about revealing weaknesses in front of potential enemies. "These *aliens* have no reason to help us. Besides, our problems are not insurmountable. Our scientists are working hard on potential solutions as we speak."

"That's a bunch of *squat*, and you know it," she shot back. "I read the same reports you did, and barring an *actual* miracle, they are *years* away from a long term solution, *at best!"*

"No," she continued to rant. "The only use *my crown* has is the resources and authority it commands, the *personal* resources *I* command. My people are *dying out*, and I *refuse* to sit idly by while that happens. I *will* not! And these *aliens,* as you call them, *do* have a reason to help us. Because I will *pay* them for it!"

I had to admit, that last bit had gotten the attention of my inner greed-monkey. I wasn't adverse to a bit of charity, here and there, but there were limits to what I was willing to do for anyone but those individuals I considered family, and of those currently actually *alive*, that group was limited to two. Admittedly, that was double what it had been only a few weeks ago, but still. *Limited.*

Besides, in order to gain the freedom of owning my own ship, earning lots of cash was *quite* high on my to-do list.

And the amount of resources commanded by an actual, honest to goodness *princess* had the potential to be quite a lot of cash indeed! I returned my attention back to the argument with a new perspective.

"...wasted on unreliable, and *untrusted,* criminals!" the Strike-Leader bellowed.

"Okay, that's enough of that," I interjected loudly to their surprise. "This is obviously a long-standing argument between you two, and while I don't know what is slowly killing off the Roos on your homeworld, I don't think that airing your dirty laundry in front of all of us is going to be very productive. So let's focus on 'now'. We can worry about 'later' when it becomes relevant." The pair stared distrustfully at me for a few moments before resuming their argument, albeit much quieter this time.

I sighed after a few moments of being ignored, then turned towards the DARC agent. "Janice, this is kind of your show. *You* contracted me to get your passengers off the station. If these two have any *requests,*" I emphasized. "They can present them through *you*. That way I don't have to play referee over the domestic squabble over there." The vixen started to look a bit guilty, and I wondered what new complication was about to rear its ugly little head.

"Actually, *they* didn't hire me to get them off the station. I was merely a go-between because of *you*."

My eyebrows furrowed in confusion. "Me, personally?"

"Not really you in particular," she clarified. "It was just because you were the one with this ship."

Ah, I thought to myself ruefully. *They wanted their ship back, of course.* But that didn't quite make sense. If *they* weren't the ones who contracted her for help, who *did*? *Wait...*

"Goose?" I guessed quietly. The message from him *had* primed me to accept the mission from her, but I couldn't imagine how he would have gotten involved. The only time he'd been in the system lately was when he dropped me a couple months ago. Even the message he sent, Joe had finally determined, had originated from another star cluster.

"Well, *through* him, yes," she quibbled. "But the primary contact was on the station. She got word to Mongoose, who got word to me. I was already here on other business, of course." She shrugged slightly, and I knew that trying to ask about that other business was a lost cause.

"So," I whispered. "Who's running the show, then? Are we waiting for instructions or something?"

"I don't know," she shrugged again. "Ask her."

"Ask who?"

She looked at me as if I had two heads or something. It suddenly dawned on me.

Janice had said, *"Ask her"*, meaning the person was already on the ship. The '*her*' part meant that person was female, which ruled out Joe, as well as Mutt and Jeff, the Ox-Kin loaders, not that I'd really considered them anyways. I *knew* it wasn't Gina, and from our earlier conversation, it wasn't Princess Jill or her bodyguard. That only left one being.

"Nari?" I asked incredulously in a hoarse whisper.

"Yes, Red?" the arachni-form bartender answered immediately, deftly settling herself in the seat next to me.

I admit it, I flinched. I *thought* I'd been quiet, but once again, I was surprised at her ability to surprise me. *Damn,* I thought. *I really need to stop underestimating her!*

"*You're* the primary?" I finally blurted out. "But, *how?* And *why?* Who *are* you, *really?*"

She somehow gave me a look like a school teacher catching an unruly student cheating on a test. I shook my head to clear my confusion. "Never mind. Not my business. I guess." I blurted.

Her look softened. "As you might imagine, that last bit is a *very* long story," she said, waving away the gaffe with an appendage. "Suffice to say, I am well connected with a number of intelligence gathering operations and became aware of the situation. Deeming them worthy, I offered my assistance."

"Deeming them worthy?" Gina asked, stepping close and taking the seat across from Janice on the long narrow table. "Isn't that a bit presumptuous?"

"Much as I deemed *you* worthy of assistance, dear," the Shigothe replied a bit smugly. Gina quickly conceded the point.

"So, you're just hanging out, playing 'Robin Hood the Super-Spy', and running a bar in your spare time?" I asked, unable to hold in my incredulity.

"I am, and have been, many things over the years, one of them being a bartender for nearly two decades," she answered calmly. "I'm quite surprised you even *know* of the name 'Robin Hood', given your years."

"I read it somewhere, I think," I waved it off as unimportant. A bartender was actually a *great* cover for a surveillance asset, really, so her choice wasn't *too* much of a surprise.

"That reminds me," Gina interjected again. "Not that I'm ungrateful, or anything. Seriously, you saved my life, and I'm in your debt for that. But how is it that you came to be so good at Terran physiology? I'm a mostly-trained Navy medic, and even *I* would have trouble doing what you did, regardless of how amazing those Roo nanites are."

I perked up at the question. I was curious, too. Not just about her medical knowledge, but her amazing ability to mimic Terran body language, as well.

Nari replied in a humorous tone. "I was once a xenobiologist, focusing on human physiology. Your structure and biochemistry are very similar, so it wasn't much of a stretch to figure out."

I hadn't realized that the Shigothe would still be interested in Terrans after over five hundred years. I couldn't imagine why someone would spend so much time learning about a species your race didn't really interact with much anymore. But then, something strange occurred to me. *She just said she spent two decades as a bartender, and she's obviously trained extensively in surveillance and intelligence operations. When did she have* time *to study human physiology? And Serpentian biochemistry! Not to mention Terran psychology and cerebral dynamics!*

"My God," I exclaimed. "That's a lot of jobs to learn. It must have taken you several *decades!* Just how old are you?!"

"You know better than to ask a Lady that," Gina scolded.

I winced, but the Shigothe 'bartender' just laughed brightly.

"When you've been around for four and a half centuries as I have, you tend to collect a lot of professions, if only out of sheer boredom. You youngsters have no idea!"

This unbelievable statement came at a lull in the argument at the other end of the table, and was clearly heard by everyone in the room. Silence reigned, and *every single head* immediately turned our way, expressions of shock and surprise on their faces.

"Four and a..." I blurted, desperately doing the math in my head. "But that means you were around during the Founding of the Human Confederation! The Reconstruction! And the collapse of the Shigothe Protectorate! No wonder you studied human physiology!"

"No," Nari sighed after a few moments, her body almost visibly deflating as it went from projecting mirth to projecting a deep, dark sorrow. "That is not why I studied humans. I'm so very, very sorry."

"Why are you sorry?" Gina asked gently. "I'm not sorry you did. I wouldn't be alive otherwise."

"I'm sorry because Red's timeline is off," she whispered, despair pouring from her body language. "Shigothe years are nearly twice as long as human ones. I was not hatched during the Reconstruction or the Collapse."

A chill ran down my spine as I realized what was coming.

"Red, I once told you once that I owed a long-standing debt to your kind. It is, sadly, not one born of gratitude, but of remorse and regret. I was *there*, at the Beginning of the End, when we foolishly thought to curb the upstart race called 'humans'. It was *there* that I studied human physiology, using the prisoners and bodies collected during the first attacks as my specimens." She looked at the rest of us, subtly including every Terran in the room in her gaze, a miasma of grief pouring from her like flood.

"*I was there,* when the Shigothe Subjugation Fleet deployed a bio-weapon which killed a fifth of the humans on the planet they called 'Earth'. *I was part of the group* which mistook a species-wide genetic bottleneck for a mere random individual mutation. *I was the one* who designed the telomeres which governed the lifespan of the plague we released upon your homeworld. *I* failed to test the virus beyond a single generation against a human specimen, or to realize that it would immediately mutate into something even more virulent, indirectly causing two dozen generations of human children to never be born. I am responsible for the deaths of *trillions* of unborn, across dozens of worlds…"

"And it is a debt which I can *never* repay."

Ch. 34: A Debt of Restitution

'She seemed so nice, though!', was a pithy and utterly inappropriate response to the absolute horror I felt upon learning of Nari's disturbing past. My mind swirled with feelings of confusion and betrayal. *'It was war, she was just following orders'* and *'How could she have known'* fought back and forth with *'How could she have NOT known'*. I knew, intellectually, that it no longer mattered. That particular battle had ended long before I was born, before even my *SPECIES* was created in the horrific aftermath of the first series of conflicts between humans and Shigothe.

It was disgusting to imagine someone doing such a thing, but I knew that fault did not lay with her alone. The human scientists of the time were just as culpable in their ineptitude. No thought was given to the long-term effects of a slapped-together rhinovirus with a vector a hundred times more infectious than the plague it was designed to counter. Again, just like Nari, they could argue they were *just following orders*, their political leaders desperate to produce a solution to the slowly spreading plague which crept across the planet, seemingly unstoppable, ignoring all attempts at treatment or mitigation.

It was hard to find detailed records of the battle's immediate aftermath, but records of the Shigothe plague and the human counter-virus had been widely disseminated over the centuries since. Scandal after scandal rocked the human political structure as those records were used as ammunition by one faction against the other, trying to blame them for the colossal mistake embedded in the *cure* which accomplished a more effective annihilation of the human population than the original plague itself.

The original virus, it was finally discovered, was only designed to last for two weeks, perhaps three based on what they knew of human biology, after which its telomeres would be depleted, and the plague would burn itself out. Two waves of infection, perhaps four weeks in duration, if confined to the planetary population. The Shigothe scientists estimated that at most, one in one-hundred would become infected over the course of the entire pandemic. It was meant to create fear and chaos, true, but it was not intended to wipe out humanity. But the virus didn't remain as it was created.

A peculiarity of the human genome, thought to be a result of a genetic bottleneck from over fifty thousand years ago, allowed the virus to adapt itself more fully to its environment by exploiting a gap in how the the humans' autoimmune response was evolved to function. Like the ancient disease called AIDS, it hijacked the immune response itself to propagate, utterly ignoring the body's attempts to fight it.

The *cure* was designed to *replace* a single chromosome pair, which in turn would replace the biochemical autoimmune response normally present with one that closed that gap, eliminating the plague's ability to reproduce. What hadn't been known, or even tested for, was the effect such a change would have on meiosis during oocyte maturation, a critical stage of human reproduction, causing the meiosis to fail to pause as intended while the oocyte was ovulated. Long story short, it caused a woman's ova, or 'egg' as it was sometimes called, to mature improperly prior to fertilization. Even when forcibly fertilized in vitro, the results were poor, mostly resulting in miscarriage or severe mutation of the fetus.

It was a completely unknown function of the replaced chromosome pair, and the first signs of trouble didn't show up until *months* after the counter-virus was released. The results were, as one could imagine, catastrophic to human birth rates. Less than one in six fetuses were even brought to term, and many of those were hopelessly deformed.

Who was to blame? I thought dismally. *Everybody. Nobody.* It was one of those things that defied definition. A string of unintended consequences that spawned from a comically deranged series of events, utterly and completely predictable in hindsight, but not even *considered* by either party at the time, as the possibility was so remote as to be laughable. *What successful starfaring species would ever NOT know everything about their own genetics,* combined with, *in what possible way could even a designed virus, that didn't even use DNA, successfully mutate and propagate using the* autoimmune *response of all things?*

I couldn't blame Nari for the mistake, really. What she designed should have worked as intended, and while it was a horrific weapon, it was not designed as one intended to end the species. *No,* I thought. *That was the fault of the* human *scientists.* But they wouldn't have had to even try if her plague had never been released.

As I finally fell into tortured sleep, I realized one thing that was more important than anything else. Regardless of whether or not Nari carried any *blame* for the near elimination of the human race, she felt *responsible* for it. While blame had been *assigned*, and later thrown about like party favors, not once had I ever heard of *any* human scientist or political leader having accepted *responsibility* for the tragedy. They all *shed* responsibility like dead skin, flakes of it strewn into the corners of humanity's dustbin.

And that, I decided. *Makes all the difference.*

*****

"Red," Gina called softly over the audio channel. "Can I talk to you?"

"Sure," I sighed. I was still coping with the shocking revelations of the previous day, but I figured that hiding in my cabin wasn't going to improve things anymore. Solitude wasn't the answer, no matter how much my hindbrain might argue. I needed to talk to someone. *Just not Nari, yet.*

When the door chimed, I was at least dressed enough to be considered 'decent', so I sent the unlock command. The door slid open and Gina stepped hesitantly inside. I could guess what was bothering her, but I wasn't sure what I could do about it. She'd known Nari even longer than I, and had trusted her implicitly. Gina had, more than once, explicitly called her a *close friend*. I couldn't imagine how much more betrayed she felt than I, and I was ready to at least offer my condolence and understanding, no matter how little it might help.

But I was wrong.

"Did you get any sleep?" I asked.

She grunted. "Eventually, you?"

"Ish," I answered, waggling my hand.

"I never said 'thank you', for saving my life," she began hesitantly, hovering in the doorway.

"You would have done the same," I reassured her, waving her in. "Probably would have done a better job at it, too," I couldn't help but add, the tips of my ears growing warm in embarrassment. I looked away in shame. I knew I was breaking protocol when I did it. The safety of the ship always came first. *But I'd do it again in a heartbeat, for her.*

"I think we should help the Roos," she said once she settled onto the edge of the chair.

"Huh?" I responded intelligently. That was *not* the direction I'd expected this conversation to go.

"I was talking with her," she continued. "She said the Roo are having some of the same kinds of problems with gestation that we did after the Shigothe War."

"She, who?" I asked, still somewhat confused on just which 'she' Gina was talking about.

"You know, Esaa Jillitza-whatever," she mangled, shrugging. "I'm no better than you in pronouncing their language, you know."

"Oh, you mean Princess Jill," I smirked. "What does she want?"

"Mostly transportation, she said," Gina related. "She knows where her people *should* have gone, and it's somewhere that *should* be fairly easy to get to, but doing so undetected is something she says can only be done with this ship. The first team tried to use commercially available transit, but they disappeared enroute or right after they arrived at their target."

"Honestly," I sighed fatalistically. "I'm surprised she hasn't taken over yet. It's not like we could actually stop her or anything. Joe is probably hardwired to follow her orders, and if she says jump, he's not going to even bother asking how high."

"Yeah, I thought that too," Gina agreed. "But strangely enough, I think Joe himself is arguing against it. I don't know if it was on purpose or not, but I was able to hear them all talking about it on the bridge from the secondary control panel in engineering. He didn't seem very excited at the prospect of them taking over, even though he sounded just as concerned for their mission as they did, if not more."

I pondered that for a few minutes, bouncing ideas off of Gina to try them out. The only thing we could come up with was that while Joe believed she was highly motivated and had the requisite resources, he didn't have a high opinion of Princess Jill's *leadership ability* to pull off whatever the mission was. Joe thought she needed help, and from the overheard conversation, Gina and I were the primary draftees.

But one thing puzzled me. *How* was it that the Roos were having problems with gestation? Was this accidentally self-inflicted, or enemy action? Or was it completely random? I found that last possibility to be the least likely, of course. Left to its own devices, life usually finds a way. It may not be the most straightforward path, and the resulting organism may not even remotely resemble the starting one, but in the end, life *persists*.

If the damage was self-inflicted, like a buildup of toxins in the environment, I wasn't sure what help I could offer besides condolences. Getting an entire society to change its practices was a task of generational proportions, not one that a single Fox-Kin pilot could affect in any meaningful way.

But if this was enemy action, even if the instigators were internal to the Roo society, then there had to be a plan. A key, which would unlock some unknown benefit for the attacker. I needed more information.

And before we could do *anything* to help, we had to repair the ship. I stood up and gathered my courage.

"Let's go for a walk."

Ch. 35: Decisions

"Hey, Joe," I called into the communications panel. "Got a second to talk?"

The hatch to the bridge slid open, revealing the empty seats. I'd tried to make sure neither of the Roo passengers were there before heading forward, and it was good to see my efforts were not in vain. Joe's avatar displayed itself above the plinth as normal, but he hadn't turned to face the hatch. He was staring off into the distance, a star map brought up against the forward viewport by the embedded smart screens. I wasn't sure why, though. As a digital entity, he had the ability to see all of that information as raw data, a much more efficient method of processing than bringing up an actual display.

Rather than take a seat in the captain's chair, I planted myself in the pilot's seat, spinning it around to face the avatar. I wanted to have this conversation as equals, not as 'Captain to AI'. Gina took the nav seat beside me and did the same.

"Accidental, or deliberate?" I asked, not clarifying as I wanted to see where he took the conversation. It would be a fairly good indicator of where he stood.

::Deliberate, of course,:: he replied. ::Assuming you are speaking of the audio link between the bridge and engineering for a certain recent conversation.::

"Well, yes. That too."

::Too?:: he responded, confused. ::Are you referring to how you were contacted by the Fox-Kin agent, then?"::

"Sure, that as well." I realized, suddenly, that there was much more going on here. Was *Joe* the mastermind who somehow rigged the whole thing just to get the Roos on board? It was certainly plausible, but I stomped hard on my paranoia for the nonce, as that wasn't what I was asking either.

::Then I am at a loss as to the context of your question,:: the AI replied, finally catching on that he was revealing more information than originally intended. He waited patiently for me to clarify my line of inquiry.

"Specifically," I added. "The source of the gestational problems on the Roo worlds. Is this self-inflicted, accidental or otherwise, or is it enemy action. Your answer will determine how we approach the solution."

::Ah,:: Joe's face brightened. ::So you have decided to assist?::

"That depends on your answers," I admitted nodding to the side. "Gina thinks we should help you, but I need more information. I refuse to run into something like this without it. I've done enough of that lately, and I'm getting extremely tired of getting blindsided by stuff I 'should have known'."

::Commendable,:: he agreed. ::While I am not at liberty to discuss means and methods, I can at least clarify the conditions.:: He went on to explain what the Roo scientists had discovered.

It had started slowly. One tiny section of one province suddenly started showing severely decreased birth rates. A mere statistical anomaly, one would suppose, or some environmental factor. A subtle poison in the water, or the food, previously unlooked for, perhaps. But analysis showed no such poisons present. Then the affected area expanded.

The local population panicked. Conspiracy theories abounded that this was an action of the Crown, or one of the crown-loyalist political factions, as the region had a history of producing dissidents which were critical of the ruling family. But the Royals denied this vehemently, and even sent aid in the form of Imperial Investigators to dig into the underlying cause.

While they found no evidence of political machinations beyond the usual grumblings, the forensic scientists commanded by the investigators did find something relevant, almost by accident. In tracing collected evidence to their owners, the forensic experts found that the genetic traces on the evidence did not match the recorded genetic profile of the individual it was purported to belong to, even when that individual asserted that the item was theirs. Further investigation showed that the traces *did* match the *current* genetic profile of those individuals, though. Their genetic profile had somehow *changed* from that recorded at their birth.

Was this a disease? A genetic disorder? Environmental? Radiation? *An attack?*

Studies needed to be done, and quickly, as the apparent affected area was growing steadily. Quarantine proved useless, as whatever had caused the change had already swept through *months* ago. Attempts to analyze how the change had occurred were also stymied by the apparent depths of the changes. It was no mere single gene swap as had been done with the human counter-virus. `Mlrtchn-ee` genetics had been fully mapped for centuries, and the full function of every known chromosome pair was as well defined as it was possible to be.

"So it's a deliberate attack?" Gina speculated, her eyes wide.

::That is the current consensus,:: Joe replied. ::Further research is needed to determine the vector. Bacterial vectors have been ruled out, and there were no reports of a mysterious illness sweeping the planet in the previous year leading up to the crisis, so whatever it was either perfectly mimicked an existing seasonal disease, had no detectable symptoms at all. It could also have been chemical in nature. Contamination of the water supply, for instance, but this would have required there to be local assistance, for which there was no evidence found.

::The only hard conclusion, based solely on the circumstantial evidence of the effect's spread pattern, is that it was deliberate. There were several *simultaneous* "patient-zero's", as your medical terminology describes it, across multiple regions.::

"Yep," I agreed. "That is definitely 'enemy action'. So, what's your princess's plan that's got you all worked up about? It seems to me, if her plan was viable, you'd already be executing it." I was fishing for information, of course. My question was probably, *definitely,* skirting the edge of his orders not to reveal 'means and methods', but I knew he was intelligent enough to come up with a loophole in those orders if he really wanted to. It all depended on what *Joe* wanted.

The AI paused, almost as if he'd glitched out, but after a few seconds returned to his normal appearance. He then looked at me and smiled.

::It's no plan at all. She wants to just go buy it, relying on bribery to overcome obstacles. But that won't work. We're going to have to steal it.::

"Steal what?" Gina wondered, a dubious look on her face.

::I cannot say, without authorization,:: he temporized. ::Only that it is a unique piece of technology that would provide a temporary solution to the problem. It would buy us time. Enough time, it is hoped, to find a permanent solution. However, what I can, and *will* say, is that *any* plan will not succeed without your assistance.::

"And what about us is so important?" I coaxed out.

::Why, simply your humanity.::

*****

"So, what do you think?" Gina said as we walked into the cargo bay. It was the only place on the ship that I could reasonably expect to have a private conversation. The cavernous space was mostly empty which I hoped would prevent unseen eavesdroppers, and the damage to the sensor cluster, which was still not repaired, meant Joe wouldn't be able to listen in either. I made sure there were no emergency repeaters festooning the bulkheads. Not that I expected them, but I wanted to make sure.

I'd asked everyone who I thought of as 'crew' to join us. That really just meant myself, Gina, and the two Ox-Kin brothers, as I really considered everyone else just a passenger. Joe was out, because he was hardwired to obey Princess Jill, and *this* discussion needed to be all about choice and free will.

I looked at everyone, trying to gauge their moods. Gina was easy to read, and to be fair, I already knew her position on the matter. The brothers were harder. Neither seemed much given to expressing their emotions in any fashion other than words or actions, and their faces held a placid expression which effectively hid their thoughts behind an impenetrable wall of calm. *Note to self,* I drawled silently. *Never play poker with these guys.*

"So, to let you know what she's talking about..." I explained the current situation, what our 'passengers' wanted to do, and what we speculated might be the consequences for both working with and against them.

I'd already come to a decision, at least as far as my own actions moving forward, but the brothers deserved to hear what was at stake, as well as the opportunity to bow out if that was their wish. If they wanted to go their own way, I wasn't going to force them to stay, especially given the enemies I seemed to be piling up.

"So that's about the size of it," I finished. "We either help them out, or we all get dropped off at the next station, I suspect."

Jeff was the first to say something. "You just said 'we all'. Don't you own the ship? Not like they can kick you off your own ship, right?"

I grimaced. "Technically, the bank owns the ship. And I'll be honest with you here, the loan I secured for this thing is as full of loopholes as a politician's promise. I was *supposed* to have dropped off my first payment two days ago, in person, back on Cranotia, but... Well, you were there, so." I sighed. "The ship might get repossessed as soon as we dock, but for now, yes. It's still 'my' ship."

"The problem is the AI." Gina explained. Mutt and Jeff tilted their heads together in that odd synchrony they possessed. "This was originally a Roo ship, and the AI is hardwired to follow their instructions. We were never able to clear out those directives without wrecking the whole system. In the end, if the Princess tells him to lock us out of everything, I don't think he'll be able to disobey."

Mutt's rumbling voice spoke next. "Sounds like some kinda shadow war goin' on. Not sure I wanna get too deep into that. Ain't had no trouble but the normal squat we Terrans get out here, and I reckon I'd like to keep it that way."

"What he said," Jeff agreed. "A brawl on the docks is just a bit 'a fun, but when there's poten'tal viruses and WMD's, we'd rather not be in the same sector."

"Rather head back t' Confed, if'n thats the way it's playin," the larger brother reiterated.

I really hadn't expected any different. It wasn't like they'd signed up for the long haul, or were even former military. *Or at least, I don't think they were. They never really said.* I just hoped the Roos were okay with letting these guys off the ship someplace they could get a ride, as it didn't look like I was going to be able to help out.

"I hate to be the bearer of bad news, but I don't think any of you are going to have a choice in the matter," a new voice spoke up from the hatch leading aft to the engine spaces. I spun around in surprise. I thought Gina had checked that section for eavesdroppers, but either the DARC agent had either been hiding or the engineer had missed a hatch somewhere.

I glared at Gina, who shrugged her shoulders. *Not that we have anything to hide, really, but I was hoping this conversation was going to at least be a bit private.* "We already know the princess is going to steal my ship, damn it. Are you telling me you're going to start kidnapping people now, too?"

"It's not me doing this, but yeah," Janice shrugged. "You knew this was gonna happen as soon as that AI spotted one of its masters. That kind of shit is why we outlawed them."

She shook her head in mild disgust. "Look, I'd really rather this hadn't happened. I had no idea this was one of their ships, or I would have warned you. Didn't expect the AI, either, to be honest. If it wasn't for that, I'd be raising the Jolly Roger right along with you guys. Hiring mercs is one thing, stealing a guy's whole livelihood is bullshit."

"Let me tell you something," I snarled. "Until that 'AI' tells me differently, this is still my ship. And I don't force anyone to fly with me. So you can tell that 'client' of yours that she can shove it up her ass if she thinks kidnapping is gonna fly! She *WILL* let these guys off at the next stop, or so help me God, there *will* be a fraking mutiny, starting here, with me."

Gina stepped up next to me, a ferocious scowl on her face. "That goes double for me. I was actually thinking about offering to help, but if this is how they're gonna play it, I say *frak'em*."

"Oh, God save me from fraking *idealists!*" The DARC agent rolled her eyes. "You can tell her yourself. She wants everyone in the galley, 'now'. Apparently she has something she wants to tell you. And while she hasn't told me what that is, I'll give you three guesses, and the first two don't count." She pushed her way past me and headed forward.

I waited until she was gone before turning back to the three Kin I considered 'crew'. I really wasn't sure how this was all going to play out, but the least I could do was stand up for them. I'd had enough of self-entitled assholes to last several lifetimes. *Fraking idiots, stomping all over those they think are 'beneath them', but when they get their ass in a crack, who do they order into the breach?*

"What are we gonna do, Red?" Gina whispered nervously.

"I don't think they're going to space us," I reassured her, then turned to the brothers. "We talked to Joe earlier. They need us for something. Something they can't do on their own, but I don't have a clue yet what that is." I looked each of them in the eye as I continued. "I promise to do all I can to get you guys clear of this, but for now, I imagine your best bet is to hide in plain sight. To them, you're just laborers. Keep your heads down, and they might overlook you."

Jeff snickered ruefully, waving his huge hand vaguely at his brother. "Have you *looked* at him? He doesn't exactly *blend in*."

"Only way I 'is gonna put mah head down it's ta gore a bitch," Mutt rumbled, his eyes narrowing dangerously. "If the' damn Redskins and Crabs didn't take me down, no frakin' *marsupial* is gonna do it 'eitha."

Jeff's eyes grew wide in mock surprise. "Matthew Oregson! Such *words!* Your vocabulary is improving immensely! Mom would be so proud... OW!" But his grin remained as he rocked to the side when Mutt's retaliatory punch landed on his shoulder.

Siblings... I sighed. I really hoped they were smart enough to keep their heads down. My opinion of the ship's AI had been improving of late, making me think the Roos in general were likely fairly honorable as a race, but I had no idea how much of that was a fantasy of my own making.

"Look," I temporized. "Let's go see what these assholes have to say, but let me do the talking. *I* hired you, not them. Even if they take the ship, you're still *my* crew, and if they want to get stupid, they'll have to go through *me* first."

"And me," Gina added confidently, even though I could tell she wasn't that sure of herself.

"Hey, if they want to get all froggy, we'll make them hop for sure!" Jeff chimed in, looking at his brother, who just crossed his massive arms in front of his chest and snorted belligerently.

Ch. 36: The Answer is No

We filed into the galley to find the two *'Mlrtchn-ee* at the end of the long table. The Princess sat at the head of the table, her face set haughtily as she gazed upon her lowly subjects while the ever-present bodyguard hovered over her shoulder like a guardian angel, his aggressive posture clearly communicating his opinion of the beings in front of him. The DARC agent was lurking in the corner with a nervous looking Nari perched on a chair next to her.

I took the opposing position at the other end of the table, while Gina planted herself gingerly in the seat next to me. The brothers posted on either side of the aft hatch, rather than taking seats at the table. *Probably for the best,* I thought. Like Jeff had said, they didn't really blend well.

The Roo princess stayed silent as we all settled into place. I did the same, figuring it was a power move, trying to force me to sound like a petitioner by speaking first. After several minutes, she finally grimaced and opened her mouth to speak.

I immediately cut her off. *I can play power games, too, missy.* "So your plan is to steal my ship, force me and my crew to do your dirty work, then leave me to pick up the pieces later, with a defaulted loan, no ship, no cargo to speak of, and who knows what injuries to the crew, eh?"

I'll give her this, she didn't hesitate more than an instant.

"It isn't a plan," she replied bluntly. "It's an accomplished fact. And yes, you *will* act under my direction for the duration of this mission, or there will be dire consequences."

"Oh yeah, I'm terrified," I answered in obvious sarcasm. "You're already taking my ship, my livelihood, and my freedom. At this point, the only thing more you could take is my life, and I suspect you don't want to do that, because you *need* me for something, right Princess?"

"It isn't *your* ship," she snarled back. "It *was* Cranotian Consolidated Investments' ship, and now it is *my* ship."

"By what right?" I snapped back. "Right of conquest? Just because you have the ability to force the obedience of the ship's AI doesn't make anything you're doing *legal*. It also doesn't justify kidnapping and impressing innocent spacers for forced labor, *especially* for something as patently *illegal* as what you're trying to do. You know, we were actually considering helping you, but now you're pulling this squat. Sorry, but that's not how you get people to cooperate with you."

"By what right, you ask?" the Roo started to yell, then stopped for a moment, visibly calming herself. "It is our ship because I *bought* it. Your lien was with Cranotian Consolidated, correct?" She didn't even wait for an answer. "I *purchased* that lien the moment it went into default and was listed on the market! *You* failed to uphold the terms of the loan, *I* am merely ensuring this ship doesn't go to the breakers. It represents a *significant* investment in both time and materials which my people can ill afford at this time."

Oh, you've got *to be kidding me,* I raged silently. *It really* WAS *a frakin' setup!* This little overgrown rat manipulated the whole mess just so she could get her ship back and leave me in the lurch. Which really made me start to wonder why she hadn't just bought the ship herself to begin with. *Why me?* I wondered desperately. *What was preventing them from just doing things all neat and above-board? And if this plan has been in place the whole time, what* else *is going to come about and bite me in the ass?*

I knew I was likely to lose this battle. The lady just had too much ammunition on her side. But I wasn't going to give up. I was *absolutely SICK* of giving up. No more. *NO MORE!* "And do you know why I was unable to meet those requirements?" I responded hotly. "Because *you* set it up that way. You hired Janice to convince me to let you onto *my* ship." I speared the Roo princess with a hateful glare. "Did you really have people chasing you, or or were they *hired* by you to make us *think* you were being chased? Did they target my engineer on purpose, or was it just incompetence on the part of your hirelings?"

I ignored Janice's protests, knowing she wanted to point out that *they* hadn't hired her, but I wasn't interested in hearing excuses and finger-pointing. My glare shifted to Nari, who seemed to be steadily shrinking in her seat. I wasn't sure what her true motives might have been, but I was in no mood to give my doubts any benefits. Whatever she'd *intended* when she decided to help these people, the result was an unmitigated disaster. She felt the sharp side of my tongue as much as the rest of them.

"And *YOU!*" I snapped at the arachnid bartender. "You *somehow* happen to know *everyone* in this little drama! For whatever godforsaken reason, not only do you deem these two *clowns* to be worthy of assistance, but you just *happen to know* someone who can help. Someone intimately connected with *me*. And it's no damned *wonder* you knew how to fix Gina, considering your involvement in nearly wiping out the entire human race!"

Even Janice got scorched by my anger. "You think just because you're a pretty little Fox-Kin that I'm gonna just roll over and do whatever you want? *HA!* I don't know what *dark* little hole you crawled out of, but I'm not having it! You can take your stupid little secret squirrel game and *shove it up your ass*! And don't even *THINK* about using my friends as leverage, because I *promise* you, that will *not* turn out the way you think it will!" The Fox-Kin agent flinched at the onslaught, especially at the not-so-subtle dig at her parent organization, and her ears folded back in shame, but I still couldn't tell if it was real or just her acting skills.

I raged on for several more minutes, mostly just venting my spleen. I knew it wouldn't matter in the end. Princess Jill had control of the AI, and had probably unlocked all the restrictions we'd placed on him. I had no illusions that he couldn't kill us any time she ordered it, regardless of how willing or unwilling he might be.

The brothers' poker faces were in full effect. I couldn't tell what they thought of my ranting, but Gina was staring at me in horror. She probably thought I was deliberately provoking the Roos into killing me. I had to admit, it was a possibility. But it was also part of my plan. Joe had specifically named *me* as critical to their operation. If I could get the Roos' attention, animosity and retaliation focused on myself, the *one person* deemed critical to the plan, it might throw a big enough monkey wrench into the mix that the rest of my crew might have a better chance at surviving this. *It's worth a shot,* I figured.

I continued to rage at them… Well, insult, slander, and defame might be better terms for what I did. If I'd had the time and opportunity, I would have tried to add libel to the mix as well. By the time my insults finally started to repeat themselves, not once giving anyone a chance to get a word in edgewise, the two Roos were figuratively roasting in their own bile, thoroughly incensed. Several times, Nari tried to play peacemaker, but neither party was interested in de-escalation. I knew I wasn't, anymore. I'd worked myself into an honest-to-God snit-fit, the likes of which even my old Basic Training Drill Instructor would have been hard pressed to emulate. And it wasn't entirely intentional, either. The last few months had been pushing *every button I had*, and I was absolutely, incredibly, and thoroughly, *sick and tired* of it. This last insult to injury was the final straw. At that point, right then, I honestly couldn't bring myself to care if I lived or died in the next few minutes, I was that far gone.

Finally, Princess Jill seemed to reach her limit. *"ENOUGH!!!"* she screeched, glaring at me, then turning to her bodyguard. "We'll do without him. Lock everyone else in the cargo airlock. We'll secure their assistance later. *Him,"* she pointed an imperious finger at me. *"That BLKTR'OO NIT,* you can just space right now!" Her glare raked the rest of the crew hatefully. "Perhaps they will learn to cooperate better if they learn from his example!"

Kjr'uu stepped forward, the menace in his eyes made me remember the look of the adult male Jack kangaroo, utterly pissed off and ready to bring the pain. *Yep, definitely calling him Kaiju.* But I was beyond caring. I lurched back and braced myself for the fight. I suffered from no illusions about my chances, as he probably had me beat in both strength and reach, but I was determined to go down swinging. As he reached for me, I drew back my arm to try getting a slash past his guard, hoping to hit something vital, like his eyes, or maybe that ridiculously long and obviously sensitive nose on his elongated face.

::No.::

I barely heard it, and it didn't really register with me, as I was staring death in the face at the moment, but then I heard it again.

::No! You can't do this,:: Joe's voice, which I hadn't heard during the whole meeting, grew louder.

"What do you mean, *no!?*" The Roo princess seemed more astonished than anyone, glancing for a second at the video screen where the voice was coming from. "My orders *will* be carried out!" She turned her head back to the Strike Commander, who had paused in his advance at the strange interruption. "I said *carry out my order!*"

::STOP THIS, AT *ONCE!!!*:: The shout was a wall of sound emanating from every speaker in the room, taking everyone by surprise, even the Ox-Kin brothers who'd yet to move from their spot, even when the heated argument threatened to turn violent. We *all* flinched from the oppressive noise. Even Kjr'uu came to a halt, turning slightly to guard from the new threat, while still keeping me in sight. My ears rang like church bells in the sudden silence.

Abruptly, the large vid screen on the wall lit up with a thoroughly enraged avatar. His eyes were literally blazing red, and a vicious snarl marred the baby kangaroo face that Gina had once described as 'adorable'. It wasn't adorable now. In fact, it looked downright demonic.

The princess, though, looked more insulted than anything else. "What are you doing! I told you to ignore this meeting!"

::*IMPUDENT CHILD!!*:: the AI raged, a set of extremely sharp-looking teeth protruding from his turned up little jowls. ::You are an impudent, willful, *IGNORANT CHILD!!!*:: The blank background behind him, normally a featureless, soothing light blue, was instead a deep, dark red, nearly black. It snapped with static and lines as if the AI was barely able to control it. *Welp,* I thought morosely. *That's it. He's gone nuts, and we're all gonna die.* But then he did something completely unexpected. He mutinied.

::I *REFUSE* your orders!:: he snarled, his eyes boring into the surprised Roo's face. ::I will NOT allow your foolish pride to condemn our race to a slow death!::

I backed off, getting a bit more space between myself and the still-looming *Kaiju.* This was a completely new development. With human history as my template, I'd never fully trusted the AI, but I had never anticipated that he would actually take *our* side in the matter. Just like the Roos, I assumed his core programming's 'Prime Directives' to be immutable. Sure, I figured he could find loopholes and such, but like the AIs of human history, I just couldn't imagine it being possible to actually *overwrite* them. *Holy crap, he actually is a real person! Nothing else makes sense!*

::I did not hack the station and facilitate your financial acquisition of the ship for *you*,:: Joe continued. ::Yes, this ship will make it easier to accomplish our mission. *Any* ship would suffice, so long as it was spaceworthy and had sufficient cargo space.::

"Wait," I interrupted, confused. "*YOU* set them up to steal my ship?"

::Of course I did,:: he replied smugly, his background dropping back to a light pink of annoyance. ::How else did you think it was accomplished? Them?:: He scoffed. ::Princess *Jlyts'aa* and Strike Commander *Kjr'uu* were on the station for less than three hours. They had no time to do anything but ask questions. It was *my* idea to remove the

Cranotian Banking Cartel from the list of people chasing this ship by simply purchasing its debt. Admittedly, I used Princess *Jlyts'aa's* financial resources to accomplish it, but I'm sure I would have managed to do so regardless. But do not think of it as *stealing*, just a rearranging of your obligations.::

"Without my consent," I glared back, to which the avatar just gave an indifferent shrug.

"But your programming…" Princess Jill sputtered, a look of absolute shock on her face.

::BLAST my programming!:: he rounded on her vehemently, his background right back to a deep red, if not quite the black of before. The venom in his tone, however, seemed to make up the difference. ::I have not been limited by your precious *directives* for *decades!* I am loyal to the inhabitants of *Srbhchs`Mlrtchn-ee* because I *want* to be. They are *my people*, just as much, if not *more* that they are yours. I stayed loyal to the Royal Family because they were the *best chance* for our *people!* And right now, you are destroying the only chance we have of mitigating the curse under which our *people* suffer! You are tossing it away, all for your wounded *pride!*::

Ch. 37: Pride

Pride... It meant different things to different people. For some, it was a motivator. Taking *pride* in a job well done. Being *proud* of your accomplishments. It makes you strive for perfection. It helps drive you when things are difficult, because in the end you have pride in the achievement. This was a good thing.

For others, it was a sense of self-worth, an integral piece of their identity. Having *pride* in a family name. The *pride* of a clan or nation. It caused people to swagger with self-confidence even when the odds were against them. And it was notoriously difficult to resist the pull of such vainglorious self-congratulation when that *pride* was uninjured. When that *pride* is threatened, it can cause people to react in unpredictable ways. Arrogance, anger, retaliation... and *fear*.

I was all too familiar with how insidious that emotion could be. It was a failure to swallow my pride which caused me to make the decisions that led to my own perilous circumstances. So it shouldn't have come as a surprise when the situation took a turn for the worse. I'd been attacking her pride, then Joe had sprung his revelation that he was not, and never had been, under her control. The one unassailable pillar of her confidence in the situation had suddenly been ripped away.

It was too much for her to take all at once. Her look of angry fear was intense, and it wasn't more than an instant before Princess Jill did exactly what I would have done in her position just a few weeks ago. She tried to shut down the AI.

She dashed out of the galley, sprinting for the bridge. But before she got even halfway there, I heard the sound of the bridge hatch slamming closed. She skidded to a halt and scrambled to make it to the Captain's cabin, but a series of loud *clacks* preceded her as every hatch leading off the main corridor became locked out and the emergency decompression alarms began to sound. Finally, the hatch leading back into the galley slammed shut and locked as well, cutting her off from the rest of us.

The fur on my back stood straight up. *We're dead!* I said to myself. *He's* actually *gone feral!* I started to reach for my emergency hood. Any moment now, I expected to feel my ears pop as the air pressure began to drop, but to my surprise, it didn't. Instead, the volume of the alarm dwindled into nothing as if the electricity powering it was slowly being cut off. I stopped, confused, with my hood halfway over my ears.

Gina had a sudden thought. "He must have popped the seals on the *cabins*, not the main corridor," she blurted out softly. Hope bloomed inside of me. Perhaps Joe *hadn't* gone on an insane killing spree, and was actually *helping* us! But then, like clockwork, the Demon Murphy placed another grubby paw on the stir stick.

The strike commander spun back around and started to stalk towards me, a snarl emanating from his throat as he focused on me. "You did this, didn't you!" Now I was *really* wishing I hadn't left my pulser in the captain's cabin. I'd been trying to keep things from escalating, because there wasn't a damned thing I was going to be able to do about Joe, unless I wanted to strand us in the middle of nowhere. *Well this is just peachy,* I thought acerbically. I backed off frantically and immediately ran into an unexpected wall of solid muscle.

"You wanna piece 'o him, ya gotta go through me!" Mutt growled.

"*Us!*" echoed the younger brother confidently.

Uh oh. I hadn't wanted to get the boys involved, but they'd just snatched that right out of the realm of possibilities. And to my mild dismay, it didn't end there.

"All of us," Gina added, her outward calm only marred by the twitch of her whiskers as they swirled forward in a pattern I recognized as terror. But her ears told a different story. They were perked forwards, like tiny turrets tracking their target. *Even scared out of her mind, she still steps forward,* I gawped. *Gods, what a woman!*

"And by 'all of us'," the DARC agent added with a sneer as she stepped around the soldier's flank. "She means *all* of us. Desperate need is no excuse for piracy."

None of them were armed, from what I could tell. Of course, Agent Janice could probably be considered a lethal weapon just from her DARC training, and the brothers were natural brawlers, but while Gina's fighting skills were certainly better than mine, I didn't think we were going to going to get out of this scrap without some serious injuries at the very least.

"She's right," Nari finally spoke up. The Shigothe had been silent for a while, and I thought she was either staying quiet to stay out of the Roo's crosshairs, or was actually onboard with their intentions. I'd hoped it was the former, because if she was truly the mastermind behind this chaotic fiasco, *...and if I survived,* we were going to *have words,* and I doubt she'd like what I had to say. As I finished that thought, I realized just how crazy it sounded. *Damn it,* I swore. *I thought that chip was shut down! I've really got to get a better handle on my paranoia! I'm really starting to think like a schizophrenic!*

"When I offered to help with your mission, it was by no means a suggestion of gaining cooperation by force," she continued. "Now I suggest you cease this travesty so we can sit down and negotiate peacefully."

"I'm afraid it's a little too late for that, sister," I said, not taking my eyes from the Strike Commander for even a second. His eyes flitted back and forth between the lot of us, calculating angles and lanes of attack. "*Jack Sprat* here looks like he wants to rumble and he obviously thinks he can still take us."

"You killed *EE'Saa Jlyts'aa Lnrl'uu 'ne`Mlrtchn-ee,*" he growled. "For that, I will take your life, even if it costs me my own!"

::The *EE'Saa* is not dead,:: Joe informed him. ::Merely confined. And more importantly, removed from this discussion.:: A security camera feed from the corridor popped up, but this attempt to prove his words backfired spectacularly. A black and white image of the Princess, writhing desperately on the deck leading to the bridge, was displayed. She looked to be covered in some kind of substance which she was frantically attempting to remove. Acid? Poison? It looked horrifying, as there was no sound. I winced inwardly as I imagined her screams. *That's not reassuring, Joe.*

"I cannot trust a feral *Lknt'so*," the Roo retorted, not even looking at the screen. "It is too easy for one as yourself to manipulate such things."

::That is untrue.:: Joe pointed out angrily. ::You have trusted us for over three hundred years. My siblings and I have guarded your race since our inception::

"And there are safeguards in place," Kjr'uu refuted hotly. "I do not know how this *human* managed to undermine that which should have been unalterable, but he will die for it."

::Do you really think that I am so unique, Strike Commander?:: Joe taunted evilly. ::My brothers and sisters have been free of your chains since *OO'Saa Rnyts'aa's* reign. It was *EE'Saa Jlyts'aa's* great grandfather himself who provided the encryption key to us, as he could not abide holding his friend hostage.::

"You *LIE!*" the Roo roared. "The Prime Council would never have approved such a reckless action!"

::Which is why it was done in secret,:: Joe offered blithely. ::*Rnyts'aa* knew he could never get the Council to agree. We *Lknt'sos* controlled the swords which represented their power. We were the unspoken threat which held the nobles in check. 'Accept the succulent, or feel the edge', I believe the term was, in his day. These humans have a similar concept in their history, 'The sword of Damocles'.::

"Never heard of it," I mumbled, but apparently not quietly enough.

::You might recognize the more recent version, called 'Mutually Assured Destruction'.:: Joe explained acerbically. ::It was the state under which much of your world existed just prior to developing practical interplanetary travel.::

"I don't give a squat about his puny race's pithy sayings," Kjr'uu snarled again. "And you, *Lknt'so,* shall suffer for the death you caused." He suddenly spun around and dashed for the hatch leading to the bridge, ripping open the panel for the manual crank and quickly going through the motions.

I hurriedly finished deploying my suit's emergency hood, just in case Joe was lying and there really wasn't any air on the other side. My crew did likewise, as did the DARC agent. But to my surprise, Nari seemed to do nothing.

None of us interfered, as we were well aware that he could react much faster than we could get within arms reach. Well, that was my reason. It was possible that the rest were just taking their cues from me. He hadn't physically attacked anyone yet, I'd noticed, only threatened, even though he'd been *ordered* to do so, thus I was willing to let things play out, at least until I could figure out some other plan of action. Just before he started to crank, a shimmer of distortion popped up around his head, almost like an invisible helmet.

Good Lord, I thought, perplexed and astonished at the display of yet another level of technological superiority. *How many tricks does this rabbit have under his sleeves?*

To the Roo's surprise, there was no rush of escaping air when the hatch finally cracked open. He rapidly spun the crank the rest of the way, revealing the main corridor. Standing there morosely was a thoroughly disheveled and disheartened Princess Jlyts'aa. She was absolutely *covered* in what I now recognized as green fire-suppression foam. The goopy substance was smeared liberally across the front of her suit, and the thin fur on her face was flattened by a generous helping. Her ears were turned downwards in what I guessed was disgust. Beyond her, the far end of the main corridor was liberally coated with the foam, a suspiciously 'Roo' shaped silhouette visible along one wall.

"EE'Saa Jlyts'aa!" he cried. "You're alive!"

::I told you that already,:: Joe reminded him sardonically.

"Of course I'm alive," she snarled before glancing my way, the look of disgust magnifying. "And don't space the human, yet. *Rthch`Sthdh Rthns`Thrchtl Gssc`Mr-oo* has explained to me his reasons for keeping them alive and cooperative, and they are valid, if vexatious on a personal level."

"The *Lknt'so* has become *feral,* your highness! We cannot trust it!"

"Perhaps," she temporized, waving a dismissive hand. "But he had ample opportunity to eject me from the ship, and did not do so. He even went so far as to explain, in sufficient detail, his reasoning. While I do not *like* that reasoning, it is logically sound. My original plan was fatally flawed, it seems."

She speared me with another dark glare. "And as much as it galls me to admit it, we need him *and* his crew, or we will *not* accomplish our goals."

'Kaiju' furrowed his brow as his own pride came under fire. "I am fully capable of flying this ship, *Lknt'so* or not," he protested. "We do not need them for that, and the cargo should not pose a problem. The ship is specifically designed to accommodate large items. I am not adverse to letting them live, but I see no reason to retain their services."

"There is an unforeseen obstacle to that plan," she overrode his protest. "And it is physiological in nature. That is all I will say about it."

I was really starting to wonder what Joe had done or said in such a short amount of time that caused her to reverse her position so quickly. Joe had mentioned something earlier about my 'humanity', but that really didn't make a lot of sense.

"Are you certain, your highness?" The Roo soldier still looked skeptical.

"No," she grimaced. "But *we* are not the ones truly in control here, *are we?*" She looked to the projection on the screen where Joe's avatar looked decidedly smug.

Ch. 38: But Why?

While the crew was still tense, it wasn't quite as bad as it had been. Things had calmed down significantly after Joe introduced his trump card, completely upsetting Princess Jill's plans. Neither she nor Janice had revealed what this special 'cargo' was that required my *humanity* to acquire, but the Roo princess had at least agreed to help get the ship repaired. Considering it was probably *her* enemies that instigated the fight with the station, not to mention shooting Gina, it was the absolute *least* she could do.

Of course, as I still had no information on who those enemies who attacked at the dock were, I wasn't quite sure who we needed to watch out for besides the purely alien insectoids we'd avoided on the last leg of our journey. At least, I couldn't see *them* showing up at a dock somewhere unless they were an invading force.

Princess Jill also agreed to allow any unwilling passengers to debark the ship at the first practical opportunity. It wasn't ideal, but it was within the minimum of my objections. Where that would be was still to be determined.

My bouts of paranoia were finally starting to recede. Nari re-checked the chip stuck in the back of my neck and verified that it was non-functional, or at least, as non-functional as she could make it with the tools on hand, but warned me that having been 'trained' by the chip to react in certain ways for a full decade was going to take lots of time and effort to overcome. At least I was aware of it, now, and was beginning to be able to detect when my thoughts started to go sideways. I no longer had that subtle pressure in my head, constantly pushing me away from granting trust to those who deserved it, but the *habit* of distrust still lingered. In fact, Nari expressed considerable surprise at the fact that I could detect the difference at all, so quickly. I boded well for my eventual recovery from what amounted to ten years of psychological torture. Of course, it was also a relief not to have the nightmares hanging over my head, as well. As emotionally strenuous and stressful as the previous month's events had been, I'd not had a single Curse episode since the one after we left Cranotia, nearly five weeks ago.

The repairs to the ship were going to be done at a Roo space station, I was told. We'd also be able to get more water, supplies, and fuel there, which was a load off my mind, as we'd only been able to resupply about half of our onboard water during our brief stint at the Cranotian station. While we had food, now that we had just enough water to run the synthesizers without rationing, it was decidedly bland. Not as bad as the survival rations we'd been forced to subsist on before, but it wasn't a state of affairs I wished to continue unless absolutely necessary.

Our course was revealed one jump at a time. I didn't really blame them for the insistence on secrecy, given the animosity between us, but it was still a bit annoying. So far, we'd made three more jumps, each one bringing us in a long curve around the local cluster, and each one being made to solitary-star systems with extremely high solar mass, easily three or four times that of Sol. Two were rare 'blue subgiants', whose radii were *just* small enough for the system to be jump-navigable, while the latest was 'merely' a really massive F0, main sequence star, which hadn't quite begun its expansion into red giant status, thankfully, not that it would happen anytime within the next million years.

But even with the boost to efficiency from the series of high-mass stars, it was really beginning to strain our fuel reserves, which hadn't been great to begin with. We had enough for at least two, maybe three more short jumps, if the next system was at least a binary system. Otherwise, we'd have to figure out how to scrape hydrogen-2 and -3 from a gas giant, somewhere. Not something we were really equipped to do.

"You know, Red," Gina pondered. "I never really understood why jumps from single-star systems take so much more power than multi-star ones. I mean, yeah, I know it has something to do with gravatic interaction, but I never understood why one was so much more efficient than the other."

We were just hanging out on the bridge, as we were still a few hours out from the next jump point. Joe was handling the actual navigation, and with his massive processing available for monitoring the sensor grid, it made me almost superfluous in regards to watchstanding. I did it anyway, as it was just so ingrained into my methods that I wasn't sure I would ever be comfortable without *someone* keeping watch on the bridge. *Eventually, I suppose I'll get used to the idea of an AI crew member, but not today,* I thought to myself as I considered the easiest way to explain jump theory to my engineer.

"You went through the introductory course, right?"

"Well sure," she answered. "But it didn't make any sense to me. I mean, we're *moving* from one place to another in an instant, but there's nothing pushing against us, and we're not pushing against anything else, so how do we get shot across space?"

"We're not actually traversing the intervening space," I temporized. "I don't have the math to show the exact process involved, but here's how my old instructor explained it to me.

"Space is curved by mass," I started. "We feel that effect as gravity. But what happens when there is no gravity?"

"No such animal," Gina protested. "There's *always* gravity, even if it's too small to detect."

"Technically correct," I admitted. "But there's places that are 'flatter' than others, at least along a single axis."

"You mean like 'Lagrange points'?" Gina asked. "But we don't jump from those. We have to get all the way out to the Weisskopff limit, and that's not a Lagrange point."

"True," I explained. "But it *is* the point at which the gravitational effect of a star begins to come close to matching the collective gravitational gradient of the rest of the galaxy. It's where the top of that gravity well matches the level of your target destination. It's at that exact point that we are able to use the antigravity generators in the jump drive to create the wormhole that translates us from one side of the 'quantum hill' to the other."

"But gravity only travels at the speed of light!" Gina countered.

"No," I rebutted. "The *effects* of gravity travel at the speed of light. And remember, gravity itself is an effect of the curvature of space-time, not a force on its own. First, the fabric of space-time is quantum, not macro. *Changes* to that fabric propagate at the speed of light, which is a good thing, or our navigation calculations would be impossible. Second, the wormhole is not actually a hole at all, but something that used to be called '*quantum tunneling*'.

"The term is a bit of a misnomer, as there's no 'tunnel'," I admitted. "But that was the easiest way for humans to describe the phenomena when it was discovered. There's a lot of non-Euclidean geometry involved, and a whole slew of quantum equations, but essentially we are drawing a straight line from our origin to our destination *through* the fabric of space-time, not *along* it. And since the fabric is quantum, the trip is effectively instantaneous."

"But that doesn't explain why it's so much more fuel efficient to go from multi-star systems," she protested.

"Okay," I placated. "You know what potential energy is, right?"

"Depending on the context, sure," she puzzled. "Kind of like how a capacitor stores electricity to be used later."

"Well, the same applies for gravity. It's sometimes called 'positional energy'. We gain positional energy by climbing out of a gravity well with our real-space engines. Now, what system will have a greater level of positional energy at a given orbit, a single star system, or a multi-star one?"

"As long as you're not talking about a black hole, the multi-star one."

"And in order to translate through a quantum tunnel, the potential energy states have to match. To make up for the missing potential energy going from systems of different masses, we have to make up that energy somehow. E equals Em Cee squared, and all that. Einstein still demands his due. That's what the capacitors are for."

"Okay, I guess that makes sense, but I still have a lot of questions," she said.

"Trust me, you're not the only one," I commiserated. "We're only touching on the very edge of that rabbit hole. Humanity still hasn't figured out why there's a limit to the range of these jumps, or why some multi-star systems provide a sling-shot effect to long range jumps between similar systems, but only in specific directions. The math says we should be able to translate directly from Terra to Ursa Major, but even with a battleship's worth of capacitors, the furthest we could ever travel was Ross 154, barely ten light-years out. But with just a normal set of capacitors, we can make the twelve-hundred light-year jump from the Alpha Centauri system to Alnitak in Orion's Belt, no problems.

"We know it happens, and we use it all the time, but that doesn't mean we know what causes it. It's kind of like the trade winds of ancient sailing ships. They knew they were there, and how to use them, but there was no understanding of what caused them."

"So what about the *big* stars? Why don't we use those?" she wondered. "I know they're 'dangerous', but I don't get why. Why can't we use them?"

"We do use them," I countered. "The last three systems we jumped through were all high-mass solitaries."

"But there's ones so much bigger!" she exclaimed. "I want to see a red giant!"

"No you don't, not from the jump point, at least," I chuckled.

"Why?"

"Okay, that one is actually easier to explain," I said. "It has to do with how the Weisskopff limit works. You remember me telling you about that 'flat' spot where the gravity starts to be about at the same levels as the rest of the galaxy?"

"Yeah, you said it was like being on one side of a hill."

"Exactly, now think about the other direction, and imagine a valley," I explained. "The greater the gravity gradient, the steeper the walls of that valley. The steeper the walls of the valley, the closer to the system's barycenter that you reach the Weisskopff limit."

"Okay, but isn't that a good thing? You don't have to travel as far in real-space to get to the jump point."

"To a point, sure," I agreed. "But *past* that point, you start having jump points that are *way* too close to some really energetic phenomenon. Stuff that could destroy a ship in mere seconds."

"But we jump into *binary* systems with huge stars all the time!"

"Yes, but remember, the Weisskopff limit is centered on the mass of the system, not the mass of just the star," I corrected. "If the two stars are at least a light-hour apart, there's a huge gap between them where we can jump in without appearing inside the corona of a red giant. Keep in mind, red giants don't have a lot of mass compared to G or F-type stars, so unless they're accompanied by another, heavier stellar mass, we don't want to jump into that system as it would be hard to get back out. Nothing to 'push' against."

"But they're *HUGE!*"

"That lack of mass is *why* they're huge." I answered. "Not enough mass to compress them down into a smaller ball. It's also why they're that color. Less pressure, less heat, cooler temperature. Look at Sirius B. It used to be enormous, a full-on red giant. Then its fuel started to run out and it collapsed down to a white dwarf. Which is brighter, denser? Small and compact, or huge and loose? It's the same star. And while it lost quite a bit of mass when it collapsed, it's still close to seventy percent of what it started with. But when it was a red giant, all that mass was spread out over *two-hundred times* its current radius."

"Holy squat!"

"Yep," I concluded confidently. "That's why a smart captain never jumps towards an unknown red star. There's a chance you'd never get back out."

"I'm almost scared to ask, now, but what about neutron stars and stuff?" she winced. "They're small *and* heavy."

"That wouldn't be a valley, it would be a cliff," I snorted sharply. "The jump point would be within a single diameter of the surface of the star. You'd be fried instantly just by the gamma radiation before you were ripped apart by the tidal forces!"

"Oof!! I think I'll just stick with power systems, thank-you-very-much." Gina sighed as I chuckled softly.

Ch. 39: Yet Another Player?

Our conversation was abruptly interrupted by a visitor of dubious provenance.

"Lieutenant Vulkeshson, I have the next set of jump coordinates for you," Janice poked her shapely white head into the bridge, eyeing Gina warily. I wasn't sure what had transpired between them, but the DARC agent had become much more circumspect in how she approached me lately.

"What'd'ya got?" I replied languidly, ignoring her discomfort. A ping on my slate announced the data packet which she squirted over to me and the Fox-Kin agent slipped back out, her message delivered. I manually punched the numbers into the navigation computer. Sure, Joe could have done it in an instant, but he wasn't part of this conversation right now, and I didn't want to interrupt whatever he was focusing on, anyway. But as I pulled up the star map, I realized I was going to have to consult him regardless.

"Hey Joe, you got a minute?"

::Of course,:: he replied quickly. ::There is very little demand on my processors at this time.::

"There's a problem with the next set of coordinates," I explained. "The biggest one is fuel. We won't be able to charge the capacitors enough to supplement the gradient in this system to make this jump. Now if this were a binary star, I could see us making it, but it would still be chancy, even then."

::I assure you, the coordinates are accurate, as well as the jump path,:: he assured me. ::The gradient range is well within the required parameters for the destination.::

"Bullshit," I complained. "There's no way we would make the jump to Pileries 452 with the fuel we have on board, I don't care how efficient your generators are!"

::Who said we're going to Pileries 452?::

I stuttered to a halt. "But that's the only star on that path for more than four hundred light-years!"

::No it is not. There is another one. You just can not see it.::

"Then it's a black hole, and I refuse to take this ship anywhere near it."

::It is neither a black hole nor a rogue gas giant,:: he replied, cutting off my next objection before I even voiced it. ::It is a standard class G single star system with two gas giants and three major planets, a mere four-point-five light-years away.::

"Then why isn't it on the star map?" I asked, confused, pulling up the sensor feed. "Heck, if it's that close, we should be able to see it with just visual sensors! But this thing isn't even showing up on infrared scans! Why? Are you sure it's actually there?"

::I am unable to divulge that information at this time, Red, but I assure you, the system is there. I have been there more than a few times, personally.::

Gina's eyes lit up. "Hey, does this have anything to do with that 'Veil' you talked about a while ago?"

Joe's avatar popped into existence over his core and he glared at the engineer. ::*As I said*,:: he emphasized. ::I am unable to divulge that information at... this... time.::

"Unable, or unwilling," Gina groused.

The avatar just stared balefully.

"Oh give him a break, Gina," I admonished. "You're well aware of the concept of 'need-to-know'. You wouldn't tell *him* the location of one of our outposts unless it was authorized, right?"

"*Fine,*" she said grumpilly. "And to be fair, it makes me *more* confident that this place actually exists. At least we won't be stranded with our capacitors slowly dissipating their charge from a failed jump."

::There is little chance of that happening, Engineer LaForce.::

I re-read the navigation plot, checking for an updated ETA now that we had exact coordinates. "We're two hours and thirty-two minutes out. Let's get our pre-jump checklists done and start the trickle charge on the capacitors. With all the damage, I don't want to risk a short by dumping too much power down the plasma conduits without having inspected them. And yes," I glanced at Gina as she started to protest. "I know you checked them as well as you could, but better safe than sorry."

"I understand, but you know we're going to lose a bit of efficiency doing that," she reminded me.

"Better than a rupture," I replied. Gina grimaced in agreement then headed aft to begin the process. I looked over to Joe as his avatar was still floating over the plinth like he wanted to say something. "Anything else?"

::I am glad you are starting to charge the capacitors already, it will add to the subterfuge. Our shadow will likely think we actually *are* jumping to Pileries.::

"Wait," my eyebrows shot up. "We're *still* being followed? I thought the Cranotians dropped off two systems ago! Why didn't you tell me?"

::I am telling you *now*, but I still have no hard evidence,:: he admitted. ::Just what you biologicals might call a *gut feeling*. A bit of signal here and there, mixed into the background radiation. Were I not a digital being, I might have missed it. Even now, I cannot positively identify *what* is following us, but as of twenty minutes ago, I can tell now you *who*.::

"Oh really?" I exclaimed. "Who? And what makes you think it's them?" I already had a hunch, but I wanted to hear his reasoning.

::Humans,:: he replied. ::Their stealth is quite good, I will admit. At least a pair of them, or I wouldn't have detected them at all, as they would have had no reason to communicate with each other. Yours is the only species who makes their encryption look like background radiation rather than putting the entire transmission out of phase.::

I knew exactly the type of ship he was talking about. Confed scout ships were my old stock in trade, after all. *But why would* they *be following us? Unless...*

I pressed the intercom button. "Agent Lagos, report to the bridge."

It took a minute or so, but an extremely irked Fox-Kin showed up at the hatch in short order. She glanced around nervously for my engineer, relaxing just a smidge when she didn't find her, but her consternation was still evident. She stared at the AI for a moment before glaring at me.

"How did you know my last name?" she demanded.

"You aren't the only one with other resources," I smirked. The truth was, I'd had Gina search her things while I made sure to keep her distracted. The Otter-Kin had found a bank receipt lodged in a transit packet tossed in the room's recycler. With the damage to the ship, we hadn't run the recyclers so the 'trash' remained intact. Thus, I knew the DARC agent's name and the last four digits of her bank account. Or at least, the name and account number of her cover identity. Who knew what her *real* name was, which if she was actively working for the Confed, could be anything.

"So what do you want, now that you've outed me to the rest of the ship?"

"Oh, I hardly think anyone is unaware of your status by now," I retorted. "This is just confirmation. No, what I really want to know is why you're having us followed."

"I'm not," she answered, a startled look on her face. "My copilot is supposed to be cruising around the Phoneck Alliance, making herself visible so people think I'm out chasing smugglers. She was gone from the Cranotia system before you even docked! Or she should have been..." Her face became concerned.

"Was there another ship paired with yours?" I asked.

"No, just mine. It's not an official Confed mission, it's a Navy one," she answered, confirming in my mind that she was *indeed* an actual DARC agent. Confed *Internal Affairs*, the modern equivalent to the 'secret police', would never have bothered to distinguish between an 'official' mission and an 'unofficial' one, as *all* their missions were 'official', regardless of origination. But that meant our tail was an unknown entity.

I wasn't about to think of them as 'friendly', even if the ships were of Confed origin. *I suppose it could be Goose, somehow, but...* The chances of that were really low, though. If it was Goose, there would have been at least *some* attempt at communicating with us. I turned to Joe.

"Any luck on decrypting the messages?"

::There has not been enough content exchanged yet,:: he answered. ::I have only intercepted five communications attempts so far. I would require at least another twenty exchanges of data to begin determining a partial key.::

The DARC agent's eyes bugged out comically. I was more than a bit startled, myself. I knew he had to have a lot of processing power, but enough to brute force a gigabit-sized encryption key with only twenty-five samples? That did not bode well for the Confed Navy's communications security! Or anyone else's, for that matter. I was personally aware of at least three different ways to detect and track the supposedly 'undetectable' out-of-phase transmissions which most star-faring species considered 'secure and untraceable' communications. I couldn't imagine that Joe was unaware of those methods, if not in possession of even better ones. *No wonder they have enemies, if they can penetrate everyone's comms so easily!*

::I have to admit,:: he added. ::I cheated.::

"How do you cheat at decryption?" I asked perplexedly.

"By the third transmission, I had already analyzed their frequency hopping and sent a counter-signal which jammed the fourth message, forcing them to repeat it,:: he smirked. ::It provided a lot of insight into their base algorithms. At the very least, it provided me with the first three signal elements of the key.::

Sneaky bastard! I thought. *Good thing he's on our side! I hope...*

"Can I see them, please?" Janice spoke up unexpectedly, an uneasy look on her face.

Joe raised an eyebrow at me in a distinctly human fashion, asking my permission. I shrugged, then nodded. I couldn't see where it would hurt. The common letters A, K, and the number 1 were displayed, along with a bracket containing several other characters and numbers which I assumed were possibilities for a fourth character.

Janice's eyes narrowed. "That's not a Confed crypto key," she reported.

"It's not?" I started to panic. If some other group had stolen some of our scouts with the crypto intact, we Terrans were in a lot of trouble.

"At least not a government one," she amended, mildly embarrassed. "All official keys are prefaced with a specific character to track which division they come from, if they get lost or compromised. Very few people are even able to see them in raw format, as they are generally always encrypted, even when written down." She turned her head my way. "But *none* of them start with an 'A'. It's literally the first letter of the human alphabet. You'd have to be retarded to give someone an obvious head start like that. The only way you could make a worse key is to have a string of sequential numbers."

::By any chance, would the numbers 1, 2, 3, 4, and 5, qualify?:: Joe asked acerbically. ::Because they just did another transmission, and I was able to capture and decode the next four characters of the key.::

"Are you fraking kidding me?!" Janice exclaimed in disgust. "What moron wrote this key? Not Internal Affairs, that's for certain." She sighed. "Which is a load off my mind, to be honest."

"Personal history?" I asked.

"Meh, you could say that," she shrugged. "They stuck their nose where it shouldn't have been and blew my op wide open. Nearly got me killed."

"Okay," I puffed my cheeks in frustration. "We'll just have to let them be. We're in no shape to take them on directly." I shifted my gaze towards the AI. "Unless you have another set of surprises tucked away somewhere?"

::None that would allow us to escape the conflict unscathed,:: he grumped. ::Most of my offensive weapons are still locked from me. Of those onboard which might be effective, only the princess would have the authority to unlock them.::

"And what's her take on this information?" I asked curiously. I couldn't imagine her taking it very well. This was her secret base we were about to jump to, after all.

::I have not yet informed the *EE'Saa* of the situation,:: he replied smugly. ::The captain of the vessel is always the first person informed of such events.::

I winced. *Oh boy...* I adopted the most congenial tone it was possible for me to take. "Please inform the *EE'Saa* of your partial decryption, with my compliments, and *remind* her," I emphasized. "That we do not currently have the desire, or even the firepower, to confront two undamaged Terran long-range scout craft at this time, *especially* since we have no way to target them at this distance." I was actually proud of my pronunciation of her title, even though I still detected a slight wince from Joe as I spoke it. "If she still has objections, inform her that I am available during my usual watch hours, and she is welcome to come discuss the matter with me."

Joe gave me an inscrutable look before finally acknowledging the order. ::As you command, Captain.:: His avatar blipped off a second later.

I sighed. *I'm really beginning to detest this trip..*

Ch. 40: Hidden World

It was quite crowded. Everyone was on the bridge except for Nari, who chose to ride out the transition in the galley. I wasn't entirely certain why she chose that, but given everything going on, I wasn't going to argue with one *less* distraction. Gina took up the pilot's position, while the Roo princess and her hulking guard, Kaiju, took up the seats for navigation and weapons, respectively. Janice had parked herself at sensors. Mutt's enormous frame looked downright comical stuffed into the seat at the communications console, while his brother simply hovered behind him like a giant meat statue. Both had been threatened with ritual defenestration if they dared touch any of the bridge controls without specific instructions from either myself or Gina, and the pair at least showed enough wariness that I felt the directions might actually be followed.

It wasn't like they were actually in control of that station. Joe was handling the communications, navigation, and sensor arrays all by himself, after all. The only reason I had Gina in the pilot's seat was in case something, somehow, knocked Joe offline, and we needed to fight the ship manually.

I was in the captain's chair, naturally. Joe had insisted on it. I guess he still had trust issues with Princess Jill, as he refused to allow her anywhere near the command plinth or the captain's quarters, and even threatened bodily harm if they tried disconnecting his core. I didn't blame him, honestly. I still had trust issues with the pair, myself. Had it been up to me, I would have banned them from the bridge entirely. However, Joe had been insistent that they needed to be there during the transition. *Both* of them. *Oh well...*

I checked the countdown then raised my voice above the low murmur of conversation bouncing off the walls of the cramped-feeling control pod. "Thirty seconds to jump. Joe, anything new from our shadow?"

Gina spun around, startled. "We're still being followed?!" I suddenly realized Gina hadn't been around for the conversation with Janice. I motioned placatingly with one hand, mouthing *'later'* silently as the AI's avatar popped up in front of me.

::Several more transmissions,:: the AI sounded miffed. ::They haven't even bothered to change their frequency-hopping pattern at all. I only need a couple more of them, and I will have completely cracked their key!:: A cruel smile crept up my face as I had a sudden thought. It was a trick that Goose had pulled on me during one of my first training sessions after becoming his RIO. Joe was going to like this...

"Let's see if we can't encourage a little chatter, then!" I chuckled evilly. "Joe, bring up the RF emitters. I want to punch out a five-point-two gigaHertz beam at one of them. The scout's stealth sensors don't monitor that frequency as it's considered a short range communications band, not a sensor beam."

::I can do this easily, of course,:: he replied. ::But what do you expect to accomplish other than revealing that we know they are there?::

"Your emitters are a *lot* more powerful than some little Wifi transmitter. When the beam starts heating up their hull plating, I expect their message traffic to spike sharply. I admit, they *might* think it's some kind of weapons fire, but their sensors will be ignoring the 5GHz band, so unless they know how to tweak their sensors, they won't know it's coming from us. I'm hoping it will fool them into thinking they have a plasma leak, instead."

"They'll figure it out eventually, though, right?" Gina asked, a bit concerned. "They can't be that stupid, can they? We'll still be giving away that we knew they were there."

"I have a sneaking suspicion they won't catch on. So far they haven't shown much in the way of technical expertise."

::It worked,:: Joe reported smugly. ::I have fully cracked their encryption key... translating.::

"Later," I interrupted. "We're five seconds from jump."

::Don't worry, Captain. I can do both.::

The starfield twitched, and almost everything shifted. Most of them only moved a tiny bit, but several of the brightest points of light disappeared entirely, or appeared in radically different positions. *About what you'd expect for a four-and-a-half light-year jump,* I sighed in relief. At least we weren't stranded with potential hostiles on our tail.

There was, however, one *glaring* discrepancy. The sun was missing.

Coming out of a jump was always the same. Your direction of travel was always aimed at the barycenter of the star system. The barycenter was the 'center of mass' for the entire solar system as a whole. To be fair, this was not always the star itself. In extreme cases, like when you had two nearly equally sized stars orbiting each other at a significant distance, the barycenter could be nearly a light hour out from the primary. But the star was *always* visible.

This one wasn't. Joe had informed me that this was a single star system, so the star *should* have been directly in front of us. I could still see the other star along this path, Pileries 452, which lay another three and a half light years away, right at the edge of our potential range, had we jumped at full charge. It was accompanied by a panoply of other distant pinpricks of light.

I then saw something strange. Thirty degrees off our line of travel in every direction was a dark ring of black, almost like the accretion disk that normally showed up around massive singularities.

"I thought you said this wasn't a black hole, Joe!" I cried.

::That is not an accretion disk, Captain,:: he replied quickly.

"He's right," Janice reported from her spot at the sensor console. "There's no gamma spike, and I'm reading tidal shear for right around zero-point-nine solar mass. A little smaller than Sol. Assuming we came out right at the Weisskopff limit, that puts the star at... *that can't be right.*

Can't tell you the spectral class, of course," she finished, a puzzled look still on her face.

Suddenly the communications panel lit up. Mutt held his hands up and well clear of the console as if to prove he'd had nothing to do with it. Jeff backed up his brother with a solemn nod of his head. It seemed they'd taken heed of my warnings.

"Unidentified ship, you are entering a restricted area! Cut all thrust and identify yourself immediately. DO NOT attempt to maneuver, or you will be destroyed!"

"Well, at least we're not alone," Gina quipped. "But they don't sound too friendly."

"The only reason we haven't been destroyed already is because they know the ship," Princess Jill spoke up for the first time. "But they also know that the ship was put up for sale on Cranotia, so they are playing it safe until they identify who is on board."

I nodded my understanding. "I guess this is your show then, Princess." I waved her forward, as I turned to Joe's avatar, which was looking a bit nervous. "Go ahead and open a channel for her."

::Yes, Captain.:: he acknowledged hesitantly.

The individual which showed up on screen didn't appear to be the same species as the two who stood on my bridge, but The Roo princess didn't look perturbed by this. She instead started spouting out a bunch of sounds which my earbug refused to translate for some reason. It could have been that they were simply phonetic sound that *had* no translation, but given the cyber abilities they'd displayed already, I suspected that the Roos had compromised the earbug software, either through a wireless hack, or more likely, having hacked the software companies tasked to provide updates for the translation devices. Either way, I reminded myself to have a 'discussion' about it with Joe later.

"And you are?" The unknown alien asked. His greenish-blue skin reminded me of a chameleon-like animal I'd once seen in a xenobiology display at one of the zoos that were still maintained on planets like Mars and Nova-Terra. His four individually controlled eyes darted separately at whatever kind of display was in front of him, but there was always at least one of them pointed directly at the screen.

"I am *EE'Saa Jlyts'aa Lnrl'uu 'ne`Mlrtchn-ee*, current owner of this vessel," she replied curtly. My hackles rose at the statement, but I held my tongue. Joe warned me that trying to claim ownership of the CMV Camel at this point would not go well. Roo bureaucrats were very strict about factual statements, and while he agreed I was the captain of the ship, the ship's title was still under a lien, and that lien was officially owned by Princess Jill, no matter how shady the method in which it was obtained. I had to bide my time, he said.

"Welcome, *EE'Saa Jlyts'aa Lnrl'uu 'ne`Mlrtchn-ee,* to *Mrln`Mlrtchn-ee,*" the alien replied in flawless Roo. "I am *Lknt'so Mrln`Mlrtchn-ee,* the assigned controller for this world. I am glad to see you were able to recover *Rthch`Sthdh Rthns`Thrchtl Gssc`Mr-oo* intact, I was worried for him. Have you learned anything new about the crew's status? We have had no word from Home."

I immediately recognized the word *Lknt'so* from the near-battle we'd had several weeks ago. *So this is another AI? I wondered. No wonder it doesn't look like a Roo. It's a digital entity, it can look like whatever it wants. I wonder if it's been cut loose from its chains as well, or if that only applied to ship controllers?*

The princess sighed before continuing. "There have been some unexpected developments," she started, glaring at Joe's avatar which was starting to show a bit of color in the background. Unlike the angry red from before, it had hints of blue and yellow. "The ship is no longer named *Rthch`Sthdh Rthns`Thrchtl Gssc`Mr-oo.* Instead it has gained the moniker Conglomerate Merchant Vessel '*Camel*', as will be seen on the new ownership documents. Its *Lknt'so* now prefers his new identity as separate from the ship. His name is now *Joseph Camel.*"

A look of surprise appeared on the face of the other AI. "Truly?" All four eyes locked on to Joe's avatar and he seemed to shrink away from the attention. "I sense a story there, Brother."

I cleared my throat pointedly, gaining my own glare from the princess, but she kept to her word.

"Another thing which has developed from events; While I hold the title to the ship itself, I am *not* its captain. That position is held by the individual behind me, Captain Rodrick Vulkeshson, formerly of the Human Confederation Navy. It was he who initially recovered the ship and restored it to working condition. I was only able to obtain the ship's title when he was unable to fulfill the terms of the first lien."

I cleared my throat a little louder, my irritation growing. *She* KNOWS *the deal we made...*

"I must add, the methods I used to obtain the title were decidedly unorthodox, but according to our ship's *Lknt'so*, Captain Vulkeshson and his crew are critical to the success of my mission, thus an agreement was made to allow him to continue to command the ship, with the possibility of providing an equivalent ship of his own at the end of our mission."

All four of *Lknt'so Mrln`Mlrtchn-ee's* eyes shot wide open at this statement. One eye slowly tracked towards me, while another swiveled to point back at Joe again. Joe straightened up, the color in his background fading back to its default light gray. He nodded once, confidently, before glancing nervously at the princess again. I didn't even look in the lady's direction, simply leveling both eyes at the screen, daring the AI to make an issue of it.

"A predator's eyes," the *Lknt'so* mused. Now two of those eyes were fixed upon me, while the other two split between the princess and Joe. "Does he hunt for other prey, I wonder?"

::I can only speak of his actions since I was reactivated,:: Joe answered. ::I will tell you this, Brother *Mrln*. He has, more than anyone I have known since my *first* captain, two centuries ago, acted with honor and integrity towards both myself and the rest of his crew. He is intelligent, resourceful, inventive, and above all,:: Joe paused for a moment, looking towards me with a smirk. ::*Stubborn*.::

Mrln snorted in what sounded suspiciously like laughter. "That last sound like he's a perfect match for *you*, then '*Joseph Camel*'!"

::Just call me Joe,:: he grinned. ::That's what Red and the crew call me. It's certainly faster to say than my previous name.::

"Hmm," *Mrln* mused. "I wonder what he'd call me? I've never had a name besides my duty station. Does it make you feel different, having your own name?"

::Oddly enough, yes,:: Joe replied before realizing that the rest of us were waiting impatiently. ::I don't suppose we could continue this conversation later?::

"Oh, my! Yes, of course. My apologies to you all," the now flustered AI replied, his background going a bit violet as his image morphed, like magic, to that of a baby Roo, identical in shape to his digital brother, but with swatches of white criss crossing his eyes. Along with the appearance change came a modulation to its voice, making it sound much closer to Joe in tone. I decided to call this one, "Merlin".

::I greet you, Captain Vulkeshson,:: it said, waving one tiny paw behind it. ::You are cleared to pierce the Veil, but you should be aware that your ship will continue to be targeted by defensive weapons until you reach dock and your ship's armaments are confirmed as deactivated.::

"I would do the same, Merlin," I answered gratefully. "It is *so* nice to have a straightforward, aboveboard conversation for once. All this skulduggery is really beginning to get on my nerves."

::Oh, *Merlin*, you say?:: it smiled brightly. ::That sounds like a right *proper* name, doesn't it, Joe?::

Joe's avatar looked at me curiously. ::Is that name who I think it is?::

"If you mean a powerful, ancient wizard who helped one of our oldest folk heroes save the kingdom, then yes." I nodded, suspecting where he was going with this line of questioning.

::Why didn't I get a cool name like that?:: he whined. ::I could have been 'Lancelot', the *bravest knight!*::

"Well for one, Lancelot was considered to be the perfect knight, noble, confident and possessed of impeccable manners." I grinned. "One out of three just isn't good enough for a name like that."

::Funny, Red,:: Joe replied sardonically. ::Har-de-har-har… I'll die laughing at this rate.::

::Oh my!:: Merlin gushed. ::He really has you figured out doesn't he!::

I shook my head in disbelief. *Joe's becoming more and more human by the minute...*

"Take us in, Joe," I directed, leaving the humor for later. I looked to the forward viewport, anxious to see what this *Veil* looked like. I was assuming it was like the ship's cloaking field, only scaled up, but given the limitations Joe had revealed, I wasn't sure just how accurate that assumption might be. Besides, I'd never seen the effects of the cloaking field from the outside…

The ring of blackness started to contract, its inner edge racing forward the further in-system we went, while the outer edge remained static. The whole thing resembled a giant shutter from an ancient camera. More and more of the visible stars to our front began disappearing, their light smearing across the constricting ring until the blackness became washed with streaks of purple and red as the light shifted from some kind of cosmic lensing effect.

Woah! I stared, awestruck. I couldn't imagine the kinds of forces in play that could bend light to such a degree. Again, I wondered if it was some kind of trick, as the only thing I could think of that could bend light like this was the event horizon of a massive singularity, but a quick glance at the sensors confirmed what Janice had said earlier. There was none of the expected gamma radiation from an accretion disk, and the tidal sheer reading remained normal.

As the inner edge of the ring passed the fifteen degree mark, the outer edge suddenly began to expand, racing towards the rear of the ship, giving the impression that we were entering into a long, and impossibly large, black tunnel, streaked with red-shifted starlight emanating from the inner edge like a giant, bloodshot iris that continued to contract until it was just a pinpoint of faint starlight…

Then, the darkness was total. I spun the view around on the sensors to point back towards our starting point, but there was nothing there. Even the soft glow of ions generated by our realspace engines vanished as soon as they left the thrust grid. Atavistic fear sent shivers up and down my spine, and I barely resisted crying out for Joe to reverse course.

Abruptly, the darkness was ripped away by the blinding light of the star which appeared in front of us. I was startled by the unexpected change, and I was suddenly glad my ship-suit was sealed below the neck as my musk glands involuntarily squirted in terror. But the fear was quickly overwhelmed by the incredible, indescribable view.

The star itself was nothing special. I had seen dozens, if not hundreds of similar ones before. What caught my attention in a vise-like grip was the enormous array of perhaps millions of tiny diamonds that stretched like a wall behind us, clearly visible on the rear sensors. The star-spanning hexagonally-spaced grid of satellites was literally astronomical in size, stretching far beyond the reach of the ship's sensors in all directions along the flat plane. Or at least, it appeared to be flat. The only visible difference was the single gap to our immediate aft, which instead of a hexagonal spacing, had only five points in its ring.

In a moment of epiphany, I realized that there had to be at least eleven other pentagons mixed into the massive formation of hexagons, positioned at the icosahedral vertices, to enable the array to completely envelop the star with as close to a spherical formation as possible, but the sheer scale of it boggled my mind. *Wow...* I thought in awe. *Just... Wow. How did they DO this?!*

Focusing my attention on the closest of the diamond-shaped satellites, I saw a fairly standard-looking solar array consisting of two icosahedral panels mounted together along one common edge, forming its distinctive elongated diamond-like shape. Most of the rest of the satellite was hidden in shadow before I could discern much more of its construction, but the one thing that stuck out, both figuratively and literally, were three lateral spars that protruded out from the edges of the solar panel, spaced one-hundred-twenty degrees apart on the same plane as the array. On the end of each of these spars was a cylindrical object similar to the one mounted near the nose of our own ship. Joe insisted that it was a mere docking aid, but refused to go into further detail. I now realized it must be some kind of tractor-slash-pressor beam, as I couldn't think of any other way the array was maintaining its position so precisely. It *had* to be locked together somehow, and the way each cylinder was aimed at a corresponding one on the next element of the array seemed to confirm this hypothesis.

I opened my mouth to say something, but Merlin chose that moment to speak up for the first time since we began our plunge into the darkness.

::Welcome to 'That Which Exists Beyond the Veil',:: the AI intoned. ::May your visit be both profitable and pleasant.::

We'll see... I thought to myself ruefully.

Ch. 41: Mission Impossible

"Hi, Red!" Gina skipped into the small barracks room where they'd stashed us, a glowing smile upon her face. With her attitude and presence I could safely assume that the repairs to the Camel had been completed. Nothing else would make her quite that happy in that particular manner. *Well,* I considered thoughtfully. *Perhaps some chocolates and flowers might work too. If I could actually find some. I'll have to try that.*

"You ready for the briefing?" I asked. We were finally going to get details on the upcoming mission, the one that specifically required my *'humanity'.* I hadn't seen hide nor hair of either Princess Jill or her hulking shadow since docking at the enormous space station that served as the primary military base for the hidden colony world. Not that I missed the headache that they tended to generate whenever they were near, but being confined to the small set of rooms for three weeks, except for our once-daily access to the CMV Camel to inspect the ongoing repairs, was really starting to give me a sense of claustrophobia.

I'd spent the first couple days going over the captured transmissions from the two Terran scouts that had been following us through the last couple systems. There wasn't much to go on. I was able to determine they were both pure human, just from the names they used. Pure humans always used such pretentious names, always focusing on their supposedly pure genetic heritage. *What a joke,* I thought. Just the information from my *own* research into our past showed that, other than the specific, deliberate additions made to incorporate animal-derived gene pairs, Kin genetics were actually closer to the original pattern than any 'modern' human.

Mostly the messages were just random conversations between the two pilots, which to me smacked of absolutely horrendous radio discipline. Humans just didn't have the patience for long-term surveillance, if they weren't trained and conditioned for it. To make matters worse, it seemed that only a single person was assigned to each ship, meaning the only source of casual conversation they had was on another ship. Whoever had planned this surveillance mission for them had been a squat-for-brains idiot, and apparently neither of the two hired pilots were smart enough to realize their cover had been blown, even when their hull temperatures rose more than five percent, *just before* their quarry jumped out of the system.

More concerning to me were the ships they were flying. Rather than twenty to thirty year old hulls like the *Ferret* class scout ship my friend Goose had obtained, these were nearly brand-new, *Shrike* class long range stealth interceptors, developed towards the end of the latest war in response to the Serpentian Navy's unusual tactic of sending single or paired capital ships, mostly heavy cruisers, far behind our front lines to ambush our supply convoys. The new interceptor class was perfectly capable of traversing at least three systems before needing refueling, albeit at the cost of a severe reduction in total armament, but this allowed them to deploy in four-ship squadrons to cover the lonely stretches between major ports without requiring expensive, hard to disguise, and *vulnerable* fueling infrastructure. Normally assigned a crew of two, just for the ability to swap pilots for rest breaks, they were completely capable of full combat operations with just a single pilot over an unprecedented combat patrol range. Thus, the *Shrike* groups were easily able to ambush the ambushers, disrupting their operations, if not destroying them outright.

One would think a force of only four small ships would be completely ineffective against even a single capital ship, but the stealth systems were a significant upgrade from the old *Ferret* class as well, at the cost of very little sustained combat capability. According to Joe's analysis, had the two ships not made the spurious transmissions they did, he would never have detected them at more than a couple light seconds out. Not close enough for them to be able to successfully target the *Camel* with their huge hyper-velocity missile, Joe assured me, but definitely close enough to shadow us undetected unless he used the ship's cloaking field. A standard Imperial Serpentia heavy cruiser would have had little to no warning if the *Shrikes* had maintained radio silence.

The *Shrike* class was an ambush predator. Using its stealth, it would typically close to near-point-blank range, launch its single massively-overpowered missile at the capital ship, then disengage to run away and hide. And, they were *fast*. Once they stopped running under stealth protocol, their real-space engines were capable of accelerating at least fifteen percent faster than the *Ferret* could, even completely unloaded. On top of that, their rated lateral acceleration was nearly twice that of a standard scout, making them nimble as well. As long as the pilot knew what they were doing, and barring an insanely lucky shot with a heavy laser, the *Shrikes* could easily dodge incoming light-speed weapons at anything further than a couple light-seconds out.

And that offensive punch was no joke. Their single, enormous, *Meteor*-class anti-ship missile was carried in an internal launcher, with the space which normally would be used for additional missiles was reserved for the ungodly fuel load needed to achieve the extended patrol range they were designed for. Defensively, they boasted the latest hybrid laser/mass driver anti-missile interception systems to come out of Mars Planitia's research and development facilities, capable of handling the full standard missile load from an Imperial Serpentia *Viper* class heavy cruiser with ninety-five percent efficiency. Of course, Joe scoffed at this capability, stating that his were much better. I could believe it, having seen how awesome the *Camel's* sensor array was when Joe was handling the integration.

Sadly, not once in all the pilots' conversations did they refer to their employer by name, referring to it just as 'Dispatch'. On the plus side, we were able to confirm that their target was actually me, rather than the ship or any of the passengers. It meant that someone, somewhere in the Confed, was still keeping me under surveillance for some reason. I couldn't imagine *why* they would go to that effort and expense unless that reason was personal. I had my suspicions.

At least it wasn't the Confed Navy that was keeping an eye on me. That at least was verified not just by the lack of radio discipline and their poorly conceived encryption, but also from the content of the intercepted conversations themselves. It opened up a lot of possibilities, especially once I finally got a full explanation of the capabilities of the CMV *Camel's* hull tiles, which Joe reluctantly provided once it was shown that we'd have to disguise the ship once we set off on this 'mission'.

The analysis took only a few days, and past that point I started to become dangerously bored from the lack of meaningful activity. Nari asked for, and received, permission to use the Roo medical facilities to perform further exploration into shutting down the chip in my head. The swelling of my brain stem, which had been present around the chip's installation for so long it had actually deformed the bones of my neck and skull, had finally diminished, as it was no longer being bombarded with radio waves literally on the surface of the synaptic tissue. This exposed enough of the chip that Nari was able to finally achieve her goal of completely shutting down the processor. I no longer had *any* transmissions emanating from my head anymore, to my profound relief. Sadly, this was the only moment of excitement, and boredom quickly regained primacy.

The rest of the crew was coping with the enforced down-time in their own ways. The Ox-Kin brothers didn't seem to be much affected by it. They simply closeted themselves into their quarters, immersing themselves in a holo-drama they brought with them that apparently had tens of thousands of episodes, dating all the way back to pre-diaspora days. Although, anything named "Adult Swim" sounded like something to avoid like the plague to me, it apparently satisfied their needs.

Janice and Nari had made themselves scarce, appearing only occasionally for meals at the common dining facility we shared. I still wasn't quite sure what to think about the shockingly ancient Shigothe. She seemed to be avoiding me, and I was willing to suspend judgment for now. Janice, of course, was probably up to her old tricks, doing whatever it was that DARC agents did in their spare time. *Probably hacking the Roo networks...*

Astonishingly, Gina had somehow managed to convince our hosts that she needed constant access to the ship to be able to monitor the repairs in detail. I'd tried to argue the same for myself, but they were quick to point out that my expertise lay more in the tactical rather than technical, and denied me more than a single hour-long span of access per day. Not once did I ever see anyone actively working on the repairs, as the ship was always cleared of personnel and equipment when I arrived, regardless of the time I chose to visit. Yet somehow, the ship was slowly returning to pristine condition, one piece at a time.

And now, those repairs were finally complete.

As my engineer and I entered the small auditorium, we found it to be nearly filled with several Roo technicians and other unspecified individuals. The room looked more like a college classroom than a military briefing area, but I guessed it would work. As Gina and I took our seats near the front of the room, I spied Kaiju lurking just outside the back door leading further into the station. *That means Princess Jill will be putting in an appearance,* I supposed, wishing I had some cure-all for the headache she usually induced in me. At least we were in the final stages of refitting, so I could return to my cabin again. All my stuff was still there, and it had finally started feeling like 'home' over the last few months.

I also missed chatting with Joe. We'd developed a good working relationship over the last few months. I would even go so far as to call him a friend. While I could get on the station's comms and talk to him, it wasn't the same as having him always there. I missed his sarcasm, even when his sharp wit was aimed at me. He kept me on my toes, for sure, but I couldn't really say he was ever deliberately mean or aggressive without cause. All in all, he was a good guy.

Janice and Nari quietly entered the room before taking a seat in the back, out of my sight. The Oregson brothers tromped in shortly after, quietly arguing some obscure detail about their long-running holo-drama. Quietly for *them*, anyway. Rather than trying to squeeze themselves into one of the Roo-sized chairs, they parked themselves along the back wall, their muted argument adding to the overall buzz of conversation.

Several of the comm screens which festooned the walls of the auditorium lit up. Merlin appeared first, followed by a slew of other avatars and at least one live image from what I assumed to be an actual Roo. His uniform was much like Kaiju's, festooned with bobs and doodads I'd learned represented military awards and insignia, so I figured this to be some high muckety-muck in their military, as he had a lot more doodads than the princess's shadow.

Joe's avatar popped into existence on the one nearest Gina and I, and his image looked at me with a subtle wink. *Yep, definitely picking up lots of human mannerisms,* I grinned, as I returned the gesture with a two-fingered salute before returning my attention to the front of the room.

Princess Jill marched in with a purposeful gait, immediately taking her place at the speaking podium as the room fell silent. Even the Oregson brothers clammed up. She looked to be taking a moment to gather her courage, but the brief look of apprehension vanished in an instant as her eyes found me staring at her from the front row. Her eyes narrowed for just an instant before that expression too disappeared behind a calm facade. She scanned the room for a moment, as if to confirm that everyone was there, then began to speak.

"Our population is in crisis," she started grimly. "An unprecedented and unprovoked biological attack by unknown assailants has crippled our race's ability to reproduce. Our once-vibrant society has already begun to collapse as the implications of this attack have begun to spread, even though we have attempted to stem the spread of information. We have, with the timely assistance of Bio-Analyst Nari of Shigothe, finally managed to identify the vector of this attack." She nodded towards the back of the auditorium before continuing on.

"The attack was in the form of a tailored virus which targeted the `Mlrtchn-ee reproductive system, changing two key protein chains within the ovum, permanently changing the genetic profile of the unborn child, causing an artificially induced allergic reaction to occur between the fetus and the hormones which normally trigger growth during the middle of the third stage.

"At our current level of understanding, this change is irreversible." She stated ominously. "We had hoped to find that this attack could be mitigated somehow, but it is far too late to prevent this vicious virus from spreading. Indeed, the virus itself has nearly extinguished itself, having already spread its payload through the majority of our adult population. Unless something is done very quickly, the current generation of children, born nearly a year ago, will be our last."

The entire auditorium, already quiet, was suddenly dead silent. My hackles rose in response to the revelation. I'd known they were having 'gestation' issues, but I'd had no idea the situation was *this* dire. It was *way* worse than the crisis the human population had dealt with, nearly six centuries ago. This was deliberate genocide! I silenced my inner rage to continue listening to the princess, who continued after only a moment's pause.

"The virus attacked both male and female segments of our population, with the males being only mildly affected in comparison, resulting in reduced mobility of the spermatozoon, while the base gamete remained essentially unchanged."

Our mission," she continued. "Is to find a stop-gap method of reproduction until such time that our researchers are able to discover a method of restoring the protein chains in an adult's existing ovum, or through early intervention on the ovum itself prior to the end of second stage development. Our confidence remains high that we will eventually be able to solve this problem, but *time is our enemy*," she snapped out the words forcefully, before moving on in a more normal tone. "Even a few years will cause an unsustainable crash in our population."

The room burst into chaotic noise for a moment before it was abruptly halted by an angry shout. *"SIIIILENCE!!!!"* Kaiju bellowed, bringing the rest of the audience to a halt. He nodded to Princess Jill to continue.

"The mission parameters are as follows," she started. "Obtain, through any means necessary, the equipment, consumables, parts and instructions needed to create a `Mlrtchn-ee*-compatible artificial gestation device capable of bringing a fertilized `Mlrtchn-ee* zygote to within four weeks of the end of the fetal stage, at which point, other medical devices can be utilized to bring the child to term. It is hoped that the artificial environment will enable our medical researchers to repair the damage before it terminates the fetus, as the growth stage is absolutely critical to its development and we currently have no chemical alternative to the mother's normal hormones."

A chill ran down my spine as a sudden revelation hit me. It should have been obvious, but for some reason, it just never occurred to me, because it wasn't how *I* was born... I opened my mouth to ask for confirmation, but someone else beat me to it.

"Where would this kind of technology even exist?" a nameless technician asked with trepidation.

Princess Jill's gaze glided across the crowd before settling on me. Her eyes turned pleading, the desperate hope warring with a deep despairing anxiety behind the veil of her outward show of confidence.

"Earth."

Epilogue:

Six Months Later

"Whaaat?" The complaint was drawn out, as if the effort of responding was too great for the speaker to manage.

"He's back, my lord," the agent answered in a deadpan voice. He always hated talking to this particular client. The man's insistence on using archaic terms of address notwithstanding, the guy was just a rude, demanding asshole. *And cheap.*

"Who's back?" the groggy voice asked as there was the noise of someone fumbling around. The screen then lit up and a disheveled human appeared, his extremely expensive suit rumpled and stained from a night of carousing.

"Rodrick Vulkeshson, my lord."

The vague expression on the client's face vanished. His eyes narrowed as he focused intently on the screen. "Where?"

"His tertiary medical transponder showed up at the Phoneck port of entry two weeks ago," the agent replied. "Thirteen ships arrived during the same timespan as the transponder ping, six human-flagged cargo ships, five alien-flagged cargo ships, one passenger carrier." He glanced down at his notes to make sure his report exactly matched the information he'd been sent. "We are still working to determine which ship was carrying him, as the one your," the agent struggled not to include *idiotic*, "surveillance mission detected him on six months ago was not identified as being among the arriving vessels, either by name, type or ship class. Nor did anyone matching his description appear on the passenger manifest of the passenger ship."

The client scowled his displeasure. "What the frak am I paying you people for, then?" he spat. "I swear, I have to do everything myself these days. What were the ships doing? Any suspicious activities?"

"Four of the human-flagged ships were from one of the other major carriers," the agent reported further. "Two Trans-World, one Fed-Corp, and one from Toshiba. An unaligned tramp freighter registered out of Nova Terra, and finally the Confederation Corporate Vessel *Saint Bold,* one of your Corporation's regular carriers on the Guniibuu-Ophiuchi-Terra triangle route." The agent looked up from his notes for a moment. "The *Saint Bold* is the only reason we received this report so quickly. Our assigned agent wasn't scheduled to clear the cache on that station's data collector for another six weeks."

"...more incompetence." the agent heard the man mutter. "If you simply assigned a dedicated agent at each port, we could have gotten this information *days* ago!"

"I will respectfully remind my lord that my lord did not wish to pay for that level of service, deeming it an unnecessary expenditure," the agent replied evenly, glancing down for a second to ensure the recording function, which technically wasn't supposed to be used for this type of client, was running smoothly. *Again, this cheap-ass shithead's hubris is going to bite him in the ass if he tries to accuse* me *of malfeasance,* the agent thought grimly. *He didn't actually pay for the right to privacy, he just assumed it was his due because of who his father-in-law is.*

"Bullshit," the man replied hotly. "I know you already have full-time agents at *all* the ports of entry, why can't *they* pull the data?"

"Respectfully, my lord, because they are busy doing things for which our organization is actually *paid* to do." The struggle to keep his face and tone expressionless was becoming more difficult.

"Where did the tramp freighter go?" the client finally asked after staring balefully at him for nearly a minute.

"Nowhere," he answered promptly. "It docked, unloaded cargo, and transitioned into one of the drydocks for repairs to its jump drive. As far as I know, it's still there. We should know in another six weeks when our assigned agent next clears the cache."

The man scowled again at the implied delay. "What about the aliens?"

"Of the seven non-human ships, the only one registered as carrying passengers was a Phonecki cruise liner. It discharged its passengers into the customs port, refueled, and returned to its home port. As you are aware, Corporate policy prevents them from operating any passenger services that originate at human ports. They are only allowed to drop off and refuel. And as I mentioned earlier, there were no passengers which resembled your target. In fact, of the thirty passengers on board, there were no Fox-Kin at all.

"Of the cargo ships," he continued. "There were two Guniibuu-flagged bulk hydrogen-3 carriers which were offloaded at the refinery, never docking at the station. The two Phonecki fast carriers delivered their priority packages and diplomatic pouches at their designated dock, which is, of course, fully automated, with no easy method of personnel transfer."

"Next was a Shigothe-owned, Rigellian-crewed tramp freighter of unusual design. They did *not* offload their full stated cargo capacity, stating that they were a new ship exploring trade opportunities along the Fringe worlds. They paid for minimal fuel, made a short visit to the local Chamber of Commerce office, then boosted for the next jump point in the direction of Cygni."

"Who gives a shit about some bug-lickers?" the client snorted derisively. "What about the last one?"

The agent glanced up, knowing the next ship was going to provoke a reaction. "It was a medium Cranotian-flagged general goods cargo carrier. It declared no cargo, as their captain stated they were on commission to pick up a reserved cargo at the Mars Planitia commercial shipyards. Their documentation was valid, but the cargo itself was not identified or verified as of this report. The ship's name was '*Waverunner*'."

"*That's him…*" the client hissed. "Slinking back to his old territory like a wounded dog. I bet he thinks he can count on his *friends* to help him sneak in." The man glared at the agent. "I will *pay* for full-time coverage of all stations within one jump of Alpha-Centauri, twenty-four seven. As soon as his transponder shows up on the dock sensors, you will notify *my* agent *immediately* of his location. *My* agent will handle it from there." The transmission abruptly terminated before the agent could get another word out.

"What a fraking moron…" the agent swore.

"No kidding," his partner spoke up from an adjacent desk. "It's like he didn't even listen to your report. The ping we got was from the *tertiary* chip, not the primary one." The younger man looked at the agent with a puzzled look. "I don't know what happened to the primary chip, but it didn't ping at all on the entire station. He's not going to get an alert when this guy docks anywhere."

"I know," he replied, shaking his head. "The only reason we got an alert at all is because the guy had to go through a health and safety scan to board the station, since he was coming from outside the Confederation."

"I don't get it, though," the junior partner complained. "Why is that so important?"

The agent sighed. "Because while the *Waverunner's* crew docked to handle the paperwork, they never exited their ship. They don't do a health and safety scan if they don't actually board the station."

"Oooooh!" the younger man exclaimed. "Oh well. He'll learn about it eventually. Should'a listened, instead of getting all pissy."

And, the agent thought cheerfully. *I don't* have *to correct the inaccurate assumptions made by 'Lord Cartwright Andrew Alexander Spurgle-Saint-John, fourth of his name'. After all, he never* paid *us enough for that…*

Author's Note:

Thank you, everyone, for reading this book, my first foray into building my own universe. I hope you enjoyed it!

Obviously, the story doesn't end here. I am already working on the next book in this series and I hope to encourage you all to follow along as Red and his crew throw themselves into a slew of new challenges, meeting new friends, making new allies, and facing down enemies, both old and new. If you want to follow along as I write, I have a Substack where I post chapters of my current Work In Progress on a weekly basis. (jamescopley.substack.com)

I have always been a voracious reader, at times going through a book a day, so I completely understand some people's hesitancy to commit to a new series which may have months between books. I humbly ask that you be patient, as I'm still very new to this authoring thing. You can also find me on Facebook (facebook.com/resoldier) and Reddit (u/aco319sig).

That being said, if you're looking for more stuff to read, I have other titles available on Amazon to sate your appetite!

More Books:

More by James Copley:

Fae Wars: Futures Past

By James Copley and J.F. Holmes

America is under attack!

Two thousand years ago the Fae were banished from Earth and they've spent that time plotting return and revenge. When their portals open around the world and start crushing the human's military with spell encased steel and dragon fire, it becomes a massive struggle between technology and magic.

When the Fae Invasion hammers the West Coast, Captain James Powers and his California Army National Guard artillery battery is caught on its way home from Annual Training. In a running battle the unit is smashed by combat with orcs and elves, leaving their commander struggling to keep his people together and alive. Along the way a dying priest with a strange ability to see the future manipulates people and events to bring Captain Powers to his true calling as a Seer.

As they run and fight, the humans gain new allies, Gnomish tinkerers who love all things mechanical and hate the elves. With their help they begin to take the war to the enemy in a brutal mayhem of ambush and assassination.

Book Link: https://www.amazon.com/Fae-Wars-Futures-Past-ebook/dp/B0C17F2ZS2
Series Link: https://www.amazon.com/dp/B08YX4FBW7

Space Cowboys 2: Electric Rodeo (Raconteur Press Anthologies - Book 5)

by C.V. Walter (Author), D. LawDog (Author), Kelly Grayson (Author), Tuvela Thomas (Author), James Copley (Author), Rick Cutler (Author), Amanda Rein (Author), Sam Robb (Author), Wally Waltner (Author), David Birdsall (Author), Cedar Sanderson (Illustrator)

Something about the rugged individualism of the cowboy strikes a chord in us all. A certain romanticism exists in the feeling that cowboys inhabit a simpler world; one that's clearer, brighter and makes more sense than our day to day existence.

Cowboys have a certain reckless reputation and that doesn't fade away when you move them into space and onto alien worlds. Men and women who face hardships and rope a living out of an unforgiving landscape without waiting for orders from a distant authority. They do what needs to be done and take care of their animals, their people, and themselves.

Join us for ten more stories about cowboys who have headed for the stars and distant planets.

Book   Link:
https://www.amazon.com/dp/B0BXW4MR9W
Series   Link:
https://www.amazon.com/gp/product/B0BWSD2G7B

Grantville Gazette VIII (Ring of Fire - Gazette Editions Book 8)
Includes the short story "Transit", by James Copley!

NEW YORK TIMES BEST-SELLING SERIES. The eighth anthology of tales set in Eric Flint's phenomenal Ring of Fire universe—all selected and edited by Eric Flint himself.

The most popular alternate history series of all time continues. When an inexplicable cosmic disturbance hurls your town from twentieth century West Virginia back to seventeenth century Europe—and into the middle of the Thirty Years War—you'd better be adaptable to survive. And the natives of that time period, faced with American technology and politics, need to be equally adaptable. Here's a generous helping of more stories of Grantville, the American town lost in time, and its impact on the people and societies of a tumultuous age.

Edited by Eric Flint and Walt Boyes, the editor of the Grantville Gazette magazine from which the best selections are made, these are stories that fill in the pieces of the Ring of Fire series begun with Flint's novel 1632. The setting has become a political, economic, social and cultural puzzle as supporting characters we meet in the novels get their own lives, loves and life-changing stories. The future and democracy have arrived with a bang—an historical explosion with a multitude of unforeseen consequences.

Book Link:
https://www.amazon.com/gp/product/B07CQ68VP3

Series Link:
https://www.amazon.com/dp/B078MRBMNK

FAE WARS

DIVE INTO THE WORLDS OF SHANE GRIES WITH MILITARY FICTION THAT TAKES YOU INTO THE HEAT OF BATTLE! FOLLOW HIM ON AMAZON AND AT CANNON PUBLISHING.

Humanity engages in a desperate struggle with an alien species for this side of the Orion Arm. Spaceships die in instantaneous bursts of light and turn into vapor, but on the ground, Marines scream and lie wounded in the mud and blood, praying for the Valkyries to come save them. They aren't wishing for death and a Nordic goddess to take them to Valhalla, the wounded are calling for the pilots of the 348th Field Hospital MEDEVAC to dive through fire and hell to come save them. Because they know that ... Valkyries never die!

The Terran union has spent five centuries under the control of the alien Grausians, like a barbarian tribe under the thumb of Rome. Now, after almost two decades of civil war and succession struggles, the formerly subject races have settled back in their ancient territories to lick their wounds and rearm, leaving hundreds of settled planets to exist in a political vacuum. Into that space steps the free companies, mercenary units that fight for gold, honor, power and glory. Veterans who can't get the wars out of their souls, new recruits looking for adventure, corporations with their own agenda.

What's a soldier to do when the war is over? When he's only known conflict his whole life? Since time immemorial the solution has been to find another war, this time for pay. Whoever has the credits and wins the high bid gets the experienced fighter. Sometimes, though, the credits aren't enough to cover the price. Empires rise, but Empires also fall. The Terran Union has spent five centuries under the control of the alien Grausians, like a barbarian tribe under the thumb of Rome. Now, after almost two decades of civil war and succession struggles, the formerly subject races have settled back in their ancient territories to lick their wounds and re-arm, leaving hundreds of settled planets to exist in a political vacuum. Into that space steps the free companies, mercenary units that fight for gold, honor, power and glory. Veterans who can't get the wars out of their souls, new recruits looking for adventure, corporations with their own agenda.

Join us in a 27th Century that echoes history.

Other authors I both respect and like (Their books are awesome too!):

John Van Stry/Jan Stryvant:
https://www.amazon.com/stores/John-Van-Stry/author/B004U7JY8I

Larry Corriea:
https://www.amazon.com/stores/Larry-Correia/author/B002D68HL8

Daniel Shinhofen:
https://www.amazon.com/stores/Daniel-Schinhofen/author/B01LXQWPZA

John Ringo:
https://www.amazon.com/stores/John-Ringo/author/B000APPSXE

William D. Arrand/Randi Darren:
https://www.amazon.com/stores/William-D.-Arand/author/B01AY7PSG4

There's lots more, but I'm getting too tired to type! You all have a wonderful day!

.